SHOW DOWN

Jorge Amado

SHOW DOWN

Translated by Gregory Rabassa

BANTAM BOOKS

TORONTO · NEW YORK · LONDON · SYDNEY · AUCKLAND

SHOWDOWN
A Bantam Book / February 1988

Library of Congress Cataloging-in-Publication Data

Amado, Jorge, 1912–
  Showdown.

  Translation of: Tocaia Grande.
  I. Title.
PQ9697.A647T7413   1987   869.3   87-47789
ISBN 0-553-05174-1

Published simultaneously in the United States and Canada

Bantam Books are published by Bantam Books, a division
of Bantam Doubleday Dell Publishing Group, Inc. Its
trademark, consisting of the words "Bantam Books"
and the portrayal of a rooster, is Registered in U.S.
Patent and Trademark Office and in other countries.
Marca Registrada. Bantam Books, 666 Fifth Avenue,
New York, New York 10103.

PRINTED IN THE UNITED STATES OF AMERICA

FG   0 9 8 7 6 5 4 3 2 1

For Zélia, from house to house.

For Alice and Georges Raillard, Anny-Claude Basset and
Antoinette Hallery, in the city of Paris.

For Lygia and Fernando Sabino.

For Itassucê and Raymundo Sá Barreto, in memory of
Basílio de Oliveira.

"Certain entries in dictionaries and encyclopedias, certain biographical notes, have me born in Pirangi. It really happened the other way around: I saw Pirangi born and growing. When I went through there for the first time, standing on the pommel of my father's saddle, there were only three lonely houses. The railroad station was far away, in Sequeiro de Espinho."

—J.A.
—*Bahia Boy*

Cacao—main fruit of your troubles;
Cacao—useless life and proper death.
Hélio Pólvora
—*Sonnets for My Dead Father*

People could make it against flood and pestilence; but not against the law: they went under.
Lupiscínio, a survivor

The celebration of the seventieth anniversary of the found-ing of Irisópolis and the fiftieth anniversary of its elevation to city, regional center, and municipal seat received rather good attention in the press of the southern part of the country. If the dynamic mayor brought forth a solemn proclamation because of all that, he should not be criticized: everything that can be done to promote the fine qualities of Irisópolis—its epic past, its splendid present—merits applause and praise. In addition to the paid advertisements, Rio and São Paulo papers printed stories about the principal events that sparked the festivities, with special attention devoted to the ceremonies, both solemn, for the unveiling of the bust of Colonel Prudêncio de Aguiar and that of Dr. Inácio Pereira, each mounted in one of the public squares, opposite City Hall and in front of the Mother Church.

Following the sudden political turnabout which eclipsed the rule of the elements that had seized control after the death of the Andrades, father and son, the landowner commanded the municipal administration for decades, as intendente him-self or through an agent of his choosing, a relative or close friend. Proofs of the colonel's administrative capacity and of his dedication to the exercise of power can still be seen and admired today within the city limits, including the street paved with English cobblestones—imported from England, yes sir! —the pride of Irisopolitans, while accusations of the diversion of public funds were forgotten with the passing of time.

As for the medical man, in the capacity of brother-in-law and adviser, of a citizen of singular aptitudes, he filled the highest positions, assumed the most responsible duties, having presided over the commission created with the worthy objective of collecting funds destined for the construction of the Mother Church, a magnificent Catholic house of worship, another source of pride for the population: symbol of the faith and idealism of those valiant people who, goaded by the intrepidness of the two worthy pioneers, collaborated in the laying of the first cornerstone of the settlement. A competent administrator, the doctor found a way to build simultaneously the church and the elegant bungalow where his descendants still live today; and even at the height of the political storm none of the many calumnies raised against his honesty could be documented. Easy accusations, difficult proofs.

Laudatory articles were written that, with the requisite emphasis and rhetoric, recalled the deeds of the colonel and the doctor: pages of civic virtue, lessons of history, examples for generations to come. Words that served as a splendid model for emulation by notables, intellectuals, youth—the hope of the nation—in short, for everybody capable of recognizing and applauding these eminent forebears' heroism and devotion to the public cause.

So all Brazil, from the Amazon to Iguaçu, can gaze, in the light of the commemorative bonfire, upon the glowing face of Irisópolis, a community born out of the rainbow on a distant day of well-being, peace, and brotherhood among men, as was proclaimed in the poem written in blank verse by the principal bard of the region, whose name you have certainly heard on the lips of his admirers.

In their commemorative literary, political, and journalistic texts, they almost always leave out the original name of the town; it is relegated to oblivion, for obvious reasons. Before being Irisópolis, it was Tocaia Grande, the big ambush. . . .

THE PLACE

Natário da Fonseca,
A Man of Trust,
Sets up an Ambush in
a Pretty Place

1

BEFORE ANY HOUSES EXISTED, the cemetery was dug at the foot of the hill, on the left bank of the river. The first stones served as markers for the shallow ditches where, toward the end of the morning, at noontime, the corpses were buried when Colonel Elias Daltro finally appeared, riding at the head of a few gunmen—four miserable types, the ones who had stayed on the plantation—and realized the extent of the disaster. Not a single thug was left to tell the story.

The colonel looked at the blood-spattered bodies. Berilo had died revolver in hand. He hadn't had a chance to shoot; the bullet had torn away the top of his head. The colonel turned his eyes away. He understood that the carnage there meant the end; he no longer had the means to go on. He kept his affliction inside his breast, showed no signs of it, wouldn't let others see it. He raised his voice in command, gave orders.

In spite of the storm—a lashing rain, black clouds, thunderclaps dying off in the woods—some buzzards, attracted by the blood and the exposed intestines, flew over the men who were busy carrying bodies and digging graves.

"Hurry up, before the stink gets worse."

2

THEY WERE RIDING IN silence up to the beginning of the
small bridge, when Natário, in the vanguard of the escort
that had gone to meet the colonel at the railroad station in
the hamlet of Taquaras, reined in his mule, came abreast of
the master, and spoke in a soft voice.

"I know a very suitable place, Colonel. I can show you if
you'd like to make a small detour, a matter of half a league.
It's a bit ahead, upriver."

Suitable place? Suitable for what? The half-breed's information was so much to the point that Colonel Boaventura
Andrade was startled. Dona Ernestina, his sainted wife,
knowledgeable in matters of spiritualism, held that certain
people had the gift of reading the thoughts of others. The
colonel preferred not to get too involved in unknown things
like that: of an almost legendary bravery, nothing in this
world frightened him; he did feel, however, an uncontrollable fear when faced with the forces of the supernatural. He
was in need of a suitable place; how could Natário have
guessed?

He stared at the foreman's face, questioning. Natário
gave a hint of a smile. The broad Indian face, straight black
hair, high cheekbones, small, cunning eyes.

Careful of social niceties, the colonel avoided speaking
of an armed struggle, any mention of skirmishes, ambushes,
bloody encounters with dead and wounded. Fierce as the
discord might be, to speak of it he would use a word that
seemed more civilized to him, less violent: *politics*.

"Politics are coming to a boil, Natário. We've got to
take measures; if not, they'll put an end to us, dangerous
politics!"

He'd gone a little further in the conversation he'd had
with the foreman a week earlier on the porch of the big
house of Atalaia Plantation, commenting on the proven news
of preparations by his rival, Colonel Elias Daltro, the political boss, owner of Cascavel Plantation, whose cacao groves
bordered those of Atalaia. Once friends and associates, the
two colonels had become sworn enemies, each considering
himself the sole owner of that immense spread of vacant

land of thick woods that extended from the beginning of the backlands to the banks of the Rio das Cobras, the river of snakes.

"Our neighbor has lost his head; he's sent for hired thugs from as far away as Alagoas. Sergipe is full of them, more than you can count. Watch out, Natário. . . ."

"I'm watching, Colonel."

"Either we take care of ourselves, prepare an adequate reply, or we go under. I've got to be careful; nobody can stand up to our neighbor in open country." He said *neighbor* so as not to mention his enemy by name.

He limited himself to those vague references because he still hadn't drawn up the plan, laid out the trap. Only in Ilhéus would he arrange the details. How was it possible, then, for the foreman to refer to a specific place, responding to his concern, answering the question he hadn't yet asked?

A very suitable place. Colonel Boaventura felt his heart beat faster: could Natário have the gift of reading his thoughts? When it was a case of dealing with people of Indian blood, you never knew.

"Suitable for what, Natário?"

The smile on the half-breed's calm face broadened. If it weren't for his small, penetrating eyes, he could have passed for a docile, peaceful individual, a simpleton. Only those who were close to him, those who had seen him in action at critical moments, knew how much capacity for decision and judgment, for courage and command, hid behind that static face.

"For a showdown, Colonel, I don't know of a better place."

A coincidence, no doubt; there was no other explanation.

Fortunately so, because if Natário could guess other people's thoughts, the colonel would have no choice but to have him liquidated.

"Any old place is good for a reply." The colonel avoided using the word *ambush*. "All you need is a well-placed tree and a gunman who's a good shot."

Natário broadened his smile even more.

"You're right, sir, but I'm talking about a large ambush, which is what we need. Word's going around that the men Colonel Elias hired will arrive in Itabuna any day now, maybe today, maybe tomorrow. Over twenty men . . .." He raised his voice. "We can't go off half-cocked, no, sir."

They were on to Colonel Elias's game, the recruitment of thugs, some coming from far away, especially chosen to guarantee the swearing in of the little two-bit lawyer elected administrator with the support of the governor. Why the hell was the governor taking sides in that dispute, which was of interest only to them, the landowners of the region? Why was he butting in, since it was none of his business? Colonel Boaventura didn't want to get on the bad side of the governor, but the office of administrator of Itabuna was a local matter, to be decided by the colonels, for better or for worse, by agreement or by arms; whoever was stronger or smarter would name the candidate. He would only have to legalize the accomplished fact—the farce of an election would follow the decision, never precede it. The neighbor, thinking he was shrewd, had moved up the date of the election, proclaimed the little lawyer the winner, and was trying to have him sworn in. Pettifoggers' tricks; Colonel Boaventura hated them.

The legal remedy was to annul the election—election, crap!, nomination by the stroke of a pen, thugs taking the place of voters—but in order to do that, a petition to the judge wasn't enough: like the election, the cancellation would have to come after the accomplished fact. During the past few days, in Ilhéus, from where he was returning, Colonel Boaventura had set up alliances, offered promises, made threats, oiled jammed wheels in registry offices, and, as usual, had satisfied himself on the firm bed and in the warm lap of Adriana, a mistress he kept with apparent exclusivity in Loreta's house. With the plan laid out in all its details, the measures indispensable to its success having been taken, all that remained was to find a suitable place and make sure of the day when his neighbor's men would set out for Itabuna, keeping always one jump ahead in craftiness.

After the bend in the river, Natário reined in his mule.

"We can't go on horseback, Colonel, there's not enough room."

They left their mounts with the two henchmen, and Natário took out his machete and opened a path. The heavy landowner held on to the trees, slipped on loose stones: would all that effort be worth it? But when they got to the top of the hill, he couldn't hold back an exclamation of surprise as the immense space opened up before him, the valley extending along the two banks of the river, a magnificent view, dazzling.

"What a pretty place!"

Natário nodded in agreement.

"It's where I'm going to build my house, Colonel, when the fighting's over and you keep your promise, sir. This here is going to be a town someday. I'm so sure, I can see it now." He was staring into the distance; he seemed to see beyond the horizon, beyond time.

Once more the colonel felt the gnawing of doubt: could the half-breed really be a soothsayer? Maybe he was one without knowing it: there were cases; Dona Ernestina knew of more than one. Adriana believed in telepathy and soothsaying, too, the two of them were alike in that, his wife and his mistress; in everything else, what a difference!

Natário went on.

"I've been getting word that Colonel Elias's hired guns are going to come this way to reach the river without crossing at Atalaia. See that path, Colonel? There isn't any other. If you just give me the order, I'll station myself up there with a handful of men and I guarantee you not one of them will get to Itabuna." He smiled. "It looks like God made this place just on purpose, Colonel."

Colonel Boaventura felt his heartbeat speeding up. Along with his supernatural forces, Natário sometimes startled him by the ease with which he would make God the colonel's ally and accomplice! He was lucky to have him in his service; he was worth ten men, with his coolness and his visions.

"You were born to be a soldier, Natário. If you'd enlisted in the army and there was a war, you'd end up with an officer's stripes."

"If that's what you think, Colonel, and you think I deserve it, buy me a captain's commission, then."

"Captain in the National Guard?"

"You won't be sorry, sir."

"Then it's a promise, starting right now. From today on you can consider yourself a captain."

"Captain Natário da Fonseca at your service, Colonel."

3

BEFORE LEAVING THE PLANTATION, Natário inspected rifles
and shotguns, carbines and revolvers: first-class weapons,
carefully chosen, worth their weight in gold; well-oiled from
end to end. He kept going over his calculations, hoping to
avoid any surprises. He couldn't allow any slips, nor could
he depend on dubious arrangements; he promised Colonel
Boaventura that not a single gunman who left Cascavel
Plantation would complete the trip to Itabuna—his word
and his rank as captain were at risk. The landowner went to
await the news in Ilhéus.

The rain continued for more than a week. The roads had
become quagmires—it was hard going, fatiguing, every league
became three. Hoping to limit any waiting in ambush to a
minimum, Natário decided he would move his men only
after news of the departure of the band armed by Colonel
Elias Daltro had reached him.

The news was slow in coming because the bastards left
the refuge of Cascavel Plantation two days late, waiting in
vain for the storm to let up. Since the rain was now heavier,
there was nothing for them to do but make the trip under
those bad conditions: they were in a hurry, they had an
appointment to keep. Impatient—it was already well into
morning—Colonel Elias, watching their departure, gave Berilo
final instructions: In Itabuna he was to present himself to
Dr. Castro and place himself under his orders. As for the
route, Coroinha would guide them: a trailman and a hunter,
an experienced guide, he knew those flats like the back of
his hand; he would keep far away from the borders of Atalaia
Plantation. The expedition had been prepared with the greatest secrecy so that news of it wouldn't reach the ears of
Colonel Boaventura or his people. Except for Berilo and
Coroinha, the rest didn't know where they were going. Gunmen paid to fight, they weren't to be taken into anyone's
confidence or given a free hand; the less they knew, the
better.

"What in hell are you doing?" Berilo asked Coroinha
when they left the road at dusk to go along the path. "Do
you see something? Or are you scared?"

"I'm getting my bearings so as not to lose our way."

It might have been so. The mud had erased the cart road opened by animal tracks toward the river. Coroinha got down, smelled the ground, moved ahead. Every step was an effort; fatigue weighed like heavy sacks on their backs. Peccaries and agoutis crossed in front of them, rattlesnakes hissed. Berilo had settled with Colonel Elias on the place to spend the night, the other side of the small bridge; it was going to be hard to bring it off: night was falling and they were still lost in those wild woods, depending on the wisdom of the guide, more and more shit-scared. Berilo, wary, kept his eye on the ferret.

While this was going on, Colonel Boaventura Andrade's men were heading down the main road; and even so the going was hard. Still, they arrived right on time to set up the ambush and lie in wait.

4

ALL EARS TRY TO make out the sound of steps in the midst of the chaos of the storm—the whistling of the wind, the rumble of thunder, the fearsome noise of the fall of a tree struck by lightning. Waterlogged, covered with mud, fanned out behind the trees on top of the hill, the gunmen wait, tense. Used to the long waits of ambushes, tempered in danger and fighting, intimates with death, yet even so they can't escape the foreboding of a last agony in the face of nature's fury, or of an end to the world. They try to keep their calm, control their nerves; they're even more afraid of Natário: they can escape the storm with their lives, but from the foreman's bullet not even a miracle would help.

Clutching his big pistol, Natário lies motionless. The first shot will be his—the signal for the gunmen to open fire, the sentence of death for that Berilo, a gunfighter recruited in Alagoas, a criminal famous for his sadistic ways, the leader of the expedition. Then he'll take care of Coroinha, the guide, if the poor devil escapes the first burst, or if he hasn't run off. He can't feel sorry for Coroinha in spite of having known him for a long time: a man who serves two

masters, who sells himself, doesn't deserve any pity. Born
and reared on the lands of Colonel Elias Daltro, a person of
his esteem and trust, the guide had furnished his enemy
with precious information for a pittance, had given the
exact number of those making up the troop—twenty-seven,
an army!—the kind of weapons they carried, the day and
hour of their departure, even agreeing to give an owl hoot as
they approached. Maybe he'd go through with the deal,
maybe not.

Natário tries to make out suspicious noises: a twig broken as someone passes by, a slip in the mud, a voice, the
whisper of conversation. Coming along the trail the gunmen
will be careless, certain that danger is far behind, left at the
distant boundary line of Atalaia. He might hear the owl
hoot right there, who knows, but he has his doubts. What's
most certain is that Coroinha, when he gets near there,
will take off; an inveterate hunter, he knows hiding places
and detours. That's what he imagines and that's what
happens. If he'd trusted the Judas, he would have lost the
best moment for the attack; the renegade didn't keep his
word.

With a keen ear the half-breed makes out, almost feels
the slight splash of feet in mud, careful footsteps; with his
hand he cautions the men. He sharpens his eyes; in the flash
of lightning he makes out Berilo. He readies his weapon,
but he's in no hurry, he lets the black Indian advance so the
rest of the troop will be in their sights. Why in hell is the
son of a bitch coming along holding his revolver and walking so cautiously, looking all around?

Berilo raises his eyes, peering about. Natário lifts his
arm, steadies his aim—*with your permission, Colonel*—shoots
for the head. The firing breaks out on top of the hill and
confusion reigns in the mud below; the gunmen return fire
at random, not knowing where to aim their weapons.

A carnage, as Colonel Elias Daltro confirmed. No one
had ever heard of an ambush that size, not even during the
time of the early battles, those between Basílio de Oliveira
and the Badaró family. It would go down in history—*tocaia
grande*, the big ambush.

5

NONE OF COLONEL ELIAS'S gunmen escaped, famous gun-
fighters brought from the backlands, from Sergipe d'El Rey,
the land of brave men, some even from Alagoas, professionals all. When the men went down the hill, following Natário,
there wasn't much work for them to do: finishing off the
wounded, bringing down a few who tried to seek shelter in
the trees and sell their lives dearly from there, chasing two
or three who attempted to flee the way they'd come.

Hunting for these last, black Espiridião found Coroinha's
body near a rock behind which he must have tried to hide:
Natário understood then why Berilo had his revolver out
and came along with such caution and watchfulness.

Coroinha had been done in with a knife. His heart had
been cut out and his balls cut off, a custom, it would seem,
much to the taste of the deceased bully from Alagoas. Natário
thought it was right for them to have done him in. If Berilo
hadn't done it, he would have taken care of the job himself.
He even agreed with the choice of weapon: a traitor isn't
worth the cost of a rifle bullet. But he didn't approve of
perversity: getting rid of a Judas with a bullet or a knife is
one thing, mocking the poor devil is quite another.

Second-hand weapons aren't worth much. Natário
wouldn't let them collect them. While it was still the dark of
night, they left the place. Under the command of Espiridião,
the gunmen returned to Atalaia Plantation. Natário crossed
the bridge and went on to the railroad station; from there
he would send a telegram, as had been arranged. With a
small change in the sender's name: instead of Natário, Captain Natário.

On reaching the bend in the river, Natário looked back,
back, remembering; he smiled in contentment. He wasn't thinking, however, of the showdown, the fallen bodies, Berilo with
his head blown off. Coroinha castrated, stabbed with a knife,
his heart outside his chest. He was thinking back, and in his
memory held the sight of the countryside at night, in the
storm: the hills and the valley swept by the rain, the belly
of the river swollen, as if it were pregnant, so much beauty!
A prettier place, by day or by night, in sunshine or in rain,
didn't exist in those parts; no place where the living was better.

Venturinha the Degree Candidate Enters Public Life

1

HIS FACE SHOWING ENTHUSIASM, an easy and satisfied smile, Venturinha—who'd come to spend his St. John's holiday on the farm—commented, on embracing Natário at the station in Taquaras, "So, Colonel Elias dropped his drawers and asked for a pot. . . ."

The half-breed corrected him.

"A man like Colonel Elias Daltro doesn't ask for a pot, Venturinha, he asks for a truce."

He had no inhibitions with the boss's son. Venturinha hadn't even been nine years old when Natário took refuge on the plantation and became the colonel's right-hand man. The boy attached himself to the young henchman, rode on the pommel of his saddle, learned bird calls with him and how to handle weapons. His first whore was brought by Natário: the freckle-faced Júlia Saruê, a traveling madam, plying her trade from plantation to plantation, well-versed in popping young boys' cherries. Better than she, only the mare Beautiful Flower.

"One way or another," the student went on, after mounting and getting on the road, "Elias is all through as a political boss. He was lucky to be dealing with the Old Man, who's got a soft heart. If it had been me, I'd have finished that swine off once and for all: torn down his house, burned his groves, left him with a cup in his hand to go begging with. But Dad felt sorry for him, eased off. Don't you think the Old Man should have gone all the way, taken advantage of the occasion?"

Natário didn't change his voice, he knew the boy's outbursts.

"Maybe yes, maybe no. But if you think the colonel didn't finish him off out of softness, you're wrong: it wasn't softness, no, it was wiseness. We need peace so we can cut down trees and plant the land; there's a lot of ground, Venturinha. If Colonel Boaventura had set fire to Colonel Elias's groves, we'd be fighting half the country in a war to the death. Burning cacao is just like burning money; those days are over. Your father knows what he's doing, that's why he's on top, giving the orders. When it was time to fight, he didn't hesitate, he didn't want to hear about any deal. But people should fight only when they can't find a way to live in peace."

"Are you the one telling me that? You, who've spent your life with your finger on the trigger? Colonel Boaventura's Natário?"

Natário smiled, his tiny eyes almost closed.

"You're about ready to come out of the university, a lawyer with a doctor's degree, but you've still got a lot to learn. Every time has its use: a time for shooting, a time for dealing. The colonel wants you to be his ace in the hole when he deals with the people in Itabuna. He told me: 'Venturinha has got to get rid of his jackassishness. This time he's the one who's going to settle everything, I want to see how it comes out.' You've got to remember that everybody in Itabuna dances to Colonel Elias's tune, one's a close chum, another his godson; there are people who will agree to pick up their guns only if he orders it. You don't talk about setting fire to Colonel Elias's groves there, or you'll throw everything away. You're too hotheaded; save your heat for the girls. . . ."

"Speaking of girls, Natário, I didn't tell you . . ." And he proceeded to tell him.

Natário didn't explain that the colonel had decided to send his son instead of going personally, because the hardest part had already been resolved, the main points of agreement had been set up and accepted. The survey would be registered, the election annulled, they'd choose a new date and a new candidate. Besides, the candidate might still be the governor's little lawyer protégé. The colonel joked with Natário, commenting on possible candidates.

"Don't you want to be intendente of Itabuna, Natário?" He laughed at the harebrained idea.

Natário didn't laugh; his voice was calm.

"Not of Itabuna, no, sir. The last one in charge of Itabuna is the intendente; yesterday Colonel Elias gave the orders, today you do. When I govern a place, even if it's the last backwaters of the earth, the one who's going to give the orders is me. Me and nobody else."

2

ORDERED FROM RIO DE JANEIRO, his commission still hadn't arrived, but that didn't prevent Natário from being called captain all the time during the peace mission to Itabuna. He was accorded the title not only by half-breeds and hired hands, but by merchants, landowners, doctors, and functionaries of the law, too, starting with the district judge. Words spoken with all the respect due the title and his fame.

In the letter to the magistrate, drawn up with the help of Venturinha, Colonel Boaventura Andrade put forth the merits of his representatives. He was writing and reading. Venturinha and Natário listened.

" '. . . my son, a student of law—' "

The boy interrupted.

"Not a student of law, Dad. I'm in the last year at law school. I graduate in December; I'm a degree candidate."

" '. . . I mean 'degree candidate Boaventura Andrade *Filho*—' "

"Not *filho*, Father. Put in Junior. That's the way I sign my name, it's more up-to-date."

"For me it's *filho*, son, and that's that; I've already written it, I'm not going to scratch it out. I don't like these foreign things: you're not some English or Swiss bastard!" He closed off the discussion, went on with his writing and reading. " '. . . and Captain Natário da Fonseca, rural property owner, my right arm . . .' "

"Captain and property owner," so the colonel was showing himself not to be ungrateful or tightfisted. With the
opportunity of the survey of the new lands for future regis-
tration in the proper office, he'd ordered the inclusion of a
few sections in Natário's name, enough for some cacao groves.
One couldn't compare them with the holdings of the colonel, one of the largest, if not the largest, landholders in the
region, but it was a good start in life. The colonel wasn't
tightfisted, but he wasn't generous either, because the survey and registry of that immense tract of virgin forest had
actually taken place the night of the big ambush, and the
ready notary had been Natário. At the registry in Itabuna
they were only going to legalize a de facto conquest, the
accomplished fact, following the laws of the land, so much
to the liking of the colonel. First the ambush, then the deal;
more to the point, first the reply, then the law.

It looked more like an expedition of war than a mission
of peace: fifteen men, armed from head to toe, commanded
by black Espiridião. They really weren't necessary, because
Colonel Elias Daltro had withdrawn from the fray and, so
they said, from politics, releasing past commitments. Men
and arms were merely a show of force on the part of the
master of Atalaia, a display of wealth and power. Necessary,
according to him, to guarantee the recently negotiated peace.

Captain here, captain there, a merry-go-round in Itabuna.
Everything went nicely, the judge was soft as silk, treating
Venturinha like a colleague, they had him in the palms of
their hands. The little lawyer, the same Dr. Castro whom
Berilo was to have presented himself to, who would have
been a cause for pity if he weren't so disgusting, was going
to be intendente in precisely the proper and desired measure.

At the land office, whose wheels the colonel had oiled in
advance, there wasn't the slightest difficulty with the regis-
tration of the survey and the filing of the titles that legiti-
mized the possession of the immense plot by Colonel
Boaventura Andrade and a piece of ground for Captain
Natário da Fonseca.

In boardinghouses and whorehouses the activity remained intense, day and night. The gunmen from Atalaia
squandered money; the prestige of the new political boss
was growing, it was God in heaven and Colonel Boaventura
on earth.

On seeing Natário cross Rua do Umbuzeiro, Maria das

Dores, sitting in the doorway, pointed to him and informed
Zezinha do Butiá, a novice from Lagarto, "That's Natário,
Colonel Boaventura's strongarm, a bad one, there's none
worse. He can't even keep track himself of the crimes he's
committed. Well, you may not believe it, but he's got women
crazy over him. God spare me and keep me away from
him." She spat with contempt.

A mincing mulatto girl with a round behind and pigeon
breasts, Zezinha do Butiá, in spite of being a newcomer,
seemed well-informed.

"I heard different. That that's Captain Natário, moneyed,
brave, and good-hearted. They say he never mistreats women."

She sighed coquettishly, following Natário with her eyes.
Zezinha do Butiá was, as they say, in the flower of her youth
and beauty. Men fought over her. She shouted to a black
boy busy eating dirt, "Manu, run after that fellow going
along there. Ask for his blessing and tell him I'll be waiting
for him; he can come whenever he likes. He doesn't have to
bring any money."

3

BEFORE LEAVING THE PLANTATION to spend the last days of
his vacation with his mother, Dona Ernestina, the model of
all virtues, Venturinha wanted to get to know the place
where the event had happened. He wanted to see with his
own eyes, to know for certain, so he could tell his friends at
the university and his fellow revelers in the capital, exaggerating details. Natário took him.

"You're going to have a look at a piece of heaven."

Among the stones of the improvised cemetery, the underbrush was pushing up impetuously: bushes crowded, papaya sprouts pushed through the undergrowth, flowers
bloomed. The news of the deed, as it spread and grew from
mouth to mouth, drew the curious from the main road. The
path opened by animals grew wider from the steps of men,
became a road. Aiming to shorten its route, a mule train
loaded with sacks of cacao had made a path. The first.

Venturinha insisted on climbing to the top of the hill, an effort for him: stocky, just like his father, fat, just like his mother. He stood behind the mulungu tree, took out his German pistol, spotted a chameleon, fired. The shot echoed through the ravines.

"It must have been exciting, eh, Natário? It gives me goose pimples."

Did Natário hear him? His gaze was lost beyond the horizon and beyond time.

"The Old Man should have a plaque put here, the way they do on battlefields."

What for? Wasn't the name on the lips of the people enough? The place of the big ambush. With time and with inhabitants it became just a name, Tocaia Grande.

A PLACE
TO SPEND
THE NIGHT

The God of the Maronites Leads the Peddler Abdala to Paradise

1

THE PAPAYA TREES SPROUTING over the graves in the improvised cemetery were giving off their first fruits when Fadul Abdala, having lost his way, discovered that beauty of a spot. A Lebanese of gigantic stature, everything about him outsize—hands and feet, barrel chest, and pumpkin head—he had picked up the nickname of Grand Turk in the cabarets of Ilhéus and Itabuna, but on the roads in cacao country he was known as Turk Fadul or, more simply, Mr. Fadu in the mouths of the field hands, who saw divine providence in him. Dazzled by the sight, he thought he had come to the plains of Eden described in the holy book he carried with him in his peddler's pack, because when there was the occasion and the need, Mr. Fadu was always ready to baptize children at bargain prices.

He dropped the heavy pack, heavier every day, the folding ruler he used as a rattle to announce to rich and poor the presence of commerce and fashion in those boondocks. In the pack he carried silks and calicos, cottons, ladies' boots, buskins, thread, needles, and thimbles, ribbons and lace, soap, mirrors, perfumes, tisanes, colored prints of saints, and scapulars against fevers.

He took off his jacket and his shirt, his pants and drawers—the marks left by the straps of his pack on his back, calluses on his shoulders—took off his sandals, dove into the river that spread out there in a pool of clear water

running over black rocks. He swam, splashing the way he
used to as a child swimming in the stream by his native
village. He found the two places alike, except that the palm
trees growing on the hills and in the valleys now weren't
date palms. He satisfied his hunger on fragrant, sweet papa-
yas, manna from heaven, the gift of God, the God of the
Maronites.

Ripe hog plums lay scattered on the ground under trees
that sheltered him from the sun. He inspected the fruit,
laughing at himself, a great big naked man; he remembered
himself as an urchin in a djellaba picking up dates: big and
disjointed even then. It was going on fifteen years since he'd
left. The wild acidic taste of the hog plums, so different from
the soft, smooth taste of ripe dates, both fruits created by
God for the enjoyment of men.

He'd changed a lot in those fifteen years, his uncle
Said Abdala, a Maronite priest famous for his advice and
appetite, wouldn't have recognized him, Fadul pondered,
tasting the hog plums one by one; he'd changed inside and
out, preferring hog plums to dates and not missing grapes:
jackfruit was good enough for him, the soft ones preferred.
He'd been reborn in those woods, the boy wearing his djellaba
had been left behind forever on the other side of the ocean.

God divided men's lives between duty and pleasure,
tears and laughter. The unbounded pleasure of being there,
sucking on a hog plum in the late afternoon breeze, listening
to the birds, watching them fly, jewels from the chest of the
Lord. Resting from the labors of the past weeks, from the
endless walking, the dangers at every moment, a peddler
knows no Sundays or holidays. God had made him lose his
way so he could have a day of rest, relief for his body and
his soul.

Why not stay there forever in that idyllic valley, just
like the animals, who warm themselves in the sun, stretched
out on stones? He'd learned from field hands to eat teju
meat and savor it, licking his lips and his fingers. There was
more than enough to eat, plenty of game and fruit, fragrant
jackfruit; pure water flowed down from its source—paradise.
Fadul Abdala gave a rough, noisy laugh, frightening parrots
and lizards: in that paradise the main thing was missing—a
woman.

Thinking about women, he thought of Zezinha do Butiá,
cheating on him in Itabuna at that moment. But he couldn't

demand that she keep her twat—a canyon!—locked up just
because in a moment of madness he'd left her two ten
milreis notes and a framed mirror for her to look at herself
and sigh. Sigh? She laughed in his face.

"Worthless Turk, raw-onion eater!"

"Not Turk, hold your tongue. Grand Turk, my oda-
lisque, your master and your slave . . ." He was given to
gallantries, too bad his accent was of no help.

2

HE LIKED THE PLACE so much that he spent the night
there. He gathered some kindling wood, lit a fire to frighten
off the snakes, put on his drawers and his shirt, lay down on
the dry leaves. He took a while to fall asleep, thinking. On
the riverbank, announcing the moon, a *cururu* toad was
singing.

Fadul had come to Brazil fifteen years before, to work
and get rich. Getting rich is the goal of all men; in order to
attain it, God gave them a soul and intelligence. Some fulfill
the Lord's commandment literally; they earn money and
become established; others don't manage it, small-souled
with limited intelligence, or without much disposition for
work, lazy, vagrant.

He still hadn't gotten rich, far from it. He hadn't even
become established, as he'd set out to do, with a business
house in one of the settlements growing up along the cacao
trail at plantation crossroads, where droves and drovers
passed. Still, he couldn't complain: he was putting a nest
egg together. Especially after he'd begun to practice a little
usury as well.

The stars increased far off in the sky. Fuad Karan in
Itabuna, who read books in Arabic and Portuguese, an en-
lightened citizen, better educated than any half-dozen
lawyers—responsible for that nickname of Grand Turk made
up when he saw Fadul surrounded by hookers in the cabaret—
told him that the stars seen here aren't the same ones that
twinkle in the skies of the East where they'd been born. The
Grand Turk didn't doubt it, but he couldn't figure out the

difference: stars are all alike, beautiful and distant precious stones; one of them would be enough to make the fortune of one of God's children. As for the moon, reflected on the water of the river, it was the same everywhere: a dark gold medal, fat and yellow, minted with the image of St. George riding his horse against the dragon. The East mentioned by Fuad, the native land, had been lost in the distance; in order to find it again he would have to cross the ocean in the hold of a ship. The stars were different, the fruit too; he didn't miss them: he preferred hog plums to dates and he did all right by the stars.

A citizen's homeland is the place where he sweats, weeps, and laughs, where he toils to earn a living and build a place of business and a residence. Alone with the night and the stars in that unknown resting place where the hand of God had led him, Fadul Abdala recognized and adopted his new homeland. He didn't see the light of day for the first time in it, nor was he baptized there. Foolish, insignificant details: more important than the cradle is the grave, and his will be dug in cacao country. Not a shallow grave like the ones in the cemetery up there—for whom, when, and why? Ah! It will be the tomb of a lord, in marble, the *Here Lies* in gold letters. During those fifteen years the big boy from the East, on becoming a man, had become a Brazilian.

So true was it that he'd already discussed with Ubaldo Madureira, a clerk at the registry office and a comrade in revelry, the price of his naturalization papers, at a discount. A Brazilian with his official papers, an established merchant, married and the father of children, his business growing, money piling up on top of money: all that quite soon, God willing. He would fulfill his destiny as set forth by his uncle Father Said when he gave his blessing during that sad and happy moment of all good-byes, when laughter and tears mingle.

"Go fulfill the will of God, Fadul, son of my departed sister Marama, go earn money in Brazil; things are hard here and I can't support you anymore. Go get rich; a rich man is respected by his fellows and well looked upon by God."

He made the sign of the cross in the air, gave him his hand to kiss. Lifting up his shepherd's crook, the adolescent went down the mountain, started on his way. The God of the Maronites is the same there and here.

3

FADUL TOOK A WHILE getting back to that place; many months had passed.

He went on with his peddler's chores, bent over under the weight of his pack, in sun and rain. He was always greeted by his customers with excitement and affection because, in addition to everything else, he was a pleasure to talk to. He liked to listen to and tell stories, mingling them with exclamations of surprise, broad, convincing gestures, and gales of noisy laughter. He'd earned the fame of a fibber, but he told the tall stories with fun and feeling, brought out undiscovered emotions in his poor and avid audience, devoid of any entertainment in those parts.

"What a cock and bull story. I even cried. . . ."

"I pissed laughing at the bit about the woman and the monkey. That thieving Turk makes up a good one. . . ."

Fadul's clientele was vast and varied: plantation owners, their wives, their children, people with money and position; hired hands and field workers almost without a penny to their name; thugs and their mistresses, swaggering and bragging; whores, his best customers, the ones buying the most. The wayfarer made no distinctions as to class or caste. He accepted with the same pleasure invitations to have lunch in the big house as in the huts of the hired hands.

He enjoyed great popularity among the ladies of the evening. He wouldn't turn down payment in kind for a box of face powder, a jar of pomade, a bottle of cologne water, or the IOU from a small loan. There were cases—rare, it's true—of free items on freewheeling days when, full of love, the Grand Turk lost his senses: metal rings sparkling with glass stones; fancy earrings, pretty ornaments. Trinkets accepted with feeling, more appreciated than a five-milreis note because they were gifts, symbols of affection and not intentional payment. Sentimental, Fadul suffered frequent infatuations. He had a predilection for fleshy girls with protruding breasts, great mounds to be squeezed in his enormous hand. A skinny woman isn't worth anything to

him, bones are for a gravedigger, people say, and they're so
right.

Prudent, conciliatory, there were those who mistook his
modesty for timidity. Such a big body and such a big coward, an opinion that got one nowhere. Armed with just a
pocket knife, Mr. Fadu collected a debt from Terêncio, a
half-breed who was a bad character, a thug. Fadul squeezed
his throat till he was bug-eyed, pricked his Adam's apple
with the sharp blade—used to peel oranges and scrape boils—
and got the three milreis, the interest, and the apologies on
the spot. When he heard about that set-to, Captain Natário,
dying with laughter, found him especially comical. Still,
holding the peddler in high esteem, he gave him a revolver
as a present: sometimes the strength of one's hands and a
jackknife aren't enough. Hot lead brings respect, old friend.

He freed himself of the reputation of softness, but never
that of thief. That grew and spread everywhere, notorious
and unanimous. At the market improvised on his arrival on
plantations, they called him thieving Turk while they complained about the price of the merchandise laid out, inviting
and coveted. Pretending to be wounded, in his honeyed
tones Mr. Fadu threatened to gather up calico and pins,
combs and brooches, ribbons and pouches—the irresistible
seduction of his business—and go sell somewhere else. The
negotiations went on amid exclamations and curses, smiles
and sighs, insults and praise: from *robber* to *my dear, dear
Turk.*

They called him thief to his face, but without anger,
with no intent to offend; it was part of the bargaining, the
wheedling, the pleasure of buying and selling. A sharper
without doubt, but a good man, as he, too, never tired of
declaring himself in a loud voice.

"Thieving Turk is your little mamma. I'd like to know,
if it wasn't for Fadul, a good man, a Godfearing man, who
would come to this asshole of the world to take care of you
people? Instead of complaining, you should thank me and
offer me a drink, you ungrateful people!" He wouldn't turn
down cane liquor, but in cabarets he drank vermouth laced
with brandy.

In the big houses the colonels, filthy rich, wouldn't
complain any less because of that.

"Turk, you're robbing us blind. Where did you ever see
a cheap old nickel watch—not a grain of silver—cost a pile

of money like that? It's highway robbery; there isn't enough cacao in the world to pay with . . ."

Fadul swore that in Ilhéus a watch of that quality, genuine silver, would cost twice as much. His pack open under the greedy eyes of the ladies of the house, he kept an eye on the bustle in the kitchen, where the smell of boiling things emanated; in matters of appetite, he took after his priest uncle.

In the cacao groves, whoever wanted to earn some money without the advantage of owning a planted plot had to count on many skills. A carpetbagger, carrying his shop on his back, Turk Fadul frequently practiced medicine, did priestly duties when necessary. He operated on abscesses, lanced boils; cleaned wounds with peroxide, burned them with iodine. In his pack were four infallible remedies: Miraculous Elixir, Woman's Health, São Lázaro Pomade, and castor oil. With them he would treat any illness—except for black pox and the nameless fever; for them there was nothing that could be done. He nursed and cured many people in those backlands where there were no doctors or drugstores, no help to call for.

A sacristan in his Lebanese village, altar boy for Father Said in his religious duties, he didn't hesitate to baptize babies who, without his help, would have died pagans with no right to the kingdom of heaven. He blessed couples living together, removing them from the sin in which they were living, giving them a new social status and the pretext for a revel with cane liquor and dancing. Mr. Fadu appreciated a little thigh-bumping led on by an accordion; a first-class dancing partner, in the opinion of the girls.

With the interest he earned, he watched his nest egg grow and saw the time coming to throw off his peddler's pack forever, build a shack, and set up shop. All he needed was to choose the place with the most promising future, a new settlement where there still weren't a lot of people.

4

ON DESCRIBING THE SPOT where he'd gotten lost and rested, Fadul Abdala was told that the name of that place was Tocaia Grande, because it had been the scene of a shadowy ambush and a cold-blooded killing a few years before, during the pitiless fight between the colonels for the possession of the last woodlands—in those parts, along the Rio das Cobras, not a foot of land was left that didn't have an owner.

In the heat of the narrative, untrustworthy types, bad-mouthers, mentioned names involved in the notorious ambush, but Fadul knew to give proper value to treachery and intrigue: they went in one ear and out the other.

Other information—which was of interest—Turk Fadul picked up in the houses of field hands, on the colonels' verandas, and from the mouths of travelers. The drovers who came down from the plantations bringing cacao to be loaded onto the train at Taquaras were, little by little, abandoning the old road, detouring by Tocaia Grande, an ideal spot to spend the night. After a certain time, traffic through the shortcut became heavier than on the main road.

One day a drover he had dealings with, Lázaro by name, blind in one eye, as he listed the advantages of resting at Tocaia Grande—the animals could quench their thirst without danger in the pool formed by the river there, could find food in the thick vegetation, and had no place to run away— was sorry that in such an ideal spot there still wasn't a canteen, small as it might be, to sell a drink of *cachaça*, a plug of tobacco, a biscuit, some *rapadura*, a handful of salt. The smart fellow who establishes himself in Tocaia Grande would get rich overnight.

Fadul listened attentively, continued along on his trail of offerings and collections. But when he returned to Itabuna with the dual purpose of replenishing his stock and seeing Zezinha do Butiá—more than a sweetheart, a curse of destiny, because she wasn't even fat or teaty—he found a way to pass through those parts, accompanying a cattle drive. He wasn't surprised to find that Tocaia Grande had ceased being wilderness. In addition to the wooden hut, a storehouse for dried cacao, a few adobe houses had been built, others were under construction. Whores were making a living, there was no lack of customers, workers from nearby groves—foresters and field hands—passing gunmen, drovers spending the night. The night was rich with the sound of accordions, of singing, bodies panting in the shelters. In the morning, with the drovers' departure, the activity lessened, only to begin again at dusk.

The last time he was there he realized he'd been brought by the hand of God. While he thought he'd gotten lost, the Lord was leading him, guiding Fadul's steps. Not just to take it easy on a day of rest, as he had thought then. But to show him the place where he was to honor their deal and fulfill his destiny. He mustn't think twice. Before continuing on his way, Fadul Abdala made the necessary arrangements.

Captain Natário
da Fonseca
Visits His Domains

1

A VERBAL AGREEMENT, MORE than sufficient. Between them a written and signed agreement, besides being unnecessary, would mean an insulting lack of trust, proof of a lack of esteem. Through the arrangement, Natário received the title of administrator of Atalaia Plantation—foreman is no position for a captain in the National Guard—with the right to spend a few days each month on the property he had begun to clear on the lands received as payment for his good services, services that no salary could repay. Good-natured, the colonel had closed the deal.

"Between us now, Natário, there's no such thing anymore as boss and employee; we're flour from the same sack."

"For as long as you live, sir, I'm your man, whatever the job."

"I know that, I know your devotion, and I've tried to match it."

Natário, his face serious, still had something to say.

"There's one more thing I'd like to ask of you, sir, if you'll let me, Colonel."

Something more? Surprised, the colonel stared at the half-breed.

"Go ahead, I'm listening."

"Zilda's got a big belly again. I want you and Dona Ernestina to be the godparents when the kid is born."

"Is that what you're asking for?" He held out his hand.
"Well, put it there, *compadre*. We'll have a great big party
the day of the baptism. It's the fifth child, isn't it?"

"Yes, sir. I've already got two roughnecks and two
petticoats."

"What about elsewhere, Natário?"

"A fair share, Colonel, I've lost count. All of them with
my face, which is no saint's."

The captain's visits to his lands generally lasted three
or four days, enough to pay the half-dozen hired hands,
check on things, and fill his eyes with the sight of the
thriving fields. But on a certain occasion he lingered there
for three weeks, at the head of his workers clearing out some
forest that still remained on the property. If it were up to
them, God knows when the burning would be completed.
Under his command, not a single machete lay idle in a
worker's hand.

It would be a small spread, according to those who
knew, a farm yielding no more than eight tons a year,
counting harvest and premature fall, and that was it. Of a
different opinion, however, the captain treated it as a plantation: the Boa Vista Plantation. In the words of its owner,
Boa Vista, a couple of years after the first flowering, would
produce at least twice the eight tons predicted by the envious. Planted in fertile soil, set up perfectly by someone who
for years had taken care of—and still took care of—someone
else's property, familiar as no one else with the secrets of
growing cacao, it was a plantation for no less than fifteen
tons, and Natário was prepared to bet money with anyone
who doubted it.

The sections that Colonel Boaventura Andrade had registered in the name of the former gunman were located near
Tocaia Grande, no one knew whether on purpose or by
coincidence. The reckless speculated about the name Natário
gave to the property—Boa Vista: "Grand View" Plantation—
hinting that he must have been inspired by the sight of the
valley beside the river when, on a distant stormy night,
six-shooter in hand, he lay in ambush: a grand view in spite
of the darkness.

When he learned of Colonel Robustiano de Araújo's plans
for a warehouse, Natário advised him to build in Tocaia
Grande. A big plantation without limits, where, besides growing cacao, the colonel raised cattle, Santa Mariana was

located near the headwaters of the Rio das Cobras, on the edge of the brushlands, far from the railroad. For that very reason the colonel had decided to build a storehouse at an appropriate site where he could keep his dry cacao and turn it over to the exporters; let them worry about getting it to Ilhéus. The landowner liked the spot, he followed the suggestion, and since it worked out well, he was already talking about putting up a corral where the cattle could rest on the way to the slaughterhouses in Ilhéus and Itabuna. Worthy advice; the grateful colonel had then sent a heifer to the captain.

The captain was present when the workers dispatched by Colonel Robustiano piled up clay, cut poles, and built the first huts; he was present at the arrival of the first lady of the night, Jacinta, better known as Coroca, the hag, because she was on in years. Her age no longer allowed her to look for customers from farm to farm; she settled there to serve the ever more numerous drovers, for Tocaia Grande had become an overnight stop for many.

2

CONTENT WITH LIFE, CAPTAIN Natário reached Tocaia Grande in the middle of the afternoon. Having been away from Atalaia longer than planned, he was in a hurry. He hadn't intended stopping in the valley, but the unusual activity, a number of men busy cutting down and carrying tree trunks, made him stop his mule in front of Jacinta's hut. Had Colonel Robustiano decided to begin building the corral? The whore, aged and worn out, appeared in the doorway, the remains of her breasts showing through holes in her slip.

"Good afternoon, Coroca." Natário greeted her without dismounting from his mule.

"Good afternoon, Natário...." She bit her tongue. "... Captain Natário." In days gone by, when he was a young man, they'd gone to bed lots of times, sometimes on the cuff; when she saw him broke and in need, Coroca would open her legs for him on credit, but lately he couldn't handle all the women offering themselves to him: "On your way back? You spent a lot of time there. Have you set up a new whore?"

"Only if the blade of a machete is a whore. . . . Tell me, if you know, what's all this fuss about? Is it Colonel Robustiano's corral or what?"

"Mr. Fadu hired a bunch of people to build him a house. A wooden house, not a mud hut thrown together like mine. The people are there inside working; you can see them through the openings."

"Turk Fadul? Going to set up a place of business?" He was thoughtful: "Where? Show me the place."

"The one who should know is Bernarda; it was her he slept with here the night he made up his mind."

"What Bernarda? Florêncio's daughter?"

"The same. She came a couple of weeks ago. She ran away from her father's bed and came here with a mule train from Boca do Rio. She's something new, the men want to go to bed only with her."

Before spurring his animal, Natário asked, "Need anything, Coroca?"

"I'm not begging. I'll starve to death first."

The captain laughed, his eyes narrowed. The goddamned thick-necked old woman.

"I still owe you some favors, remember? From the old days."

"Could be."

He gave her some coins, went off after the workmen, and from them learned about Fadul's plans. The peddler had left money with Bastião da Rosa and orders to cut down and prepare enough wood to build a house with two doors in front and three rooms inside. A small palace like that in those parts could be found only in Taquaras, beside the railroad tracks, and that would be pushing it! Besides, Lupiscínio, the carpenter, had come from Taquaras, sent by Mr. Fadu to build a counter and some shelves. A lot of work to be done in a hurry; Bastião da Rosa gave his opinion.

"The Turk's gone crazy, Captain. Tocaia Grande's no place for all this lordliness."

Natário shook his head in disagreement. Crazy? He didn't think so. He knew for certain that sooner or later Tocaia Grande would be a city alongside which Taquaras wouldn't be more than a miserable village, a pesthole.

3

JACINTA'S SHACK WAS A mansion compared to the straw
hovel where Bernarda took shelter: half a dozen palm fronds
poorly put together, four stumps of wood stuck into the
ground. Inside, a cot, a clay pot on three stones—that was it.

Natário dismounted, glanced around. The girl, wet from
head to toe, was coming up from the river, the clothes she
went to wash in her hand: drawers and a petticoat. Her
cheap cotton dress, soaked against her skin, clung to her
dark body and showed it off; water ran down from her hair,
dripping on the back of her neck. When she recognized the
visitor, she stopped, then broke into a run with her arms
held out toward him. In Natário's eyes the one running was
a girl of two leaving the mud puddle where she'd been
playing to come hang, naked and dirty, around his neck.
When he hid out at Atalaia, he'd stayed for a spell in the
house of Florêncio and of Ana, his mistress. Florêncio didn't
work in the groves; he was occupied with jobs of greater
importance; he took care of weapons and gunmen.

How old could Bernarda be? he wondered, when the
image of the child blended with that of the girl glistening in
water and sunlight. He'd known her when she was a suckling babe, hanging on her mother's hip; in a sense, Natário
had helped to rear her. In the small living room of the little
two-room house, Ana had set up a hammock for the guest;
on the floor, in a crate made into a cradle, the child slept.
She would wake up crying in the middle of the night, but
rarely would Ana wake up to give her her breast. Dead with
fatigue, sunk in a leaden sleep in the next room, she didn't
even hear her daughter whimpering. Natário would take the
child out of the box, put her in the hammock, and lull her to
sleep with the swaying, lying on his chest.

She must have been five when Colonel Boaventura
brought Father Afonso to bless the chapel that Dona Ernestina
had had built on the plantation in payment of a promise to
St. Joseph, her protector, to whom the colonel owed his
life—to St. Joseph and to Natário, who'd squeezed the trigger on time: *With your permission, Colonel.* The festivities
lasted two days: a crowd of guests, people came even from

Bahia. The priest celebrated mass, consecrated the image of
the saint, married all those living together, baptized a whole
raft of children and a few grown men, still heathens.

Natário took advantage of the festivities to marry Zilda,
with whom he had been living for more than a year. He'd
found her wandering on the Água Preta road, pale, skinny,
and frightened, an orphan, both parents dead from smallpox. A troop of renegades was dogging her heels, a pack
after a bitch without an owner. More for amusement than
for appetite, Natário entered the competition, sent Mané
Bragado, the freckle-face, to his grave: the blowhard didn't
know him and pulled out a gun. Since the skinny girl had
cost the life of a man, he took her with him and right away
she gave him a child.

Quiet and submissive, hardworking and neat—the house
was always clean as a whistle—Zilda took on weight and
coloring, consideration and affection, and stayed on. Where
did she get up the courage to tell her lord and master that
they had to get married? By a priest, so as not to be living
against God's law; she didn't need any judge, no.

When he picked her up, Natário was still living in
Florêncio's house; he got her pregnant in his bachelor's
hammock; in full view of Bernarda, in a manner of speaking. Bernarda still slept in the living room, but with Zilda's
presence she lost her place in the hammock, on the swaying
and comforting chest.

On the occasion of the collective baptism, Ana invited
them to be the girl's godparents. Skillful, Zilda made a rag
doll for her godchild out of some old cloth. Natário didn't
give her anything except what she wanted most: to be able
to call him godfather, kiss his hand, and receive his blessing.

While Florêncio stayed on at Atalaia, Bernarda lived
more in her godparents' house than in her parents'. She was
going on ten when Florêncio—having had a misunderstanding with the colonel over some trifle, and having the arrogance of a gunman who refused to do hard work—moved to
the Boca do Mato Plantation, where Colonel Benvindo was
looking for a capable thug to ride herd on his sharecroppers.
Natário and Zilda offered to take care of their godchild;
Florêncio wouldn't think of it. They needed Bernarda to
help take care of her little sister: Ana had popped out another daughter in the meantime, Irará by name, nicknamed

Irá. Afterward, when it happened, Zilda thought that even
back then Florêncio had had his eye on the child.

When their friends moved away, Natário only rarely
saw Bernarda again. At the age of thirteen she was a fine
young woman, pretty, coveted. Lust for a woman in the end
of the earth that was cacao country had no brakes or limits,
for there was no female available except for a few rare lucky
fellows; anything in a skirt had charm and usefulness. Not
to mention receptive mares, mules, and donkeys.

A stroke laid Ana in her bed, mute and deaf, crippled for
life. She became a burden with no other value except to
cause expense and work, while Bernarda was developing
with opulent and visible seduction. From the bedroom, lying
beside the cripple, Florêncio could hear his daughter's heavy
breathing in the living room, a powerful call. What could
the old sot do? He gobbled the kid up before someone else
might get her. Nobody wanted to delve into the matter; it
wasn't worth the trouble. A bandit hired in the backlands of
the São Francisco River when the battle over possession of
the land began, Florêncio had established a macabre record
of service. The daughter belonged to him, and it was up to
him to take care of his family as best suited by his head. Or
his balls.

4

ADDING UP IN HIS head while he tightened the cinch of the
saddle, the captain concluded that Bernarda must be fourteen or fifteen years old. If she'd been living in Ilhéus, she'd
still be a silly girl, playing with dolls; here in the backwoods, she was a mature woman, a prostitute with an open
door.

She came running with arms outstretched, dropping
the clothes she'd just washed, but as she approached, she
stopped short and lowered her eyes. Leaning on his animal,
Natário looked at her and even without wanting to, ran his
squinty eyes over his goddaughter's entire body: agile and
slim, compact bronze flesh. A confusion in his breast, where
feelings and emotions were running into each other, contra-

dictory, as if he were two different people. The warm voice still came from the past.

"Give me your blessing, Godfather."

But reality imposed itself immediately.

"You got my message, didn't you?"

"What message? I just found out you were here right now, from Coroca. What's up?"

He let go of the mule, who went off looking for something to graze on; it wouldn't go far. Without waiting for an answer, he went through the doorway into the hut, sat down on the cot made out of two planks. Bernarda went with him and stood before him: there was so little room that she was almost touching his knees.

"Tell me, what happened?" In the apparently cold and neutral voice a touch of concern showed through.

Bernarda raised her head and looked straight at her godfather.

"I couldn't take any more. Papa did only two things when he came back from the groves: drink and beat us." The words came out slow and heavy. "And do what you know he did, Godfather."

With her hand she smoothed her skirt, the only sign of embarrassment.

"There wasn't anything to eat at home, he bought only cane liquor. We didn't starve to death because of the neighbors and because I went into the bushes with anyone who'd pay me, taking a chance: if Papa found out he would have killed me."

Natário listened without comment. Bernarda sniffled, weeping threatened to break out, but she caught it deep in her throat, her spirit had been tempered in a slow fire. She lifted the hem of her skirt to daub her burning eyes. The captain noticed her firm thigh, saw the curve of her behind; his goddaughter had walked on coals. Overcome by sorrow— *the poor girl!*—he felt his heart soften, but his eyes remained staring, hazy with lust, until the child let go of her skirt and went on.

"Papa made me his mistress, his own daughter, everybody knows that. While Mama was still alive, unable to talk or move like she was, I put up with it, I wasn't going to let Mama die alone. But after we buried her, I ran off." She looked at her godfather again to declare, "Anybody who thought I agreed to it was wrong. I stayed at the house without wanting to, because of Mama being the way she was."

She remained in that house without wanting to, the plain truth, but Natário only said, "I didn't know that *comadre* Ana had died."

"She left us about twenty days ago. I sent you a message at Atalaia. Didn't they give it to you?"

"I was away. I'm only on my way back now. What about Irá?"

"She stayed with Papa."

"What if he does with Irá what he did with you?"

"With Irá, Godfather? But she's too little, she still isn't eleven years old and she hasn't bled yet."

"Do you think *compadre* is a man to worry about foolish notions like that? In Luíza Mocotó's house in Rio do Braço there's a girl ten years old selling herself. They say it was her father who broke her. What we've got a lot of here are cacao trees and hungry dogs."

He summed up without commenting, that's how it was and that was that. In the heavy silence of intentions and thoughts, the captain pushed the palm fronds that served as a door with his foot. He held out his hand, touched the cotton dress clinging to his goddaughter's skin. Bernarda didn't move or lower her eyes.

His goddaughter. A little girl came running, naked and dirty, to hang around his neck. Natário offered her a penny, but she refused. What she wanted was to ride on the back of his neck, hold on to the brim of his leather hat, play. She grew up sleeping in the hammock, breathing heavily against the gunman's chest, laughing when he tickled the soles of her feet. The child's universe was made up of her godfather; except for him there was nothing but a desert of desolation and indifference.

More than a godfather, almost a father. So what? Her real father was Florêncio, and she hadn't refused when the old man wanted to sleep with her. She'd bedded with him for more than a year, if not with pleasure, with resignation. Natário put the palm of his hand on Bernarda's belly; she remained motionless, but when his fingers touched her breast, she gave a trace of a smile and lowered her eyes. The captain pulled her onto the cot.

After the strangled sob, the moan of anxiety and joy, the cry of victory, Bernarda passed her hand lightly across her godfather's face, trembled, smiled, and said, "I always thought that someday I'd lie with you like this."

She snuggled up to his sweaty chest, just like the girl in the hammock.

"It happened in my dreams, lots of times. When I want something, I dream about it. Do you too, Godfather?" She started a conversation to keep him there in her lap.

"Dreams are lies, dreaming isn't worth the trouble. When I want something, I do it or take it." He softened his voice to conclude: "It's better having it than dreaming about it. I was wanting too."

Blessed, happy words. Her godfather had been wanting as well, dying with the urge to lie down with her and penetrate her. The desolation and meanness of life were crumbling; there was no place for them in the luminous world of kisses and caresses when bodies and souls undress and offer themselves without embarrassment, without shame. *Oh, how wonderful, Godfather, let's fill ourselves, I need it to make up for the endless days, the nights of fear and disgust! Oh, Godfather, so much rotten time! So much sad time! Let's fill ourselves, don't leave!*

"Godfather, don't leave right now. You won't, will you? It's still early." She excused herself. "I haven't got anything to give you. Only myself, if you still want to."

They both wanted to and they lingered in their lassitude, making it last until the sun went to sleep in the river and the mule brayed outside. While he was putting on his boots, the captain wanted to know, "What did the Turk say?"

"He's going to set up a store here. He says it has a future. He's probably on his way back."

"When he gets home, you tell him to come talk to me at Atalaia. But tell him right off that the hill by the bend in the river, that highest one, is mine, and has been for a long time."

The godfather's word was truth and law; Bernarda asked the question only in order to have a minute more of conversation, make him stay and make her happy.

"Did you buy it along with the fields?"

"The fields I got from the colonel because I earned them. I earned that headland, too, but I don't know who gave it to me in payment: whether it was God or the devil. I know only that it's mine and nobody lays a hand on it or sets foot on it."

He didn't offer her any money when he left: it would have demeaned her if he had: instead of a copper penny the little girl had only asked for pleasure. But, before hitting the trail, the captain arranged with Bastião da Rosa and Lupiscínio to take what was left over from the lumber cut for Fadul; they would use it, at his expense, to build a three-room house where his goddaughter and Coroca could live and practice their profession. Whoever wins power and authority also takes on obligations. He must fulfill them.

Black Castor Abduim da Assunção Assaults a Plantation Owner After Having Cuckolded Him Twice Over

1

BLACK CASTOR ABDUIM DA ASSUNÇÃO brought the nickname Tição Aceso, Burning Ember, with him from the Bahia Bay region where he came from, and he held on to half of it, rarely answering to the name he was baptized with; he got to be just Tição, a happy-go-lucky boy. At the time of his escape, he left behind forever the epithet "ebony prince," repeated by Adroaldo Muniz Saraiva de Albuquerque, baron of Itauaçu, with an obvious mocking tone, but which Baroness Marie-Claude Duclos Saraiva de Albuquerque, or simply Madame, would always pronounce with a roll of her eyes, a trill of her tongue, and a wiggle of her ass.

Her ass, not her hips, thighs, buttocks, or rear end, Rufina, the mulatto girl, declared in the kitchen of the big house, bringing on laughter and gibes: since Madame's lacked such meaty attributes, she could hardly shake them. In compensation, her enormous eyes were always imploring and perturbing, and beneath the lacework of her transparent organdy blouse, with the brazenness of a foreign woman, she flaunted a pair of tiny breasts, firm, however, and haughty, more pink than white in their glow, pure coquetry. When young Castor, in his gaudy servant's livery, would appear in the living room bearing crystal glasses on a silver tray, Madame would whisper: *Mon prince*—and her voice would melt away in pleasure.

Rufina's voice would also melt away in pleasure when

she saw him in the pantry, all yellow-green, with red touches
on his puffy sleeves; she would sigh: Tição Aceso, oh, my
Tição!" Rufina, with a body worthy of the whims of an
opulent plantation owner or a reverend and magnanimous
canon—bare legs, bare shoulders, full breasts, color of mo-
lasses, overflowing opulence peeping through the low-cut
neck of a cotton gown, not brazenly, but fearfully. Her small
behind like the stern of a sloop, she was sailing along at
high tide, strutting under the nose of Castor, the burning
ember who was lighting fires in her insides.

Castor didn't feel too comfortable in the servant's livery
sewn under the instructions of Madame, who had copied it
from an old French pattern book. He preferred the piece of
cloth between his legs and tied around the waist and the
heat of the forge in the smithy of his uncle Cristóvão Abduim,
his only relative. The baroness had taken him away from
the anvil in order to turn the apprentice blacksmith into a
page, an attendant, a favorite: a servant has no will or
choice. Even so, in spite of the burlesque costume and his
domestic slavish state, Castor maintained the proud bearing, his perennial, contagious laugh. Careless youth, burning ember, or *prince noir*, he made Rufina lose her head,
ready to face the direst consequences, and drove Madame
into a frenzy.

2

MARIE-CLAUDE HAD LEARNED about the incomparable qualities displayed by blacks in the exercise of *bagatelle* from
Madeleine Camus, née Burnet, her schoolmate, her *aînée*. At
Sacre-Coeur, beautiful and dissolate pupils of the nuns, *amies
intimes*, they exchanged information, projects, and fantasies, talked about religion and whoredom, anxiously awaiting their liberation.

Returning from Guadeloupe, where her husband, a lieutenant colonel in the artillery, had commanded the garrison,
Madeleine made two peremptory declarations: a) all lieutenant colonels are born with an irrevocable vocation for
passive cuckoldry, and not even the greatest simpleton of a

wife can prevent them from fulfilling their destiny; b) blacks, in matters concerning the boudoir, are absolutely unsurpassed. There was no better proof of the first assertion than Madeleine's husband himself: it was he who had brought home, as an orderly, black Dodum, precisely the best proof, the most splendid example, of the second revelation.

Proclaimed baroness and mistress of a plantation due to the happy act of matrimony with a nobleman more or less colonial, more or less of mixed blood, but very rich—regarding his fortune there was no more or less, only more and more—Marie-Claude traveled to the distant and mysterious tropics, where her soft green realm of sugar cane and servants was located. In her baggage she carried chic dresses, a boatload of medicines, concerned maternal advice, and exciting information from Madeleine. At first everything was novelty and bustle, a reason for parties and laughter, but it was not long before monotony descended.

One day, while they were discoursing about the purity and beauty of equine and other breeds, and passed by the sugar mill, Baron Adroaldo pointed to an adolescent black boy wrapped in sparks in the smithy, calling Madame la Baronne's attention to that magnificent specimen of a purebred animal.

"Look at his torso, his legs, his biceps, his head, *ma chère*: a beautiful animal. A superb example. Observe his teeth."

She looked, obedient and interested. Her moist eyes lingered on the superb example, on the beautiful animal. She observed his white teeth, his mocking smile. *Malheur!* A strip of cloth hid his primacy.

The baron really was an authority on breeds, he'd inherited the ability from his father, an expert in the selection and purchase of horses and slaves. But Marie-Claude had learned with the nuns of Sacre-Coeur that blacks also have a soul, acquired with baptism. A colonial, second-class soul, but sufficient to distinguish them from the animals: God's goodness is infinite, Sister Dominique explained, while talking about the heroism of missionaries in the heart of savage Africa.

"*Mais, pas du tout, mon ami, ce n'est pas un animal. C'est un homme, il possède une âme immortelle que le missionaire lui a donné avec le baptême.*"

"*Un homme?*" The baron burst out laughing.

When the master of Itauaçu laughed in French, putting
on the pose of a cultured and ironic aristocrat amusing
himself with human foolishness, he became even more intolerable in his affectation and arrogance. A namesake of his,
Adroaldo Ribeiro da Costa, a university graduate and intellectual from Santo Amaro, on hearing him horselaugh as he
mercilessly massacred the language of Baudelaire, beloved
master, began to call him Monsieur le Franciú, to the enjoyment of his listeners and behind the baron's back. The poet
may have had his head in the stars, but had enough sense
not to expose himself to the wrath of the big boss.

"Don't be angry with me, *ma chère,* but what you're
saying is nonsense. Where did you ever hear that a black is a
man? He is a beautiful animal, I repeat, certainly less intel-
ligent than your horse Blue Diamond."

"*Très beau, oui. Un homme très beau, un prince. Un
prince d'ébène!*"

Ebony prince! *Vous êtes drôle,* Madame. Permit me to
laugh." And he gave off a superior and definite horselaugh.

The vulgar derision, the arrogance, *le ricanement sardo-
nique* of the baron ended up convincing her: destiny is destiny, drawn up in heaven. The baroness adopted Castor and
didn't regret it. If the plantation owner noticed the interest
that caused the change of status from blacksmith's apprentice to serving him at table, he looked the other way; he
himself was busy pulling down half-breed girls around the
sugar mill, using and abusing them as if slavery were still in
force.

A feudal lord, he popped a lot of cherries, but only with
Rufina did he maintain an extended relationship; in the
kitchen of the big house she took on the airs of a mistress, a
concubine covered with gold and silver—trinkets, bracelets,
earrings, necklaces, gold braid—in addition to the mother-of-
pearl cross that the most reverend canon had given her. The
baron's generosity knew no limits: as if the expensive gifts
weren't enough, he insisted on instructing the mulatto girl
in the practice of the refinements of foreign women, without
success, because she preferred natural play: insatiable gluttony doesn't require any sauce or seasoning.

To make a long story short, then, because the complex
plot of the double cuckoldry, or double *cocuage,* of the master of Itauaçu is too long in its telling for the importance it
has in the history of Tocaia Grande, let it be stated right off,

what became public domain in a short time: fighting on two
fronts, that of Madame, all gold, and that of Rufina, all
copper, with the strength and innocence of the nineteen
years he was about to complete, Castor Abduim placed a
double pair of powerful and comical horns on the baron's
aristocratic head.

3

THE PAMPERED AND PERFUMED belly of Madame la Baronne
tightened with appetite, became dewy when in the solitude
of her boudoir, broken by the baron's snoring, she thought
about her ebony prince and sketched him out with lust:
*thick lips, teeth for biting, rough tongue, broad chest, strong
legs, and the rest, oh!*
   Pardon the dirty word, which obviously doesn't belong
in madame's lexicon. She would never say *the rest*, she
would never use a term so vulgar and indelicate to name
that unique and prime magnificence, the very sight of which
obliterated Rufina's brain and moistened Madame's most
intimate parts. *Parts:* another unfortunate word, common
but current among the people of the kitchen from whose
gossip she prayed that God would spare and keep her.
   In spite of showing sensitivity on the surface, the baroness remained lucid even during moments of ecstasy, zealous
of her Gallic logic and exactness. With proper pertinence
she addressed the beautiful and remarkable tool according
to occasion and usefulness: with both hands she grasped *le
grand mât,* satiated herself sucking *le biberon,* opened herself
up to receive front and rear *l'axe du monde.* Agonizing with
the baron's snuff and refinements, disdaining the balms of
the compassionate and magnanimous canon, Rufina sought
consolation and supply on the same broad chest where the
skinny baroness rested the ringlets of her blond hair: the
chest of Castor Abduim da Assunção, Tição Aceso, Ebony
Prince, *servant de luxe,* ex-apprentice at *maréchal-ferrant* at
the forge of his uncle Cristovão Abduim, both with their
heads made by Xangô.
   In the cane fields, in the sugar mill, on the plantations

of the bay area, in the towns of São Félix, Cachoeira, Muritiba, and Santa Amaro, in Maragogipe, and even in the capital, people commented upon the case, saying that the brotherhood of St. Cornelius, patron saint of the antlered, had a new and illustrious president, the baron of Itauaçu, *Monsieur le Franciú*, the cuckold squared, cuckold supreme, cuckold emeritus, lord of laissez-faire. *"Un gentil cocu,"* to use the definition that sounded pleasant and friendly in the mouth of his wife, the baroness. Ah!—the baroness's mouth could only be compared to Rufina's twat, two masterpieces, two works of art, an opinion shared by Baron Adroaldo Muniz Saraiva de Albuquerque, nobleman and plantation owner, and by black Castor, born a serf in the cane fields. It was proven once more that truth is imposed on scholar and illiterate, alike on rich and poor, on nobility and peasantry.

4

IN ORDER FOR ADROALDO Muniz Saraiva de Albuquerque, baron of Itauaçu, not to be judged badly, nor to have attributed to him the defects of a terribly backward plantation owner—butt of vulgar prejudices, unworthy of having a civilized European wife—it must be said that the contretemps with Castor, from initial outrage to final flight, did not have as its pretext the intimacy current between the baroness and the blacksmith's helper. From all indications, the horns coming from Madame's bucolic pastimes didn't bother the baron in the least. He bore them with dignity and nonchalance, as a shining example for the barbarian sugar lords with their summary justice: they would kill missies and misses who dared anything with blacks, and they would have the blacks killed only after having them duly castrated.

What made the baron raise his arm with the whip and leave a slash of blood across Rufina's naked back was the indignation provoked by the half-breed girl's behavior: her ingratitude, her complete lack of respect. He felt himself attacked in what was most sacred to him, his sense of property. He'd spent experience and money on the ungrateful wretch—he'd bestowed on her the honor of deflowering her and persistently fornicating with her; he'd sought to instruct her in the more refined sexual practices, which the stupid no-good refused to accept; he'd given her the status of concubine, raising her to the position of house ward, of domestic animal, in addition to the articles of clothing and accessories, so many of them. The mulatto girl's betrayal pained him deeply: it wasn't a matter of the momentary whim of a bored wife, laughable giddiness, venial sin; this was a serious crime, a vile affront, a humiliating mockery of lord and master, an unpardonable fault, a mortal sin. To tolerate such an outrage would have meant shaking the foundations of morality and society.

So, when on returning from his morning ride he surprised Rufina being possessed in the rooms of the former slave quarters by Castor in the elementary way of the untutored, the mulatto girl underneath and the black man on top, the baron was furious; it was no trifling matter, we must agree. The black king took to his heels, but came back, almost immediately, when he heard Rufina's wail. Out of his head, the baron was making an example of her. Castor pulled the whip from his hands, broke it in two, and threw it away. In return he got the punch, the insult, and the threat.

"I'm going to have your balls cut off, you prince of shit, you dirty nigger."

His face burning, his sight hazy, the prince—whatever he was—of ebony of shit grabbed the baron by his riding jacket and filled his face with blows. He stopped hitting him only when people came from the big house and the sugar mill in an uproar that had something festive about it: it wasn't every day that they got to see the spectacle of a plantation owner being slapped around.

Head and balls at stake, Castor took off. If he had lingered, not even the baroness would have been able to save him. Not that she wanted to: sick over the black man's betrayal—*Aie! Madeleine, le plus beau noir du monde, le plus vilain des hommes!*—Madame fell ill, kept to her bed for melancholy days, but soon recovered and readied herself for a trip to Europe in the company of the baron on a second well-deserved honeymoon.

The fugitive reached the state capital after coming down

the Paraguaçu River in a sloop loaded with sugar and cane liquor. Mãe Gertrudes de Oxum, who took him in, thought the city of Bahia was too close to Santo Amaro to guarantee the life of a black man accused of such crimes: he'd dared raise his eyes to the irreproachable and virtuous wife of the master; rejected, he'd tried to violate the poor defenseless servant girl; prevented from carrying out his base intent, he'd tried to murder the plantation owner. Police agents were looking for him with an arrest order; *capoeira* footfighters from around the bay were combing the streets for him with orders to kill.

Hidden in the hold of a two-masted schooner, he traveled from Bahia to Ilhéus. At the temple in a coconut grove between Pontal and Olivença, where he took care of his African gods, his *orixás*, Pai Arolu took him in and recommended him to Colonel Robustiano de Araújo, whose wealth didn't prevent him from offering food to the gods and receiving the blessing of the *babalorixá* priest. In the eldorado of cacao, Pai Arolu had as much or more prestige as His Grace the bishop: he'd got there first and he possessed incontestable powers over sun and rain.

5

CASTOR HAD BEEN WORKING for five years as a shoer of horses on the Santa Mariana Plantation when, following behind a mule train, he chanced to spend the night at Tocaia Grande. His destination was the town of Itabuna, more exactly the side streets full of thriving whorehouses, where he would quench his thirst of so many long weeks. For someone who liked to have his fill, enjoying rich viands, native and foreign delicacies in the feasting on sugar plantations around the bay, the cacao farms in the southern part of the state left much to be desired in matters of women.

Otherwise, he was satisfied; he didn't miss anything except his uncle. Even if he could, he wouldn't have gone back. Back home he was nothing but a slave, with only the right to obey without raising his voice. Treated as a prince, putting horns on the baron in the luxury of linen sheets, lace bedcovers, satin pillows, not even in Madame's bed did he feel himself a free man. In order for that to happen, it had been necessary for him to hit the master in the face, risk his life, go out into the world and reach the cacao lands, where everyone had his own worth and, good or bad, was paid for what he did.

He made up for the lack of women on the plantation by going along with the mule trains: in stopping-places, villages, towns, he found the warmth of whores. He'd matured into a calm and cordial black man, conserving his simple ways and his proud bearing, his friendly character. When he was a long time in coming back, some of the girls would complain about Tição's long absence: there was no one like him to liven up a party.

A capable and skilled craftsman on the primitive forge set up at Santa Mariana to take care of the needs of the plantation— branding cattle, shoeing saddle and pack animals, sharpening machetes, repairing work tools, shovels, hoes, scythes—Castor, for his own enjoyment, made knives, daggers, harness bells, rings to give to women friends, *candomblé* instruments that he sent as gifts to Pai Arolu: Oxóssi's bow and arrow, Oxum and Iemanjá's *abebês*, a double-bit ax for Xangô. The colonel poured out his praise for the skill and expertness of the blacksmith, an artist in his eyes. Tição had given the plantation owner a pair of stirrups, forged with care and craftsmanship, a valuable set.

A good person, Colonel Robustiano de Araújo. Rich and powerful, he didn't put on airs, didn't look down on his workers. Even so, Castor's dream was to set up a smithy in one of the new towns and work for himself, not serve a boss, no matter how good he might be.

With Coroca's Help, Tição Abduim Extracts a Molar for the Mistress of the Famous Bandit Manuel Bernardes

1

SUDDENLY, PIERCING WAILS DROWNED out the usual sundown gabble in the large encampment that Tocaia Grande had become. They came from far off, in a crescendo: desperate cries of pain. Somebody was calling for help and talking about death. The accordion fell silent in the hands of Pedro Gypsy, who wandered about at random with no fixed destination, doing a little bit of everything and not much of anything. The determined card players stopped dealing, drovers and workers awakened, stood up, came out to see what was going on. Alongside Coroca in the army cot, black Castor half-arose, alert.

"It sounds like someone's being killed," the lady of the evening commented.

"I'm going to take a look," the black man said, pulling on his pants. "I'll be right back."

"I'm going too." Coroca sharpened her ear. "It's a woman crying."

A legend of danger and violence still hung over Tocaia Grande—it hadn't got its name by accident—every so often a shooting, a knifing, fights over a greasy deck of cards. Even so, people who lived there and people passing through Tocaia got alarmed whenever they heard cries of pain, calls for help.

Three figures appeared from behind the shed where the cacao from Santa Maria Plantation was stored and where the drovers who brought it and the gunmen who guarded it were resting. Coroca and Castor could make out the still-youngish woman in the light of the full moon, a dark mulatto girl with thick curly hair, a fine piece of womanhood if she hadn't been so distraught: she was holding her hand over one cheek and moaning without end. She was accompanied by a thin half-breed man, on in years, and an old woman. Coroca went up to meet the people: nothing serious, just a sick woman on her way to Itabuna in search of treatment. She couldn't be in such bad shape because she was walking on her own two feet and not being carried in a hammock on people's shoulders, half-dead. The whore's mocking laugh could be heard.

"All that fuss over a tooth? Waking people up out of their sleep over foolishness like that? Disgraceful."

Worried and angry, the old woman confronted Coroca.

"I'd like to see if it was you, missy. The poor thing's been doing nothing but suffer for three days. She's had no rest. It started the day before yesterday and all it's done is ache, worse and worse. The poor girl hasn't had any relief."

She raised her voice so the onlookers could hear.

"We're on our way to Taquaras to see if we can find somebody to pull out her tooth. If we don't find anyone there, we'll go on to Itabuna. She's my daughter, his wife."

She pointed to the man, who remained silent. The old woman was spilling her insides out. She was all ready to repeat the explanation on their way out. She went on.

"I think they put a curse on her. That woman from Aparecida who—"

"That's enough! You talk too much, ma'am."

He had a dagger at his belt and a repeater slung over his shoulder. Even without the old woman's explanation, they knew right away that the girl was his property from the worry and care reflected in his sullen face, which grew soft when he looked at the whimpering woman. He stood in front of Castor when the black man came over and offered his services.

"If you're looking for someone to pull out your tooth, ma'am, you don't have to go to Taquaras. It can be done right here. Come along with me."

The man wanted to know, "Where to?"

"To Colonel Robustiano's warehouse, so I can take a look at the shape the tooth's in."

"You know about toothaches?" More than the question, the tone of voice contained suspicions and warnings.

Castor didn't hesitate, he opened up in a smile.

"I know, yes, sir. Let's go, ma'am."

At a signal from the man they went to the cacao warehouse, the gunmen making way for the group, all interested in the details of the event. The audience grew with the presence of Pedro Gypsy, Bernarda, Lupiscínio, Bastião de Rosa, workers, and drovers. They exchanged whispers, looked out of the corners of their eyes at the armed man; the carpenter made a sign, Bastião da Rosa answered with another, confirming what it meant. They'd recognized the morose stranger: he'd grown older and had gotten hitched, which made him all the more dangerous. Lupiscínio felt a shiver go up his spine, a chill in his muscles: anything could happen.

Tição asked the woman to sit down on some cacao sacks and open her mouth, but she didn't move; she kept on moaning, waiting for a decision by the half-breed, who repeated the question.

"You really know?"

The black man laughed again, playfully and well spoken.

"I already told you, sir."

I'm nobody's sir, yours or anybody else's. I'm Manuel Bernardes, from Itacaré, and I don't like horsing around. I'm going to tell her to sit down, and the risk is yours." He softened his voice when he spoke to the woman.

"Go sit down, Clorinda. Open your mouth and show the boy which tooth."

Lupiscínio and Bastião da Rosa had identified him before he proclaimed his name, a knife fighter and a threat to be watched. He had been a thug in the service of Badarós during the battles between them and Colonel Basílio de Oliveira in the final siege. When he ran out of ammunition and found himself all alone with a bullet in the shoulder, bathed in blood, even then he didn't surrender, didn't give up; armed with his knife, he still wounded three more. When he was captured and tied up, they meant to put an end to him in the underbrush, but Colonel Basílio wouldn't allow it: you don't kill a tough man like that in cold blood. He ordered them to let him go, shook his hand. Manuel Bernardes went to live in Itacaré, where he planted corn and manioc and had a flour mill. The only one whose fame could rival his was Captain Natário da Fonseca.

At that moment they were all afraid for the life of black Tição, a hardworking and boastful young man, highly thought of by all. A blacksmith with a steady and strong hand when he pounded a nail, an ironworker with agile and skillful fingers when he worked metal. He seemed to possess only one serious defect: he was a busybody, he stuck his nose everywhere, tried to solve everything, a real devil. He was going to pay dearly for his boldness; who told him to butt in? He certainly had no competence or experience, all he was was a well-intentioned, easygoing nigger.

"Pleased to meet you, Mr. Manuel. My name's Castor Abduim; they call me Tição because I'm a blacksmith. I've got other nicknames I could tell you if you want to hear them. Now, let's give some relief to your lady. In this world there's nothing so bad that can be compared to a toothache, that's what I've heard say. I never had one, thank God." He laughed from one side of his mouth to the other, his white teeth glistening.

2

"IS IT AN UPPER or a lower? Which side, ma'am?"

"Lower. This one here."

The onlookers came closer, they all wanted to see, their eyes went from the gunslinger to the black man, from the woman to her old mother. Tição asked Coroca to hold the lamp up to Clorinda's face. He could barely manage to see in the flickering and smoky light: he was feeling with his fingers on the right side until the patient moaned louder and he felt the cavity in the molar. He announced, "A back one! If the lady wants, and if somebody can get me a pair of pliers, I can take it out."

Manuel Bernardes's voice sounded again, still doubtful and threatening.

"Have you ever pulled one out?"

In that asshole of the earth, a horseshoer ended up being a horse doctor. Castor had pulled teeth from donkeys and horses more than once. Not from men and women yet, but what difference did that make?

"I can't keep track of them all."

In the tool chest in the warehouse they found the pliers. The black man asked them to bring him some cane liquor.

"So the girl can take a swig to dull the pain."

A drover brought a bottle that was more than half full. Tição tested it, praised it: it's good stuff. He explained to Clorinda, "It's going to hurt some, but if you want me to pull the tooth, you've got to bear it." His smile brought on confidence. "But it's only one pain, then it's all over, finished."

"Do me the favor, then."

Politely, the black man held the bottle out to the half-breed, offering it to him.

"A sip? It's good to calm the nerves."

"I can do without." Alongside the woman, he was gripping his repeater, impassive.

Castor pretended ignorance.

"You can do without? Don't you like it, or are you a Protestant? The girl's the one who can't do without it, whether she likes it or not."

From the way in which she took the bottle, it could be seen right off that Clorinda never refused a good drink. She even stopped moaning.

"Now open your mouth, ma'am. The light, Coroca!"

He probed the gums of the moaning woman, who squirmed with each touch of the uncomfortable hand. In the heavy and tense silence, alarm and apprehension hovered over the group, who hung on every word, every movement. The old woman took the bottle out of her daughter's hand, had a drink herself. Tição laughed and remarked, "What's this, Granny? Are you going to have a tooth pulled too? Hold these." He handed her the pliers, turned to the impolite fellow. "Loan me your knife, Mr. Manuel."

"What for?"

"You'll see. I've got to move the gum back so I can grab the tooth with the pliers."

He took the weapon, prescribed another shot of *cachaça* for Clorinda.

"She'll get drunk like that." The old woman was alarmed.

"The drunker she is, the better off she'll be."

With a nod of his head, Pedro Gypsy approved and

praised the loosening up of the moaner; she was guzzling the bottle willingly.

"Get ready, it's going to hurt a little," Castor warned.

"It can't get any worse than it is." The *cachaça*, if it hadn't got her drunk, had given her courage.

Asking Coroca to move the lamp so he could see inside the open mouth, the black man pried away the gum from the tooth little by little, with the tip of the knife; trickles of blood ran down from the corners of the woman's mouth. Manuel Bernardes looked away, staring straight ahead. Besides the muffled moans, not the slightest sound could be heard. Clorinda twitched from time to time when she felt the prick of the knife.

"All set!" Castor stated. "Pass her the bottle, Granny."

He returned the knife. Manuel Bernardes wiped off the blood on his khaki pants. Tição waited for the woman to stop drinking and made her open her mouth wide; even so he had a hard time getting the pliers in. Nor was it easy to get the molar between the prongs: in spite of the delicate touch and the skill shown by the shoer of horses, the pliers bit into the damaged gum two or three times, making Clorinda flinch. Taking advantage of a moment when the black man took out the pliers in order to push back the gum with his fingers, the woman gave a jerk and leapt up. Without even looking at her, Manuel Bernardes said, "You wanted it, now you've got to take it. The young fellow warned you. Go sit down and don't get up again."

It was an order, but delivered with softness. His voice wasn't raised, he never raised it when he spoke to Clorinda. The half-breed was in love, Bernarda reflected, and worried about Tição: if the black man damaged the woman's mouth and didn't get the tooth out, they were going to witness a different kind of trouble. She looked around and read the same agony on the faces of the others, *oh, Virgin of Capistola!*

The woman quieted down and Tição finally managed to get the molar between the prongs. He dug his feet into the ground, gave a strong pull, but the patient moved, the tooth resisted, it didn't come out with the tool. The black man patiently began the delicate task all over again, in endless minutes. The onlookers pressed in. Somebody, maybe Bernarda, let out a sigh. Manuel Bernardes's voice, angry and harsh now, demanded, "Get it over with!"

Castor smiled in the light of the lamp and went on

calmly until he felt the tooth tightly held by the prongs gripping it at the root. He asked the help of two men to hold Clorinda still, to stop her from moving. Before anyone could come forward, Manuel Bernardes declared, "You don't need anyone, I can do it myself."

He laid his rifle against the sacks of cacao, clutched the back of the woman's head with his two hands. Then the black man firmed his body, pulled with all his might, the might of a blacksmith used to shoeing animals, hammering red-hot iron. The pliers came out dripping with blood. Castor held them up with the molar between the prongs, a giant tooth that was a delight to see.

"There's your chopper, girl."

Clorinda spat thickly, cleaned the red drool with the back of her hand. She picked up the bottle of *cachaça*, drank what was left as if she were drinking water, then thanked him.

"God save you, boy. Please excuse my bad manners."

Manuel Bernardes slung the rifle on his shoulder. He came over.

"Shake." His hand was outstretched. "Excuse my suspicions, but you looked so green. A damned hard job. What do I owe you?"

"You don't owe me anything. I don't pull teeth for a living."

Another bottle of cane liquor appeared, no one knew where from. It went from hand to hand, finally reached them. Manuel Bernardes held it up by the neck, swallowed two measured swigs, wiped his mouth with the sleeve of his jacket; he laughed for the first time as he handed the bottle to the black man.

"I'm no heathen, no, God save me and keep me, but I didn't feel like drinking with you back then." He took his leave. "If you need me someday, you know where I live."

A bouncy sound could be heard, it was coming from Pedro Gypsy's accordion, a *coco* from Alagoas that made people's feet thump and their blood pound. The old woman went wild and got into the quick, small steps of the dance: an old woman made devilish from the *cachaça* and the black man's dance. A circle formed around her, hands clapping to the quickening rhythm. Bastião da Rosa, a white man with blue eyes, took Bernarda into the center of the circle and danced with her. Clorinda, her suffering over,

invited the half-breed at her side with a look. Manuel
Bernardes smiled again, his heart relieved of the pain of his
companion and the temptation to kill. He took the repeater
off his shoulder. From the sacks of cacao a strong smell
arose that mingled with the stink of sweaty bodies—familiar
smells, basic smells.

"Dr. Tição . . ." Coroca joked, hanging the lamp on a
hook by the door.

They'd left the party together, had come back to the
army cot. Coroca wasn't the perfumed and stylish baroness,
nor did she possess Rufina's slim young body, but for taking
care of an emergency she was as good or better than anyone: she had the wisdom of Madame, the fire of the mulatto
girl. A peerless pussy.

3

A DAMP, TORRID UNIVERSE of mud and dust punctuated the
cacao calendar. The rains, just as absolutely necessary as
the sun, lasted half a year, heavy, endless, easily turning
into tropical storms. If they went beyond their useful time,
however, the rains could turn deadly, making the buds,
hungry for light and heat, rot on the trees. Colonels and
foremen, gunmen and hired hands lived with their eyes
turned to the sky, searching for signs that sometimes
portended wet weather, sometimes dry, praying that the
arrival of rain would make the cacao trees burst into blood
and the heat of the sunshine would help the sprouts grow
strong and ignite into gold. So the legend of that blessed
region could hold its own, with the incredible news of such
fertility traveling far and wide, tales that startled the entire
nation.

In search of work and fortune, down from the north, up
from the south to the new eldorado came a mixed and eager
humanity: workers, criminals, adventurers, ladies of the evening, lawyers, missionaries impatient to convert the heathen. They came from across the ocean too: Arabs and Jews,
Italians, Swiss, and Germans, not to mention the Englishmen
of the Ilhéus–Conquista Railroad—the State of Bahia South

Western Railway Company—and of the British consulate, with its Union Jack, staunch phlegm and sturdy drinking. The English consul had left his family in London, taken on a silent Indian woman as a maid for all tasks in Ilhéus. In bed, in her small nakedness, she seemed a forest goddess, and perhaps she was. The honorable consul gave her a beautiful son, a half-breed with blue eyes, a chocolate-colored gringo.

The people in those newly worked fields, rich and blood-thirsty, had little religion, although they brought up God's name in every proposition, pronouncing it in vain, even invoking His protection for their ambushes and swindles. Men of easy promises, the colonels renewed agreements every year, striking compromises with the celestial court for the sake of the rain, for the sake of the sun, trying to buy the goodwill of the saints and forgiveness for their crimes—if the accidents of conquest can be called crimes.

In the days of the colony, when cacao still didn't exist, St. George, brought over by the white men in the altars of their caravels, was proclaimed the patron of the captaincy. Mounted on his horse, his lance upraised, a warrior saint, quite precisely, a protector. In the recesses of the jungle, brought by slaves in the hold of slave ships, Oxóssi, lord of the jungle and of the animals, rode on a spiny pig, a gigantic peccary, a wild boar. The saint from Europe and the *orixá* from Africa blended into a single divinity, ruling sun and rain, receiving offerings and chants, masses and *ebós*: on a litter in processions, on the main altar of the Cathedral of Ilhéus, or in the hut of Pai Arolu, who had been born a slave and had taken refuge there to guard his free-dom. In the *peji*, displayed side by side, the bow and arrow, symbol of Oxóssi, worked on the anvil by Castor Tição Abduim, and the brightly colored print of St. George crush-ing the dragon in the moonlight, an offering from the Arab Fadul Abdala, a Godfearing man when business permitted.

Mule trains carried the dry cacao from the plantations to the railroad stations or to Ilhéus and Itabuna, where the headquarters of exporting firms owned by Swiss or Ger-mans were located. The older animals stayed behind on the plantations, carrying the soft cacao from the groves to the troughs. The drovers crossing those trackless and risky paths chose places that would offer favorable conditions for spend-ing the night, gathering-places that with time and traffic almost always gave birth to a settlement. Some developed into hamlets and villages, future towns, others only vegetated—a row of houses with a whore and a cane-liquor store.

With the passage of time, Tocaia Grande became the favorite place to spend the night for drovers who came from the wide region of the Rio das Cobras, where a great many landholdings were located, among them some of the largest plantations in the region. The news of the construction of a store ordered by Turk Fadul, an astute man, a man of vision, sparked the construction of additional dwellings: huts, cabins, shacks, some of adobe, others of wood, the poorest made out of dry straw.

The first house of stone and mortar was built by black Castor to shelter his hammer and anvil, months after he pulled the tooth of Clorinda, Manuel Bernardes's good-looking mistress. According to gossip, Colonel Robustiano de Araújo loaned the blacksmith some money without interest or terms.

"That black man's a smart one. If he doesn't fall into a snare, he'll get rich. He's got drive, he learned things from foreign women, that's why sometimes he gets into trouble; but I never saw him stick his nose where he shouldn't."

A ROW OF HOUSES

In a Time of Lean Cows, Fadul Abdala, a Victim of Nightmares, Attempts to Get Himself a Mistress

1

THE TIME OF FAT COWS was late in coming, subjecting Fadul's patience and spirits to difficult tests and mounting hardships. He stood firm, however, faithful to the agreement that had been made: he was fulfilling his part, God couldn't fail to keep His. Fadul never lost a chance to remind Him—almost always with a humble prayer, but with an angry curse when he grew desperate—of the solemn promises He made: the Lord had led him by the hand to that place to establish himself there and get rich, fulfilling his destiny.

On certain occasions, though, his doubts pushed him to the brink of giving up. Other horizons offered themselves with immediate prospects, attractive visions, while he suffered the limited and sluggish gestation of Tocaia Grande. Ready to win Fadul's soul, the devil outdid himself to convince him: Satan laid out brilliant schemes, made attractive propositions, lighted up mirages to hurry the hermit along to his domain.

In order to conquer him, the unworthy one used and abused the fatal picture of Zezinha do Butiá. The cruel woman, brazen and bold, invaded his bedroom to disturb his rationed, meager hours of rest. It would happen invariably on nights after the most arduous work when, following the insane bustle, Fadul would throw himself onto his bed like a lump in search of needed rest, of rehabilitating sleep,

of a pleasant dream in which he might see himself rich and
respected. On the contrary, his dreams were filled with
anxiety and aggravation. No sooner did he fall asleep than
she would bounce in, bare and beckoning.

Clouding his closed eyes would be the sight of Zezinha's
twat, paradise itself, motherland of delight, manna and nectar. Exhibited and forbidden. The bitch went overboard in
her provocation, carrying on and going wild in a devilish
way in order to take him off the straight and narrow. First
an imperious invitation with its voluptuousness, its flirting,
its endearments; then a violent rejection with disdain and
curses—a serpent's tongue, a viper's.

*What are you doing in this dirty hole, this out-of-the-way
place? You ignorant Turk, you imbecile! Before, at least, you
used to come to Itabuna and rest your peddler's fatigue on my
breast. You used to be a good-time boy, they called you Grand
Turk, and you could choose anyone you wanted. Today, you
almost never leave your den of snakes and lepers, no sooner
do you arrive than you're on your way back. Not counting
your buying time, the minute you've got left is barely enough
for a sigh, you poor devil, you dumb jackass of a Turk, God's
fool.*

He would try to grab her, but she'd slip away, flee from
the bed; from enticement to enticement, the battle went on
all night without his being able to touch or move her. With
the sound of the first bray, Zezinha would disappear into
the fringe of morning.

Fadul would wake exhausted, covered with sweat, tense
with frustration. In the hazy dawn he could still make out
breasts and thighs, the bold behind, the fuzzy stomach, the
disappearing pussy. Tomorrow I'm going to drop everything
and take off. Braying and whinnying echoed up and down
the valley. The drovers didn't take long in appearing for
their morning drink before taking the road.

On his way back from Itabuna, Fadul begged Zezinha
for the favor of a visit to Tocaia Grande, offering her the sky.
She took something on account for traveling expenses, promised to show up soon: surely, one of these days, the feast day
of St. Someday.

2

IN THE MISERABLE ROW of houses, snakes and outcasts abounded. An ever-present danger, the snakes, poisonous for the most part, came out of the underbrush and the bog, a deadly and daily menace. Trash thrown away along the road, the rejects gathered in Tocaia Grande, the few worn-out whores were barely enough for the impatience of drovers in need, for the urge of woodsmen and hired hands on their way from one plantation to another. Only two or three abstaining days away from the plenty of Ilhéus and Itabuna, but those in a hurry couldn't stand the awful wait. There wasn't much to choose from in the row of houses, but a man starving to death will eat manure and lick his chops.

All except for Bernarda, completely the opposite of the others, a delight. A beautiful girl, young and clean, a vigorous body, a doll with shiny dark skin and a black mane, a wild filly. The path of life had stuck her there, or had she chosen it on purpose? She showed no desire to go away, to work better places. If she had, there certainly would have been no lack, in Ilhéus or Itabuna, in Água Preta, or Itapira, of colonels ready to set her up in a house and to open accounts for her in the town's shop for the privilege of having her there. There were those who wanted to get her to leave Tocaia and try her luck elsewhere. "I like it here," she would say, and smile.

Soon after he was established, after weighing the pros and cons, Fadul had proposed that they get together, invited her to come live with him, help out with the chores of his business, share his enormous bed. He'd told Lupiscínio when he ordered the bed and mattress: "Take a good look at my size and remember that most of the time there's going to be a girl there having fun with me."

Bernarda thanked him and turned him down. She was his to command whenever Mr. Fadu needed, felt like sleeping with her, in whatever house he chose, whatever bed he preferred, all he had to do was wave. He could pay if he wanted to: going to bed with such a courteous gentleman, such a warm and well-endowed man didn't call for any payment. Living together, however, thank you very much, she didn't want that, no. Not with Fadul, or with anyone else, no matter who. She passed the news on to Coroca.

"You know? Mr. Fadu gave me a bottle of perfume. Mr. Fadu's a good guy. He asked me to live with him."

"Be his mistress?"

"Just what I'm telling you."

"Live with the Turk. You've got it made, you've got the damnedest luck."

"I turned him down. I don't want to get tied up with him or with anyone."

"Why not?"

"You can live only with a man you love. Really love."

"I thought you had eyes for the Turk."

"Could be. But I'm not going to live with anybody just as a girlfriend or for money." Thoughtful, looking at the ground, she explained, "Living together, not even as man and wife, only for a love that lasts a lifetime, with ups and downs and from the heart. If it can't be that way, it's not for me. It's much better being a whore."

New in the place and living together, the two of them had known each other only a short time. Coroca didn't make any comments; she swallowed questions and advice. Bernarda looked up, laughed, and pondered.

"Tocaia Grande is a place with nice men. Mr. Fadu, Pedro Gypsy, Bastião da Rosa, and, nicest of them all, my godfather."

Bernarda reigned as a favorite. Everybody's favorite, captivating; fought over at night by drovers, not always available for Fadul's appetite. Every so often, when he was weary of the poor choices left, the Arab would have a whore come from Itabuna, but it cost him a pretty penny.

3

HE FINALLY WOKE UP behind the bar as he served the first *cachaça* liquor to the drovers. That was the hardest money he earned: at dawn, before sunup, without time to relieve his belly or wash his body. As soon as he could, he would leave that money grubbing to someone else and dedicate himself only to broader profits and less annoying chores.

He defecated in the woods, watching for snakes. He dove into the river, cleaning off the sweat, the stink of bedbugs and his nighttime visions. He cleaned his teeth by rubbing them with a plug of tobacco; he blew on the embers to revive the coals under the iron trivet, an Asian luxury acquired at cost in payment for a debt in Taquaras. He put on some water in a tin pot, to boil for coffee. At peace with himself once more, he pondered life and its difficulties. Not easy yet, but he had been through worse. He was sure that if he quit, he'd soon repent: the grace of God isn't meant for men of little faith. In order to earn it and become a rich and respected merchant, he had to show that he was worthy of the harsh challenge.

A breeze was coming off the river, the wenches were resting from the night's activity; Tição went out to bring in his catch and reset his traps. The half-breeds in the cacao warehouse and the workmen building the corral for Colonel Robustiano de Araújo still hadn't begun the day's chores. Only the trilling of the birds broke the silence of Tocaia Grande. Fadul's favorite time: having drunk his strong hot coffee, he would sit on the doorstep, light his hookah, run his eyes over the pleasant surroundings—the valley, the river, the hills, the trees, the clump of houses—the Grand Turk surveying his empire.

He wouldn't take one step out of there, not even at some doctor's advice, a bandit's threat, or a woman's lures. The female hadn't been born yet who could make him change his mind, veer from the course of his destiny. A man who loses his head over a female to the point of giving up the use of his reason will end up penniless, the demoralized butt of laughter and gibes. Let Zezinha do Butiá come at the head of a parade of the finest ladies from the cabarets of Ilhéus and Itabuna, not even then would she succeed in making him do anything foolish. No skirt, whether Zezinha, a lady of the evening, a back-alley cat, whether Aruza, a good match, or Jussaro Ramos Rabat, a rich widow, all prospective brides, all seductive and enticing. Unlike and unequal are the temptations a good Christian is subject to, all charged with false enchantment and real danger.

While he was strengthening his resolve, he kept the riverbank in view, especially the stretch known as the "ladies' bidet," a name given by Castor, who'd picked up some Frenchiness, a pool formed out of stones, with a water-

fall, where the whores went to bathe themselves and wash
their clothes. Who knows, maybe Bernarda would show her
grace in bloom after her bath and would accept filling the
emptiness of morning with a feast of pleasure.

Bernarda, a dark enigma. He'd got the idea before that
she gave him preference in the swarm of those in love with
her attributes because she'd let herself spend hours on end
listening to stories from the thousand and one nights, nur-
sery tales, Bible episodes, the Turk's specialties, and in bed
she would writhe in passion, melt into laughter. There
were those who talked about infatuation between the two.
Bernarda, however, hadn't accepted hanging her clothes
next to his, ceasing to be a fallen woman and rising to the
status of a respected mistress. She'd preferred staying a
house whore available for all passersby. Fadul couldn't understand it: as undecipherable as a verse from the Koran,
the enigmatic book of the infidel.

In conversation with Coroca about life and its complica-
tions, he asked her in passing if she knew of any explanation
for Bernarda's absurd behavior. Coroca avoided answering.

"Who can figure it out! A woman's mind is a dark well;
it's not easy to see to the bottom. I dropped my jaw when I
heard it. But if I told you, Mr. Fadu, you wouldn't believe
me. In Itabuna I knew a woman who left her rich husband,
a shopkeeper, crazy about her, to go be a whore in a madam's house. Her name was Valdelice, she was a hefty woman,
and she enjoyed being a *puta*. The world is more mixed-up
than people think, Mr. Fadu. That's all I know."

A Band of Gypsies Sets up Camp in Tocaia Grande on the Night of a Full Moon

1

DURING THOSE FIRST STAGES as a hamlet, the passage of the Gypsy caravan left fond memories in spite of all its trouble. People remembered it for a long time, even though in the space of a day and a night little had really happened. An irresistible fascination persisted, however, a mystery to be unraveled.

The Gypsies had appeared in the middle of the afternoon and set up camp in the tract of land on the opposite bank. They must have lost their way at the small bridge or did it on purpose, who can say?

They unhitched the wagons covered with colored cloth and with leather tops, crammed with geegaws. The women took care of lighting the fires while the men went to water the animals, horses and donkeys, at the riverbank. Only Josef, the oldest, curly white hair, earrings, rings on his fingers, dagger in his wide sash, vest instead of a jacket, immediately crossed over on the rocks and went to Fadul's store. *The carriage of a king*, Coroca thought when she caught sight of him.

2

WHAT WAS SAID AND repeated on the coast and in the backlands, everybody knows: Gypsies are a race apart and a people not to be trusted. They don't mix with the natives, or

with anybody else for that matter, not with Sergipean or
Turk, Portuguese or half-breed, nor any other flock whatsoever. Whoever heard of a marriage between a Gypsy and
people of the country? It's yet to happen. A nation apart, a
race of wizards and confidence men, Gypsies live by trick-
ery, by swindles and wiles.

On the back of stolen horses, the men look like nobles,
counts and barons, dukes and marquesses. Reclining on
grimy mattresses in the wagons where they live, dressed in
flowery rags, long flouncy skirts, covered with bracelets and
necklaces, the women could pass for princesses and queens
were it not for the fortune-telling, the chattering, and the
bare feet. Carried away by appearances, there are those who
say and even write that Gypsies are the remnants of the
royal court of Babylonia, wandering throughout the world,
fulfilling their destiny. Whatever it might be, it's best to
keep your distance, use caution in business dealings, hide
your most precious belongings from them. A people without
a home, where were the likes ever seen? No one can trust
them.

3

THE COINS TINKLED ON the counter. Josef was getting ready
to pay for the provisions in cash, in case it became absolutely necessary, in order to avoid doubts or mistrust. In the
boondocks of those backwoods it wasn't wise to cheat: he'd
seen more crosses in the cemetery than shacks lined up
along the road. But the unhappy hour for unloading his
pockets hadn't struck, the discussion had only just begun.
Josef tried to pick up the conversation about the quality of
the animals.

"I've got good ones, the best. First-rate mounts."

Fadul had let a vague interest in the purchase of a
donkey be understood, but he hadn't shown any hurry to
discuss terms, letting the matter die out: business with a
Gypsy calls for shrewdness. He changed the subject.

"Do you plan on staying long?"

"Here? What's there to do? Not even any pots to repair." He spat, showing his gold teeth. "Who can I do business with besides you?"

"You'll see how things liven up later when the drovers get here. And the hired hands after the whores. The place'll fill up."

"I don't intend staying too long."

"You're going to spend the night, aren't you?"

Josef didn't say yes and he didn't say no, he bargained.

"To see the place fill up? Would it be worth the trouble? Excuse my frankness, but I've got my doubts."

He offered another solution, an easier one.

"You come with me, sir, and pick out the donkey right now. Before someone else buys him."

Fadul was unconvinced.

"Not now. Customers will be coming in soon. Come back tomorrow morning; if I get a chance, I'll take a peek at the donkeys."

It was no use pushing it, Josef was used to that game of caution and craftiness. If the rules didn't change with others, you can imagine that with a Turk . . .

"If that's how it is, I'll spend the night here in order to take care of you, sir."

"Stay if you want, but not for my sake."

The Gypsy piled his coins on the top of the counter, put his hand into his pants pocket, took out a kerchief tied by the four corners, unknotted it, and beside the pile of coins he poured out the golden temptation of jewelry. Fadul scorned the trick.

"I was a traveling peddler for many years. I've still got stuff like that put away here. Would you like to buy some? I'll give you a good price."

"Peddler?" Head down, Josef tied up the kerchief, put it into his pocket, repeated, "Peddler!"

He recovered right away, however, and with a quick motion placed a small package wrapped in dark paper on the counter: where had he gotten it from without Fadul's noticing?

"Well, then, take a look, sir, and tell me if you've got this in your assortment."

He unfolded the paper, revealing a reliquary fastened to a chain. It was hard for the Turk to hold back the exclamation that came to his lips and, with difficulty, he turned his eyes away. Josef declared, "You wouldn't find the likes of it even in Ilhéus."

Holding the chain in his fingertips, he lifted the reliquary to the level of the merchant's eyes: the sunlight sparkled on the grooves, heightening the value of the jewel.

"What have you got to say, sir?"

It was no good for Fadul to show indifference, Josef had noticed his interest from the way the shopkeeper held out his hand to grasp the reliquary, from the care with which he handled it: a piece of jewelry just the right size to hang from a pretty woman's neck.

"What a nice present to give to your lady, sir. Solid gold. Take a good look at the workmanship."

"I'm not married. I don't even have a whore." No whore, not even Zezinha do Butiá was worth a gift like that.

He didn't dismiss the piece, didn't say it was ugly or a fake. A veteran peddler, experienced in dealing with metal goods, Fadul knew how to recognize worth. He wouldn't give anything for the chain, not worth a cent. The reliquary, however, was genuine gold, a high-priced piece, stolen no doubt. He opened it up to look inside, hefted it in his hand. He didn't put it down, but said he had no use for it.

"I don't even want to know if it's real gold. I haven't got anybody to give it to, and I wouldn't know what to do with this dingus. It's no use to me. What would I do with it?"

"What would you do with it? You could sell it later on, make some money. You're teasing me, sir, you know it's gold and of the best quality."

Fadul then asked, his voice neutral, devoid of any hidden meaning, "It's not that I don't want to buy it, it's just that I don't have anyone to give or sell it to. Just out of curiosity, tell me how much you're asking for the reliquary. Just the reliquary, without the chain."

Josef displayed the jewelry on the counter. For just an instant, because with an unexpected move he put it into the Turk's hand.

"Keep it until tomorrow, check the gold, the grams and the carats. Tomorrow, when you come to pick out the donkey, you can give it back, sir, or keep it if you want; you set the price, sir, whatever you think it's worth." He put the item in Fadul's hand. "We'll settle it all tomorrow, everything together."

Before the storekeeper could answer or react, Josef picked

up the bag with his purchases, gathered in and kept the money set aside for payment, and went through the door without looking back.

"None of that!" Fadul shouted when he got his voice back. "Come back here! Take your junk with you."

Too late: the Gypsy was far off. Fadul examined the jewelry again, slowly and minutely. Anyone who sells to a Gypsy on credit is a sucker, soft in the head, but no matter how small its value might be, that piece was worth many times over the price of what had just been bought and not paid for: dried meat, beans, sugar, and a bottle of *cachaça*. There wasn't any risk of getting cheated; if anyone was to lose, it would be the Gypsy. Just to be sure, when it was time to settle up, he'd wear a revolver on his belt.

Coroca, who'd just come in, clapped her hands when she saw the reliquary.

"What a pretty thing! Dona Marcelina, Colonel Ilídio's wife, had one but it wouldn't hold a candle to this." She turned to the Turk. "Did you buy it, Mr. Fadul? Who are you going to give it to? Thinking about getting married?"

4

AN EXCITED CLIENTELE EAGERLY paid for the good fortune read in the lines of their hands and whispered into their ears in that Gypsy half language. Gypsy women are born with the gift of prophecy. Even some whores with high-flown airs, who swore they didn't believe in that knavery, held out their hands with a twenty-cent piece.

In order to remove doubts, to insure confidence, the fortune-tellers began by telling something real that had happened in the woman's past, talking about it as if they'd witnessed it themselves. For a nickel or more they foretold the future, guaranteeing boyfriends, their being kept by rich plantation owners, important colonels, driving away rivals, predicting exclusive and eternal relationships. They supplied dreams and love at bargain prices.

At the fortune-tellers' fair at sundown, Bernarda drew the oldest and evilest of the Gypsy women, the grandmother, tired of so much repetition of vague and exact fortunes. Taking the hand the girl held out—she was still a girl—the Gypsy spoke about the pursuit of an old man; there's always an old man who chases girls. Right on target: with that simple reference she showed a perfect knowledge of what had happened, leaving Bernarda open-mouthed.

"That's it exactly. I know who the old man is."

It couldn't have been anyone but her father, but she didn't want to remember him or those days.

"What I want to know is afterward, from here on. I want to know if my man is going to love me for the rest of his life."

"Your man?"

She raised her eyes from Bernarda's hands to her eyes, noted the anxiety and the passion.

"You want him to be yours, don't you? For him not to go with anybody else. Put two hundred reis in my hand and I'll say a prayer and he'll never again want to hear about anyone else."

"Why should I want him to be only mine?" Bernarda was startled. "He can have as many as he wants."

Surprised, the Gypsy woman looked at the girl's tense face again. What they all wanted, without exception, was to be the only one, the first, with no one as second; they would request curses against their rivals, pay for prayers and sorcery. She looked for an explanation of the absurdity in the girl's afflicted face, and asked, confused, "What do you want, then?"

"I want to know if he's going to get tired of me, stop seeing me. If he's ever going to get tired of me."

"Give me two hundred reis and the Gypsy woman will tell you everything." Craving for the nickel, she added, in order to convince her, "I see blood and death . . ."

Bernarda held on to the two coins.

"Tell me once and for all. Is he going to love me all his life?"

Such affliction in the girl's speech penetrated the Gypsy's breast, reached her blunted heart: casting aside the repeated formulas, always the same, she predicted only what the poor girl wanted to hear.

"All his life."

"You talked about death, ma'am . . ."

"You're going to die in his arms," she whispered.

5

FADUL HAD PROMISED JOSEF a night filled with drovers, woodsmen, and farmhands filling up the clearing, with money to spend. "Excuse me, sir, but I've got my doubts," the Gypsy had answered. It looked as though he were more than right, because that was one of the poorest nights for people stopping over at Tocaia Grande.

Apart from the two troops with their three men and one kid, there were three woodsmen and a farmhand, the four of them after women. Add to these eight living souls the mulatto Pergentino, who had arrived at nightfall driving two donkeys with merchandise destined for Atalaia, where preparations were being made for lunches and dinners. At the Turk's "erection"—the drovers called the construction his erection to tease Fadul and listen to him carry on—Pergentino wanted to know if the merchant could tell him the whereabouts of Captain Natário da Fonseca. The administrator of Atalaia was to meet him in Tocaia Grande.

"It's by way of an errand he asked me to do for him and bring from Taquaras. He said he'd be here today and tomorrow."

"He hasn't arrived yet. If you want, you can leave the order with me. When the captain shows up I'll give it to him."

"I'll leave the order and if you'll let me, I'll leave my load too. I'm not crazy enough to unload baskets right now under the eyes of those Gypsies. Things Colonel Boaventura ordered from Ilhéus. They're for the festivities," he explained.

The Turk brought the rumor that was going around out into the open.

"That means the doctor's really coming this time, doesn't it?"

"For sure."

"What doctor?" Valério Cachorrão butted into the conversation. He'd come with Maninho to toss one down and buy a strip of dried meat to roast on the coals under the straw shelter and eat with some flour and *rapadura*.

"The colonel's son is a law doctor. He's been away for six months."

"Where was he? Doing what?"

"In Rio de Janeiro, enjoying life."

"And he does a good job of it. I've heard that he's got a lot of guts," Valério Cachorrão went on, always ready to talk about brave men and brawls.

"He had someone to take after," Maninho put in, joining the conversation. "Colonel Boaventura never knew what it was to be afraid."

"And besides having balls that way, he's a regular stud."

It was mulatto Pergentino's turn to state, "He favors his father in that too."

Passing by the Row of Houses, Attorney Andrade Junior Is Pessimistic As to the Future of Tocaia Grande

1

IN ACCORDANCE WITH THE arrangement made with mulatto Pergentino, Captain Natário da Fonseca dismounted in Tocaia Grande in the morning. A short time later, spotting the Gypsy encampment on the other side, he crossed the river. Just in time to prevent Fadul Abdala's being taken in by Josef and buying a seemingly fine-looking donkey whose appearance had captivated the Turk.

Knowledgeable in matters of gold and silver, shrewd at peddling wares, but naive about mule or equine affairs, the Turk had proposed paying exactly half the price the Gypsy had asked at the start of the transaction. It was no small matter to follow the stages of the bargaining, to fathom the circumlocutions and evasive statements in the give-and-take between the two slickers—an endless wrangle. Now angry shouts of protest and accusation; now whimpering appeals. They mutually proclaimed themselves victims of the greed, avarice, and bad faith of their adversary. In the midst of the arguments, words and phrases in Arabic and Romany came out—if really that gang of Gypsies spoke Romany, as Fadul had heard from the wise mouth of Fuad Karan while telling him the story at the cabaret in Itabuna.

Declaring himself swindled, cheated out of his inheritance, Josef was still ready to accept the merchant's offer when the captain, joining them, ruined everything. After shaking hands with Fadul and greeting the Gypsies with a nod—Josef's companions Maurício and Miguel were watching the animals nearby—Natário asked, "Are you buying the donkey, friend Fadul?"

"What do you think, Captain?"

"I'll have to take a look."

He went over to the animal, ran his hand over its haunch, opened its mouth, examined its teeth under Josef's suspicious eyes.

"Do you want to throw your money away, *compadre,* buying a donkey with dentures? Have you gone crazy? Are you worse than Dr. James, who bought two of these at one time and thought he had a real bargain?" He smiled, remembering the innocence of the spendthrift fellow who had resolved to devote himself to farming and raising vegetables.

"Dentures? What's that? Never heard of it." Having recognized Captain Natário da Fonseca, Josef preferred to play ignorant rather than contradict him. "I don't know what you're talking about."

Natário lost no time in answering. As a result, feeling insulted by the Gypsy's attempt to trick him, Fadul blew up, went wild, carried on. Josef admitted nothing. The Turk knew as well as he that selling someone a bill of goods was part of dealing in animals.

"If that one's not right for you, pick out another."

After walking among the troop being watched by Maurício and Miguel, the captain, a noted connoisseur of donkeys and horses, advised against any deal. The only animal he noticed worthy of any attention was a colt that might grow into a fine mount in the future. But that was of no use: to carry goods over the holes and ruts between Tocaia Grande and Taquaras, what Fadul really needed was a strong, healthy donkey, with no defects.

"At the fair in Taquaras you can find a donkey in good shape. It would be safer," Natário suggested.

He didn't venture an opinion, however, in the debate over the reliquary, whose price had been set before the discussion: he didn't understand anything about jewelry. Josef tried to cancel the agreement, start all over again.

"Without the donkey, it's a different bargain."

"What? Different? What do you mean? It was all settled."

"Without the donkey, my dear sir . . ."

"My dear sir can fuck your mother . . ." Now Fadul was really furious. "What's one thing got to do with the other? I'll pay what we agreed on, not a penny more."

He had the advantage of having the jewel in his possession. He took a roll of old patched bills out of his pants pocket, licked his finger, began to peel them off.

"I don't want to sell it anymore," Josef declared.

"Too late. I've already bought it." Fadul held out the amount agreed upon, having just finished counting it.

Josef, his hand on the hilt of his dagger, pondered the situation. Maurício and Miguel came over and stood alongside him. If the Arab had been alone, in spite of his size, his scowl, and the revolver at his waist, they would have tried to jump him and settle the affair by brute force. Even the Gypsies, however, knew the name of Captain Natário da Fonseca and about his exploits. Josef ended up accepting the bills and he insolently recounted them. He had his pride to cover too. He turned his back without saying a word, but the captain wouldn't let him go.

"What about the whip, don't you want to sell it?"

A curious riding crop, a masterpiece, was hanging from the Gypsy's wrist. A strap of braided horsehair held by rings—silver or cheap metal? Inlay worked into the handle—bone or ivory? Josef turned around slowly.

"I've already lost a lot of money today. I don't want to lose any more."

"Tell me right off how much you want for the whip. If the price is right, I'll take it."

Silver and ivory, metal and bone, once more the Gypsy and the Arab plunged into speculation and haggling with visible pleasure. The captain interrupted the argument and with no further ado bought the crop at a price Fadul considered expensive. Almost immediately the Gypsy wagons began to move, heading in the direction of the small bridge.

2

"WHAT ARE YOU GOING to do with that, friend, sell it? Give it away as a present?" Captain Natário da Fonseca wanted to know, admiring the reliquary resting on the folds of dark paper that Fadul had opened up on the counter.

The shopkeeper laughed his thick, satisfied chuckle as he poured some *cachaça* from a special bottle.

"It cost a wad of money, but it's worth a lot more. That much I know. Where the son of a bitch was going to screw me was on the price of the donkey. If it hadn't been for you, sir. God sent you, Captain."

He looked through the door at the other bank. The wagons had already disappeared in the distance.

"The Bible is right when it says that he who lives by the sword shall perish by the sword. Everything's written in the Bible, Captain. The Gypsy tried to rob me, and he got robbed."

"Is it really worth that much?"

"I can sell it in Ilhéus or Itabuna for a lot more than I paid. All I have to do is offer it for sale in a cabaret. There's bound to be some colonel who'll want to buy it." He nodded his big head. "Give it away as a present? I haven't got a girlfriend or a wife, and even if I did, I'm not a millionaire to give a present that's worth as much as this. It was a good deal. Captain, you're the one who paid too much for that whip. You were in too much of a hurry. If you'd held out, the Gypsy would have let you have it for less."

"Could be, but I haven't got the patience to haggle. I bought it to give as a present, *compadre*, and to a man at that."

"I know. For the little doctor, right?"

Calling a man of his size little doctor might have seemed to be a joke in poor taste, a sign of disrespect, but Natário had known him since he was a boy and Fadul had seen him when he was a youth. The news of Venturinha's return after a prolonged vacation in Rio de Janeiro dominated the conversations in the bars of Itabuna and Ilhéus, at the railroad stations in Água Preta, Sequeiro de Espinho, and Taquaras, in villages and towns, in big houses of the plantations.

"Venturinha's going to have a hard time, going all over the place, eating dust, getting all muddy. Besides being a lawyer, the colonel wants him to take an interest in Atalaia. He's already bought him a saddle donkey and a *campolino* mare. I even helped him pick them out. Two first-class mounts, with Venturinha the only one to ride them." His eyes lit up. "The colonel's crazy about his son, you can imagine, old friend."

Full of memories, the thread of a smile appeared on Natário's mouth.

"To think I carried him on my shoulders . . ." The crop

swirled in the air. "He's going to like this whip, it's real fine."

An incomparable whip, worthy of an elegant lawyer, the son of a millionaire, a cacao colonel who had a powerful voice in politics, laid down the law in court, gave orders in chambers. In lawsuits that dealt with matters of land, there was no lawyer in the whole Bahia region who was a match for him, could stand up to him: Venturinha had everything and more.

"Now's the time for the colonel to call the tune. It's good that you're with them, Captain, and that I'm your good friend."

They touched glasses, drinking to the return of Dr. Andrade Junior—that's how it read on the diploma from the Faculty of Law: Bachelor Boaventura da Costa Andrade Junior. At last Colonel Boaventura Andrade would be able to carry forward his ambitious political plans, drawn up on the occasion of his son's graduation six months before, in December of the previous year.

3

ON RUA DO COMÉRCIO in Itabuna, the gate in front of the steps of a town house, property of the colonel, had displayed since December a shiny plaque that read: DR. BOAVENTURA DA COSTA ANDRADE FILHO, ATTORNEY-AT-LAW. Andrade Filho, as it said on the baptismal certificate: Junior was a gringo invention, and the plantation owner hated foreignisms. The ground floor of the town house served as a depository for dry cacao. The drovers from Atalaia Plantation brought their loads in a continuous flow of men and animals. In spite of living in Ilhéus, the colonel was of the opinion that Venturinha should set up an office in Itabuna, a new and progressive city adjacent to the rural properties that one day would be his—a fact that wouldn't prevent him from practicing law throughout the region. In May, at last, the young barrister arrived to take over, or so it seemed, the office and the many heavy responsibilities that awaited him.

Venturinha's graduation had been an event sung in prose

and verse. Months had passed, but the memories of the magnificent celebration still lingered. The festivities, begun in the capital, continuing on in Ilhéus and Itabuna, culminated at the plantation.

On the morning of the glorious day of his graduation, the archbishop of Bahia, primate of Brazil, had celebrated a high mass in the cathedral basilica, and in a verbose sermon summoned the graduating class to the "unyielding defense of law and justice, the sacred mission of those who had chosen the indomitable career of advocacy." In the silence of the cathedral the colonel muttered as he listened to His Grace's words: pretty, but empty. Lawyers were nothing but a bunch of hornswagglers, good at putting on airs, useful, no doubt about that, even indispensable, precisely in order to legitimize violations of law and justice. Very expensive to boot. Now the colonel had one at home, at his disposal.

The ceremony to award diplomas took place at night in the faculty auditorium, presided over by the state governor. In black gowns, with cap and tassel, the new graduates took the oath and received from the hands of His Excellency the tubes with their diplomas. Dona Ernestina didn't stop weeping and Colonel Boaventura Andrade, hide and soul tanned by so many dangers, snuffled, hiding a tear with the cuff of his jacket. A new suit, navy blue, cut from English cashmere.

The following day, a Sunday, the ball given by the new graduates to their families and to the Bahian society was held at the Cruz Vermelha Carnival Club. Matrons and young ladies displaying expensive outfits, the men in starched Irish linen suits. The colonel and Dona Ernestina entered, all decked out in their fancy best. She with her fat squeezed by the whalebone of a corset, he strangling in his starched collar, clenched by his patent leather shoes. Even so they were bursting with pride. They poured out French champagne and Madeira brandy, fraternizing with the Medauars and the Sá Barretos, relatives of the other two south Bahian boys graduating in the same group: the cacao groves were beginning to harvest doctors.

The dance was followed by the monumental early-morning revels at the love nest of Madame Henriette, whose Marseille origins were attested to by her accent, her expertise, and her nest egg. A bash offered by Venturinha for his most intimate classmates: the colonel had generously loosened his purse strings.

Madame Henriette had no equal when it came to organizing a high-class frolic, *une féerie*, as she herself proclaimed. A discreet house, an aristocratic rendezvous, chic madams, recruited for their weight in gold among mistresses and kept women of gentlemen of quality: noblemen from the Bay area, wholesalers from the Lower City, merchants from the Upper City, circuit judges, high military officers, powerful politicians—clergy and nobility. Properly mannered and voluptuously endowed, each one more desirable than the next, beginning with the delectable Mistress of the Whorery herself, so French and so blond. Calculating and mercenary, *la sage* Henriette divided her working time among three first-rate customers, rich and prodigal; romantic, *la folle* Henriette reserved all her leisure time for the young and handsome Jorge Medauar, who, it so happened, had been graduated along with Venturinha, his friend and confidant, his fraternity brother. Medauar was the poet of the group, applauded and sought after, the darling of young women and whores. He composed verses and published them in the newspapers. At family parties young girls would recite the "Moonlit Sonnet of Your Hair," dedicated to the anonymous "H., lascivious and ardent flower of the Mediterranean." Henriette's light blond hair—a field of moonlit wheat, goldglowing springtime in the rhymes of the sonnet—loose and luminous, ruled over the party, her party as well, to be sure. Too busy, therefore, to corner the host and faint in his arms, she had to delegate this responsibility, as lady of the house, to auburn-haired Rebeca, she of the wine-colored *pudenda*, *soi-disant* exclusive property of the captain of the port. All of them, without exception, *soi-disant* exclusive properties.

Mass and ball, graduation and festivities, past joys, but always present in the memory of Colonel Boaventura Andrade, who recalled them with justifiable pride and a certain melancholy. He had knelt during the high mass, been amused at the hypocrisy of the sermon, been sincerely moved at the graduation ceremony, let himself go at the ball, his wing collar and patent-leather shoes notwithstanding. He had heard all about the orgy and sanctioned it when, on the seventh day, he finally rested from festivities, solemnities, and emotions in the dusky arms of Domingas Beijaflor—*soi-disant* exclusive property of Monsignor da Silva, prior of the cathedral, holy man, paragon of virtue.

4

IN SPITE OF HIS well-known ill feelings toward lawyers'
tricks, chicanery more despicable than shotguns and carbines, Colonel Boaventura Andrade on that December of his
son's graduation didn't try to hide his satisfaction. A doctor
son, still a rarity in southern Bahian lands, in addition to
pleasing his parents' hearts, a reason for pride and respect,
meant the impending conclusion of long-conceived projects.

The studies had cost a lot, the price of lawbooks and
trustworthy whores was deadly—blessed cacao! Carrying
the expenses of a student was no joke, maintaining him in
the capital with the largesse called for by a scion of Colonel
Boaventura Andrade—the fame of the plantation owner's
fortune echoed across Bahia: endless groves, thousands of
tons of cacao at each harvest, blocks of real estate in Ilhéus
and Itabuna, and impressive bank accounts.

Even so, he was glad to pay the bill: the title of lawyer
was worth as much as a good plantation, the key that opened
the doors of politics and could bring an auspicious marriage. With his lawyer son at his side, the colonel would no
longer need the services of other attorneys to take care of his
interests in court and law offices, nor would he have to rely
on funding the elections of third parties to sensitive positions, through whom he could delegate orders. He would be
safe from slander and lies, any sort of surprises: only the
law itself was more deceitful than politics. That's why they
would always go together, hand in hand.

Venturinha, however, had other plans for the coming
months. After so many years of study, written tests, oral
exams, going blind over textbooks, he deserved a vacation.
Not the usual student end-of-the-year vacations in Ilhéus
and Itabuna, picking up third-class whores in cabarets, but,
indeed, the vacation of a newly graduated lawyer off in Rio
de Janeiro. He'd previously visited the federal capital only
poorly and briefly, during a trip with a student delegation.
This time he planned to linger for the months of January
and February, leaving before New Year's, coming home after carnival. A person who'd applied himself so well to his
studies—repeating only one semester in the whole course of

studies—he was worthy of a commensurate reward, a vacation in Rio de Janeiro with a full wallet.

The colonel listened and agreed: after all, two months more or two months less didn't matter that much. In the colonel's plans the essential thing was to see his son finally shining in the courtroom, defending cases, addressing the jury, managing the plantation, entering politics, a candidate for state deputy or *intendente* of Itabuna.

5

BEFORE LUNCHTIME, CAPTAIN NATÁRIO da Fonseca got on his mule in front of the little wooden house, said so long to Bernarda and Coroca, waved to Fadul in the distance, and went to the station at Taquaras to meet the lawyer Andrade Junior returning to his home ground. The boy was coming in the company of Dona Ernestina, who had met him in Ilhéus. In order to hide the excitement that was burning within him, the colonel had purposely stayed behind, waiting at Atalaia. But Natário had witnessed the landowner's emotion when he opened and read the telegram Venturinha had sent—relayed from Taquaras by a messenger—announcing his landing and setting a date for his arrival at the plantation: time for the colonel to make preparations for a proper reception for his doctor son, who'd finally decided to come back from Rio de Janeiro. He'd promised to return right after carnival, in February; they were on the eve of St. John's Day, in June. The joy had been reflected on the long face of the colonel, who was speechless, reading and rereading the message. Finally, laughing with his mouth and his eyes, with his whole face, he announced the news.

"He's coming, he's already in Ilhéus. Our doctor, Natário."

The captain was going about thinking of such things, when he spotted the figure of a woman on the road ahead. A small bundle on her head, a bouquet of leaves and wilted wild flowers in her hand, a jubilant smile on her lips, Maria Gina, barefoot, was wandering down the road.

"Where are you off to, Maria Gina?" the captain asked.

"Yonder, Captain, sir." She wasn't about to reveal her secrets, she kept them to herself, but Natário had helped her once and she hadn't forgotten.

The sun was a hot coal, marking the hour; if the train wasn't late, Venturinha should be getting off in Taquaras in a little while. Would he still remember Maria Gina?

Natário first knew her on Atalaia, already a crazy girl, with a vague look, smiling for no reason, careless of her body. Venturinha had only just tried a woman, had to hold himself back, he couldn't resist a skirt.

"Do you remember Venturinha, Maria Gina?"

The whore stopped walking, stood in the road, clutching the branches, making an effort; her memory came from far away, from the other side, confused, a mixture of dreams and visions.

"Who, Captain, sir?" She did remember the captain, yes, when the werewolf had begun to attack her, he'd intervened, taken the side of the defenseless woman, cut the werewolf into three pieces, and the devil never mistreated her again. "No, I don't remember."

"Venturinha, the son of the colonel, back there in Atalaia. A long time ago."

"I don't remember the son, no. I remember only the colonel; he liked going to bed with me, he was so kind."

There were people who didn't like to go with her because she was loony. With a fear of punishment from heaven, because those crazy people are God's favorites, anyone who abuses them will pay dearly, here on earth or later on, who knows where. Venturinha didn't believe in omens, he pulled Maria Gina down under the platform amid the smell of the cacao laid out to dry. Natário had never heard about the colonel, but he didn't doubt it.

"Colonel Boaventura?"

"He had a hairy chest, good to run your hand over."

She started her slow walk again, her eyes lost once more, her lips open in a smile as she put the coins that the captain had put into her hand in the waistband of her skirt.

Captain Natário da Fonseca spurred his mule, moved on. If the train was on schedule, Venturinha wouldn't be long in arriving. A full-fledged lawyer. Would he still remember Maria Gina?

6

NOT IN DECEMBER, NOR in May either. The colonel's plans saw themselves postponed again. How long? The question remained up in the air, Venturinha hadn't fixed a date. The post-graduate course had no set time for ending. It could go on for a few months, five or six, how many he didn't know exactly, until December at most. But how could he miss an opportunity like that? It doesn't come along every day and the few openings had been fought over by candidates from all over the country and even from abroad. The colonel should know that there were Argentinians among the candidates. Argentinians, yes sir! He, Venturinha, had managed to enroll because of the good relations he'd established with famous professors during that short stay in Rio de Janeiro. Short? Five months the colonel counted on his fingers: January, February, March, April, May.

The colonel had become aware of Venturinha's intentions through the long letter full of considerings and therebys in which the boy informed his parents of his decision to continue his studies, enrolling in the pertinent course on Law of Property Ownership, indispensable for anyone who wanted to practice successfully in the region; it would be most useful to him.

Stumbling over the sibylline language in which the letter was couched, pure lawyers' jargon, the colonel, submerged in doubts, ordered his son to come to Ilhéus to explain himself better, because he didn't intend, nor did he think it possible, to decide such a matter through correspondence.

In his view, having finished his course at the Faculty of Law, with a ruby on his ring finger, his diploma and certificate of admission to the bar hanging on the wall of the waiting room, Venturinha was ready to begin his career and tread the road laid out for him: to practice law, marry a girl from a wealthy family—as wealthy as his at least—get into politics, and assume the responsibilities and positions that befitted him. That was what the colonel had worked for like a slave, fought with weapons in his hand, shed blood, risked his life. He didn't see the need for any new courses, hadn't he graduated and received the title of doctor already?

Backed against the wall, Venturinha could do nothing but break off his stay in Rio and come to argue in person.

"I interrupted the course, I'm missing classes!" he lamented.

Moved, Dona Ernestina stood up in support of her son. Usually she didn't dare argue about her husband's plans when she knew about them, which wasn't often. But on that occasion she broke out of her habitual compliance to demand, with unexpected energy, the colonel's understanding and indispensable financial support so that her boy could stuff himself with knowledge. What the boy wanted was to study, a praiseworthy intention; how could he stop him?

"A course taught by famous teachers, the best specialists," Venturinha exclaimed, his arms in the air.

The colonel could see him in the courtroom, his ringing voice, his quick rejoinders, his finger in the air, his son the lawyer. He listened in silence to the boy's arguments, his wife's foolishness: illiterate like her father and mother, she could barely sign her name, what the devil did Ernestina understand about courses and curriculum? In the end, harried, the colonel grudgingly ended up giving in and agreeing to everything.

"Until the end of the year, go ahead. But I want you here in the new year, I'm getting old and tired."

The open seminar on the law of land ownership, available to all graduates who wanted to join, was especially meant to furnish credits for those who intended to compete for civil positions in the Ministries of Agriculture and Justice, and the magistrature. Venturinha had learned about it quite by accident, had run over to sign up, but rarely attended classes. As for the Argentinian lawyers, not a single one had actually come to bathe in the enlightenment of the eminent Brazilian scholars.

In an indirect way, the course had most benefitted the Argentinian Adela La Porteña, better known as Adelita Chucha de Oro, "straight from the theaters of Buenos Aires, where she had reaped applause and ovations," to slaughter tangos in the cabarets of Rio de Janeiro: she charged the price of a diva and not a whore. A foreigner and a performer, having her as his private property was for the boy from Bahia the greatest, the highest glory. Besides, she was crazy about him, madly passionate: "*¡Por vós yo me rompo toda!*"

7

THE ARAB FADUL ABDALA came to know about Venturinha's most profound studies from the scholar himself when, days later, the traveler stopped in Tocaia Grande, in the company of Captain Natário da Fonseca and two armed men. Having to visit Itabuna in order to fulfill the colonel's demands—stop by there, receive his friends in the office, tell them that at the end of the year he'd be back bringing still another diploma, doctor of lands—he couldn't arrive like a shyster in search of law cases, a poor devil with no escort. He was, after all, Andrade Junior, the son of Colonel Boaventura Andrade, the political boss of the district, a man of substance and strength. He couldn't do with less: his entourage must include the captain, the two gunmen, the *campolino* mare, and the riding crop.

Natário had convinced him to go by way of Tocaia by mentioning the reliquary. In the idleness of Atalaia, Venturinha, gnawed at by longing, full of vanity, had confided to the captain about his Argentine lovemaking, falling into his old habit of bragging about his conquests. The half-breed had always been an attentive and interested listener. This time Venturinha wasn't talking about just any woman, whether a concubine cuckholding her generous protector with him in a room at a brothel or a girl from a good family, coy and wise, going only halfway, masturbating him in the doorway of a country house. He was referring to the sublime Adela, queen of the stage of the Río de la Plata, *"la patética intérprete del tango arrabalero."* A dream of a woman, big and white, white as milk, a Junoesque body: standing, she was a statue, in bed an earthquake. Her pink pussy— "Oh, Adelita's pussy, Natário, what can I say!"

He had complained of not having found any item in Ilhéus worthy of La Porteña: a necklace, a bracelet, a diamond. He had gone into all the shops, but it was useless: costume jewelry was all they had. He was going to look bad to the diva, since he'd promised to bring her something special from Bahia. The captain remembered the reliquary the Turk had bought from the Gypsy: who knows, maybe it would solve the problem.

Venturinha dismounted right beside the hitching post
next to Fadul's store. The Arab ran out quickly, bowed with
pleasure, happy with the unexpected visit by the colonel's
spoiled son.

"I heard from the captain about your arrival. Does it
mean you're going to spend some time with us here . . ."

"I didn't come to spend any time, Fadul; my studies are
going to keep me in Rio for a while."

Hadn't he finished law school already, gotten his degree? The merchant's surprise, contained as it was, didn't
escape Venturinha and he deigned to give him an explanation, which he was putting together to answer the inevitable
and whimsical questions of his colleagues and acquaintances in Itabuna.

"Specialized studies, property law. Another title to add
to that of doctor."

"Doctor twice over!" Natário concluded.

Only a partial explanation; even so, Fadul clapped his
big hands in celebration.

"What can I offer you to toast it with? The only good
stuff here is *cachaça*. There's brandy, but I wouldn't recom-
mend it."

Venturinha ran his eyes over the stock of drinks, most of
it cheap bug-killers for farmhands and drovers. But Fadul
reached for an almost full bottle hidden at the back of a
shelf. He took out the cork, wiped the top, nodded his big
head in satisfaction.

"A specialty. Manioc liquor made by black Nicodemos
in Ferradas." He held the bottle up to the morning light: the
liquor had a bluish cast. "Reserved for those who deserve it.
The captain can tell you about it."

"First class," Natário confirmed. "Strong as hell."

"I've got a cure for that too. . . ." The Turk laughed and
went out the door.

At the rear of the house a cashew tree was growing,
loaded with ripe fruit, yellow and red. Fadul picked four or
five.

"After drinking, suck on a cashew fruit and the effect
goes away."

"I don't need that . . ." Venturinha was almost offended,
and he swallowed his drink in one swig.

"Where's that piece of jewelry you bought from the
Gypsy the other day, old friend? The doctor would like to

see it." Having emptied his glass, Natário was sucking on a cashew, and the juice ran down the corners of his mouth.

"I'll go get it."

Venturinha poured himself another drink: manioc liquor was something else again. It had no smell and it tasted good, it burned your chest. When Fadul displayed the piece of jewelry on the counter on top of a handkerchief, Natário gave him the bottle to put away.

"Before we finish it. It's still a fair piece to Itabuna, and this manioc stuff is like a sock on the head. While you people are talking and doing business, I'm going to pay a visit."

He didn't want to be the go-between in the buying and selling of the jewel, and he knew that Bernarda was expecting him, impatient Bernarda, prettier every day.

8

AT A PRICE FOR a friend, a little more than double what he had paid Josef, Fadul turned the reliquary over to Venturinha. In Ilhéus, in a waterfront bar, in Itabuna, in a cabaret, he could get a much better offer. But, as he explained, the doctor more than deserved it. He had let Venturinha himself, who took pride in his knowledge of jewelry, set the price, repeating the Gypsy's maneuver.

"Your price is mine, Doctor. Pay whatever you want."

Venturinha called for another drink of manioc liquor while he counted out the new, crisp banknotes.

"And the captain, where'd he go? He took the mare with him."

"To Bernarda's place, it could only be there."

They crossed the clearing: under the shed, coals smoldered in the ashes of the fires from the night before. Birds came to peck at the remains of the drovers' meal. They reached Baixa dos Sapos. The women in the doors of the huts, half-naked, stared curiously. Who hadn't heard of Venturinha, the colonel's son, who'd studied to be a lawyer? Guta came over to them.

"Don't you know me anymore, Venturinha?"

Venturinha shook his head, he did not recognize the brazen woman, so many had he gobbled up in those brambles.

"It's Guta," the Turk explained.

The whore came over, putting herself in front of the visitor.

"You used to like my smell, don't you remember?"

Sweet smell of tobacco, he remembered. And having remembered, he put his hand into his pocket and gave Guta a five-milreis bill, a fortune. With three shots of manioc liquor rising up from his gullet to his head, the little doctor—a grown man!—felt lighthearted and generous. They were all his serfs there. As for Adela, she smelled of sandalwood. He touched the reliquary in the pocket of his riding jacket. Before giving it to her, he would put a picture of himself inside, so she could carry him on her white bosom, between her breasts: oh, Adelita's sumptuous breasts!

At the door of the little wooden house he found his *campolino* mare. He turned down the coffee Coroca offered, good-naturedly joking with her.

"You still alive, Coroca? And still fornicating, you old devil?" They were all his serfs there.

Coroca was nobody's serf and fornicating could only mean something bad. The old woman gave it back to him.

"Now you're a lawyer you talk fancy, people can't understand. But once you were just a boy who came to go to bed with me. Who was it taught you everything you know about women? Wasn't it this old devil?"

Five more milreis thrown away. With her he had learned how to enjoy himself with his partner, linger lazily: the ones before Coroca had taken care of him in a blink of the eyes. Things from the past.

"Good-bye, Coroca."

From up on the fine leather saddle fastened by a silver breastband, on a proud mare, casting his glance over the row of houses, huts, and people, Dr. Andrade Junior shook hands with the Arab Fadul Abdala in farewell.

"I don't know what you're doing in this filthy dump. If you want to make money, why don't you give up this hole and go to Itabuna?" They were all his serfs there. "You can count on me if you want to. There's no future here, this will never be more than a pigsty."

Captain Natário da Fonseca did not hear him expound those opinions: he was pulling back on his pants, his boots. In bed, naked, Bernarda smiled at him.

9

THE CAPTAIN LEARNED OF the lawyer's pessimistic prediction several days later when he passed through Tocaia Grande again. Venturinha had left for Rio de Janeiro, where the open seminar, with the wisdom of the scholars, the boring lectures, and Adela La Porteña, Adelita Chucho de Oro, with the wisdom of whores, and the long nights of tango and revelry, awaited him.

Sipping a drink of manioc liquor, Natário referred to the young doctor's stay in Itabuna, where he was so regally feted.

"You'd think the Christ child had arrived."

In spite of his usual discretion, and knowing that Fadul was a friend of Fuad Karan, he told of a very amusing incident that took place in the cabaret during one of those nights of celebration. When Venturinha repeated for the hundredth time that he was going back to Rio to finish a scholarly course specializing in land ownership, Fuad Karan beseeched the heavens.

"What for? My God, what for? Who knows more about land ownership than the colonel, your father and my friend? The laws here that determine such rights were laid down by him, weren't they? You can't fool me, Venturinha, this story of yours must have a woman behind it. Come on, tell us."

Without disparaging the importance of the open seminar, Andrade Junior, lawyer and dandy, just back from the metropolis, spoke with knowledge and enthusiasm about the bohemian life of Rio and exalted its women, so cosmopolitan and refined. In the cabaret in Itabuna, among brutish colonels and greedy lawyers, the star of the theaters of Buenos Aires, the Goddess of the Footlights, Adela from Argentina, twinkled for a moment.

Nights on End in the Wilderness of Tocaia Grande, Fadul Abdala Deflowers the Virgin Aruza

1

YES, AS HAS BEEN said before and is proven here, diverse and varied are the temptations the devil offers a devoted follower of the Maronite rite, all the more so if he is a petty merchant sent by God to the ends of the earth and forgotten there: a pigsty, as Venturinha had called it. Merchant? Contemptible shopkeeper would be closer to the mark.

Awake or asleep, in his drive to get rich quick, Fadul Abdala underwent temptations of all kinds during the desolate times of lean cows. Pondering by candlelight, business, profits, gains, lots of money, a furniture store, dry goods. In the Turk's broad and lonely bed in Tocaia Grande, the cherry offered by Aruza Skaf, proffered fiancée, and the heat offered by the widow, Jussara Ramos Rabat, beautiful, both fiery, were nothing before the lascivious nudity of the ladies of the evening, led by Zezinha do Butiá.

A virgin in heat, a widow in need: each alternative guaranteed making him a prospective cuckold. Some choice! The one who fills the hole is the mason's apprentice.

Jamil Skaf, a devoted father, and Jussara Ramos Rabat, a merry widow, had their differing ideas regarding a husband and marriage, but both concurred as to the commercial calling and ability of the Arabs. Therefore they saw in Fadul the ideal candidate, the best of them all. Aided by ambition, one of the worst of demons, the two were on the

verge with slight difference in timing of leading him to the
priest and the judge. It was a close call in both cases.

2

STOPPING IN ILHÉUS, WHERE he had gone to replenish his
stock, make some payments, and see the ocean, Fadul Abdala
was invited to dine in the company of Álvaro Faria, at the
home of Jamil Skaf, a countryman who had come up in life,
owner of the Select Shop, a prosperous business in furniture
and mattresses.

Fadul was surprised by the invitation, given at the Bar
Chic, near the waterfront, because although he had known
Jamil for several years, he hadn't been on close terms with
him. They saw each other now and then, in bars, in cabarets, in houses of prostitution, and exchanged handshakes,
friendly greetings: nothing beyond that.

Sipping his apéritif at the Tacho de Bibi, killing time
until lunch, a *moqueca* of prawns and lots of beer, Fadul
was enjoying some moments of profound spiritual enlightenment listening to Álvaro Faria, a man given to much knowledge and little work. Only Fuad Karan was the equal of
Álvaro Faria for a good philosophical discussion, some fine
talk, the one in Ilhéus, the other in Itabuna, each more
knowledgeable and witty than the other, two luminaries.

"You eat and drink well at Jamil's house," Álvaro whispered to him, "and his daughter is dazzling." Short and with a
mustache, animated, talking up a storm, his countryman
Jamil, upon extending the invitation, added that after dinner
they could go to Tilde's house, which had just opened on
Unhão, with the added attraction of some recently arrived
Frenchwomen.

3

IN SPITE OF THE fact that the two of them, Álvaro and
Fadul, were the only guests, the dinner had the air of a

banquet, such was the variety of Arab and Brazilian dishes and the quality of the desserts. Fadul ate his fill.

On praising the fine quality of the kibbe and the sublime taste of the *araife,* an almond cake with honey sauce, his favorite sweet, he discovered that dinner had been prepared by the daughter of his hosts, the student Aruza—an outstanding cook both at the oven and at the stove. Aided, of course, by a battalion of servants.

During dinner, Aruza was shy, with nothing to say, replying with monosyllables when the conversation was directed her way. She did not even smile when the others burst into gales of laughter at the witticisms and remarks of Álvaro Faria. Before they sat down to dinner, Fadul listened to Jamil extolling the qualities of his daughter, of whom he was very proud.

"In December she graduates as a teacher, she plays piano, recites poetry from memory. A good education, I didn't spare any expense."

He was silent, as if calculating how much he'd spend on the education of his heiress, but then he continued enumerating her virtues.

"Devout and hardworking, obedient."

Since he hadn't referred to her beauty, Fadul had a shock when he saw her enter the living room. Jamil made the introductions.

"This is my daughter Aruza, friend Fadul."

Fadul held out his enormous hand, smiled courteously. Álvaro Faria had been right: Aruza was really dazzling. Curly hair, fleshy lips, large eyes, small waist, full breasts under the white blouse, strong hips under her blue skirt. Not too taken with frail and fragile bodies or delicate shapes, Fadul found himself face-to-face with the personification of his concept of beauty. A lucky dog, the one who'd marry her. Jamil finished the introduction.

"This is my friend Fadul Abdala. I told you about him."

Aruza granted him only a quick look and an almost inaudible voice.

"How do you do?"

Too beautiful, there couldn't have been a prettier girl in all Ilhéus. Fadul searched his head for the exact expression to describe her. He found it in the Koran: *begum.* Begum, a Muslim princess.

4

WHEN DINNER WAS OVER, after belching with satisfaction, Jamil invited them to have coffee in the guest parlor, opened up for the occasion.

"Where are you going, Aruza?"

Aruza was slipping off down the hallway. She stopped and answered without looking at her father.

"I'm going over to Belinha's. I'll be back in a little while."

"You're not going anywhere, no, miss. We have company, your place is here."

Aruza turned around, came and sat down. When the coffee cups were taken away, Jamil told his daughter, "Open up the piano and play some music for our friends."

Resigned, the girl obeyed. She began with "La Prima Carezza." Álvaro Faria clapped his hands in apparent ecstasy, but in reality he was stuffed. "Over the Waves" and "Für Elise" followed. Aruza wanted to consider the concert finished, but Jamil demanded, "What about mine? Aren't you going to play it?"

She sat down at the piano again, attacked the "Marche Turque." The enthusiasm was general. When she finished, while Fadul and Álvaro were applauding, the girl got up, asked her father, "May I go now?"

Obstinate, Fadul thought, feeling the tension grow in the room. Jamil's voice let a touch of anger show through in spite of the smile under his mustache.

"Not now and not later. Sit down and talk with our guests."

He then got into a heated argument with Álvaro Faria about local politics. Aruza and Fadul exchanged a few words, and he tried to interest her in the Bible and the Koran, but without success. She didn't even act as though she were listening to him; she was biting her lips. Was she a student in coventry or a frightened damsel threatened in her dreams and plans?

With a worried look, Dona Jordana, her mother, broke out into smiles for the guest; she didn't let the silence last and Jamil noticed it. She found a subject to Fadul's liking,

Arab sweetmeats; she recited recipes, spoke about the details of honey and sesame.

Outside in the street someone was whistling a lively part of the "Marche Turque" over and over again.

5

ON THE WAY TO TILDE'S house to see the Frenchwomen, phony perhaps but great still the same, the ne plus ultra in matters of refinement according to Álvaro Faria, Jamil Skaf halted and, taking Fadul by the arm, nervous, wanted to know what he had thought of Aruza.

"A beauty, a begum. Not to mention her education."

Then his countryman asked abruptly, "Do you want to marry her?"

He went on, his voice stumbling, almost out of breath.

"The store is going full steam, I'm going to open a branch in Itabuna, and I've planted cacao in Rio do Braço. Aruza is an only child." He repeated, "Do you want to marry her?"

Such an untimely offer left Fadul bewildered to the point of not paying due attention to the protocol of the Frenchwoman who fell to him. But afterward, in his room at Mamede's small hotel, he realized that Jamil Skaf had decided to pick out a husband for Aruza.

That Jamil should choose a husband for his daughter and impose him on her was a normal procedure, correct and proper, worthy of applause. An extremely loving father, concerned about Aruza's future happiness, he was proceeding that way in order to insure her a blessed home, a peaceful life, and continuous well-being. The fine tradition, tried and true, uncontested, ordained that parents, responsible for the destiny of their daughters, should select from among the available bachelors in the realm the very best and propose a marriage and dowry to him. Some were lax in their paternal duties, leaving the choice and decision in such a serious matter to the sighing, lighthearted, immature maidens themselves. The result of such neglect was inevitably an unhappy marriage: weeping wives, broken homes, squandered inheritances, ruined fortunes! Jamil Skaf, with diligence and drive, looking for the best man in the realm of cacao, had finally found Fadul Abdala from out there at the ends of the earth.

Fadul kept thinking. On his next trip to Ilhéus he would give his answer. In the meantime, however, he thanked Jamil for the honor and the trust.

6

THE NEXT MORNING, ON his way to the station to take the train, Fadul Abdala, by chance or by intent, followed the unusual route that took him to the bottom of Conquista Slope. Up on Conquista, Our Lady of Mercy School, of the Ursuline Sisters, turned out primary schoolteachers, furnishing degree and diploma to all the rich girls of Ilhéus and the cacao region who studied there as boarders or as day students. Each morning and afternoon the day students went up and down the hill in wild juvenile excitement. At the foot of the slope swains loitered about like restless bumpkins.

On seeing him carrying his valise, the unmistakable look of a peddler about him, his hand to his hat in greeting, Aruza let out a small cry—it could have been of despair or excitement—and pointed him out to a schoolmate, who must have been Belinha, her neighbor and confidante. They were talking about him. Fadul went on his way to the station, carrying the vision of the girl in the blue and white uniform in his eyes.

During recess, in her favorite corner under the mango tree, Aruza bathed herself in tears. Belinha was of no help, but Auta Rosa, a second-year boarder, crafty and resourceful, immediately suggested a solution to the poor impassioned girl's problem, to get her out of marrying the husband chosen by her father. Belinha had seen Fadul standing at the base of the hill and confirmed matters: a huge, ungainly greenhorn, a hick, just the opposite of the elegant lawyer whom Aruza sighed over and who sighed over Aruza.

7

IN THE SOLITUDE OF Tocaia Grande, Fadul Abdala thought
about Aruza Skaf on countless occasions, with softness or
with violence, patiently or avidly, asleep or awake.

Alone in bed or covering one of the whores from the
place, Fadul had her, insatiable. It lasted about two months,
the period between his arrival from Ilhéus with the devil
whispering in his ear and the charms of the normal-school
student in his eyes, in his arms, in his lap, and his hearing
the news brought by Colonel Robustiano de Araújo. On
many nights he possessed and deflowered her three, four
times in a row.

Afraid of frightening or offending her, Fadul made an
effort to be delicate and prudent in his initial contacts, as he
removed the blue and white uniform. Timid caresses, furtive kisses on her shoulders, on the back of her neck, cautious touches creeping along in the discovery of guarded
treasures: the pleasure of gods. Little by little the maiden
would surrender, shame melted into desire, Aruza gave into
his advances, letting the Turk disrobe her.

The nude body lying on the thin mattress of dry grass
covered with chintz, the stink of bedbugs, in the abandonment of Tocaia Grande, Aruza surrendered. Full breasts,
pleading to be grasped and squeezed by his hands, powerful
behind, haunches like a mare's, and the glorious snatch. All
in conformity with the Grand Turk's taste and appetite. God
had finally taken pity on him.

They would change position—he experimented with all
of them—vary the rhythm, the place and time of penetra-
tion, Aruza's pussy was never the same. At the crucial moment, Fadul heard her cry out, as indispensable as the blood:
Siroca's cry and blood. For an instant, short but atrocious,
Aruza was little Siroca surrendering defenseless in the cacao grove to the peddler's strength and sweet-talk.

On certain nights, at the exact moment when Fadul was
about to pluck the bride's hymen, Zezinha do Butiá, shameless and taunting, would rise up in bed without having been
summoned. *Do you think you're the one who is going to deflower
a heavenly virgin, savor an unblemished cherry, you ignorant*

ass of a Turk, you blockhead? She was pointing with her fingers and suddenly he could see the open wound, the plowed field. Passing by there before, most certainly, had been a sweet-talking second-rate lawyer, good at whistling the "Marche Turque." Instead of unblemished virginity, a pair of horns.

What was the reason for Jamil Skaf's offering him for nothing the hand of his only daughter, the branch of his store in Itabuna, a partnership in the furniture business, and an easy and immediate fortune? There must have been some serious reason, and what could it have been? Zezinha do Butiá was laughing in his face: *You're going to cover the shame of your countryman's daughter with your great big body and your ambition, you muddle-headed Turk, you mercenary idiot. You're capable of anything for money, or do you think I don't know?*

One of those times, when, furious, he tried to expel Zezinha do Butiá from his dream, he woke up in time to spot in the dim light of dawn a green sword snake, beautiful but deadly, slithering across the foot of his bed. After quickly killing it, he began to think and reflect: Zezinha do Butiá had come to save his life. Only his life? Or to stop him from getting caught up a blind alley, finding himself when least expected carrying the litter of St. Cornelius in the procession in Ilhéus, too late to have repented and gotten out of it?

8

WHEN, AFTER MUCH REFLECTION, and weighing the pros and cons, Fadul decided to return to Ilhéus and carry forward the marriage plans proposed by Jamil Skaf, Colonel Robustiano de Araújo happened to pass through Tocaia Grande on his way to Santa Mariana Plantation. After lingering with old Gerino, he stopped his mount in front of Fadul's store. The colonel was coming from Ilhéus and he brought him a message from his friend Álvaro Faria, that amiable master of the good life who, in bars, gambling casinos, and cabarets commented with his customary sparks on the chronicles of the city. He'd asked the colonel not to forget to recount to the Arab Fadul the details of the wedding feast of Jamil Skaf's daughter.

"Who, Aruza? But two months ago she wasn't even engaged, how could she be married so suddenly?" Colonel Robustiano de Araújo placed both hands on his belly in an expressive gesture.

Pregnant? If she wasn't, she should have been according to what malicious tongues were whispering. Aruza and Dr. Epitácio Nascimento, a lawyer without clients, had faced the tears of Dona Jordana and the fury of Jamil and had confessed the evil step, fruit of desperate love. The young attorney had disembarked a short time before from a ship of the Bahia Line, ready to carve out a rapid career, and he had.

Wailing and recriminations being of no use, Jamil Skaf, a practical man, speeded up the wedding so that his daughter could walk up to the altar in garland and veil, virginal orange blossoms.

Fadul listened, didn't say anything. He left his cursing for after the colonel's mount had disappeared down the trail: *câss-âm-abúk-charmúta!* He never dreamed about Aruza again. Zezinha do Butiá returned to reign absolute in the enormous bed in the solitary nights of Tocaia Grande.

Jussara Ramos Rabat, Widow and Heiress of Kalil Rabat, Visits Tocaia Grande

1

FADUL ABDALA HAD MET Jussara Ramos Rabat, widow and heiress of Kalil Rabat, at the Taquaras fair while negotiating the purchase of two donkeys needed to haul goods to Tocaia Grande and to serve as mounts. Having chosen the animals carefully and examining their teeth and hooves according to what Captain Natário da Fonseca had recommended, he gave himself up to the pleasures of bargaining, haggling over the price with Manuel da Lapa, pointing out imaginary defects in the animals, placing obvious qualities in doubt.

"Have pity on me, Mr. Fadul, at least round it off a little higher."

"Not a penny more."

Jussara was what people call a big mama, a female to fill the eyes of any soul, a copper-colored half-breed glowing in the sun. Seeing her walking in his direction among mares and donkeys, seeing her stop in front of him, staring at him, Fadul lost his composure and the transaction was on the brink of going down the drain; he was stunned, unable to think or move. Aware of the danger, Manuel da Lapa decided to accept the price so as not to wind up empty-handed.

"Am I talking to Fadul Abdala?" she began, and then laughed a rough, bold laugh, the sound of a rattle.

Her eyes were bright, in contrast to her dull, pained voice, dying among the words as if Jussara were going to

faint, languid and charming, coquetry personified at the
Taquaras fair. Those who met and heard her for the first
time instantly felt ready to protect her, defend her against
any traps, tricks, or betrayals.

With effort the Turk finally managed to take off his hat
to greet her, deferential and courteous. He looked her over
discreetly from head to toe, trying to guess how she was
underneath her sedate clothes. Jussara proclaimed her widowhood to the four winds in the different shades of black of
her riding skirt, her silk blouse, the shawl that wrapped her
hair, protecting it from the dust. She was dressed in heavy
mourning, but in the hot coals of her eyes and the crimson
of her lips there wasn't a hint of tears or any touch of grief.
If she had bewailed the dead man at one time, she wasn't
weeping anymore: picking up her life again, she breathed
languor and pleasure, glowing in the sunshine of the fair with
promise and invitation. In her hand a whip with a silver
handle; in her fleshy mouth, half-open, her white and perfect teeth, teeth for biting.

"I've heard a lot about you." She didn't say whom she
had heard it from or what they had said, as if her statement
concealed some secret. "My name is Jussara. Did you know
Kalil Rabat, the owner of Orient House?"

Focusing his eyes, Fadul caught sight of a bloodred rose
placed behind her ear underneath the shawl, and the discovery excited him. Where had she come from, this half-breed
woman? From the depths of the woods where half-breeds
fought or from some wandering Gypsy camp? How many
bloods had mingled to produce that mystery, attain that
fascination?

"I knew him. More by sight than by contact. I heard
that he died."

"I'm his widow. I don't know anything about running a
store. Poor me."

She held out her whip, touched the giant's chest, insolent and frail at the same time.

"When you come to Itabuna, come see me. I'll show you
the store. I'm looking for someone to help me: no one takes
a widow seriously running a business. Poor me. . . ."

She turned her back, went to where a page was holding
a white-faced horse by the bridle. Before reaching the mount,
Jussara took the shawl off her head in a sudden gesture. She
let her black hair—blacker than the riding skirt, the silk

blouse, the lace, and the flounces—flow loosely down her
back to her waist. Fadul swallowed dryly, staring foolishly.
Helped by the page, Jussara put her foot in the stirrup,
mounted, and settled in the saddle. She turned her head
toward the Turk, waved good-bye. A minute later she was
gone.

Manuel da Lapa held out his hand, collecting the price
of the two donkeys, and commented, "What a woman, out of
this world, Mr. Fadu."

Riding one of the donkeys and driving the other, Fadul
set out for Tocaia Grande: poor man, *woe is me!* Proscribed
by fate, relegated to the asshole of the earth.

2

IN THE FORTNIGHT FOLLOWING the encounter at the fair in
Taquaras, Jussara Ramos Rabat, widow and heiress, filled
and perturbed all of Fadul Abdala's idle hours. What intentions were concealed in her gestures and words, her insistent looks, the languor of her voice?

In spite of the blouse with bows and furbelows, closed
at the throat, as modesty and shame require, and of the
ample and long riding skirt, the Turk could imagine the
bountiful udders, swollen breasts—good to squeeze with his
hands as he savored them—the voluptuous movement and
large size of her hips, the flat copper stomach and the mossy
mound, the fearful and wanting mouth of the world. He
took off Jussara's skirt and blouse, the endless ornaments,
too many knickknacks, and he saw her naked among the
animals in the bustle of the fair; no mare could be compared to her in bearing and grace. She whetted his appetite,
and he wanted her with such intensity that he was unable to
possess her in his dreams in spite of falling off to sleep with
only her on his mind, she with her extreme coquetry, her
rare elegance.

"Poor me," Jussara had said, and repeated again and
again, complaining about widowhood and business, two serious problems. What was she looking for with that litany?
What did she have in mind when she invited him to visit her

in Itabuna? Offer him a job at Orient House, proposing an interest in the sale perhaps, a small share in the profits? Working for others did not tempt him; he preferred to slave away without rest in what was his through the nights and dawns of Tocaia Grande without having to satisfy or render accounts to anyone.

Or, maybe, being a widow and a modern woman, she was looking for a husband who could take care of her and of the business. Young, rich, and so beautiful, she must have had platoons of candidates in the city of Itabuna, the port of Ilhéus dogging her steps; why would she have to come after a shopkeeper at the Taquaras fair in the midst of mules and donkeys? Being able to choose among landowners, merchants, lawyers, doctors with caps and gowns? She was obviously looking only for a clerk she could trust. It would have to be someone else, not him.

3

SITTING ON THE DOORSTEP, he was thinking about Jussara, a vague chimera in the smoke of the hookah, when he saw her in the flesh, getting off her white-faced horse, giving the reins to her page. Fadul Abdala had come back from a swim in the river, the sultry weather weighed heavily on his back and on the nape of his neck. In the intense light of early afternoon Tocaia Grande was drowsing in torpor and silence.

It had happened so abruptly that Fadul was not surprised or astonished, as if he were witnessing the most natural thing in the world. He even stopped looking at Jussara to watch the page, a combed and polished black boy, riding a saddle donkey, leading the horse by the bridle to the shade of some trees. But suddenly he realized the absurdity of the scene and, rubbing his eyes, faced the half-breed woman coming toward him. He barely had time to get up to welcome her.

"Why didn't you come see me in Itabuna? I waited in vain."

"I still haven't been there." It was taking him a long time to recover.

"Since you didn't go, I came here, poor me." She cast
her eyes over the surroundings. "What a depressing place.
What are you doing buried here?"

She shook her head with dismay. Her hair was curled
up into a bun, a tortoise-shell comb, an elegant touch, holding it up at the top of her head. Before the Turk could
answer, she went on.

"Are you just going to stand there? Aren't you going to
invite me in? Aren't you going to offer me something to
drink?" And she started in.

She stopped beside the counter, looking over the items
for sale, few and meager, shook her head again in a sign of
disapproval, but she didn't make any comment.

Still befuddled, Fadul followed her in. God in heaven!
Was it true, or had the sun gotten into his skull, making him
see visions in broad daylight? Not knowing what to offer
her—he had nothing worthy of her—he asked, "What would
you like to drink?"

"I'll take a swallow of water from the pitcher." Jussara
pointed to the clay jar on the windowsill.

She went around the counter, into the house, invading
his quarters, crossing the threshold of the bedroom.

"I like big beds, but I've never seen one that size."

"To fit me." Fadul said proudly, offering her a mug of
cool water.

Jussara drank in small sips, licking her lips as if she
were tasting a vintage wine, while she looked straight at the
Turk again, sizing him up and approving with satisfaction,
her moist mouth half-open, her eyes cloudy.

"Two people your size can fit and there's still room left
over."

She laughed a meaningful laugh, short and expressive,
and gave him back the mug.

"Thank you. When you go to Itabuna, don't forget to
come see me so I can show you the store. I don't know how
to take care of it all by myself; I miss things." She was
repeating what she had said at the fair: Was she offering
him a job behind the counter in the store or, who knows, her
hand in marriage? "When are you coming by there?"

She softened her voice, fell into coquetry, pleaded and
commanded.

"Don't take too long, come as soon as you can. I can't
wait for the rest of my life. Poor me."

She turned half around, ready to go out of the room and
leave Tocaia Grande. The Turk shuddered.

"Are you leaving already?"

"What can I do here? I stopped by only to see you."

Fadul's eyes grew shadowy, dark with impatience and
tension. Without even taking the trouble to close the door,
he went over to Jussara and took her in his arms. She did
not squirm away or resist him, she only said with the languid voice of someone who needs support and protection,
"Have pity, don't abuse me. Can't you see I'm a widow and I
have to get married again? If I lose my head, what will
become of me later? Poor me, even in love I have to control
myself."

Fadul didn't answer, remained silent; the conversation
could wait, not he. He was taken with fury, his eyes dim,
feeling the half-breed's body quiver. He pulled off her blouse,
her corselet—oh, those opulent breasts, so nice to grasp—
Jussara moaning slightly. Fadul pulled off her skirt, her
petticoat; he tore the laces of the panties that were tied
about the knees. The panties were black too.

He laid that royal person, that fantastic woman, onto
the mattress of grass and bedbugs, wearing only her high
riding boots. Fadul didn't waste time getting undressed: he
unbuttoned his fly, releasing his tool, impatient and rigid,
and covered Jussara.

He loosened the bun on the top of the half-breed's head;
free, the hair fell down, a black satin sheet covering the bed.
The mouth of the world, damp and gluttonous, received the
Lebanese chieftain's dong. The revels lasted all afternoon.

4

"OH, WHAT HAVE I done? My God, what an idiot I am! A
widow without any sense, I came for a husband and I leave
dishonored. Oh, poor me!"

She looked through her tears at the Turk stretched out
on top of her, crushing her breasts and thighs, when, panting, they came back from the first crossing of the desert and
the sea. Before he took off her boots, he undressed and

finally closed the door. Jussara spoke easily, in words accented by contrite weeping, pained complaints with which she accused herself in her affliction.

"Now that you've got what you wanted, you are free to despise me, mock me, call me a tramp, throw me out. It's my fault, I was fine in Itabuna; what did I come here for? To disgrace myself when what I need is a husband to look after me and take care of my store. I curse the day I saw you in Taquaras and lost my head. I didn't have the strength to resist, I disgraced myself. Oh, how I disgraced myself!"

She kept on incriminating herself while the great big man was getting off the bed, closing the door, and getting undressed; naked, he grew in size, getting even bigger. On the bed, lying down, she watched him from the corner of her eye, a husband and then some! A hard worker and ambitious, pompous, and foolish, just like Kalil Rabat, a happy boob born for a bridle and horns. But with the advantage of being big, good-looking, and in possession of that piece of timber. Jussara came with a full hand: the glow of her face, the temptation of her body, rolling in money, the best-supplied dry goods store in Itabuna, insolence and coquetry, her bonfire. What more could a dumb shopkeeper stuck in the boondocks want?

Since he did not think that was the most appropriate time to be talking about the widow's lost honor and how to restore it, the Turk listened in impatient silence to the endless, rueful litany. Jussara did not even quiet down when he freed her of her boots, a courtly gesture. Pathetic, she assumed the responsibility for the fateful mistake.

"I'm to blame, I didn't run away in time. But I don't care; it's all over."

Before she might suddenly put an end to the scarcely begun frolic, Fadul lay down beside the half-breed; with one of his outsize and delicate hands he caressed her breasts, softly kneading them; with the other he poked her behind and pinched her lightly, running his fingers over her trench. Jussara trembled and sighed, curled up on the hairy chest, felt the dong between her thighs, nearly fainted.

"You abused me, I let you, now you think I'm a fallen woman. How could you still want to marry me?" She raised her voice, making it clear and precise as she declared, "I swear by the soul of my mother that it was the first time I ever sinned in my whole life. I never had any man except my husband. I lost my head, poor me."

The naked legs were crossed, Jussara's thighs half-opened and her voice grew faint again.

"I lost my honor . . . I'm in your hands . . ." She stroked Fadul's face, put honey into her voice as she confessed, "But even so, I don't repent, you wicked man! You blinded my eyes, you seduced me."

Even in dishonor, I don't repent—nice words to hear: they inflate the chest, inflame the heart, light a fire in the balls of a man who is good in bed. In spite of the prudence with which he normally behaved in matters as relevant and touchy as those, Fadul decided to make a promise; to be fulfilled, who knows, after proper clarification and verification of some details.

"Don't worry. I'll come to Itabuna one of these days and we can talk there and settle things. Don't worry about the store."

"Really? Are you going to take over the store? Look after me?"

"Rest easy." And he didn't say any more.

5

SHE'D COME IN SEARCH of a husband, Fadul was convinced as he listened to her despair. A husband who could put an end to her uncomfortable widowhood and take over the store, generate profits. In order to conquer him, she was playing with high stakes, offering body and honor. Pure shrewdness or holy innocence? Softness or bad faith? Devouring passion or calculated risk?

With a failing voice, Jussara, noble and romantic, proclaimed love at first sight.

"I came because ever since the day I saw you at the fair, I've been out of my mind, my head was good only for thinking about you. I was cursed. Now I'm in your hands to be happy or to be disgraced forever." She asked again, "Are you going to love me or cast me out?"

Could that desperate drive, that mad possession, be a

positive answer? It must have been, because how could
Fadul live from then on as an orphan of Jussara's breathing,
sweat, smell, ecstasy? The bodies entangled, mingled, covered the sands of the desert, crossed the ocean waters, finally reached the ends of the earth in intensity and pleasure,
two unleashed powers, a wild colt, a mare in heat.

When night fell, Jussara fixed her bun and got on the
white-faced horse brought by the page—a sullen and perfumed black boy—Fadul finally compromised himself as he
kissed her good-bye.

"A few days from now we'll settle everything in Itabuna."

Before leaving, Jussara had placed her final trump card
on the table, or rather, on the bed. While she was putting on
the rags of her lace panties, petticoat, and corselet, black
blouse and skirt, a chaste and disconsolate widow, she stated
that what had happened would never happen again: whoever wanted to go to bed with her to practice the sweet and
dangerous game of nooky—that's how she put it, bashful,
lowering her eyes—would first have to take her before the
priest and the judge. She'd never known any man other
than her husband; Fadul had been the first and the last and
for one single time when, blind with passion, she had lost
her head and given in. No, it wouldn't happen again! In bed
again, whether in his arms, if he really loved her, or in the
arms of someone else, any hardworking and decent man
who would propose marriage to her—there would be plenty
of choices—only after the papers were signed, never before,
as had just happened. Wife, yes, lover, no. *Oh, poor me!*

She spurred the white-faced horse, followed by the page,
in a hurry to reach Itabuna and spread the good news. If
Fadul had not been explicit, if he had not promised categorically, Jussara knew how to read between the lines, discover
intentions by the inflection of the voice, and she had no
doubt that the Turk would come running after her. On his
skin, his mouth, his chest, his dong, she had left her unforgettable taste, indispensable from then on: the poor man
would no longer be able to live without it. She had no
doubts, she could start to arrange for the priest and the
judge.

The sun still hadn't gone to hide in the waters of the
river when Jussara disappeared in the direction of Taquaras.
No one had seen her arrive; no one had seen her leave.
Except for Coroca who, when she appeared to buy kerosene,

wanted to know, "Did you send for a whore from Itabuna,
Mr. Fadu?"

6

ONE RESTFUL DAY'S END in the young and trail-eager city
of Itabuna, after dropping his valise in the room of Zezinha
do Butiá at Xandu's flophouse and taking a tub bath—
Zezinha had heated up some water in the kettle and was
scrubbing his back with a towel gourd and sweet-smelling
soap, the wonders of civilization!—Fadul Abdala was getting ready, in the gallant words of the lovely lady, to fondle
his turtledove.

"Just look at his dovey, I'd already forgotten how fat it
was."

The size of the dove, a joy! As she played with it, Zezinha
do Butiá, nostalgic, sang a romantic *modinha* from Sergipe:

Turtledove, turtledove,
Plaything of love,
Come make your nest
Where I hold you best . . .

In the room, after his bath, having taken his pleasure,
Fadul found the whore sad and silent, as though something
were vexing her. Fadul was almost puzzled. Zezinha put so
much feeling into her impetuous surrender, fainting in his
arms, languid, loving. She even seemed like a girl in love
giving herself for the first time, or as if it were the last. Not
that she was in the custom of holding a distant and cold
pose; quite the contrary, she was an explosion of a woman.
No one else satisfied Fadul so completely as she in her zeal
and drive and even more so by showing a touch of love and
affection in the anxiety and tension of the games they played.
That's why he could never compare her to the other whores
he knew and frequented. In spite of her not having large
breasts or displaying a behind like a sauba ant, the Grand
Turk's manifest preferences, he never lusted so feverishly

after any other. It was Zezinha who inhabited his dreams in the long nights of his exile.

7

THE SHADOWS HAD DEEPENED, it was the end of afternoon. Getting out of her embrace, Fadul leapt out of the bed breathless, afraid of arriving late for his meeting with Fuad Karan at Rômulo Sampaio's bar, where his friend purveyed erudition every day, enlightening the elite of the city at the sacred hour of apéritif and backgammon. Careless about the duties of her trade, Zezinha remained lying on the bed, didn't come over to help him.

"You're late, aren't you?"

"A little. I've got to hurry . . ."

"Start running, maybe your girlfriend won't wait. Hurry up before she finds someone else and takes him to bed with her."

The strangest talk, an insolent and sarcastic voice. Surprised and suspicious, afraid of a scene, Fadul stopped putting on his drawers.

"Girlfriend? What's all this about?"

"Are you going to deny it? That's all they're talking about in Itabuna."

"About what? Spit it out."

"Everybody knows you're engaged to Jussa. Do you dare deny it?"

The mistrust that had hit him was confirmed: machinations of the widow, who was transforming the promise of a visit, the vague beginnings of a love affair, into a formal commitment of marriage. Jussa, the diminutive of Jussara; Zezinha was throwing the nickname into his face: an insult, a slap. Holding his shorts, he stopped and asked her.

"Jussa?"

"Jussa Poor Me, don't tell me you don't know her. . . . Just the other day Fuad Karan was here and he said to me, 'You know, Zezinha, your Fadul has gone crazy: he's about to marry Kalil Rabat's widow.' I was knocked for a loop, I didn't believe it. 'It can't be, I don't believe it.' But he said it was the absolute truth, that you were going to be the new king. . . ."

"Let's hear it right out. King of what?" He raised his voice, upset to find out that he had become the butt of the town's gossip.

"King of cuckolds like the late Kalil, a good man who died from wearing enormous horns all the time."

Fadul hadn't expected that, he wasn't prepared for the abrupt revelation, a whack on the head. He opened his eyes wide, dropped his jaw, swallowed.

"The dead man was a cuckold? You're not lying, are you?"

"If you don't believe me, ask Fuad; he's the one who knows all about it. Ask anybody you want. Everybody in Itabuna knows Jussara's reputation."

Fadul's hazy eyes saw the half-breed in mourning again, immaculate. In his ears the voice of coyness and chastity: *It was the first time I sinned in all my life, I never went with any other man except my husband; but when I saw you, you wicked man, I didn't have the strength to resist—what can honor do against fate?* Swearing on the soul of her mother while opening her legs, shameless whore. Everything about her was a sham, a lie, deceit: *bitch, cow, whore three times over!* How could he have believed her, he who took so much pride in being smart? Convinced, vain, he'd puffed up his chest: Fadul Abdala, irresistible stud. Drooling, he'd come running to her just the way she knew he would. He broke out in Arabic, *"Hala! Hala! Charmuta!"*

"The only thing great about you is that you're a great boob. You see a pretty woman and the promise of a lot of money in front of you and you don't see anything else, not even a pair of horns." She paused with her eyes on the Turk's face, confused, astonished. "Or maybe you're not up to it. Do you see it and close your eyes to pretend you don't know? That's what they're saying about you."

Naked, huge, and disheartened, a frog caught in his throat that couldn't swallow. *Charmuta! Arkut!* Fadul plopped down on the edge of the bed, tried to control his voice, his anger, and his shame.

"I didn't know she was like that; I live off in the backwoods."

"I shouldn't have worried about it or gotten mixed up in it; I'm not getting anything out of this. If I'd been smart,

I'd have shut up. If you marry her, you'll be a moneybags
with lots of dough; you can set me up in a house, get me out
of this life. Fuad even congratulated me, said you were
going to be filthy rich. . . ." A sob escaped Zezinha's breast,
against her will. ". . . filthy rich, stinking rich, was what he
said, do you hear?"

She paused, attempting to hold in her tears, her voice
coming out in spurts.

"If you marry her, I never want to see you again." She
started crying.

She didn't make any effort to hold back her tears anymore, keep the weeping in her breast, hold firm. Zezinha do
Butiá covered her face with her hands and let herself go.
Seeing the gleam of tears on the face of the prostitute,
listening to her weeping because of him, indignant and sad
at thinking he was going to be Jussara's husband, rich and
with a pair of horns, Fadul recovered his spirits, freed from
spite and vexation, got up again, came out of his rage and
shame unscathed.

The good God of the Maronites had come in time. It
didn't matter to Fadul anymore whether Jussara was a
chaste widow or the most fucked and famous madam of
Itabuna, he wasn't thinking about marrying her anymore.
What mattered to him, that and only that, was Zezinha's
weeping, her uncontrolled tears—the grief, the spite, the
sadness shown by the poor girl, the sign that she really
loved him.

"You mean to say that's why you're all upset? It wasn't
the sickness or death of somebody in the family?"

"Don't you think I've got feelings?"

Night had completely fallen, a cloak of black. In the
parlor Xandu lighted a lamp.

8

"I WAS TEMPTED, YES," Fadul confessed to Zezinha do
Butiá the events of the brief and malignant hallucination
that almost brought him to hitch his destiny to that of
Jussara Ramos Rabat, Jussa Poor Me, with her getting a

husband and respectability, his getting the biggest dry-goods store in Itabuna and the realm of passive cuckolds: King Fadul of Passivity. He'd escaped just in time, thanks to the good God of the Maronites, who, in order to save him, had taken hold once more of the good offices of Zezinha, raised to the status of guardian angel. Given the size of the danger, the whore had not been content to appear to him in his dreams, as at the time of Aruza; she'd come in person to save him from dishonor.

Zezinha knew a lot and she bored him with the details of the widow's carrying-on before and after burying the dead man and weeping for his horns. She listed the swains, a whole crowd of lucky guys. He knew several of them; it would be easy to prove the truth of the entanglements if that was what he wanted, but Fadul no longer had any doubts to clear up.

Later on, at the cabaret, Fuad Karan added some new facts. He spoke about the strange circumstances, enlarged the list of lovers. The most diverse citizens lumped together in the half-breed's rich chronicle. No one could have accused Jussara of having any prejudices in matters of men: if they wore pants and could lift their poles, they deserved her attention and, circumstances being right, she would take them to bed. Fuad Karan eruditely summed it up: "Jussara is a nymphomaniac, my dear Fadul, there's nothing to be done."

"A fire in her tail," Zezinha had confirmed, "there's no male who can put it out."

From all that had happened, a bitter aftertaste stayed with the Turk: the half-breed had abused him, had tricked him and exposed him to laughter and jeers. Simply withdrawing from the supposed engagement, leaving her in the lurch, wasn't enough for him; he had to show all his disdain. Then he remembered Coroca's question on that afternoon of idle talk and enticements: *Did you send to Itabuna for a whore, Mr. Fadu?*

He laid the happy idea that had occurred to him before Zezinha: send a message to the widow's house carrying the amount of money corresponding to the usual payment to a whore for an afternoon in bed. An affront, it would cleanse his soul. Zezinha agreed with the plan, but thought the amount too small, unworthy of someone who was known for his generosity to whores; the sum was much less than Jussara deserved. The half-breed wasn't just any whore with an open door on a street corner. She'd been lucky, she'd come up in life: being a widow, she'd been married, the cream of the crop, upper crust, she had a maid and a page at her service. Besides, she'd traveled to Tocaia Grande. How many times had Fadul gotten into her during the afternoon? Hadn't he liked it? Every inch a woman, a buxom belly with a fire in her behind.

The lower the payment, the greater the insult, the humiliation, the Turk argued, but he ended up giving in. Zezinha wasn't convinced: she wanted to avoid his looking like a tightwad, a cheap customer: if he was going to pay, he should pay what was right, even a little more. Fadul, sensitive to those eloquent arguments, finally decided to pay double what the whores he ordered from Itabuna got because Jussara was a widow and because she didn't practice her trade for money.

He wanted to call Vadeco, the black boy who was messenger and jack-of-all-trades in Xandu's house, to deliver the message by hand: *Here's the payment Mr. Fadul sent.* Laughing, Zezinha picked up the coins.

"Wasting your money on Jussa, you don't know what you're doing! It's the same as throwing money away: she's going to laugh and give it to her page as a present. It's better in my hands. I need something to help my family."

During the Aforementioned Absence of Fadul Abdala, the Notorious Manezinho Invades Tocaia Grande at the Head of His Gunmen

1

FADUL HADN'T CONFRONTED TEMPTATIONS of the devil only, dreaming while awake, suffering while asleep. Whores and virgins in heat offering themselves in bed, a rich widow, supposed fiancées, dry-goods stores, furniture, promises of a quick fortune, a happy life, mad fantasies! The victim of men's cruelty and greed, he'd faced other provocations capable of knocking down a less determined citizen and putting him to flight. Before he started to make money hand over fist, Fadul Abdala had purged his sins in Tocaia Grande.

Previously, with the drudgery of a peddler, he was at least master of his time. But the store, at first only a small shop, demanded the owner's permanent presence in order to sell and serve, collect and receive, impose respect. A businessman with an open door in a new settlement, the owner of the only business that took care of outsiders, he couldn't afford the luxuries of a peddler: gathering up his merchandise, putting it on his back, and leaving to roam about wherever he wished. Fadul had begun to live according to a suffocating calendar. Absenting himself from Tocaia Grande meant problems and risks.

He spaced out his trips, reduced the number of days he was away. Even so, at first he couldn't enjoy a moment of rest while he stayed in Ilhéus and Itabuna for the time strictly necessary for purchases and payments: buying was an art, the art of tricks and bargaining, paying was a science of juggling dates and promises. Even during the night, too short for conversation, gambling, cabaret, and whores, his thoughts continued to revolve on the store, on the ominous underbrush. It had happened on the occasion of his first absence; it might happen again in spite of the support of Coroca and the protective shadow of Captain Natário da Fonseca.

Only when his stock began to get low did he decide to take a few days off to replenish it at the marketplaces of Ilhéus and Itabuna. He'd gained experience about which articles to buy: which sold the most, the proper amounts, the preferred brands. Great was the sale of dried meat, cane liquor, and brown sugar, but of the dozen denim pants, he'd sold only two and at a lowered price. In compensation, he'd sold all the cotton ones and could have sold more if he'd had them.

Late at night, locked up in his house so no one would see him, by the light of the lamp he counted the wad of money, small bills, dirty, torn, glued with soap. He took a large red bandanna out of his stock and placed the bills in it in the manner of hired hands, something he'd learned from his days as a peddler. He knotted the ends and, with a safety pin, fastened it to the inside of the right pants pocket. As for coins—a lot of them, in copper and nickel—after dividing them according to value, he wrapped each pile in a piece of paper and put them in a small leather bag that he tied to his belt under his shirt. On trails and cuts, highways and by-ways along the Rio das Cobras, the fame of Turk Fadul's wealth flew from mouth to mouth: hidden money, diamond rings, gold pieces. There were those who said they'd seen pounds sterling: gleaming, dazzling their eyes. They never could have imagined that the kerchief and the bag contained his capital and profits, his wherewithal, everything he owned except for what was left of the supplies in the store.

After having taken care of his morning customers, he'd hung up in plain view at the front of the establishment a notice painfully spelled out in capital letters on the lid of a shoe box: CLOSED ON ACCOUNT OF OWNER'S ABSENCE. The two doors to the store were barred from the inside with wooden beams and, after locking up the entrance to the back room, he put the revolver in his belt and took advantage of the company of Zé Raimundo, who was driving a large train coming from Atalaia Plantation, for the trip to Taquaras, three and a half leagues through the ends of the earth.

Visiting an old friend, a certain Zelita, who plied her trade at the station, Coroca went with them. Skinny, dried-out, she weighed almost nothing. Zé Raimundo stuffed her between two sacks of cacao, astride the packsaddle on Full Moon, a strong and peaceful mule, the lead animal of the troop, with tinkle bells on her head and chest harnesses. Head held high, Coroca took on the airs of a foreman's wife or a landowner's mistress. Fadul, knapsack on his shoulder, chuckled in anticipation of the delights that awaited him in Itabuna. Only on the train, when he attempted to peel an orange, did he realize that he'd left his favorite jackknife behind in Tocaia Grande.

2

DURING THE FIRST TWO days of Fadul's absence, nothing serious happened. Drovers and helpers arrived sweaty, covered with dust and mud, thirsty, in need of a drink of *cachaça* to restore their strength, to fight the cold or heat, depending on the season. They came upon the notice. If there was one of them who could read or sign his name, he spelled out the message for the rest; if not, they got the news from the mouths of the whores. Amid curses and laughter they argued about the double-dealing Turk who was tossing them to the dogs while he went off to replenish his stock.

"Turk son of a bitch. Today of all days . . ."

"Why didn't he leave someone in charge?"

"Who might that be?"

"Pedro Gypsy's here with nothing to do."

"If the business belonged to you, would you leave it in Pedro's hands?"

They ended up going off to the women.

"Let's go see if the girls have decided to lock up their boxes. . . ."

The number of whores varied, some would come, others would go: a trollop never warms up a nest. The regulars, a half dozen of them, no more, lived in shacks clustered by the

river at the opposite end from the shed where Colonel
Robustiano Araújo stored his dry cacao. Coroca, on choos-
ing the spot for the little house that Captain Natário da
Fonseca had recently ordered built by Bastião da Rosa and
Lupiscínio, refused to have it built on the Caminho dos
Burros.

"I want it right here. . . . A whorehouse on the main
street isn't right. The main street is for family houses."

Lupiscínio was bemused.

"What families, Dona Coroca?"

With the respect he had for older people, he called her
Dona and he sent his son and apprentice, Zinho, a young
lad, to go get her blessing.

"Oh, families will be coming soon, you'll see."

"You really mean it?"

"It's best to start here right off, near the frogs, rather
than be sent away later on. Today it's all the same, it
doesn't matter, but later on, who can say."

That was how the Baixa dos Sapos, frog hollow, was
born, where drovers and helpers headed in search of a woman's pleasures; under those circumstances, with the store
closed, they arrived earlier, in hopes of a sip of *cachaça* or
coffee. Others stayed by the woods, picked a nice ripe jackfruit. To fill the gut there's no food that can come close to it
for flavor and nourishment.

3

AT DUSK ON THE third day, in the middle of a ceaseless
rain, the aforementioned Manezinho came into Tocaia Grande
followed by two other thugs, Chico Serra and Janjão. They
were riding bareback, rope lassos around the animals' necks
in place of bridles or reins: fine-looking saddle donkeys, well
groomed and well fed, the chosen mounts of colonels. They
came in shooting, to dispel any doubts.

They halted in the clearing where the drovers of the
first mule train had built a kind of straw-roofed shelter, a
precarious defense against the sun and rain. There they'd
lighted a fire, roasted jerked beef, cooked yams and bread-

fruit, boiled coffee, and talked about life and death, that is, about the cacao crop, an eternal and passionate topic. Producing his accordion, Pedro Gypsy had just proposed to the group an enticing deal: round up two or three sluts and organize a shindig in exchange for a few pennies. Lively black Dalila, looking for a customer, praised the idea: nothing better than a little dancing to start a pleasant evening. "A woman in bed is much better," argued a red-headed drover's helper, lusting after the black girl's tail. "You fresh fat-ass, where's the money to back up all that talk?" With the echo of shots and the beating of hoofs, all conversation died.

The thugs wanted to know where the Turk's shop was. "Up ahead there, but the owner is traveling, so the doors of the emporium will be closed for a few days."

"We-uns will open it. For anybody who don't know, my name is Manezinho," the one who seemed to be in command said, and after running his eyes over the group, he galloped off in the direction indicated.

Just to show how good a shot he was, Chico Serra aimed at the stalk of a breadfruit on a nearby tree and brought it down. Leaning down from his donkey, Janjão reached out and hefted the whore's behind.

"Don't go away, sweetheart, I'll be right back."

Pedro Gypsy had realized that the outsiders were aware of Mr. Fadu's absence and that was why they'd come: it couldn't have been with any good intentions. He forgot about any plans for hip-swinging; the night was starting to look dangerous.

"They're going to raid the store!"

"He's apt to," one of the drovers agreed, stirring the coals with the tip of his whip. "That Manezinho is the devil himself; he used to be a gunman for Colonel Teodoro das Baraúnas, he has his share of deaths on his conscience. Not a month ago he killed a doctor in Água Preta. He's on the run. The others, I don't know."

But the cowboy, who was on his way back from Itabuna, knew the other two by name and by reputation, as bad as could be. Chico Serra had never been good for anything except waylaying people; he'd been drifting ever since Colonel Maneca Sá had kicked him off Morro Azul Plantation, when he didn't have anything more for him to do. As for the stringbean, they certainly must have heard the name Janjão

Fanchão, one and the same. Besides being a criminal, he was off his nut, beat up on women, a fancier of queer ass.

"Oh, God in heaven!" Dalila exclaimed, and ran off to warn the whores to hide in the woods.

Having given his information, the cattle drover proposed that they all flee to the warehouse where Colonel Robustiano kept three well-armed men all the time, guarding his cacao. They'd be safe there and sheltered from the rain. He didn't want to risk his life staying out in the open; he grabbed his rifle and got up.

"Aren't we going to do anything?" Pedro Gypsy asked to ease his conscience, because not even he was thinking about standing up to the bandits and stopping the attack.

"What can we do?" The cowboy began walking toward the cacao warehouse.

"Who's crazy enough to run the risk of getting shot because of the Turk? It's his mess, not ours." Drawing back from the heat of the fire, the drover stirred the coals with the tip of his whip; he, too, got up and started out.

The others went along with him, putting aside Pedro Gypsy's suggestion that at least they should go and spy on what was happening; they liked the wily, bragging Turk, but not to the point of standing up for his cause against fierce gunmen, heartless murderers. Only the redhead, a curious and daring kid, hid with Pedro behind the trunk of a jackfruit tree from where they could watch the store. The rain had become a downpour; clouds covered the sky.

Nor did Pedro Gypsy, whose belly Fadul had filled so many times with food, and even more with *cachaça*, hide behind the tree with the idea of being of any help; he was taking the risk only because he had a hunch and he wanted to check it. It wasn't to steal beans, *cachaça*, dried meat, or rough-cut tobacco that Manezinho, Chico Serra, and Janjão were breaking down the doors of the store: Pedro Gypsy felt sure he knew what the real reason was.

4

AFTER THE FIGHT FOR the conquest of the forests, when wheeling and dealing took the place of ambushes in the conflicts among the cacao colonels over the vacant lands, laid-off gunmen wandered the roads, coming and going with no set direction, offering to kill for a trifle, or even for nothing in cases of robbery. Of the hundreds of thugs who'd come to the southern part of the state of Bahia from the tri-state backlands and from the banks of so many other rivers, putting arms and good aim at the service of the rich plantation owners, a few had marked out lands, planted crops, using weapons only when absolutely necessary. Most of them settled on the plantations and became bosses over gangs of hired hands, bodyguards, and foremen. Some, however, didn't adapt to the new conditions and roamed the countryside committing atrocities and terrorizing people.

They ended up being liquidated one by one, but for a long time there were a lot of them, of sinister fame. Among the most fearsome stood Manezinho: he'd taken part in the legendary battles fought between Basílio de Oliveira and the Badaró family. The strongman of Teodoro das Baraúnas, of grim memory, he didn't want to serve any other colonel or lay down his weapons. Lately, he planned to organize a gang to attack plantations, villages, towns. All by himself he thought and schemed: one can well imagine what he could do at the head of a gang of thugs. As a start he took on Chico Serra and Janjão.

They stole the donkeys in the pasture of a plantation they'd passed; nobody caught them—let them just try! Manezinho laughed at the warning from Chico Serra, who was still fearful of the colonels' power.

"If you're scared, get lost. I want only real men in my outfit."

Listening to the gabble of women, perhaps vain twaddle in the whorehouses of Taquaras, Manezinho had found out about Fadul Abdala's journey to Itabuna. The sluts condemned such carelessness and lack of foresight—more than carelessness and lack of foresight the laziness, the foolishness of the Turk, an idiot. He was going off on a trip, leaving behind hidden in the house in Tocaia Grande the money he'd accumulated over the years as a peddler, a treasure at the disposal of the first one with nerve enough to go look for it. They were arguing about the location of the hiding place. In the living quarters out in the back, under the mattress? In the store, up front, among the merchandise? They all agreed over the size of the treasure, a sack bulging with gold

coins, according to the testimony of people they knew and
in whom they had absolute confidence.

5

THEY TIED THE ANIMALS to the stakes by the side of the
store, tried to knock down the front door without success:
the wooden beam resisted, attesting to the competence of
Bastião da Rosa. They went around the house and found
the rear entrance. After Manezinho had tried unsuccessfully
to shoot the lock off, Chico Serra backed up, charged the
door with the whole weight of his body, and the bolt began
to give way. Janjão finished the job.

Inside the house they lighted the lamps; wind and rain
blew in through the open doorway. It seemed unnecessary
to leave anyone on guard; each one more notorious than the
others, who would dare attack them? They helped themselves to the *cachaça*, drinking from the bottles; a bottle for
each, the three of them needed it.

They combed the house from top to bottom, from end to
end. First they visited the rear rooms. In the smaller one
that served as a kitchen they didn't find anything except the
trivet and some makeshift pots and pans. In the bedroom,
on the bed, on top of the dirty bedcover, lay Fadul's jackknife.
Before putting it into his pocket, Janjão examined the long
steel blade with curiosity and pleasure: just what he needed
to calm down any whore who resisted when he went after
her rear end. Smiling, he gulped down the remains of the
cachaça and threw the empty bottle against the wall.

Manezinho and Chico Serra tore up the mattress, spilling the dry sedge about. Janjão brought out a new supply
of *cachaça*, and the three of them took apart the enormous
bed, the masterpiece of Lupiscínio the carpenter, all of it
made of top-grade wood brought from the forest, where
jacaranda, mahogany, *putumuju*, fiddlewood, pink perobas,
and brazilwood abounded. They were looking for the hiding
place where the sack of gold coins might be. No hiding
place, no coins.

The other section served as a storeroom for merchan-

dise. For a while they amused themselves by filling up
empty feed bags with knickknacks, destroying everything
that they didn't care for. They greeted the discovery of the
denim pants with enthusiasm and swigs of liquor. They took
off their cotton ones, old and mended, and pulled on those
luxurious new ones, made of expensive cloth. Chico Serra
put on two pairs, one on top of the other. They piled up
dazzling trifles, but found no trace of the treasure in the
storeroom either.

"It's hidden out front. We should have started there,"
Manezinho reasoned.

Alert, he went over to the door, looked outside: only the
pitch blackness and the fury of the downpour, no sound but
the howling of the wind. Manezinho smiled, proud of his
deserved fame: no son of a bitch had dared disturb them.
The name and renown of dangerous men had reached town
before them.

6

BERNARDA HAD TRIED TO dare, only she. When Dalila appeared in panic, urging the women to escape to the woods,
Bernarda was busy with a drover and the appeals didn't
make a dent with her. Curses, shouts, and threats were
customary at night in the settlement: the better the business, the greater the disorder. But the uproar was growing
and spreading: Bernarda, having given her partner his fill of
pleasure, put on her slip and went out to have a look. She
came back with the news.

"Bandits are raiding Mr. Fadu's store."

She didn't wait to hear the answer nor did she worry
about getting paid; just the way she was, she shot out into
the downpour. Mud-splattered, she reached the shelter
in the clearing: nobody. Where could they be? Scurrying into
the bushes worse than the women? They weren't defending the
store either, not a peep from those quarters. She went to the
shed: there, at least, she'd find the three men charged with
guarding the dry cacao. She went off, whipped by the wind;
everything calm all around—too calm, it was frightening.

One of the doors of the storehouse half-opened at the sound of her steps and Bernarda glimpsed the muzzle of the carbine. She shouted her name and the door opened wide.

Inside the storehouse, the watchmen and the cowboy were standing guard, arms at the ready. Sitting on the ground, drovers and helpers were arguing over cards: some betting, others watching, but none of them paying any attention, their minds numbed by the bandits' arrival. They looked at Bernarda, but no one opened his mouth; they went on with the game. They knew she hadn't come in search of business. The water was running down her body, making puddles on the floor: the slip, clinging to her skin, outlined her breasts and stomach, her hips and thighs. In the dim light of the lamps she looked like a vision from the other world.

"They say bandits are raiding Mr. Fadu's house."

There was no response. The cattle drover started to speak, thought better of it, stared at her as if his eyes were all lighted up: wow, he'd never been to bed with Bernarda!

"Are they or aren't they?"

Turning his eyes from the bold woman's wet breasts, the cowboy nodded, and confirmed, "João Fanchão, Chico Serra, and Manezinho, you couldn't ask for worse than those together."

"What's been done about it?"

The half-breed who'd opened the door was surprised at the question; in a flat voice he explained, "Been done? They came for the store; after they rob it, they'll leave."

"They're only three, and there are nine of you here. . . ."

In the silence she took a step forward, spat on the ground.

"Nine men shitting in their pants, they're so scared."

"No whore's going to say I'm scared. . . ." The other guard, who'd been quiet until then, was offended.

He went over to Bernarda, ready to give her a slap in the face, teach her some respect and consideration, but he stopped when he heard old Gerino's warning.

"Are you crazy, Zé Pedro?"

The card players, who'd stopped their betting, went back to dealing their greasy cards in relief. The old man lowered his voice to speak to Bernarda. Boss of the men assigned to guard the shed, he didn't seem offended by the whore's accusation; no one who knew him could accuse

Gerino of being a coward. Besides, he hadn't forgotten that
Bernarda was related to Captain Natário; if the half-breed
had tried anything against her, not even God could have
saved him. Gerino considered himself responsible for the
cacao and also for the men under him.

"Do what, Bernarda? Tell me if I'm wrong. We've got
nothing to do with that business. We're paid to guard the
colonel's cacao; if they come here they'll run into fire, that's
what we're paid for, only that."

"But they're robbing the store and they say they're
going to grab the women by force and rape us, one by one."

"We're not here to look after any Turk's goods or any
whore's cunt. What do you think this is, a city? This here is
a dump with a store, four whores, and us in the colonel's
warehouse: it's every man for himself and the devil take the
hindmost. If you want, stay here with us and nothing will
happen to you."

He walked over beside the door where Bernarda stood,
upset and tense, and told her without any rancor, "But if
you don't want to stay, if you're set on getting killed for the
Turk, you can go. We're not budging from here. If they come
here, they'll find out what lead tastes like. People have got
only one life and one death to spend."

7

NOT IN THE DRAWERS or on the shelves, not under the
thick boards of the counter—*where in hell could that bastard
Turk have stuffed his gold?* There, too, they took everything
apart, piece by piece, a tiresome and futile bit of work. "It's
got to be somewhere," Manezinho reaffirmed, controlling
the haste of his chums: on one side, Janjão, whose drinking
had increased his longing for the black woman's rear end;
on the other, Chico Serra, apprehensive of a surprise attack
by the drovers.

Where in hell? In the sacks of flour, beans, corn? They
opened the front door wide and began to throw the merchandise outside, piling it up in the rain. They strewed the
beans and the corn about, the rice and the flour, the refined

sugar, they took out their knives and hacked at the slab of dried meat. In order to drive off fear, Chico Serra shot off the necks of several bottles with his revolver; in the woods where they'd taken refuge, the whores heard the shots and were pissing with fright.

Dripping with rain behind the jackfruit tree, Pedro Gypsy and the redhead made an effort to see and understand; they could just make out the figures moving in the darkness. Janjão and Chico Serra had piled the merchandise up, Manezinho poured kerosene over the pile and lighted it. There was an altercation, their voices rose threateningly. Janjão wanted to set the house on fire, Manezinho held him back with roars. Sure that the sack of coins was there, well-hidden someplace, the leader of the gang had plans to come back soon, when the Turk had returned from his trip. Under the barrel of a gun Fadul himself would lead them to the booty. For nothing.

Janjão, who seemed to have shit in his head instead of brains, then tried to prolong their stay in the settlement, time enough to go up the black girl's ass, but Manezinho wouldn't hear of it.

"You can stay if you want to be killed by the drovers. Let's go!" he ordered Chico Serra, who wanted just that.

The two went off fast, shooting in the air as a farewell. Janjão still took a look around, with blockheaded obstinacy: how could he have spotted the ragamuffin in that darkness even if she'd stayed with her behind up waiting for him in the storm? Finally he gave up; he shot off his weapon in the direction of the clearing where he'd found her, with a curse he spurred the animal on, in a hurry to catch up with his cronies. He cursed again. A double loss: neither the treasure nor the black woman's ass.

The flames couldn't stand up to the heavy rain, and slowly went out; the strong smell of burned corn, sugar, beans, charred meat spread out in the wind. The vagrant and the redhead came out from behind the jackfruit tree and went closer. Pedro Gypsy passed by the bonfire without stopping and went into the house; who knows, maybe he'd have better luck than the bandits. He also believed as the gospel truth the existence of the cache of gold coins accumulated by the Turk: in his mind it was no sack, but a chest. The drover's helper, a greenhorn who didn't know anything about it, contented himself with what he could rescue from the fire. Then they were joined by men from the warehouse, women from the underbrush. They fought avidly over the remains of the sacking of the house and store and what they could rescue from the flames. That was how part of Fadul Abdala's fortune was consumed, the part he didn't carry on his person, the merchandise left behind in the general store.

Pedro Gypsy continued scavenging tirelessly through the night even after the others had gone off. Fortified by two bottles of *cachaça* miraculously spared from Manezinho's wrath, Chico Serra's shit-fear, Janjão Fanchão's thirst, and the rapaciousness of the hangers-on, a gang of wretches.

8

TO BELIEVE THE VERSION promulgated far and wide by Pedro Gypsy, the imprecations of Fadul Abdala shook heaven and earth, made the four quadrants of the world tremble, so terrible were they. Cuckoos and currasows, parrots and macaws fled in flocks to the most hidden corners of the woods, the coendous hid in hollow trees, sleepy kinkajous woke up startled, snakes went on the alert, coiling up for whatever might be coming.

When all is said and done, however, Pedro's version notwithstanding, the tales of other eyewitnesses about the arrival of the Turk in Tocaia Grande three days after the attack showed similar drama and grandiloquence. They pictured him beside himself, pounding his chest; then, in despair, lifting his big open hands on high, pointing in the direction of the careless, negligent, remiss God of the Maronites, to whose care he had entrusted the peace of his house and the security of his goods before he left. He opened his mouth with the roar of a beast wounded through the betrayal of his own father. He accused the Lord of having abandoned him at the most needed and bitter moment of his life, and he did it in Arabic, making the spectacle all the more pathetic. Incidentally, to talk to God, Fadul always used his mother tongue, since he wasn't sure that the Almighty knew Portuguese. In Portuguese he swore vengeance, oaths that were lost in their lack of sense: where, how, and when could he carry them out? Never.

The angry dialogue with the Almighty served to relieve him; He had only exposed his character and his faith to a much more difficult test than the nightmares with Zezinha, naked and unattainable. Fadul realized that He had saved his life by getting him out of Tocaia Grande on the occasion of the looting.

They watched him grow silent. He lingered over the disorder and the rubbish as if wishing to keep the image tattooed on his soul. Then he called Lupiscínio and gave him precise orders: start working on the counter and the shelves, there was no rush for the bed. On the same day that he had arrived and learned about the disaster, Mr. Fadu was serving his customers again.

Unless asked about it, he never brought up the subject again. When pressed on the matter, he wouldn't refuse to talk about it, but would answer carefully, making a show of calm and resignation. He didn't complain that no one had defended his residence and business, finding excuses and explanations for such behavior: only a madman would have risked his life to rescue bags of sugar, bolts of cloth. From Gerino himself he learned of Bernarda's attempt and how it had been difficult to keep her in the warehouse safe from the bandits. If they'd seen that pretty thing trying to get involved in their lives, good-bye Bernarda! Before finishing her off they would have used her in the way foreseen: all three at the same time and brutally, under the command of Janjão Fanchão, the ass-fancier. The Turk backed up the old man's conduct: he had done the right thing. Bernarda was soft in the head.

He didn't talk about going away to do business elsewhere, in a less exposed place, or going back to his life of a peddler: it was as if the looting had reinforced his decision to establish himself in Tocaia Grande. However, he'd lost the extroverted good nature, his joviality; he no longer fooled around or joked with his customers the way he used to. No smile could be seen on his face, no matter how hard people tried to bring one out. What had happened to the Turk who told loud and lively stories, full of wit and wisdom, the sweetheart of whores? Concerned, they wondered if Mr. Fadu would ever laugh and joke again.

Buried in his work, with his well-known drive and ambition, he'd overcome the shock, the rage over his considerable losses. But something kept on disturbing him, stopping him from sleeping, gnawing inside him without rest: the impossibility of revenge. It pained him to know that the bandits who had invaded his property, destroying and stealing valuable goods, were free: they were living off the fat of the land, far from the reach of his hands. Fadul felt unhappy, disgusted with his sad and ugly life.

9

A LITTLE MORE THAN a week after his return, Fadul Abdala was already sick and tired of listening to jokes and wailing, back into his habitual chores. One day toward the end of morning Captain Natário da Fonseca dismounted from his mule and tied it to the stake beside the store. Fadul hurried out from the back of the house to greet and serve his friend, ready for a long lively talk about the bad things that had befallen him.

Contrary to what was expected, the captain didn't bring that unhappy matter up. He savored the *cachaça* in small sips, spoke about this and that. He brought news of Colonel Boaventura, still strong and healthy, thanks be to God, but a little sad because Dr. Venturinha went off to Rio de Janeiro after his graduation party and didn't seem to be in any hurry to come back. He mentioned the plots that he, Natário, had begun to plant in Boa Vista; he'd see how they were going to prosper. Surprised and disappointed at such indifference, Fadul had a hard time not letting his disappointment show.

After rolling his cigarette, Natário accepted the light offered by Fadul, turned down another shot of *cachaça*, and got ready to go on his way. Moving away from the bar, he stretched, put his hand into the pocket of his khaki jacket, and took out the jackknife that the Turk had forgotten when he'd gone to Taquaras.

"Doesn't this belong to you, friend Fadul?"

He put the knife on the counter. Fadul Abdala felt a tightening in his chest.

"Yes, it's mine, Captain. If you don't mind my asking, how did it get into your hands?"

"How else, old friend?"

He went around the house, came back with the mule, put his foot in the stirrup, read the anxious question in Fadul's eyes, mounted, and replied, "I heard what happened. I found them right after. Three bad articles, friend Fadul."

The Turk's eyes lighted up, a smile grew on his mouth, and at the same time he felt an urge to cry; he wanted to confirm things.

"The three of them, Captain?"

"The three of them, all in the same hole in the ground. I'll see you later, old friend."

10

THE EASY LAUGH, THE noisy chuckle, the raillery, the singing, the pleasure of telling stories or arguing, and the appetite—the joie de vivre—had returned. Once again Fadul Abdala's hollering was heard in Tocaia Grande in mockery or gabbing and when finally, in exchange for a few pennies, Pedro Gypsy picked up his accordion, he called the ladies over, and the shindig started up, the one who put on the best show in the group was the owner of the emporium. He'd become his old self again, his heart free of the thirst for revenge.

He wasn't free of worry, however. He was still obliged to travel periodically to replenish his supplies, pay creditors, find out what was new in business, and dedicate his time to you-know-what, leaving the store locked up, in full view of people passing through, all kinds, at the disposal of burglars, thieves, and gangs of bandits.

It was quite true that the dark fate of the three hoodlums had traveled fast, with added inventions and details to curl one's hair. At least five different versions were going around, but all of them equally gruesome when it came to the death of the thugs, and gossips swore that Captain Natário da Fonseca was the Turk's partner, nothing less. When asked about it, Mr. Fadu didn't deny it; that sacrosanct rumor was a better defense of his business than any firearm.

Even so, proportionate to a decrease in the stock of merchandise were the obvious signs of worry on Fadul's face and in his actions. Oh, if he could only find a capable person, ready and worthy of confidence, to whom he could entrust the counter, the cash box, and the revolver—oh, he would go away with much more ease and satisfaction. The customers would be served without interruption, sales wouldn't undergo a paralysis, and the presence of a fearless person running the store and sleeping in the house might be enough to stop another attack. Unfortunately, in the wilds of Tocaia Grande he didn't see any citizen who embodied so many and such outstanding qualities.

For the hilarity of some, to the surprise of others, the one who undid the knot and solved the problem, who faced up to the responsibility and took on the heavy burden was— just imagine!—old Jacinta Coroca. She'd come back from Taquaras with Zé Raimundo's troop astride the pack frame on Full Moon, jingle bells ringing, in time to learn about the depredation and verify its damage. She shook her head in silence, but didn't pester Fadul with questions and suggestions.

On a certain night, when she felt the Turk's affliction to be so great that it silenced him during the course of his usually noisy and festive fornication, Coroca offered herself while she cleaned him delicately and carefully.

"If you want, Mr. Fadu, go take your trip in peace. I'll take care of the business. Leave it in my hands, I'll take your place. You can go off without worry."

Standing up, enormous and naked, water dripping from his huge member, the Turk looked at Jacinta with stupefaction as she held a piece of soap, bending over the tin basin bought on credit from Fadul himself. He took time measuring and weighing her, as if he had never seen her before.

"Are you proposing that I go off and leave the store open with you taking care of everything—selling, collecting, making change?"

Putting the cake of soap down by the basin, Coroca took a clean cloth, carefully wiped the sizable balls and remarkable tool.

"All you've got to do is write down the prices for me; I

know a thing or two. I'll sleep behind the counter till you get back."

She thrust out her bust: in the light of the lamp the curved and fragile body grew taller, the eyes sparkled.

"You?" Fadul was staring at her, startled, his mouth open.

A joke in poor taste from the Lord God of the Maronites, who was leaving him to his unpleasant fate once more. Roused up, furious with rage, he lifted his thoughts to heaven: *At this critical moment when, in desperation, I'm looking for the help of a strong, competent, serious man, is this the helper you offer me, Lord? This skinny old whore?*

Then a light went on in Fadul Abdala's mind and he understood that bravery, wisdom, and decency are not just the privilege of males, the rich, and the strong; they're the endowment of any mortal, even a skinny old whore. Wasn't Coroca good when it came to bed and to advice?

"You?" he repeated in a different tone.

"Me, yes sir. Maria Jacinta da Imaculada Conceição, who you people call Coroca. I know how to read, sign my name, add and subtract. I took care of a store once in Rio do Braço. Fear I only felt once in my life when I was in love with a man, the one who taught me to read."

She laid the cloth beside the soap and the basin. Smiling, she finished.

"And I never learned how to steal. I don't know why."

THE
SETTLEMENT

Settled down in Tocaia Grande, Black Castor Relinquishes Solitude

1

THE BLOODY BODY OF the wild boar on his naked back, the full knapsack hanging from his shoulder, a cloth tied around his waist, Oxóssi came out of the woods and headed for the river. In the sunlight, his proud bearing and his favorite prey were enough for Epifânia to recognize the enchanted one, god of forests and fierce animals. In the evening she'd spied Xangô in the distance at his forge, inventing fire. Xangô or Oxóssi, black Tição Abduim came crossing the plain armed with a hunting knife and a shotgun.

At the Ladies' Bidet, a broad basin formed by the current, Epifânia was taking a bath, wrapped in water and breeze, resting from a night of toil; on a rock lay the yellow robe she had just washed and a chunk of laundry soap. In the city of Bahia, where she'd been born in the house of iiá Quequé of the Seven Doors, she'd shaved her head on orders from Oxum, the vain one. Oxum, wife of Oxóssi and Xangô, the mother of calm waters: Epifânia shuddered, felt a chill deep inside.

The hunter dropped his burden on the ground farther on, where the river grew wider: blood oozed out of the mortal wound in the peccary's throat, turning the clay red. He untied the cloth from around his waist and laid the knife and the shotgun beside the sack. He had made the long wide blade himself and had tempered the edge. He had crafted the raw leather knapsack to carry small game. Putting out his arms, he dove into the river to clean off the blood covering his back. Epifânia raised her body from the water in order to see better.

When he came to the surface, Tição finally caught sight of her sitting in the swirling current: the figure of an *iiabá*, most certainly Oxum in person, mistress of rivers, visiting that distant province of her realm. Before the vision could disappear in a shimmer of light, he paid homage to it by touching his forehead with the tips of his fingers and repeating the salutation: *ora-yê-yêwo*. But as the spell persisted, he focused his eyes, waved an arm, and, in order to start a conversation, asked if he could borrow the piece of soap. She stood up, showing off her pointed purple nipples, her mature breasts, her slim waist, her full hips. Her black skin was so dark it shone blue. Black Epifânia, at the peak of her strength: a danger turned loose on the cacao trails, roaming from place to place, settling wherever she found excitement.

She brought the soap in her hand, teetering on the smooth and slippery stones. Her ebony body glowed; flashes of blue on the smooth color of pitch. After handing him the soap, she squatted down and stayed there, watching him wash himself: the waters were being born from Epifânia's womb. Epifânia of Oxum, wife of Oxóssi and Xangô.

When he gave back what was left of the piece of soap, the black man took her by the waist and measured the depths of her eyes.

"Tição, I've heard of you," Epifânia whispered, letting herself be led without any resistance, submissive.

They dove hand in hand into the waters. Then he led her upriver, holding her tight against his chest, swimming slowly in celebration of the meeting. Epifânia no longer felt the exhaustion of a busy night with customers. When they saw the body of the boar on the bank, she asked, so he would hear once more and notice the hoarse languor of her nighttime voice, "Were you the one who caught it, Father?"

With a nod of his head he said yes and, smiling, showed contentment: big game coming at just the right time, just the way it should. A gift from Oxóssi or Xangô, maybe even an offering from Oxalá. In some storage space in his shop he'd set up the *peji*, the sanctuary, and had placed the saints there: the bow and arrow, the two-headed hammer, the *paxorô*. He explained the reason for his celebration.

"Tomorrow's Sunday."

"So what? In this place, what difference is there between Sunday and other days?"

A newcomer, Epifânia wasn't aware of their habits and customs. There weren't many rites, but each one had taken an effort, demanded ability, and patience above all: Castor Abduim da Assunção, when he took on a task, wouldn't give up or turn back.

"I'll tell you later."

He laid the weary body of the mother of calm waters down on the bed of stone, stared at her face, and touched her stomach marked by long stripes: he didn't see or feel them. He only saw the half-open, gasping mouth, the languid eyes half-closing; he only felt her woolly pubic hair, kinky but soft to the touch. The current covered and uncovered the enchanted ones; the river carried off the chunk of soap.

2

INITIALLY, IN ORDER TO know the date of the month and the day of the week, one had to consult the only calendar in Tocaia Grande, hanging beside the door of the dry cacao storehouse. At first glance, a print that was a delight to see: a European winter landscape, mountains white with snow and a big hairy dog with a small cask hanging from his neck, a thing to be admired. Pasted underneath the print hung a small thick pad made of printed pages that told the day and date—the calendar, properly speaking—a New Year's present from Colonel Robustiano de Araújo to old Gerino, a loyal fellow.

The proud owner of such a precious item, Gerino would show off the painting to whores and drovers, repeating information he had heard from the colonel: "In foreign parts it's cold enough to bust your gut and that barrel is chockfull of *cachaça* to help anybody who might be in need of it." You couldn't want a prettier or more educational calendar, even if it was unfaithful and uncertain, because old Gerino would let days and days go by without pulling a leaf

off the pad, and when he remembered to do it, following the
colonel's recommendation, he would take them off haphaz-
ardly: one, two, never more than three, economizing on
those letters and numbers that were incomprehensible to
nearly all residents and strangers. Life went on permanently
behind time, and nobody could guarantee exactly whether it
was the end of March or the beginning of April, or if it was
Wednesday or Saturday. What about Sunday, the holy day?
In those times Sunday didn't exist in Tocaia Grande.

Without knowing whether the rains would be ahead of
time or behind, it was becoming difficult to estimate the
size of the final harvests and to foresee the amount of cacao
that would be produced on farms and plantations along the
Rio das Cobras. Confusion and disorder: some didn't care
very much, but others were restless and upset. Turk Fadul
had money to collect from customers whom he'd trusted or
to whom he'd made loans on time, he had payments to hand
over to his suppliers, both precise dates, jotted down in
Arabic in a notebook. Merência considered Sunday a day of
compulsory rest in accordance with the orders and demands
of God's law—the God of the proud potter, since Fadul's
God, less orthodox, obviously allowed business on Sunday
with a proper increase in prices and profits. Bernarda ago-
nized, trying to guess the happy days of her godfather's
visits.

Her godfather's visits, the foundation of her life. Previously, a quick stopover—oh, too quick!—coming and going
between Atalaia and Boa Vista; lately he'd come to spend
the whole night in Bernarda's company: oh, too short a
night! Due to Gerino's absurd calendar, even Captain Natário
da Fonseca saw himself obliged to alter his habits and his
timetable.

3

WHAT BRINGS ON LAUGHTER can also bring on tears, and
vice versa, the whores affirmed with good knowledge of the
reasons. Bernarda would prove the accuracy of the saying
many times over in the small and infinite course of a night.

It was only after that unbelievable night of suffering, when she felt she had lost him forever, that her godfather decided to modify his schedule and enlarge the tiny measure of their bliss. Bernarda had held her weeping in the depths of her throat, she had practice in locking up tears and sobbing in her chest cavity; but how wonderfully she finally laughed when she guessed the reason and saw the consequences.

On his monthly trip to Boa Vista, Captain Natário da Fonseca used to appear in the middle of the morning; on his way back to Atalaia he would get off his mule in the middle of the afternoon. A brief and divided occasion: everybody wanted to see him, exchange a few words, find out what was new; he spent a long time in conversation with Fadul.

In the morning or in the afternoon, while Bernarda and the captain were having their fill and their refill on the army cot, Coroca made some coffee with brown sugar to serve nice and hot during the minutes of conversation that preceded his departure. On arriving from Atalaia, Natário brought news of his family, Zilda and the children. "Your godmother sends her blessing and that piece of cloth for you to make a skirt with." On his return from Boa Vista, there was nothing to report except the progress of his newly planted plots. He went on enthusiastically about the growth of the seedings, optimistic projections: happy, Bernarda clapped her hands. If, on the contrary, he speculated, the duration of the rains ruined his predictions, drowning the sprouts. . . . Bernarda conjured away such evil prospects, announced sunshine. She didn't forget to have him ask for her god-mother's blessing at the time of parting. A painful, hated moment: she would have to drag through an endless month to feel him against her breast again, a few paltry seconds against an endless longing. When would he spend a whole night with her, from the shadows of dusk to the brightness of dawn? *When, Godfather?*

Well, if it didn't happen that on one of those distant afternoons of times gone by, while savoring Coroca's coffee, her godfather had unexpectedly announced that two weeks from then, on his way back from the wedding festivities of a daughter of Lourenço Batista, the stationmaster at Taquaras, he'd spend the night in Tocaia Grande. A whole night with her? Oh, God be praised! What a wonderful piece of news, one she'd been waiting for. It was hard to believe it was true. All aglow, beside herself, she asked her godfather to repeat the exact day. There was no way to make a mistake: Sunday after next, the following one, less than two weeks. The whole night.

There was no way to go wrong, Coroca confirmed after Natário spurred his mule and went onto the road. The pages printed in black on the little pad on the calendar told the days of the week, from Monday to Saturday, but Sunday stood out in red, setting apart the holy day, the festival. It was fortunate that Gerino's calendar existed, because in Tocaia Grande the days were all the same; there was a festival only when Pedro Gypsy put together a hoedown when there happened to be a lot of drovers passing through.

Bernarda's indifference toward the calendar hanging on the wall of the shed changed into extreme interest: she passed by daily, early in the morning, to check on the slow passage of time. She saw the first red page on the small pad of the calendar, she kept waiting for the second one, in such an impatient and afflicted way that one of the guards commented, "The kid's happy as a lark. She can't stand still."

"Bernarda's not right in the head," Gerino asserted, remembering her, wrathful and insulting, on the night of the bandits.

How could she have guessed that the gaudy calendar was three days behind? Contracted for the whole night by a hired hand—money sweated out at the end of a machete or a hoe, saved penny by penny with the intention of taking it easy, at his leisure, with the oft-mentioned Bernarda—she was doing her business in bed, underneath the guy, her godfather in her head, when she heard a slight sound at the front of the house. She gave it her attention: someone was trying to open the latch on the outside by sticking a knife through the doorjamb. Bernarda got scared, moved: the man moaned with pleasure as he felt the unexpected response, speeded up the rhythm of his entry: *What a woman!* They'd been telling the truth.

Bernarda knew immediately and with absolute certainty: it was her godfather, he'd moved up the date of his trip. She tried to get up but didn't have time. By the dim flame of the lamp she saw the shadow fall over the army cot and the shape fill the door to the bedroom, giving an order without raising his voice—the authority was enough.

"Get out of here and make it snappy, fellow."

In the darkness the hired hand didn't recognize the intruder. A fat mulatto, used to rows in whorehouses, he imagined he was up against one of those interfering drunks with lots of swagger but not much substance. Still on top of Bernarda, he said rudely, "Get out? Why? Are you crazy?"

"Because I'm telling you to."

"And who are you to give me orders?" He was getting up, ready to teach the insolent party a lesson.

"I'm Captain Natário da Fonseca." He drew back, leaving the door free; the steel of the gun gleamed in the flickering of the lamp.

"For the love of God, Captain, don't shoot!"

He snatched his pants and shirt, shot out the door, disappeared in the woods, and stopped running only when he reached the river. He'd been lucky: he'd found out it was the captain before he committed the lunacy of raising a hand against him, signing his own death warrant. With that scare, no matter how good a female she was—and boy, was she!—he'd never go to bed with her again, not even for free, God help him.

Bernarda stood up, confused, speechless; she didn't even ask for his blessing. Natário put away his weapon, his face impenetrable, his voice severe, strict.

"Didn't I tell you I was coming here to sleep tonight? Did you forget?"

"Godfather, you said you were coming on Sunday. Just today I took a look at Gerino's calendar."

Coroca's voice came from the other bedroom.

"It's true, I was with her, it said Thursday." Having said that, she went about her business, calming down her own frightened client who proposed paying her and leaving. "Take it easy, boy, don't be afraid."

The captain sat down on the bed, took off his belt, began to take off his boots.

"Go wash up."

Bernarda sped off in the direction of the river, but she ran back for soap when she was halfway there: water wasn't enough to cleanse her skin of the sweat and memory of the blockhead.

When she got back, wet and immaculate, ready and waiting for the nuptials with her godfather, she found him apparently fast asleep. He hadn't even taken off his pants. She sat down on the edge of the bed, touched his face gently with her damp fingers. Without opening his eyes, her godfather turned his back to her. Was he really asleep or was he rejecting her out of spite? In the smoke of the lamp he'd found her underneath the other one, had been offended, and no longer wanted her as his mistress.

He'd never shown signs of jealousy, hadn't reserved her exclusively for himself as a kept woman. Passing through Tocaia Grande, he would take her in his arms with ecstasy and softness, as if there were love, that at least. They didn't exchange words of affection, oaths, or promises, and they didn't have to, because they were together in bed. Rider and mount, they rode; dog and bitch, famished wolves, thus devoured each other. During breaks they would talk about farm and family, worries and daydreams, the house he was going to build for himself and Zilda on top of the hill. *When, Godfather?* There was no money involved, there was no payment, you don't pay for affection. If Bernarda might have wanted something more, at no moment did she let it be understood, hinted, or asked, satisfied with whatever he conceded and consented to.

Sitting uncomfortably on the wooden frame of the army cot, she watched over Natário's sleep during the cursed night. She didn't close her eyes. Abandoned. She had dreamed so much about having him to herself for a whole night! Without her asking or begging, her godfather had decided to come on his own. But now he was aloof, indifferent, lost forever. He'd turned his back on her; everything was over. Worse than his absence was his disdain.

When she heard him snore, really asleep at last, she got up softly, snuggled up to her godfather's chest the way she used to before: he in his bachelor's hammock, she a little girl. She remembered the good and the bad: her father's tongue in her mouth, her mother dying helplessly, hunger, running away and meeting again, the first time in the cot in the hut and the pair of earrings, gilded jewelry, a present that she'd gotten from him and that she wore proudly when they were together. In that way, step by step, she began to realize the apparent and the real and understood that anger and disdain were nothing more than a ruse and a coverup to hide jealousy and a feeling of debasement, the pain of cuckoldry. His anger was a sign that he loved her, that he didn't consider her a vagabond whore, no better than so many others he'd shacked up with in the desolation of the cacao world. Not a passing love that makes you laugh but doesn't make you suffer.

Before dawn, having pushed Bernarda's body off his chest slowly, so as not to awaken her, Natário got up, went out to piss and bathe. Excited, she leapt out of bed, put on the earrings, ran after her godfather. They met on the bank of the river, she stared into his eyes.

"It wasn't my fault."

"So you told me. Even so, I was mad."

Bernarda helped him take off his pants. The shadows and the stars dissolved; the night had come to an end. There had been no offense or negligence, injustice or threat. Only the sorrows of love, of jealousy, lingered. *Even so, I was jealous*, Natário thought; it was enough to make one cry and laugh.

When he took his leave, Natário warned, "'I'll be back in seven days to spend the night. Count them on your fingers so you won't make a mistake again."

If he was trying to give his voice a tone of scolding and warning, he didn't succeed: with his hand he stroked his goddaughter's hair, and on the godfather's motionless face, a scowl carved in wood, Bernarda spotted the faint shadow of a smile.

4

AFTER THE FRIGHT THAT had cut through her when Janjão Fanchão threatened to go after her tail, black Dalila had disappeared in search of quieter parts where she could wiggle the sought-after butt in peace. She tramped over leagues of ground: when she came to, she found herself in those dangerous precincts once more. She noted the growth of the place: more people, new huts, fewer dangers, and the lighted forge.

Informed about the evil deeds and intentions of the deceased and of Janjão's plans, Fadul informed Dalila with obvious satisfaction about the death of the pederast. The whore already knew about it: the event had caused a stir; the talk had spread out, reached her in Itapira, where she'd been stopping between harvests. That far away? What do you know!

"They say they castrated him, good job. God be praised."

Not having an interest in denying the cruel details of the contradictory versions of the fate of the bandits, quite the contrary, Fadul changed the topic of conversation.

"Is it true that you're a virgin in the rear?"

Dalila pretended not to hear, answered right back, categorically and enigmatically, "By force, Mr. Fadu, not in the front, much less behind."

She didn't say anything more; she didn't want to be a hypocrite like so many others. Sentimental, when she was sweet-talked she didn't know how to refuse; when in need, she would yield to a good offer: the blame was God's for having made her so well-endowed. She cut the questioning short. "By force, better dead, Mr. Fadu."

The Turk and the girl were having fun with those tricks and countertricks, when Castor appeared with the invitation: would Fadul like to be his partner in an enterprise of unpredictable success? He was thinking of making sun-dried meat, he'd never done it before, but it wouldn't hurt to try. On Colonel Robustiano's plantation he'd seen the backlanders salt beef on butchering days and lay it out in the sun; it turned out to be even more delicious food than regular dried meat. He'd provide the game, the Turk would supply the salt, what did he think?

Dalila shook her tail, darkening the sun, and declared that she knew all about it and had had experience. Deep in the backlands, where she'd been born, surrounded by cattle, the poor people lived off that, salting fresh meat and turning it into sun-dried meat for Colonel Raul, the same one, it might be said in passing, who'd popped her cherry. They also salted pigs and smaller animals and different kinds of birds. They'd even deep-fried songbirds to eat and sell at the market. With songbirds you eat the whole thing, even the bones.

Starting with those three partners—Tição's hunting, Mr. Fadul's salt, Dalila's expertise—the company quickly grew: if you would call it a company. Lupiscínio and Bastião da Rosa set up a line to hang the salted meat on. Other women came to help, and there was a lot of activity on the bank of the river during the pickling. They exchanged comments, wisecracks, laughter. It was all great fun: a lot of work, not

much meat, but enough so that each one had his portion.
Fadul found out that there wasn't any left over to sell in his
store, but even so he contributed his share: not everything is
money in this world.

The strong sun contributed to the success of the experi-
ment; it didn't rain during those busy days. When Dalila,
from the height of her clogs and her competence, announced
that the sun meat was ready for the fire and to be eaten,
they improvised a real banquet. In a clay pot Bernarda and
Coroca cooked part of the meat in a black-bean stew, Zuleica
toasted flour in the frying grease, Cotinha made jackfruit
sweets—and nobody thought Cotinha was good for anything! They put together a few pennies to buy a bottle of
cachaça from Fadul, and the seller himself made his contri-
bution by lowering the price. It ended up in a songfest.

That was how the idea of Sunday lunch was born. Lively
as only he could be, Tição was author of the proposal that
earned the warm applause of his tablemates: a lunch that
would bring them together once a week to fill their bellies,
talk, and laugh. At first only a few appeared, then eventually the rest joined in.

At Epifânia's Request Black Castor Abduim Organizes the Feast of St. John

1

EARLY ONE MORNING BLACK Castor Abduim was shoeing the donkey Piaçava when, as he glanced inside the shop, he noticed a dog stretched out by the forge. He imagined that the pooch belonged to Lázaro, a veteran of the Tocaia Grande trails, or to Cosme, his son and helper, a snotty brat. It must have been a recent acquisition, because he couldn't remember having seen the animal following the mule train. Mud-covered, he was taking advantage of the heat of the fire before going on his way again. Tição didn't envy him his fate: rotten weather.

They'd appeared at the blacksmith's door early, eager to reach Taquaras before the train left. While Cosme was tightening the knots on the canvas thrown over the load to protect it from the fine and persistent rain, Lázaro stopped to admire Castor's precision and skill. Heads and shoulders covered with burlap sacks converted into capes and hoods, barefoot, pants hiked up, father and son were skating in the mud, cursing the dark, overcast, sad sky.

It wasn't a matter of a sudden cloudburst, a short, quick downpour, one of those summer showers that left no trace, not even blotting out the sun's eye. Winter had begun, bringing incessant rain, nasty days, cold nights, a gray horizon, and mud and moroseness.

Well shod, Piaçava brayed, kicked up his heels, and joined the troop. Lázaro joked as he said, "He's happy with his new boots, the son of a bitch."

Cosme drove the donkeys along, Castor wished them a good trip, went back into the shop—later on, when the rain let up, he'd go hunting. Beside the forge, the dog raised his head, wagged his tail. The black man, cupping his hands to his mouth, shouted, "Lázaro, you forgot the dog!"

Lázaro halted.

"What dog?"

"The one that came with you people."

"With us? No dog came with us; you're seeing things."

If he hadn't come with Lázaro, who had he come with then? His owner will probably show up, the blacksmith thought. With the intention of figuring things out, he sat down in Xangô's chair: that's what he called a big square stone he'd brought in from the woods and placed beside the *peji*, the sanctuary. He held out his hand, the mutt tried to get up, could barely stand on his feet. He came over with great difficulty, disjointed, wagging his tail. Observing him more closely, sagging and skinny, cold and dirty, bones showing through the skin, Tição decided that it must have been a stray dog, a wanderer in search of leftover food and of a bitch in heat. He'd go off the same way he'd come.

2

EPIFÂNIA CAME INSIDE ATTRACTED by the barking, curious to see what was going on. A calico cloth around her waist, her breasts showing, she seemed immune to the early morning cold. Startled at seeing the dog, dirty and begging, she asked compassionately, "Where did that poor soul come from?"

"From nowhere. He just appeared."

How he had come, from where, Castor couldn't say: all of a sudden he was there, warming himself by the fire. All of a sudden? Epifânia wasn't in the habit of being surprised: she always had an answer for things that were most difficult to explain. Nothing seemed confused, ambiguous, or obscure to her: for her, everything was clear, easy to understand. Everything except black Castor Abduim.

"A trick of our Friend." She was referring to Exu, the

joker, always ready to play tricks. "Pay attention to what I'm telling you, take the string and untie the knot. Don't you set food out for Him every Monday? Who gets the first shot of liquor when you drink? Isn't it for Him? Answer me this: who ever heard of a hunter hunting without a dog? Exu always takes care of his friends."

She went to get some water in a gourd. The dog drank avidly. As for the meat and beans, leftovers from last night, he eyed them with suspicion: he took his time, smelling them, undecided, doubting that so much good luck could have come his way. His fearful eyes went from Castor to Epifânia, begging for permission and reassurance. On other occasions it had turned out badly for him.

Filled with pity, Epifânia pushed the clay dish with the food under the poor thing's nose: only then did he swallow the lump of meat and beans in one mouthful—before it was too late. Then he put out his tongue, licked the black woman's hand as she snuggled up beside Tição.

"Poor thing, he's starving to death."

"They hurt the critter; his hips are out of joint. He was kicked in the rear."

"With all that mud you can't tell what color he is, whether he's light or dark, but take a look: he's got a black spot on his chest, another one on his head. You'll see, he could even be pretty."

"Pretty?"

Castor laughed, incredulous: another person with a heart of gold like Epifânia hadn't been born yet: proud and deceitful, certainly, but she was good-hearted and helpful like nobody else. He snapped his fingers, calling that pour soul— that's what she'd called him out of pity—who'd taken refuge there.

"Come here, poor soul."

With an effort the dog managed to stand up, then stumbled over to them. He gave a loud bark, his tail up, and he seemed like a different creature: he'd been warmed by the fire, received water, food, and affection. From that moment on, he answered to the name of Poor Soul.

3

EPIFÂNIA WENT TO THE door of the smithy, exposing herself to the endless drizzle: the sky was completely hidden. She complained, "I've got a weight on my chest, an aching. It even feels like somebody put the evil eye on me. Who knows?"

Tição got up. He wanted to clarify something on his mind that had been bothering him for days.

"You're in a strange mood. You're—"

In the sunless morning not a ray of light, not a touch of warmth. Epifânia, who knew only too well, interrupted him.

"I've never seen such a godforsaken place; they don't even celebrate St. John's Day here. Damn it to hell!"

But he went on and finished.

"You're itching to leave, isn't that it?"

Epifânia walked over to Castor, swaying up and down, her neck and breasts damp from the rain. When she got in front of the black man, she put her hands on his broad shoulders and confronted him, a voice that complained and challenged.

"You wouldn't give the least little damn."

Wise, she brought her body up close. She knew her powers and the weaknesses of her man. He thought for a moment before answering.

"What you want to know is whether I'm going to plead, beg you to stay, and have you laugh at me. You're free to do whatever you want to. We didn't sign any contract and there's nothing good that lasts forever; you said that yourself and you've repeated it many times. Remember? But don't say I don't care."

"You don't care a bit. You don't love me or any other woman. But someday you'll really fall in love and then you'll know what pain's like. You'll have a rough time; you'll see how bad it can be." She put her arms around him.

"How can you say something like that? That I don't love you? Can't you see it, can't you feel, woman?"

She felt the stiff sledgehammer against her thighs.

"Love for you is going to bed. Me, Zuleica, Bernarda, Dalila, you even love Coroca, who is it you don't love? A pack of idiots, all of them crazy about Tição, starting with me. They say it's the same in Taquaras. You know what you are?"

The black man's body next to her, the tension growing, who had the power and who was weak? She closed her eyes. What good was it being sharp, tricky? Infatuated, overcome, she always ended up putting down her weapons at the height of the challenge.

"There are times when I think you're just a great big kid, with no brains or feeling. You don't mean to be bad, but you're the devil himself."

"You still haven't answered: are you thinking about getting away from here?"

Without releasing her embrace, Epifânia moved her body from his.

"You really want to know? Never in my life have I spent a St. John's Day without jumping over a bonfire, roasting corn, eating *canjica* sweets, dancing a square dance." She looked outside. The rain held the leaden sky in its grip. "June is coming up. For me there's no feast day that can match St. John's."

Having gotten things off her chest, she felt light-headed and sad; she leaned her whole body against him again. Even wet from the drizzle she warmed him more than the forge, her warmth burned—at that point she no longer cared who gave in first.

"I never intended roosting here this long. You hobbled me. But you never asked me to stay."

"Did I have to?"

"You've got an answer for everything. You're the devil, you are. I'd already set it up with Cotinha, but for you I'm capable of forgetting about St. John."

"You like St. John's Day that much?"

"Too much!"

She wanted the bonfires, the sweet potatoes, the green corn, the trays of *canjica*, the fritters, the honey cakes, the genipap liquor, the steps of the square dance—she deserved it. All the other women deserved it too. Tição ran his hand over Epifânia's proud behind. Black Epifânia, bossy, tricky, men eating out of her hand, crawling on their knees, whipped and spurred: melting in the arms of Tição, she had no force, no power, who would have thought it?

"If you want to, you can go do your St. John's jumping

in some bigger place, with more people. But you should
know, in any case, that this St. John's Day there's going to
be a feast in Tocaia Grande. On the eve and during the day."

"Who's going to set it up? You?"

"I like it, too, and I miss it."

"You're going to do that for your black girl?"

"For you and for everybody."

"You're a tricky one. I'll believe it when I see it."

"Well, you will."

Epifânia cooed, whined in submission, collapsed with a
moan.

"I'm shaking all over: you reeled me in, you put the evil
eye on me. You're Exu Elegbá, you're the Evil One."

"My name is Castor Abduim, the girls call me Tição, a
good boy, or don't you think so?"

The mutt followed them with his eyes when the two,
chum and chummy, laughing at each other, went back to
the room behind the shop. When he heard the hammock
creaking, Poor Soul put his snout between his front paws
and went to sleep.

4

BREAKING UP WITH LAUGHTER at the door of the shop,
Epifânia was holding the big heavy rock with both hands.

"I found it in the river. I thought it was pretty, so I
brought it for you."

A full-grown and experienced woman, body and heart
well-hardened, she had the ways of a child, full of laughter
and fantasy. A pebble, a fruit, a flower, a frightened green
lizard: a present every day in addition to herself, at any
hour, the main gift. Black, round, and smooth, the rock
rolled on the ground: the roguish laughter grew on the
whore's fleshy lips.

"Doesn't it look like a man's ball?"

It did indeed: a great big ball, enormous and black,
Oxalá's, it couldn't belong to anyone else. Tição laughed at
her shamelessness. Arrogance made her aggressive and insolent; putting aside those quirks, however, she was loving
and captivating.

"Oxalá's ball! I'll put it in the *peji*."

The *orixás* lived in the *peji*, powerful but needy gods. So that she could give it to Oxum as an offering, Castor hammered out on the forge a tin *abebê* with a small mirror set in the center; the tin plate gleamed as if made of gold, it glowed: opulent. Placed in the *peji* for the use and pleasure of the mother of calm waters, Epifânia would take it out of there whenever she wanted to fan herself and look at her face in it. Which of the two was the more vain, Oxum or her daughter?

Epifânia had a yellow necklace of African beads, her greatest treasure, and a set of magic seashells with which she could divine the future. Some of the whores were afraid of her and kept their distance; frightened, they called her a witch.

She'd ended up in Tocaia Grande between harvests, traveling on safe and easy roads, the summer sun in command of life and all creatures. The poverty of the settlement dissolved before the incomparable landscape, the beauty of the place. With no cacao to be transported, the activity of droves and drovers dwindled in the off season. With an itch up their behinds, the whores didn't warm their nests and fled for larger places with a stable clientele. In competition with fewer and less desirable colleagues, Epifânia reigned with almost absolute sway in the Baixa dos Sapos and in Castor Abduim's shop. During the hot season there was no mattress more sought out, no *puta* more in fashion—with the exception of Bernarda. But Bernarda didn't count: a young heifer, she held forth in an army cot, she lived in a wooden shack, and she behaved arrogantly—she still lacked a professional polish.

Epifânia found Fadul quite good-looking, went to bed with him the night she arrived, repeated it several times, appreciated the magnitude and skill of his tool, but didn't let herself be overcome, because she immediately fell for Tição, seeing him from a distance raining sparks at the forge, juggling the flames. A person falls in love right off, otherwise it isn't real love, it's a trick and a betrayal that ends up with cursing and crying, if not with a bullet and a blade. Epifânia considered a love affair a serious and complicated matter: good fortune and suffering, harmony and disagreement, fighting and reconciliation. Reconciliation doubles the appetite, and tempers it.

Molded by Oxum, who personified flirtation and vanity full of whims, she resembled more the daughter of Iansan, armed for battle to impose her sovereignty. Her whims Tição tolerated with a smile, finding them funny. However, as for ruling him—nobody ruled him.

On the same day of their meeting by the river, after they went to the hammock in the shop to continue their fooling around, Epifânia warmed Tição, ready to occupy the throne and lay down the law.

"Don't think you can walk all over me just because I like your ways. We haven't got any contract and nothing good lasts forever. I'm here with you in your hammock today, tomorrow I'll have my feet on the road looking for something better for myself."

"I don't like giving orders," Castor replied as he got on top of her, "or taking them."

Though pitch black, a nobody with no place to hang her hat, she insulted people as if she were a foreigner, white, pink, and rich; a whore by profession, she took on the airs of a properly married woman. She angered quickly and would gather up her skirts and arrogantly walk out.

"If you want a woman, get someone else, it won't be with me anymore."

When her anger was over, repentant, she would come back to his arms and make up for lost time. It happened on more than one occasion that she found him with somebody else: *You told me to get someone else . . .*

She would burn with rage, beside herself, threatening with sticks and stones, fatal *ebó* fetishes. Some whores sighed over Tição, a handsome black man, but they drew back, afraid to expose themselves to macumbas and mandingas. Nevertheless, there were those who took the risk: bold Dalila, for example. A trim body, nothing affected her, not snake venom, not smallpox, not a spell cast by an angry bitch. She declared herself the daughter of Obaluaiê, the Old One.

In spite of the airs and the anger, it was worth it. It was worth seeing Epifânia serenely crossing the clearing facing the sun: Castor glimpsed flashes of blue on the jet-black skin, just as once before he had perceived golden variations on the white skin of the baroness. That's who Epifânia looked like: Madame. They were exactly alike: twin sisters, identical.

At the dinner table in the big house, in the plunging

neckline of her Paris gown, the noblewoman displayed a
rare flower, picked from the garden. No sooner had the
baron gone out to smoke the cigar that annoyed her so
much than the hussy would call her servant with her finger
and tell him.

"*C'est à toi, mon amour.*" She would pull her neckline
open, revealing her breasts. "*Viens chercher,*" she whispered,
her voice falling off.

Epifânia would arrive with a wildflower thrust into the
opening of her Bahian robe, leaning over for him to take it
out and glimpse her taut nipples.

"I thought it was pretty; I brought it for you." Her voice
thrilled at its lowest range.

Identical in their boldness, vanity, flirting, whims, two
iiabás alike in their despotism. Both with the same drive: to
rule him, break his balls, put a saddle and bit on him, dig
spurs into his loins.

5

THE PASSING OF SUMMER was easygoing and pleasant.
Epifânia was by turns a merry girl, mischievous, laughing,
and a seasoned woman, fiery, clean; moreover, she was good
company in bed, at dances doing the *coco,* at Sunday lunches,
and simply to talk to. Wherever she went she was well
received, greeted with pleasure. With her around, washing
clothes in the river became an event; she knew stories, she
said witty things. Admired and feared, Epifânia took over
and imposed her ways.

But she was also feared for her witchcraft and her voo-
doo offerings. She cast her seashells, discovered what to do
to tie a man to some woman's apron strings or vice versa, to
put an end to the strongest sexual ties, to bring couples
together or break them up: infallible spells. That's what
people said and swore to. It wasn't boasting or exaggeration
and the proof was right there: what had happened to Cotinha,
Zé Luiz, and Merência. It was the subject of talk, a reason
for fear and pleasure. What else could have explained Zé
Luiz's madness?

When she arrived in Tocaia Grande, before she had her own shack—although built in the blink of an eye, in less than half a day's work by diverse volunteers, all of them happy to please the new arrival, whom Fadul furnished with a mattress, soap, needle and thread, and other notions on credit—Epifânia found a place to stay in Cotinha's hut, having become her friend. After a while, at the request of her short friend, she prepared a spell with special leaves and the heart of a ynambu bird felled by Tição and placed it on the path to the brickworks. No sooner said than done: stubby Zé Luiz began to chase after Cotinha and became involved with her at bedtime and mealtime, going on to spend with her what he had and what he didn't have, squandering bricks and tiles. They were about the same height, a pair of midgets.

The one who didn't take kindly to the success of the fetish was Merência, when she discovered her husband's profligacy. *Cachaça* and shamelessness are incurable male vices: a good wife can't prohibit them, but she should limit them, and that was what she did, furnishing her better half, on weekends, with not too many funds for such abuses: funds insufficient for an infatuated person who was behaving with the largesse of a colonel. When she caught him in flagrante, trying to pilfer from money obtained through extreme sacrifice, she applied the standard remedy to him, proven on previous occasions: she grabbed him by the scruff of the neck and beat him black and blue. The peaceable potter, cured of his passion, went back to his modest habits: more liberal drinking and screwing outside the house only on Sundays. And he considered himself satisfied.

Epifânia came and went from the river to the woods, from Cotinha's shack to Coroca and Bernarda's house, from the cacao warehouse to the Turk's store; more often than not she would show up at the smithy and remain there quietly, watching Castor work iron and tin, making sure no other woman had an eye on him, ready to offer her tail to someone who already had a commitment and a woman.

She wouldn't admit it, she even tried not to let it show, but she was devoured by jealousy when she suspected that he was seeing someone else: making it with Tição was all the local whoredom wanted, the bunch of tramps. Epifânia was on the verge of blowing up with Dalila, far and away the worst offender.

While summer lasted, luminous and light, she laughed
at everything and forgave everything. But winter came, dark,
cold, and sad. There was more activity, true: money was
pouring in. But even so it was hard to accept the mud and
desolation, even more the haughtiness of Castor Abduim,
shoer of donkeys, impenitent stud, a black faker and tricker.

When dwarfish Cotinha refused a new spell—"I can't
stand a man who is beaten by a woman!"—and decided to
go somewhere less backward to celebrate the June holidays,
those of St. Anthony, St. John, and St. Peter, three of her
favorites, Epifânia didn't hesitate.

"I'm going with you."

"Are you tired of Tição?"

She was going to say yes, but she thought better of it.

"He's the one who's tired," she reflected, looking at the
rain. "If he loves me, he's never said so."

As is known, she didn't go through with it, didn't travel.
Besides, Cotinha didn't pull up stakes either, she turned
back too. When she heard about the St. John's feast the
black man was preparing, quick as a flash she volunteered
to make the indispensable genipap liquor. After all, the fruit
was falling off the trees, rotting on the ground.

"Do you know how to make it?"

She'd learned how from the nuns in the convent kitchen
at São Cristóvão, the town in Sergipe where she'd been
born.

"You were a nun in a convent?" Castor was surprised.

"I wanted to be, but I never made it." A touch of longing tinted her singsong voice. "I was working as a maid in
exchange for meals and to serve God. Then Father Nuno, a
Portuguese monk who came every day to say mass, fondled
my breast behind the big bell." She remembered it all with
nostalgia. "A real man, God be blessed! I barely came up to
his belly button. He pulled up his cassock, lifted my skirt,
and that was that."

She sighed as she spoke about those happy times when
she was living the life of an abbess: every day she had
sacramental wine and a holy roll.

"But the sisters found out and sent me away."

6

IT'S TIME NOW TO talk about Zuleica, who, lingering in Tocaia Grande since the winter before, has received only a brief mention. According to her, the birds fell silent to listen to Castor Abduim da Assunção sing. She was a dark and pensive woman: in the cohort of busybodies hanging around Tição's smithy, Zuleica stood out as discreet and withdrawn. An almost furtive presence, with an open face and reserved manners: those who didn't know her occupation took her for a girl from a good family.

Others may have been prettier, more stylish, more showy, livelier in bed, but no one was more sought after or could be compared to her in the trade. She was delicate and timid, attentive. Nevertheless, Coroca would say that all that bashfulness was only pride, hard as stone.

"Zu knows what she wants. She's got her self-respect and she doesn't lie."

Actually, when she made up her mind about something, suddenly and without warning, no one could make her turn back. She would do so without leaving her corner, without changing her calm, dreamy posture. Anyone who thinks whores are all alike, a dirty bunch of tramps lacking in feeling or modesty, is mistaken. Jacinta summed it up.

"Each one has got her face and her disguise, her way of showing off her behind."

Before the arrival of Epifânia, bringing pride, truculence, and fits of anger in her baggage, there had been a long and peaceful relationship between Tição and Zu, never disturbed by tiffs, bad words, or disagreements. There were those who guaranteed that the love affair, placid and accepted, would end up in a permanent arrangement once the smithy was completed and the blacksmith living in a house of his own. But, vagabond and whoremaster, he didn't invite her; proud and introspective, she didn't insist, stayed as she'd always been, happy to deserve the loafer's preference. Life and love affair went on peacefully.

"I could have told you," Coroca reminded people, when, in the face of Epifânia's arrogance and excitement and Castor's interest in the newcomer, Zuleica silently withdrew. She left without fight or scandal. No reproaches or remarks were ever heard. She stopped going to the shop, cleaning his game and cooking it, eating with him. But she didn't become his enemy; she didn't turn good into bad at the first opportunity; she got along with Epifânia. She kept quiet—cautious, but not conforming; but according to Coroca: *You're wrong if you think so.*

If she stopped coming by the shop, she didn't give up her round of talk and song, drumming a lively *coco* dance, but her eyes were lost in the distance when the black man opened his chest and silenced the birds. At first Tição didn't pay much attention to Zuleica's aloofness. "All I have to do is snap my fingers and Zu will come running back."

At a matter of fact, the girl didn't refuse when, on the occasion of one of Epifânia's tantrums, the blacksmith came looking for her. But how surprised he was when he saw her, after the first round in the hammock, getting up and putting on her dress, ready to leave. Worse yet, she held out her hand to be paid. She'd come as a woman of the street; she wanted him to be aware of that, she was pointing out the difference: she wasn't staying to spend the night, to continue the lovemaking. She hadn't given herself for nothing, for love.

Taken by surprise, Castor lay there, confused, not knowing what to say. Embarrassed, he gave her some coins; she took them, but threw them down as she left the shop. She'd come peacefully and she left peacefully, her head held high.

He began to treat her with great courtesy, showing respect for her whenever possible, even though he didn't invite her to his hammock again. She kept herself aloof, and the general opinion held that the love affair was completely over, a thing of the past. It was difficult to believe Coroca when she quietly reaffirmed, "Zu is crazy about Tição; she can't get him out of her head."

The only one who said she was right—Epifânia—added a powerful argument: why hadn't the bitch made an arrangement yet to go to bed with someone else for nothing? Who'd ever seen a whore without a love affair, all the more necessary in that asshole of the earth where there was nothing else to do?

One Sunday, after the communal lunch that more and more people were coming to, all of them laughing and having fun together, Merência—a romantic at heart—asked Castor to favor the gathering with some *modinhas*: he knew so many! The black man announced that he would begin with a song that was one of Zuleica's favorites.

"One that you always asked me to sing, remember, Zu?"

"Which one? I know, 'Marie, You're Getting Married.'" She came out of her serious mood, clapped her hands.

Tição turned his voice loose, his eyes on Zuleica as if he didn't see anyone else around.

Maria, you're getting married
And I'm going to wish you well.
I'm going to give you a present, oh, oh
A lace petticoat, oh, oh
As cheap as they can sell . . .

It was enough for Epifânia, sitting next to the black man, to storm off in a furious pet. If the other girls caused her problems, what to say about this sly one? She spat on the ground and dug her heel into it.

7

PEDRO GYPSY'S ATTEMPT TO liven up St. Anthony's Night ended up with fighting, bullets, and blood. It must be borne in mind, however, that there had been no base intention, no vile money interest, in the tempting proposal made by the vagabond.

In fact, when he approached the settlement that rainy, chilly day, he didn't intend staying more than one night— asleep, if possible, on the mattress of some slut who would warm his carcass. His destination was Taquaras, or maybe Ferradas, Água Preta, Rio do Braço, or Itabuna; he wasn't sure himself. He had a craving for taking part in the June festivities, where he could have a grand good time, and for free, eating, drinking, and dancing *à la vonté*. But when he ran into the arrangements for St. John's Day in Tocaia Grande, he was carried away.

The preparations were already a party in and of themselves. For well over a week they had taken up all the spare time of the tiny population and it was hard to believe that so few people had accomplished so much. On their way back to the plantations, the drovers dropped off what they had picked up for Fadul's store: green corn, dried coconut, fireworks: flaming swords, firecrackers, as well as sparklers and other childish delights for the whores. Not to mention the balloon, because the balloon was a secret shared only by Tição and Coroca; no one else knew of its existence.

When he saw Bastião da Rosa, Lupiscínio, Zé Luiz, Guido, and Balbino busy transforming the old makeshift shelter set up in times gone by into a spacious straw-roofed shed—a rustic structure of sticks, stakes, and forked poles firmly set in the ground, a floor of tamped clay, smooth and solid—Pedro Gypsy gave up any thoughts of continuing his trip. And his appearance was timed just right, because Fadul had just received a message from Lulu Concertina saying he was sorry he couldn't accept the invitation to come play in Tocaia Grande for the St. John's feast: popular throughout the region, everybody wanted him.

The women didn't shrink from work: they helped build the shed, carried the wood the men had cut in the forest for the bonfires, gathered kindling, and improvised stoves on rocks where they cooked the *canjica* and other typical June goodies. With Epifânia's help, hard-working Cotinha took care of the genipaps, peeling them, taking out the bitter seeds, and squeezing them so the juice could be made into liquor later on. She worked at the job recalling the taste—fantastic!—of the sacramental wine and the virtues—oh, so many!—of Friar Nuno. A Portuguese and a lover, the monk would tell her in his funny way of talking, *Come here, my pretty novice.* She would obey, he would novitiate. Pedro Gypsy volunteered to test the brew when it was put on the fire: he would determine the exact time to remove the nectar. A man with well-honed taste buds, a matchless connoisseur of food and drink, good on the accordion, a wild card without rival in those parts.

They'd planned a monumental bonfire in front of the shed, in the clearing, that is, one for each night. But since there was a lot of firewood left over, they decided, as suggested by Merência, seconded by Tição, to give the rest of the logs to people who might want to build smaller fires in front of their places, where they could roast sweet potatoes and corn. Whoever wanted to could take home some *canjica*, a bottle of genipap to serve neighbors before they all got together for the beginning of the festivities, the jolly St. John festivities: to eat fritters, *canjica*, and honey cakes, drink liquor, leap over the coals with a partner, dance a quadrille.

Finding the command post vacant, Pedro Gypsy occupied it, and his proposals were concerned with enlarging the feast: pointing out a deficiency, correcting an injustice. Celebrating St. John's Day was a great idea. But why discriminate against the other June saints, since all three were equal in devotion and miracles? Why not begin by celebrating St. Anthony, the marriage saint, the patron of brides, and end by praising St. Peter, the patron of widows? The fact that there still wasn't any marriageable virgin or weeping widow in Tocaia Grande didn't mean anything: someday, by the grace of God, there would be more than enough of both. He, Pedro Gypsy, placed himself at their command with his accordion to stir up a little dancing on St. Anthony's Eve. They would light a small bonfire, taste a piece of *canjica*, have a swig of genipap liquor, dance a little *coco*, a polka, and a mazurka in a dress rehearsal for the big night, St. John's Eve. They would save the fireworks and the quadrille for then.

It wasn't hard to convince the people. In that lonely and abandoned end of the earth nothing aroused more enthusiasm than a dance, a wingding. It happened only on occasion, when Pedro Gypsy was around or when someone who played the concertina, guitar, or *cavaquinho* happened to spend the night in Tocaia Grande.

8

A WHORES' WRANGLE IS like that: a straw fire, lots of smoke and not much flame; it starts all of a sudden and ends that way, doesn't last long. It explodes unexpectedly, spreads, reaches its height, loses its drive, dwindles and stops. There's not even any smoke left over at the end.

The cat fighting started by Epifânia and Dalila at the beginning of the dance on St. Anthony's Eve didn't get to be sensational, but it did liven things up. As would be proven later on, it had some influence on the spirits of Misael, a good-looking mulatto who was well-off, as might be deduced from his snotty manners. In the company of two cowhands, an old man and a boy, he was coming back from Itabuna, where he'd left a fair-sized herd rounded up in the backlands of Conquista. They were wearing leather jackets, riding good horses, carrying weapons and money. They'd stopped in Tocaia Grande late in the afternoon. *A St. Anthony's feast? Some fun? Sounds good.*

A few couples were dancing to the sound of Pedro Gypsy's accordion, when Epifânia abruptly broke away from the arms of Master Guido and threatened to split the lip of Dalila, who was twirling with the aforesaid Misael. Breaking away from her partner, Dalila replied in kind.

"Come ahead, if you're woman enough."

Guido and Misael stood to one side to get a ringside view: who doesn't enjoy following—blow by blow, taunt for taunt, slap for slap—a row between women?

Epifânia attacked with spit. She aimed at Dalila's left eye and hit the target. They exchanged insults.

"Lousy nigger! Shithead!"

"Stinking whore! Smelly hick!"

Black and whores the both of them, lousy and smelly, but they were two first-rate women, two sought-after whores, two princesses of the settlement. In Tocaia Grande, in order to be first-rate and sought-after, in order to occupy the position of princess or the throne of queen—Bernarda's throne—not much was called for, neither outstanding manners nor good breeding, given the status of the whores lost in that settlement, a bunch of tramps. In any case, the two of them stood out, arousing envy and jealousy.

Dalila put out the hand she'd cleaned her eye with and swatted Epifânia in the face. They grabbed each other by the hair, exchanged slaps, closed in, cursing and scratching. A lively, joking circle formed, urging on the contenders.

"I'm betting on Big-Ass," Misael challenged, standing up for his lady.

"I'll bet you two cents," Guido accepted, no less a gentleman.

Without stopping his playing, Pedro Gypsy got up from

the long wooden bench, the work of Lupiscínio, where he'd been sitting in the company of Zuleica, and went over to join the circle. It's worth noting that at no moment, not even when the brawl was on the point of becoming generalized, did the musician stop fingering his instrument in a kind of low-keyed musical accompaniment. In spite of the fact that he was broke, he risked a cruzado on Epifânia, so sure was he of the outcome. Bastião da Silva covered the bet out of pure sporting spirit, to liven up the competition, without harboring any illusions about collecting those four hundred reis: Pedro Gypsy was in debt to God and half the world.

According to Guido's opinion, the bets were naturally null and void when Zuleica entered the fray, surprising everybody except Coroca. Dalila seemed on the verge of defeat; with a yank, Epifânia pulled off her chintz skirt—the old one, because she was saving the new one for St. John's Day—leaving her behind in full view of the appreciative audience. Without knowing how to react, Dalila was about to abandon the field. At that moment, getting up from the bench where she'd been following the ups and downs of the mess, Zuleica attacked Epifânia with kicks; she had the advantage of wearing clogs. Feeling herself supported, Dalila, rolling her naked behind, flew on top of her rival again. The circle applauded with cheers, clapping, and whistles.

"Two against one, you yellow bitches. I'll take you both on."

But Epifânia wasn't facing them alone: little Cotinha got into the fray on her side and showed unexpected valor. The four rolled on the ground, all tangled up; in addition to Dalila's ass, Epifânia's breasts could be glimpsed as her Bahian robe unraveled.

With Zuleica's intervention, the real reason for the squabble became obvious in the eyes of the womenfolk, a just if not sublime reason: black Castor Abduim da Assunção, who stood aside, minding his own business as if he had nothing to do with it.

They sighed, fought, and cursed over him: they ate out of his hand. A truth everybody knew, which was confirmed at once: going over to the fighters covered with dirt, scratched, and spat on, half-naked, Tição—oh, you proud black man! —ordered, without raising his voice, "That's enough for today, girls, let's have some fun."

The sound of the accordion swelled in a full, irresistible cadence. Turning his back on the valiant women, the ungrateful shoer of donkeys offered his hand to Merência, a proper married woman who disapproved of that whole catfight, and went off with her to dance. Dalila straightened her skirt, went back to the arms of Misael; Epifânia went to those of Guido. Fadul took Cotinha: the Turk was even bigger than Friar Nuno de Santa Maria, but size didn't frighten someone who'd been brought up in the service of God on high. In her usual peaceful way, with the same distant look, as if she had never even been fighting, Zuleica accepted the invitation of gold-bearded Bastião da Rosa and kicked off her clogs. On the floor of tamped clay, they went back and forth barefoot, stepping lightly, whirling in a glow of sweat, a fragrance of billy goat.

Fingering the accordion, beating his feet on the ground to keep time, Pedro Gypsy danced among the couples in the center of the shed. No one missed Lulu Concertina. The feast of St. Anthony had begun to get lively.

9

ALAS!—THE GYPSY'S WINGDING got too lively. The trouble started again with a few words passed between Guido and Misael, still disputing the bet made during the women's fight, the two pennies laid on Dalila's tail and Epifânia's teats. For some unrevealed reason or for no reason at all, just as a provocation, Misael, after having had a few drinks, declared Dalila the winner and demanded immediate payment.

They had their falling out during a break in the music, while drinking Cotinha's strong, tasty genipap. They came to ugly words and threats, but didn't take any action because Turk Fadul decided to intervene. He was used to doing it every time there was a dance: the small number of whores caused constant disputes, brought on challenges, fierce quarrels. Fadul would separate the contenders, almost always relying only on his recognized superior authority: owner of the store, creditor to many. If necessary, however, he would resort to brute force.

Without taking into consideration the silent and hostile presence of the other two cowboys, the Turk, outsize hands, fingers like pincers, grabbed each of the rowdies by the arm, placing himself between them.

"The only ones to fight in here are the women. A man, if he wants to, can go outside; there he can kill himself if that's what he wants. This is a dance hall." He opened his hands, releasing them. He looked straight at Misael's helpers, the old man and the boy, turned to Pedro Gypsy. "Where's the music, fellow?"

Muttering about what Guido could do with the two pennies—"Keep them, I don't need them, stick them up your ass"—Misael went off, followed by his henchmen. So much the better that Guido didn't hear the muttering: he wasn't in the habit of stirring things up, but when provoked, he didn't back off. In the southern country cowards don't grow up, they die in their cradle at the first sign of diarrhea.

It became obvious that Misael was looking for a fight; the more he drank, the more he gabbed. He demanded that all his favorite pieces be played, insulting Pedro Gypsy with coins tossed at him as tips, which the accordionist picked up without feeling insulted; he got into an argument with the two men from the cacao warehouse over Dalila, with whom he wanted to dance all the time; he bragged about how good his horse Pirapora was, proclaimed himself a great lover, rich and tough. "A squealing pig pretending to be a wild boar," old Gerino remarked, having known him in other parts. The challenges and boasts were swallowed by the music, the stamping of feet, the noise of the shindig, the *cachaça* breath.

The party and the night were well-advanced, when a new argument exploded in a corner where there wasn't much activity. On one side stood three cowmen: the boss, Misael, old Totonho, and the boy, Aprígio; on the other, three women: Bernarda, Dalila, and Margarida Cotó, the Stump, with her withered arm and her freckly face. What looked at first like a simple misunderstanding over dance partners was nothing of the sort: it was a matter of the perverse demands of the cattle drovers. Having to be on their way while the sky was still dark in order to gain time, they were demanding that the three whores leave the dance immediately—they had no intention leaving Tocaia Grande without a good screw. They were in a hurry, they couldn't wait till the dance was over: the way it was going, it would last into morning. *Hurry up, you dumb broads, it's time to go.*

Well, the whores, under the influence of the festivities, had decided to shut up shop, not accept any customers on nights of the June feasts: a party is a party. They intended to have a good time, dance, relax, drink, laugh, and flirt, if they wanted. Since that night wasn't like all the others—nights of hard work, lying about enjoyment, sweating on a stranger's chest, faking moans without feeling anything—the three unanimously refused the offers of the loaded cowman and his two sidekicks: *Not tonight, you'll have to excuse us, another time. Tonight, not for any amount of money.*

Misael had chosen Dalila, leaving Bernarda for the old man, Margarida for the boy. He'd hesitated between Bernarda and Dalila, but in the pupils of his eyes he still had the picture of the black girl's behind, a masterpiece. The old man was licking his chops, all excited, the boy didn't complain about Cotó's freckles or stump of an arm, birth defects: at eighteen you take what comes and ask for more.

Dalila's explanations were of no use, good as she was with her mouth, nor Margarida's push, when Balbino, a renegade black-Indian half-breed began to come on to her, nor was Bernarda's firm no. "The basket's shut, Grandpa."

"We'll open it then," the old man snorted.

The cattlemen were rather high and time was short. "Get away," Bernarda said when old Totonho tried to drag her off. With her blow and the genipap liquor, the old man swayed on his feet. Misael, who was holding Dalila by the wrist, lost his patience, fumed.

"If you all don't want to come nicely, you'll come just the same, you damned sluts!"

The music had stopped while Pedro Gypsy was slaking his thirst with a slug of *cachaça* and the threat resounded throughout the shed; the other whores came over, curious; Misael, always the great lover, rich, and tough, thought they were coming to offer themselves in place of the angry ones.

"We've already picked these here, we don't need you all." He turned to the ones selected, shoved Dalila. "Let's go!"

Epifânia stepped forward, sweat running down her black skin; she faced the cowmen, her voice hoarse, permeated with liquor.

"Not them, not us, nobody with any shame left up her

nose is going to screw with you people today. Can't you see we've got the lid on? Go stick your cows if you want to." So as not to lose the habit and also because she, too, had abused Cotinha's genipap, she spat on the ground and dug her heel into it.

A man worth his salt doesn't just go off carrying an insult to his manhood, much less one from a prostitute. Misael announced before making a move, "These three are going to take it up the ass whether they like it or not, and you're going to get one in the face, you shitty hag."

The slap could be heard all through the dance hall—dance hall: that's what the Turk called it, a place for dancing, a place for fun and not for fighting. The black girl lost her balance; the second blow, even stronger, knocked her to the ground, a thread of blood ran down her thick lip.

"You son of a bitch!" Dalila howled, an unleashed she-wolf.

10

"YOU SON OF A bitch!" Bernarda repeated, advancing too.

Before the cattle drovers realized it, they were encircled by furies from hell. Coming to Epifânia's defense, Dalila threw herself onto Misael, strangling him. What had happened to the rivalries and jealousies so important at the start of the catfight? A mixup with whores, as has been said, leaves no quarter; it's a fight with wild women.

The whores all joined forces without exception to face the drovers, to reject their dictate: if they didn't have the right to keep the lid on their basket whenever they felt like it, if they weren't owners of their own twats, what did they have left in their miserable lives? All of them who plied their trade in Tocaia Grande: Dalila, Epifânia, Bernarda, Zuleica, Margarida Cotó, Two-Ton Marieta, Cotinha, Dorita, Teté, and Sílvia Pornambuco, all of them disheveled, united for their cause. Missing on the list was the name of Jacinta Coroca, not by oversight, but by appreciation and consideration: all by herself she was worth more than all the others put together. When the inexperienced Aprígio threatened to pull out his revolver, thinking he could solve the problem of a surging wave of teeth and nails with it, Coroca gave him a kick in the nuts. The boy's outcry could be heard three and a half leagues away, at the station in Taquaras, according to the sworn testimony of Pedro Gypsy, a witness of the first order.

Old Totonho, poor devil, worthy of pity, was the most enraged of the three. He'd always hoped to spend a night riding a young heifer like Bernarda; he saw his dream undone and wouldn't accept it. Grabbing her by the waist, he finally got her down; he was trying to touch her breasts, lift up her skirt, all ready, God knows, to lay her right there in the shed, in the midst of the scuffle, in full view of those present. He was out of his mind, shaking as if he were having an attack of malaria. He softened his voice to beg, "Let's go . . ." He gritted his teeth to command, "Let's go!" He pulled off his leather jacket to give himself more freedom of action. That was his big mistake: they lost the respect for him that the leather jacket imposed. Bernarda took advantage of it to slip away and, before Totonho could get up, Two-Ton Marieta, hefty, slow, and maternal, threw her big body on top of the poor man: his joints creaked. Whimpering his last hopes, splayed on the ground, the old man pleaded, seeing Bernarda throwing herself at Misael, "Aprígio, grab her, I'm coming."

How could the young man hold Bernarda when he was doubled over, defending himself from Coroca's kicks? As for the firearm, Coroca had stuck it down the front of her dress, between her shriveled breasts: leaving a weapon within reach of a child is to run the risk of death.

In those few minutes confusion reigned. Misael was trying to escape the ever more aggressive siege; scratched and spat on, he was dealing blows; Dalila caught one in the face, but all the same he was having a hard time keeping on his feet. Nervous, he knew it was time to take off for Conquista on the back of his horse Pirapora: who needed to be insulted by the big-assed woman, not to mention cursed by the rest of them? Anyone who starts a fight with a whore is off his rocker, weak in the head.

11

IN SPITE OF FADUL'S tight face, Misael waited, confident
and smiling, when he saw the men walking in his direction.
Surely he'd find understanding and support from them,
help to tame those bitches and make the rebels fulfill the
inherent duties of their profession: to open up their pussies
to whatever customer tells them to and pays, without any
arguments over place or preference. He wouldn't go back on
that. Where had anyone ever seen a woman of the streets
who had her own say, office hours, a day off?

The Arab was coming closer, furious: willy-nilly, one
after the other, the whores walked off, leaving the gentlemen flatfooted, as if the party had stopped at the height of
its activity. He shouted at the furious women, "What the
devil are you doing there?"

But when he caught onto the altercation, he addressed
Misael.

"Is causing trouble all you can do, friend? What did you
come here for? Let's cut this out."

There was a truce in the brawl; scratches and blows gave
way to discussion. The cattleman started out by appearing
reasonable. He temporized.

"We didn't come here looking for trouble. We only wanted
some stinking *putas* to give our dicks a little relief."

"They tried to take us by force, and we've all got the lid
on," Epifânia interrupted, blood running out of the corner
of her mouth.

"I won't go even if I'm dead," Bernarda reaffirmed.

"Whores have got no say!" Old Totonho answered, moving closer to the one he'd promised himself.

Coroca stopped beating the boy with her clog.

"We're whores, not slaves," she said, and turned to
Fadul as if challenging him. "Isn't that so, Mr. Fadul? Or do
you think the same as they do?"

Convinced of the men's support, feeling that he had all
the reason in the world on his side, ready to pay for a round
of *cachaça* before going off with his cowboys and their
choices, Misael was astonished to hear black Castor Abduim
ask and threaten, "Don't you people know that slavery ended

over twenty years ago? The girls will go if they want; if they don't they won't."

Misael looked around, ran his eyes from Tição to Zé Luiz, from half-breed Balbino to white Bastião da Rosa, from Guido to Lupiscínio, from Gerino to Fadul, from the warehouse men to the drovers and transients, from Pedro Gypsy and his accordion to Merência, huge and secure. Finally he stood face-to-face with the shoer of donkeys.

"It would have been all settled if it wasn't for a fresh nigger like you. I don't know why I don't bust your face." Then he turned to the others. "If you don't want trouble, stay out of this."

With that he put his hand on his wide belt, the old man and the boy came over to back up the challenge. Before the cattle drover could reach his revolver, Fadul, after smiling at Coroca, spoke in a calm tone, as if he were exchanging niceties and not giving orders.

"Leave that gun alone, Mr. Misael: that's your name isn't it? And try to be on your way before it's too late." At the same time, he held back the restless black man. "Take it easy, Tição!"

Keeping his hand on his holster, Misael still hesitated.

"Do you people want to fight over these cunts?"

"If you try to force them, friend, you've got a fight on your hands. Just remember one thing. That's the way it is here: if you mess with one of us, you mess with us all."

"That's the way it is all right. If you don't like it, you can be on your way," put in Merência, once so jealous of her status as a married woman that she'd refused to live anywhere near the prostitutes in order to maintain her respect, keep her distance. But there she was, hands on her hips, joining the fight, as if these fallen women were relatives of hers, cousins, nieces, and sisters.

Fadul summed it up.

"It's the rule of the place."

Even if it hadn't been until then, it came to be from that moment on. The great lover, rich and tough, Misael couldn't back down.

"I shit on your rule and I shit on all of you."

He never got to grab his firearm. Tição flew on top of him, joined by Poor Soul, who had left the bench under which he'd hidden to doze to the music of the accordion, where he'd been keeping a watchful eye on the doings of friend and foe.

Only then did the wrangle look like something. Fadul trapped old Totonho by the shirt and pants, lifted him into the air, and tossed him like a sack. The women had fun tearing the clothes off young Aprígio. With so many men trying to take part, it was even beginning to look cowardly. Guido could barely control his impatience: he begged Castor to let him have Misael, with whom he had accounts to settle. But Tição wanted to demolish all by himself the loving, the wealth, and the toughness of the big talker, show him what a fresh nigger could do. Pour Soul was leaping among them, growling and biting.

To guarantee his escape as he ran off, old Totonho took a shot at random: nobody had thought to take his weapon away, an ancient horse pistol. The bullet struck Cotinha in the head.

12

IN THE HAMMOCK THAT had served for toil and rest, a gift from Zé Luiz in happier times, they placed Cotinha's body, the slim body of the rickety girl, and they carried it to the primitive cemetery where the papaya trees and banana shoots grew and bloodred cherries ripened. It had rained without letup during the night in the aftermath of the feast and the brawl, but by the morning the rain had stopped and the sun came out for the funeral.

At dawn a few men dug the grave beside a blooming cashew tree. A deep grave, the first to be opened since the place came to be called Tocaia Grande. They picked up spades and shovels after the departure of Misael and Aprígio, the boy carrying Totonho's saddle.

When the men went after him, the old man leapt bareback onto Pirapora—swift as the wind, in Misael's boast—and escaped at a frantic gallop. Misfortunes do happen, a slug in the head, a bullet in the chest, a wild shot: most times the trigger was pulled out of fear, not from any wish to kill.

That being the case, they considered themselves satisfied with the beating given Misael and young Aprígio. The cowboy and his helper had become cowed—an appropriate word in every sense. "A squealing pig pretending to be the wild boar," Gerino had said. And he was right: on his knees, Misael begged forgiveness in order to save his life.

Castor and Lupiscínio balanced on their shoulders the ends of the long bamboo pole stuck through the knots of the hammock and carried her to the cemetery. The procession mingled tears and laughter; the mourners spoke of the dead woman with kindness, they didn't mention her grumpiness, her bad moods; they praised her courage, her sincerity, her jackfruit sweets, banana chips, and genipap liquor. In the silence, on the way to the cemetery, black Tição remembered details from conversations, the convent in São Cristóvão, the sacramental wine, the big bell and Friar Nuno novitiating. He smiled as he remembered, and when the time came to lower the body into the grave, he asked, "Does anybody know a prayer? She lived in a convent; she was almost a nun. She ought to be prayed over."

They made several attempts, but nobody knew a whole prayer all the way through from beginning to end, not even a short Hail Mary. Merência had pardoned the poor sinner, as charity teaches and commands, but not to the point of appearing at the cemetery. But in spite of all that, Cotinha's soul couldn't go to heaven—if there is a heaven for whores— without the key of a prayer to open the gates.

Mixing up fragments from the Our Father and the Hail Holy Queen, Fadul Abdala's strong voice rose up. In childhood he had been an altar boy for his uncle, the priest, in his Lebanese village. He recited in Arabic with unction and feeling. It was a pleasure to hear him, it made one want to cry. Epifânia couldn't resist, and broke into sobs.

No sooner was it over than the sun disappeared and winter returned.

13

EPIFÂNIA DIDN'T WAIT FOR the end of winter to pull up stakes. She celebrated St. John and St. Peter, told everybody who wanted to listen that she'd never had such a good time.

On St. John's Eve they lighted bonfires in front of the huts, several of them; neighbors visited each other. The clearing was lighted up with rockets, snakes, Roman candles, pinwheels, sparklers, colored flares, blue, green, red, yellow, so pretty. They ate and drank their fill, the whores confessed that they were charmed: there was no leader of a quadrille who could measure up to Castor Abduim: the black man was a master of foreign tricks. Epifânia leapt over a bonfire together with Zuleica; from now on they would be blood sisters.

The great moment was the release of the balloon, a surprise for everyone except Tição and Coroca. It was drizzling a little: they filled it with smoke from the largest fire in the clearing where they were gathered. They lighted the wick, the balloon climbed into the sky and disappeared. Before vanishing, it mingled with the few dim stars: false as it was, it was the loveliest star of all.

They were still celebrating on St. Peter's Eve in order to finish off Cotinha's genipap liquor and take advantage of the presence of Pedro Gypsy and his bellows.

Days later, early in the morning, Castor had just finished taking care of the hooves of Rosedá, the lead mule in Elísio's train—after having trimmed them with his file, he nailed four shiny shoes on them—when he saw Epifânia waiting, ready to leave. They'd spent the night together and she hadn't told him anything. On her head perched a small tied bundle with clothing and slippers, her entire belongings.

"I'm leaving, Tição." She was taking advantage of Elísio's mule train so she wouldn't have to travel alone. "Can I take the *abebê* you made for me?" In her eyes and her voice was a firm decision, a touch of sadness, and her rough pride.

Tição gave her the tin mirror from the *peji* of the *orixás*, the one that represented Oxum. He didn't ask her to stay, he only said, "I'll remember you all my life."

Epifânia held out the tips of her fingers: barefoot, the bundle on top of her kinky hair, the *abebê* in her hand, she followed the train in the direction of Taquaras. Poor Soul went with her for a good piece, but when he realized that the black woman was really leaving, he gave up and came back to lie down by the warmth of the forge. He was still ugly and skinny; he'd shown himself, however, to be brave and a good hunter. He watched over the shop and Tição's steps.

Captain Natário da Fonseca Meets a Family from Sergipe and Directs Them to Tocaia Grande

1

ALL THEY LACKED TO be a band of pilgrims were the chanting and the dogs, Captain Natário da Fonseca reflected when he spotted the caravan. He stopped his animal at the approach of the ragged band in order to answer the greeting of the old man better, repeated by an echo of weary voices: *Afternoon.* The old man took off his hat to ask information. He wanted to know if they were on the right route to the plantations along the Rio das Cobras and if it was true that they were hiring laborers in those parts. *That's right, yes: the harvest was starting, cacao was ripening, it was a pretty sight.*

He didn't have to ask where they were coming from, but Natário did in order to keep the conversation going.

"From Sergipe?"

"Yes. sir."

"All one family?"

He counted with his eyes: beside the three couples a strong tall youth, a girl in braids, a kid carrying a snare to catch birds with. A woman with a kerchief around her head was carrying a baby a few months old, the other woman, younger, had a belly. Ten living souls, soon to be eleven. Perfect for what Natário had in mind.

"Yes, sir, we're all related."

"Where in Sergipe are you coming from?"

The old man took a moment to answer—what if the news had traveled this far? He made up his mind, however.

"We come from near Maroim. Have you heard of it?"

"I passed there on my way here, a long time ago. I come from Propriá."

Standing by attentively, the others followed the dialogue. Leaning on a makeshift staff cut from a tree branch, the emaciated old woman, her kinky hair sandy, more from dust than from age, took a step toward the rider; the woman with the child in her arms followed her. A countryman is almost a relative, he's not the same as a stranger. Who knows? That citizen of Propriá, well-off, riding a good-looking mule on a good saddle might be of help and salvation. He must have had some reason for prolonging the conversation in the hot sun by the side of the road.

"All you see around here are Sergipeans. But almost all of them alone. Families are rare, especially one this size. Why did all of you people come, if you don't mind my asking?"

One of the men spoke up before the old man had a chance.

"There's no work back there; they say there's a lot of it here. That's why, and that's that."

He didn't look at the captain, he looked at the others; the question had been answered, none of them had to add anything. Brusque, not very illuminating, still there hadn't been any insolence or challenge in the reply; only reserve, suspicion. Who knows? The old man had lowered his head when his son got ahead of him, taking over—precedence and respect had gone to hell in Maroim.

Natário pretended not to hear, wasn't bothered. He knew those stories by heart, all identical at the bottom. How many had he seen arrive with the gun still smoking? He moved his eyes from one to another, measuring and sizing up the four men, which of them had done the shooting? He didn't leave out the boy: youth is counted double on the calendar of insult.

" 'That's why and that's that,' a good answer. Keep your secrets, I'm no father confessor. When people land here they're reborn, they haven't got any debts to pay. They can even change their names if they want."

That was when the young man let go of his wife's hand and came over to Natário.

"They drove us off, they kicked us out. We didn't come because we wanted to. We were forced to come."

"Shut up!" ordered the older one, who'd spoken before.

The old man began a gesture, but didn't complete it. The captain lowered his eyes to the repeater on the young man's shoulder, but he didn't ask any questions or make any comments. The young one, without paying any attention to the old man's signal or his brother's order, opened up, released the affront that had been consuming him.

"It didn't happen the way you're probably thinking. They wouldn't let me . . ." He pointed to the old woman and the pregnant one, mother and wife. "Much as I wanted to put an end to the bastard." He looked at the palm of his hand. "Dammit, they tied my hands! They stopped me from doing what I wanted to do!"

All worked up, on that occasion he'd wanted to pick up his gun and do something foolish. Married only a short time, the young bride, pretty and pregnant, put her arms around his neck: *Think of me and the child!* His mother desperately snatched the repeater away from him. *I'd rather die than have a criminal for a son, arrested or wanted by the police.*

"I didn't raise my son to be a murderer or to die at the hands of a gunman." That's how her father and her brother before him had died, killed in the same useless way.

Between the two of them they drained his spirit, and the threat went to the four winds. For the senator, however, there was little difference between a threat and an attempt to carry it out, the responsibility for which belonged to all of them together and to each one separately. A strange Solomon's judgment meted out at the corral fence.

2

IN THE GLOW OF the noonday sun on the road to the woodlands they blurted out the story, each actor declaiming his part with precise intonation; in the act of repeating it, they buried the past, a painful thorn, a useless burden. They

returned to the same purity they had had before cruelty
imposed methods and terms, reason and unreason. Almost,
but not entirely: even when healed, wounds leave indelible
marks.

More than once the captain had heard the same sad
story. Men and women, from the old man to the boy, worked
the land, going halves with the owner and master, a cattle
rancher, political boss, state senator. Life went along peacefully, they planted and harvested, took the part that belonged to them to market in Maroim, sold and bartered. On
Sunday the women went to church, the men to the tavern.

One day, for no reason, it was all withdrawn. The oral
agreement, the given word wasn't worth a thing. They had
to turn over their plot of land, their horses, their chicken
coop, the well, security and laughter, for a ridiculous bit of
money.

Called to the office of the ranch, the old man came back
with the payment stipulated by the senator—*It's no use
talking about it, it's take it or leave it*—enough time to get
their things together and look for another place, a burning
in his eyes, a knot in his throat. Whom to complain to? The
bishop?

For the women, in the madness of their affliction there
was always the comfort of the parish priest, he himself
affected by the unexpected ruling that would deprive him of
fat capons, selected fruit, tender sweet cassavas, weekly
gifts from those good, Godfearing people. He advised resignation and obedience. In a certain way, he opined, half-
closing his eyes, folding his hands over his fat belly, they
should consider themselves the children of good fortune,
given the natural kindness of the senator. Owner of the
land—or did the land belong to them, maybe?—if the senator wished, he could have put them off with no payment
whatsoever, with no period of grace, no handshake. He needed
that fertile soil to turn into grazing land for his cattle,
growing hilo grass instead of manioc and beans. The herd
came first, nothing more just than that. The senator was
doubly magnanimous: first, by letting them farm and harvest for such a long time, and second, by paying them what
he didn't owe. He reminded them also of the grace period
given, time enough for them to be able to go to market on
Saturday and sell their last produce before they moved.

They ought to have thanked him. He gave them his blessing.
God is great.

If it hadn't been for the excitement and the threats, the
matter would have passed without any other aggravation.
But when he learned through indirect ways about the anger
and the empty words, the senator was deeply shocked: he
wouldn't tolerate ingratitude. He canceled the period of
grace, decreed immediate expulsion—if any member of the
family was found roaming around on his land, he would
give no quarter.

As for that hothead, the bandit who'd thought about
murdering him, that one needed a lesson. Arrested, he was
tied to a stake in the corral, without water, without food,
baking in the sun.

They had to drag away the pregnant woman, who was
holding on to her husband's legs, ready to die along with
him. The old woman stood at the door of the sacristy in
Maroim until she was received by the priest. A humble
sheep in the flock of the Lord, behold her: suddenly transformed into an insane fury, she looked more as if she had
been possessed by the Beast. "Father, if they don't let him
go, we're coming back and they'll have to get rid of all of us,
one by one, starting with me; it's going to be a slaughter."
Even the priest, of a contemplative and drowsy nature, lost
his calm, was afraid, felt a chill in his belly.

"God forgive you, woman. I'll go see what I can do."

Proving again his generous impulses, the senator listened to the priest's plea, ordered them to release the wretch
in time to join the rest of the rotten crew. First, however,
they gave him a couple of dozen whacks with the switch
used on blacks during the ancient and worthy institution of
slavery.

The senator would not allow people of bad faith on his
domains. His domains: the state of Sergipe, land and water,
trees, animals, roads, justice. He had a few junior partners,
rich sugar mill masters. The rest were serfs.

3

"WE WERE DRIVEN OFF . . ."

What good was carrying the gun on his shoulder? Too
late, the moment had passed. Better to follow his mother's
advice and forget: lock up the swelling and the sting of the
switch in his guts.

"It could have been worse," the old woman concluded.
"What happened happened. Our trials are over and we've
still got our lives. God will help us stay together."

The captain didn't comment on the events; he didn't
say yes, he didn't say no, he didn't take one side or the
other, he didn't approve or condemn. The usual story, not
much to it, the old woman was so right: what happened
happened; if they stayed together they could change misfortune into profit.

"You really want to stay all together?"

"That's our intention, but they say it isn't easy." The
old man had taken over the talking, in charge of things once
again.

"What's your name?"

"Ambrósio, at your service."

"And you, Auntie, what are you called?"

"Evangelina, but they call me Vanjé. Maybe there's no
way it can be done. . . ."

"Anything can be done this side of death."

He began by telling them his name and his title. "In
this neck of the woods everybody knows me . . ." Then he
began talking about Tocaia Grande, a settlement less than a
league away, lying in a spot that's almost too pretty to
behold. He spoke about the land on the banks of the river
where they could plant long plots of beans, corn, manioc,
land that doesn't belong to anyone, that belongs to the first
one to get there. In cacao farming it's every man for himself,
with no appeal.

"Land that doesn't belong to anyone? For real?"

The old woman had seen it happen twice already.

"This is the end of the earth, Dona Vanjé. It's not like in
Sergipe, where everything's got a lord and master. Even the
miracles of the saints."

Vanjé could see that the man from Propriá was a messenger of destiny, she felt herself freed of fears and uncertainty. Old Ambrósio, however, was thinking it over.

"The money we've got isn't enough even for a start."

"You won't need it. When you get there, look up a Turk named Fadul. Tell him I sent you. He'll help you with everything you need."

He finally explained the reasons for so many privileges.

"I don't know of a nicer place in the world than Tocaia Grande, but it's only going to prosper the day it has families living there, little kids and young animals."

The older brother, the one who'd given the brusque answer, silent since then, still wanted to know, "Are you from there, sir?"

"I was born in Propriá, like I said. But when my time comes, it's in Tocaia Grande I plan to die."

4

THE RAGGED BUNCH DISAPPEARED in the dust of the trail. Captain Natário da Fonseca's thoughts flowed out to the canyons of the river São Francisco, to the fields of poverty and indignity. In the silence of the forest he was the echo of imprecations and agony. The life of the poor was hardly worth a sigh. Not even the whipping of blacks had been eliminated, not to mention all the rest.

Why linger over such century-old disorders, aggravating himself? the links of cradle and birth had been broken forever way back. The pressing compromises of the present required his care. In place of the fowling piece of his youth he carried a dagger and a horse pistol: the guarantees of verbal agreements, the pledges of fair play.

A smile blossomed on Natário's lips: the Turk was going to have a devilish surprise when he came face-to-face with the Sergipeans bearing the message. Not by accident that morning the two had been talking and Natário had given the diagnosis and proposed the cure.

"Well, it's like I say, friend Fadul, as long as there's no

family living here, only drovers and tarts, there isn't going to be much progress. But it won't be for long. Pretty soon now I'm going to get some Sergipeans to send here. It's getting to be a need: the new plantings are starting to give cacao, and money's going to flow. Tocaia Grande's going to stop being a hole in the wall, a settlement. Pretty soon it's going to leave Taquaras behind. Write that down if you've got any doubts."

"God can do anything, Captain. When is my noble friend going to bring in the Sergipeans?"

"Any one of these days, Fadul. When you least expect."

The Sergipean Family Arrives in Tocaia Grande and Captain Natário da Fonseca Starts Building His Own House

1

IT WAS GETTING WELL into morning, and the two prostitutes, old Jacinta Coroca and young Bernarda, were warming themselves in the summer sun by the door of the wooden house that had been built for them on orders of Captain Natário da Fonseca. Jacinta was mending clothes; Bernarda was combing her thick black mane, her hair was beautiful and she knew it. She was examining it strand by strand, searching for nits.

Turning her attention away from the delicate task of rethreading her needle, Coroca glanced at her companion, broke the peace and quiet.

"A woman in this business who gets herself pregnant is an incompetent. Better to have stayed on the farm cracking cacao shells."

She said it in a low, barely audible voice. In a slow mutter she continued her scoffing conversation, her eyes fixed on her sewing, as if she were talking to herself alone and to no one else. Bernarda was listening to her in the same way: as if she didn't hear anything but the quiet of the morning.

"Why the devil did she have to get her belly big? She'll find out, and she doesn't even know who the poor devil's father is. She doesn't know a damned thing."

The breeze caressed the waters of the river, the tops of the trees, Bernarda's hair. Coroca babbled on.

"A person with no brains shouldn't choose the profession of whore, which isn't a simple profession. It's really quite complicated. She thinks it's only picking lice, flashing a smile, putting perfume in the right places, but she's so wrong. A woman in this trade is like a nun: when she enters the convent she puts everything else aside. Father and mother, brother and sister, her real name and the right to get pregnant and give birth. Except that a nun becomes a saint and goes to heaven to sit in God's hand, while we never go beyond being whores, condemned without redemption."

She looked at the horizon beyond the river and the hills; the strong light hurt her eyes.

"I ruined my eyes seeing so many kids, all shitty and blear-eyed with snot coming out of their noses, crying in the corners of a whorehouse. A whore's child is the most helpless creature there is. You'd have to be a lunatic or worse to think that a whore can give herself the luxury of a child, can bring a kid into the world. There's nothing more pitiful than a woman of the streets at her trade with a small child clinging to the hem of her skirt."

Without interrupting her litany, she stopped sewing, examined the mending of the holes in the faded blouse.

"If she didn't know what to do to avoid having a kid, why didn't she ask older women? I never had a belly, and I've been at this more time than I can say: I haven't got enough fingers and toes to count the years I've been in this line of work. They didn't start calling me Coroca just yesterday."

She fell silent for a moment, hesitant. The memories of a hard life were her exclusive privilege. But if she didn't come to the aid of Bernarda, the dummy would drag the curse of a child for the rest of her life. Bernarda could have been her granddaughter.

"I was a young one when Mother taught me how not to get pregnant from Colonel Ilídio. I was kept by the colonel, in my own place. He was the one who came to help me when Olavo, after he'd busted my cherry, died spitting blood, weak in the chest. The colonel fixed up a place for me, with everything in it and anything more I asked for. All I had to do was want something and he'd send twice as much, an old goat in heat. I was living high, Mother never got tired of saying. All I had to do was not have a child, Dona Marcolina wouldn't have stood for that. I was a mistress for more than seven years, or did you think I was born a lost woman? I fell into this only when the colonel kicked off and Dona Marcolina ordered them to give me a whipping and drive me out of Macuco. It was the first order she gave the men after putting on widow's weeds and taking over the plantation." She looked up from her sewing. "It would have been better if she'd ordered them to kill me."

Through the strands of hair hanging across her face, Bernarda followed Jacinta's look as it wandered aimlessly about. Facing the light, her eyes looked empty, like a blind person's. Coroca went back to her sewing and the litany started again.

"If she'd asked me, I would have taught her. All she had to say was, 'Jacinta, what do people do so as not to have kids?' But you think she asked? There she is with something in her belly and not knowing who the kid's father is."

She'd begun to mend a petticoat, cast another sidelong glance at the girl's swollen belly, softened her voice.

"There's no reason for her to worry either. I know the recipe for a potion made from leaves you can find in the woods; it never fails. The woman drinks it and the same day, in a few hours, she gets rid of everything, the whole load, not a trace left. She has to take it in the water, while she's bathing. I learned about it from the late Cremilda, who'd get caught right and left, not because she wanted to, but because that's the way she was, she got pregnant if a man breathed on her. That was her way: they came and they went."

She looked at the girl face-on: her companion in the house and in the trade, so young, without an ounce of good sense. Coroca couldn't permit such foolishness.

"I'm talking about you, I'm old enough to be your grandmother. I'll fix the potion today, it's got an awful taste, but it will clean out your belly. You take it in the middle of the afternoon and you'll wake up empty. Are you listening?"

Bernarda raised her head, threw her hair back, and finally faced the jabberer's stare.

"You'll have to excuse me, but I'm not going to take any potion to empty out my belly, so don't take the trouble of searching the woods for leaves. I know what you're saying is meant for my good, and that you're trying to help me. The fact is that I'm having this kid because I chose to have it, not because I didn't know any better. When did I ever get

pregnant when Papa slept with me? I didn't want a kid from
him: when Papa opened my legs, I closed off the rest of my
body."

"You didn't feel anything with him?"

"You don't have to believe it, you can say I'm lying. The
first times I was beside myself, all I did was cry. Then not
even that." She made a movement with her shoulder, chasing away that past bitterness. "I don't even want to remember. I don't care about anything now except the kid in my
belly. I've got a belly because I wanted a kid, and I'm going
to have him, nobody's going to stop me. Nobody in the
world."

She stretched, put her hands on her stomach to show
it off better; then she took Jacinta's hand and kissed it.

There wasn't anything to do; no potion could solve the
problem. Coroca nodded in agreement. Having solved the
puzzle, there was no reason for her to continue the charade—
vinegar had turned to honey in their conversation.

"I see. It's his kid, isn't it?"

She didn't have to mention the name for Bernarda to
know to whom Jacinta was referring and to open her lips in
a triumphant smile.

"It's Godfather's, yes, you guessed it." She lifted her
face, shed her anger and her reserve, her hair flowed down
over her shoulders, floating in the breeze; Coroca was looking at her in the face, toward the sun, she was proud. "What
more could I want in the world, what more could I ask of
God? I hope it's a boy, just like him."

"Every son of his has got his father's face. Zilda's own
and the rest as well."

"Mine is going to be just like him in looks and spunk."

Every living person, no matter how miserable and dis-
possessed, how sad and lonely, has the right to a quota of
joy; there's no destiny made entirely of bitterness. The cost,
the price to be paid, doesn't matter. Jacinta herself had paid
absurd prices for a whim, the flame of a desire. She'd never
regretted it even when, after the excitement and joy were
over, loneliness grew bitter and gray. After all, what does
one get out of life beyond the pain and anguish, the agony
and good fortune of being in love? It's worth running the
risk; no matter what the price, it's cheap.

"Nothing's free in this world, everything's got its price.
People can pay with their lives, I've seen it happen. If you

got pregnant with a kid because you wanted to and were
ready for it, nobody can butt in and say you're wrong.
Except that afterward it's no good complaining; you've got
to put up with it quietly."

"Complain? What about? How can you say that? Can't
you see I'm overjoyed?"

Proud heart, broad laugh, feather-brained.

"Feather-brain, you've got to get prepared for the birth.
Even animals in the woods prepare themselves to give birth."

"I was waiting for the day to get closer and arrange it
with you."

"It's best to say it right now. Where are you going to
drop it? In Taquaras? In Itabuna?"

"I'm going to have it right here."

"Here? Are you crazy? There's no midwife here to take
the baby when it's born."

Bernarda smiled again.

"There isn't? What about you?"

"Me?" Taken by surprise, Coroca was frightened, shivered.
"I've done a lot of things in this world you'd never guess;
I even took care of people with smallpox. But I never mid-
wifed a baby."

"Well, you better get ready to take care of mine."

The old woman fell silent. She'd attended at more than
one birth, she'd helped midwives at the moment of the
miracle by bringing a basin of water, towels. The midwives,
queenly, competent, serious, calm-stepping, used measured
movements, exact words: village eminences with the powers
of God in their hands. When she spoke again, she did so
with a choked voice, suddenly hoarse, coming from deep
inside.

"You really want me to bring your kid out? You think
I'm up to midwifing a birth?" She put aside needle and
thread, the items to be repaired.

"If you really want to, you can do anything."

"Taking a baby, helping it to be born, God in heaven!"
She looked at her thin, bony hands. "It could be!"

"After I give birth, you'll be the godmother."

"We're already blood sisters ever since St. John's Day,
have you forgotten? Bonfire sisters, now we'll be the same
thing in life and death."

She shook her head, scolding herself.

"And to think I wanted to kill the little bugger even
before he was born. Dumb old woman, out of your head!"

They both laughed softly, two whores warming themselves in the sun by the door of the wooden house in the settlement of Tocaia Grande at the beginning of summer. Spontaneous laughter, the old woman's and the young girl's, so like the breeze rustling the tops of the trees, rippling the water of the river, a laugh of pure contentment.

2

"IT HAS TO BE here," Ambrósio stated, halting.

The flatland spread out on both sides of the river, surrounded by steep hills. A kind of low hedge of thick creeping vegetation covered the completely uninhabited left bank. In the distance on the right bank they could see huts scattered aimlessly about and, closer by, the row of shacks lined up along the road. A few tile roofs loomed up, a scattering of wooden structures, one straw roof, and a broad shed in the clearing.

"The man was right when he said it was nice," the old man murmured.

"The captain," old Vanjé corrected him. "He said he was a captain, Captain Natário."

Old Amrósio, and old Evangelina, otherwise known as Vanjé, were both stooped, skinny, gray-haired: he couldn't be over fifty; she still hadn't got there. Two old farm workers thrown off their land, looking for a few acres where they could plant and harvest on their own. They looked at the virgin forest before them, vigorous and eternal. All about, vacant land, a matter of arriving and taking possession. Mightn't it be another trick, a dirty swindle? Why should the man, a captain, lie to them? The tragedy had happened far away, in Sergipe, in a captive land. That was water under the bridge.

Dinorá stood alongside Vanjé, the baby in her arms. She turned and smiled at her husband, João José, called Jãozé. When the pilgrimage ended they could reestablish their roots, finally build a home. She'd never again thought that they would find a place to settle down in, somewhere where they could work the soil, plant, raise pigs and chickens, bring up her son, get pregnant again. She'd been afraid the child would die in her arms on the way: the emaciated little thing would whimper softly and slowly, without the strength to cry.

Her husband took a step forward, stood between his mother and his wife; he responded to the smile by stroking his wife's weary face. He, João José, had forgotten how to smile. Before the events in Maroim—was it yesterday or had many years gone by?—Dinorá had filled the house with singing, her bright face, her shining eyes, beaming, lively. At night he would take her in his arms, they would laugh and sigh together.

Rough fingers, a callused, dirty hand: the unexpected caress didn't touch only Dinorá's face, broadening the timid smile on her parched lips. A miraculous unguent, it spread out over the wounds, outside and within, in what was exposed and what was hidden. The tips of the fingers touched every fiber of her being: a soft balm, a hungry call. Dinorá felt herself reborn, once more a woman ready for toil and bed.

In the sun at the curve in the road, they stood gazing at the promised land, eyes fixed on the hills and huts, hearts throbbing. Hesitating between disbelief and certainty, they recalled their fear and their doubts, but they were trying to rid themselves of suffering and bitterness. They clung to the captain's words: fertile land and lots of it.

They started walking again, old Ambrósio in front with his staff, restored in respect and command. Vanjé carried the child so that her daughter-in-law could walk hand in hand with her husband. Agnaldo offered his arm to the exhausted, panting pregnant woman.

"We're getting there, Lia. Only a little ways to go." She shouldn't give birth before her time. "Why are you crying?"

"I'm happy."

"I wonder which one's the Turk's house?"

Diva, the girl in braids, answered her brother's question.

"It must be that one." She was pointing to the handsome smithy, made of stone and mortar.

"Come on, everybody!"

There they went, weary, forgotten people from Sergipe, between fear and hope, disappointment and expectation. The boy and the teenager went past the group, running toward the river.

"Where are you going?"

"Let them go, Ma. I'd like to go too," Diva put in. Her hair was stiff with dust, her face grimy, her smell pungent: her body begged for a bath.

"Me too," the one with the belly agreed.

"Later. We've got to talk to the Turk now."

3

TWELVE EMACIATED YEARS OLD, the boy reached the pool by the bank of the river where the rapids began. He took off his clothes and dove in.

Aurélio, his brother, looked back, didn't see anybody except his people raising dust on the road. He pulled off his shirt and began to unbutton his pants when he heard waves of laughter. Downriver he caught sight of a lively group of women in a stone pool. Aurélio was motionless, holding his pants. The uninhibited whores, some half naked, others completely nude, were scrubbing clothes, bathing, or lost in idle conversation. Bewildered, the adolescent didn't know what to do or how to stop his prick from growing inside his fly. A full and fruitful land: a prodigality of thighs and teats, behinds and pussies. Aurélio was, not surprisingly, seventeen years old.

Nando, the boy, was taking possession of the river, the initial conquest. Later would come trees, marmosets, and birds.

4

IT'S EASY TO RECOGNIZE a Turk by his hooked nose, his curly hair, his botched language. In the building of stone and mortar they found a very dark black man hammering red-hot iron, the greasy hide of a peccary hanging from his waist. No Turk that color had ever been seen: Diva couldn't hold back her laughter.

Tição stopped working; he didn't know why the girl was laughing under her braids, but he laughed, too, relaxed. Then he caught sight of the old people and the rest of the group. On the horizon, coming from the river, Bernarda was crossing the clearing. Diva felt at peace and confident. Hers was the slender body of a child, the look of a girl hardened by life.

"The Turk's house is that big wooden one. The store's in front, the living quarters behind. Right about now Fadul is either sleeping or figuring accounts. I'll go with you."

Curious, he accompanied the group to the store. Leaning over the counter, Fadul Abdala was studying names and dates written down in a notebook: a list of debts and loans, and their due dates.

"It was Captain Natário who told us to come see you. He says the land is good for planting and you could furnish what we need."

The Turk looked them over, one by one.

"Do you come from Sergipe?"

"Yes, sir."

Then he did something the wanderers didn't understand: the great big man kneeled down, raised his hands to heaven, and cried out in Arabic: he was talking to someone in his confidence, to God Himself. His face was jubilant, he shouted expressions of praise: old friend Natário never went back on his word. In the morning he'd promised that he'd soon be sending some families from Sergipe to populate Tocaia Grande. The afternoon still wasn't over and the first contingent had arrived that very day. God be praised!

To show the satisfaction that had taken hold of him, he began to pour *cachaça* for the men. Thinking of the old woman, the new mother, the pregnant wife, and the maiden immediately thereafter, he went to his cupboard for a bottle of genipap liquor left over from all those put up by the late Cotinha for last winter's feasts. He served the mother and the girl: the pregnant one asked for some water to quench her thirst, the old woman preferred a shot of *cachaça*. Counting the baby in arms, there were eight of them, but they informed him that the two youngest had run off to swim.

"His Sergipeans!" the Turk roared at no one in particular.

He placed himself at their disposal. The land was there, untended; all they had to do was cross the river. There wasn't any bridge or canoe, you crossed over on the rocks along the rapids; in winter it was harder because of the rains. The finest quality land, just waiting for someone to cultivate it.

"And it doesn't have any owner? Really doesn't?"

"It does now, you people, my friends, it's just a matter of picking out the piece you want. Isn't that what the captain said?"

"Is he an official, a notary?"

"The same as if he were."

João José still had a touch of doubt.

"And who are we going to sell our crops to?"

The Turk opened his huge arms.

"Out beyond the woods it's all planted with cacao that's just starting to come in. Customers won't be lacking."

That was what his friend had told him that very morning and only a lunatic would dare doubt Captain Natário da Fonseca.

5

WHEN SHE GOT OUT of the ox cart, the only reason Zilda, Natário's wife, wasn't greeted with fireworks was because the captain had forgotten to tell Fadul about it far enough in advance. Nevertheless, the event was as celebrated as the arrival of the Sergipeans two months earlier. The news that Captain Natário da Fonseca had finally decided to start building his house caused a sensation and marked off another step in the life of Tocaia Grande. The new cacao trees were flowering in the neighboring groves on the eve of the first harvest.

Days before, Balbino and Lupiscínio had opened a path and climbed up to the top of the hill to study the site for the house; Bastião da Rosa and Guido took care of the troughs and drying racks on Boa Vista Plantation. Zilda had come to consult with the masons and carpenters about the shape and the details of the construction. The house was a big job; the owner wasn't a nobody and he had a large family, a wife and eight children, five legitimate, three adopted. Curiously, all eight looked so much alike.

When the cart was still creaking in the distance, the inhabitants gathered noisily in the clearing to greet her. But Natário, in front of the team of oxen, riding a black mule with a slow trot, led the delegation to the wooden house where Coroca and Bernarda lived. The two of them were waiting by the door.

Zilda had brought two sons with her: Edu, the eldest, a lanky lad of thirteen, the spitting image of his father, and the last one, born at the end of the fighting, a short time after Natário had got the acres of land to plant his cacao groves, the godson of Colonel Boaventura and his plump and sainted wife, Dona Ernestina. In honor of his godmother, he received the name of Ernesto at the baptismal font.

Delicate of body and fragile in appearance, but healthy and strong in reality, Zilda descended the cart holding the hem of her skirt. Her goddaughter kissed her hand.

"Your blessing, *madrinha*."

"God bless you, child. Good morning, Coroca, you look stronger every time I see you."

"I'm doing as well as God allows."

Natário dismounted, loosening the cinch on his mule. He planned to continue on his way as soon as he'd shown Zilda the hill where the house would be built, at the foot of a mulungu tree. Ernesto got out of the cart dragging a puppy leashed with a rope. Frightened, the animal tugged and bared its teeth. Touching the hand extended by Castor Abduim, also present at the reception, Zilda told him, "It's a young bitch I brought as a present for you, Mr. Tição. I heard you had a dog, here's a wife for him."

"You're going to have to wait till she grows up . . ." the black man advised Pour Soul, who was jumping about restlessly.

Tição patted the puppy's snout, scratched her stomach, and put her on the ground. Poor Soul touched her with a paw, snorted for play. *"Oferecida,"* the offering, Tição said, calling her that because he'd got her as a present and from seeing her, tiny and bold, hop about and stir up the mutt.

Pulling Edu by the ear, Natário also spoke to Castor.

"As an added bonus, you're going to get this kid here, my oldest, Eduardo. He's going to stay with you to learn the trade. Make a blacksmith as good as yourself out of him."

"You can leave that up to me."

"Come on inside," Coroca invited.

The fire warmed a can with freshly brewed coffee. The food sat on a table improvised out of a kerosene crate: cooked breadfruit, grilled dried meat, manioc flour, yams, soft jackfruit, and ox-heart mangos, green in color, tastily ripe, big, incomparable. They barely had time to taste the banquet before Natário hurried them on.

"Let's go, I want to get to the groves. You'll have plenty of time for talking."

Before accompanying her husband and the parade of inhabitants on the way to the hill, Zilda gave Coroca a pair of floppy slippers with red pompoms, a deluxe item brought from Ilhéus, and Bernarda a small bundle containing baby clothes: a lace-trimmed camisole, crocheted booties, a blue bonnet with a white ribbon, everything knitted by her, skillful like no other.

Bernarda's belly had swelled. "They're going to be twins," Zilda joked, touching her goddaughter's stomach. Big-bellied, legs swollen, Bernarda wasn't up to accompanying her godmother on the climb. Wielding machetes, Lupiscínio and Balbino widened the recently opened trail.

Natário hadn't been back to the top of the hill since he'd climbed up there with Venturinha, a short time after the night of the storm, the night of the showdown, the big ambush.

THE
HAMLET

Old Jacinta Coroca is Initiated into the Esteemed Profession of Midwife

1

FOLLOWING IN THE FOOTSTEPS of the Sergipeans from Maroim, two other families had settled on the opposite bank of the river, cultivating and planting, raising chickens, goats, and pigs. Because of the abundance of poisonous snakes, they built their dwellings on stakes and put their pigsties underneath. The layer of fat that covered the pigs made them immune to the bites of the snakes, whom they killed and ate. At the request of the new settlers, Guido and Lupiscínio were planning the construction of a small bridge at the narrowest part of the stream. Having lost more than one head of cattle to the current, Colonel Robustiano de Araújo showed interest in the project. The captain too.

The family of José dos Santos, coming from Buquim, had five people: him, his wife, and their three daughters. That of Altamirando, the couple and one daughter, had come from the backlands, where the drought had struck; the daughter, Ção, retarded from birth, had just turned thirteen. Every two weeks Altamirando would buy a steer from Colonel Robustiano's herd—on credit, to be paid in the next two weeks. He would slaughter it and sell the fresh meat on Sundays and salted whatever was left over. In partnership with Ambrósio, José dos Santos planned to build a flour mill: the manioc patches were thriving.

2

BY MAY THE FIRST donkeys from Boa Vista Plantation had already entered Tocaia Grande. Captain Natário da Fonseca, in person riding the black mule, was driving the tiny train on whose backs came the first cacao picked from his groves. The happy moment resulted in a feast that couldn't help but happen.

His harvest was a few bushels: a trifle, certainly, if compared to the production of other plantations, but all the money in the world couldn't pay for the ex-gunman's emotions: his tiny eyes flashed on his stolid face, the hint of a smile played on his lips. The celebration developed into a solid wingding with plenty of free *cachaça*. Bernarda was happiness incarnate. In spite of her big belly, she spent the night rolling around in her godfather's arms.

3

IN PREVIOUS SEASONS, TIME had passed slowly, stationary for months and months. But with the groves producing, the days sped along and yesterday became remote, the day before yesterday lost in the distant past.

Belonging to the past, then, was the Sunday when the dugout canoe—made from the trunk of a young, flourishing mahogany tree—brought young Aurélio and Diva across the river with some produce to sell. The old settlers saw what they had never seen for sale in Tocaia Grande laid out on burlap sacks: string beans, chayotes, okra, turnips, eggplants, and squash, all in small quantities. There were those who couldn't believe their own eyes.

Each week the variety and quantity of the products grew: Turk Fadul greeted the first handfuls of peppers with excitement: sweet peppers, round and yellow, malagueta peppers, long and speckled with green and red. Nando dealt in birds. He and Edu, partners in deviltry, had set up pyramid traps in woods teeming with seed eaters, song thrushes, flycatchers, swallows, plovers, rice finches; they built rustic bird cages to hold their catch. In Tição's smithy an oriole, ruffling its feathers, filled its breast with song and whistling.

Soon the families of José dos Santos and Altamirando joined Ambrósio's in laying out the week's picking. Ção ran after the pigs, cradled the piglets as if they were little children: her breasts were maturing under the tatters of her dress. With Edu and Nando she ran through the valley, her thin legs, curly hair, wild laughter, active eyes, loud mouth seemingly everywhere. A wild and daring girl.

The detachment of whores grew, the shacks, sparse before, increased in number, standing beside each other in busy, noisy lanes and alleys. The light fantastic started toward the end of the afternoon. Gone were the days when only Tição's lunches marked the existence of Sunday.

4

THE FIRST BABY THAT Coroca delivered, upon becoming a midwife after fifty-four years of life and toil, wasn't Bernarda's, as had been foreseen and expected.

She was sleeping soundly alongside Zé Raimundo, a long-standing customer with whom she could chat and laugh before and after the screwing—a fine, excellent screw, Coroca was zealous of her renown, she did what she could to deserve it—when someone began shouting for her, pounding on the door.

"It's for you, *comadre*," Bernarda informed her, having awakened in the next room.

"I'm coming."

At the door, soaked to the skin, without even saying good evening, Agnaldo recruited her.

"Are you the midwife? Mama sent me to get you. We've got to hurry, Lia's having her pains." He repeated, "Hurry up!"

A sudden and unexpected command: still half-asleep, Coroca didn't think twice.

"I'll be right there."

Time to slip on her rags. In the bedroom, Zé Raimundo opened one eye and wanted to know what the noise was all about.

"Nothing. I'm going out, I'll be right back."

The canoe was still being dug out of the mahogany trunk, Agnaldo swam over, Coroca teetered across on the stones. Only then, taking care not to slip on the moss and fall into the river, did she realize fully what rattle-brained chatter had brought her to the other shore, but it was too late to turn back. Bernarda was to blame for the mistake and the summons. If they asked Bernarda where she was going to give birth, with a midwife in Taquaras or in Itabuna, the fool kept singing the same tune, not in Itabuna nor in Taquaras, she'd have it right there in Tocaia Grande with the help of her good friend Jacinta.

"Does Coroca know midwifery?"

"Sure . . . What doesn't she know?"

Coroca had the reputation of an established midwife before she'd even delivered a single baby. Because of the talk, old Vanjé had remembered her in the hour of need, when her daughter-in-law began to feel her contractions. Vanjé herself had had some experience in those difficulties because she'd borne nine children, the five still living and the four who never grew up. But she was afraid of a difficult, complicated birth, and demanded the skillful and firm hand of a knowledgeable midwife, capable and experienced, for success.

5

STRETCHED OUT ON THE slats of her cot, her eyes bulging, Lia kept moaning and calling for her husband. Ambrósio and Jãozé paced restlessly; Diva didn't know what to do; Dinorá was rocking her son, half-confused. Vanjé found herself all alone, unable to control her nervousness and fear of the bad omens. Why was the midwife taking so long? Only Nando in the next room was sleeping, oblivious to the crisis.

Agnaldo came in, dripping wet, rushed over to Lia, took her hand, and sat down beside her. When she saw him, the weeping woman relaxed her body, still moaning. Vanjé demanded of her son.

"What about the midwife?"

"I'm here, Dona Vanjé. Good evening to all."

Coroca went over to the cot, ordered Agnaldo, "You, boy, get out, get away, leave the poor thing alone. With you beside her she'll never give birth, not now, not ever." She extended the order to old Ambrósio and Jãozé. "You, too, I don't want any men hovering around in this room."

She stood beside the bed like a sentry until she saw them leaving. Only then did she turn to Diva and ordered, "Bring that lamp over here, girl, give us some light."

Coroca took charge as if the only thing she'd ever done in her life had been delivering babies, a trivial matter, a routine task. Vanjé didn't feel alone anymore; she got her confidence back, placed herself under the midwife's orders. Coroca asked for a bottle. Diva brought her an empty one, still smelling of *cachaça*.

"Blow hard on it," Coroca recommended, putting the bottle into Lia's hands, taking it right back. "Not that way, don't stop. I'll show you, look how I do it."

She showed her the right way.

"Take a good look. Take a deep breath, just the way I did, and blow until you can't anymore." She took a deep breath, blew into the neck of the bottle. "Then do it again; don't stop blowing."

She told them to boil some water in an earthen jar for the sitz bath needed to speed up the labor and hasten the birth.

"There's nothing better."

She scolded Dinorá, standing there, the child in her arms, useless.

"What foolishness is that, woman? Put the child to bed, come help. Bring the basin, put it here, close by."

Coroca had never performed a delivery, however, in whorehouses she'd been present at any number of them, easy ones and hard ones. She'd helped respectable midwives in the preparations for the delivery, admiring the knowledge and practice of the wise women. But she had also seen children born dead or ones who died at birth through carelessness or ignorance. Some women claimed to be midwives, but all they did was make angels and, to top it off, they charged and collected a fee. Coroca was used to saying that no one had witnessed the birth of so many whores' children as she. But the midwife's responsibility of bringing a child into life or condemning it to a premature death was new to her. And her first case was a married woman to boot.

She felt a chill rising to her chest, but she paid no attention, wouldn't let it be noticed. Trying to give a peaceful, confident impression, she lingered in conversation about garden plots and breed animals, laying hens and the pregnant sow. She interrupted her talk to require Lia to keep on blowing into the bottle with force and without pause. The contractions were becoming more frequent, more prolonged, and the girl felt herself torn inside. *"Aah, I'm going to die!"*

Even then Coroca made her laugh in the midst of her pain.

"When you made him, you enjoyed it a lot, didn't you?"

She bullied Dinorá and Diva to warm up the water.

"Get it going. Put more wood on the fire."

In the next room Dinorá's child woke up crying, calling for his mother. Dinorá wanted to go to him, but Coroca held her back.

"Let his father go. You're busy."

"Go take a look, Jãozé. See what's wrong with him."

João José informed her.

"He's had a shit."

"Then clean him up," Coroca cut in, before Dinorá could abandon the kettle.

They poured the boiling water into the tin basin bought on credit at the Turk's store, like almost all the other belongings. They helped Lia get up off the cot and settle into the basin, her skirt raised up to her belly.

"Oh, I can't stand it! It's scalding my skin."

"The hotter the better."

Vanjé and Dinorá supported her under the arms, Coroca held her legs open so the heat would penetrate her body. The hot steam dilated her womb, the pains became stronger, the contractions became more frequent, one after the other. Lia was moaning now, crying out now; Agnaldo was peeping through the door, agonizing. Diva was biting her nails, restless.

When the water cooled off, they carried Lia back to the cot.

6

GATHERED AROUND THE COT, at the height of the moans, as the night went on, the women awaited the advent of life. The baby arrived on the edge of morning, when the men had already left for work: they had to start plowing the fields when it was still dark. With Coroca's permission, Diva went with them, carrying the knapsack with the provisions: jerked beef, flour, *rapadura*, a bunch of bananas. Agnaldo was forced to go, Coroca wouldn't let him stay.

"A father only gets in the way."

Attentive, she noticed that in the course of a stronger contraction, the labor so violent it was on the point of silencing Lia in the middle of a moan, the tiny skull, covered with black fuzz, appeared in the dilated vulva and remained motionless there.

"He's coming out," Coroca murmured.

"He's stuck. Oh, my God!" Alarmed, Dinorá was wringing her hands.

"Shut your mouth," Vanjé scolded.

So much the better that the midwife had sent Diva and Agnaldo off to work. If they'd been there, it would have been pandemonium.

Squatting in front of Lia, Coroca reached out with her two hands, placing one on each side of the patient's opening, sticking her fingers in to widen the passage. Then, with infinite delicacy, she took hold of the fragile little crown, and with skill and confidence brought it into the light of dawn in the hollow of her hands. Then she eased out the body, all coated with blood. With one last contraction, Lia expelled the placenta.

Purplish, the newborn baby didn't cry: was it dead or alive? When she lifted him up, Coroca realized that the umbilical cord had wrapped itself around the baby's neck, threatening to strangle it. She quickly unwound the cord, letting the baby breathe.

She took the piece of string that Vanjé, relieved, held out to her, measured four fingers along the length of the cord, and tied it off. Without waiting for the shears—in that turmoil nobody knew where they'd gone—she cut it with her teeth, knotting it at the navel.

A chunk of bloody meat, the infant was placed under the upturned basin: they beat on the top of it with the palms of their hands until they heard the crying break loose, the gasps that announced a life.

"Good news, my friend," Coroca said, turning the basin over and taking the baby in her hands to show it to the mother. "It's a boy."

The birth was coming to an end, the first birth done by Coroca. If they'd asked her who'd given birth, she or Lia, she wouldn't have known what to answer. The affliction over, mother and grandmother were smiling. Dinorá lost her crazy-cockroach demeanor and ran to the fields with the news: *It's a boy, a spanking baby boy!*

Vanjé heated the water in the basin for her grandson's bath.

"I've seen my share of midwives delivering babies, but I never saw anyone who could compare with you and your magic hands. Blessed hands, *comadre* Jacinta."

Magic hands, blessed hands. Unable to answer and not wishing to upset anybody, Coroca turned her back, took refuge in the other room: she sobbed softly, the tears running down her face. If anyone had announced to Tocaia Grande or the world that he'd caught Jacinta Coroca weeping, they would have called him the biggest liar in the world.

Colonel Boaventura Andrade Proposes a Toast

1

ONLY A FEW MULES, a small troop of them, were needed to bring in the first cacao from Boa Vista Plantation that season. On the other hand, many were needed to carry the first harvest gathered on the same occasion from Colonel Boaventura Andrade's new plantings. When the fighting was over, Atalaia Plantation had doubled in size, and production wouldn't be long in doubling, perhaps even tripling again.

As administrator of the colonel's rural properties, Natário had decided and had seen to it that the harvest would begin simultaneously on the small piece of land awarded to him and on the immense one registered by right of conquest at the notary's office in Itabuna in the name of his old friend and boss. He wouldn't harvest for himself before he harvested for the colonel.

If Boa Vista was a profitable spread, what could be said of the estates incorporated into Atalaia? Not even the plantations of Colonel Henrique Barreto, the reputed king of cacao, showed equal care or rendered a crop like that, in spite of employing the services of a full-time agronomist with a doctor's degree and a team of pruners working between harvests. Woodsmen and hired hands didn't fool around at work; it was impossible to do so under the orders of Captain Natário da Fonseca. In return, the pay was never late and there were no games played with the weekly figures.

There'd been only one attempt to gyp the woodsmen

and workers and it was never repeated. Slippery Perivaldo, the employee responsible for the payroll, a kind of book-keeper, had been reported to Natário by some of the more alert people: he was adding too little and subtracting too much with the workers' credits and debits. When the truth of the accusation was proved, he was sent away, but he didn't get far. No sooner had he crossed the boundary of Atalaia than he became buzzard feed: one shot, that was all he was worth.

"Was that necessary?" Colonel Boaventura had asked Natário when, alone with him, he'd learned of the incident. "Wouldn't a beating have been enough?"

"For what he did, yes: for the insult, no."

"Insult? What are you talking about?"

"To get himself off the hook, the rotten bastard was going around saying it was you who put him up to it."

"Son of a bitch! Taking something away from people who haven't got anything. My God! Anyone who plants cacao doesn't have to steal from his workers. You did right, old friend."

"With your permission, Colonel."

2

SITTING IN THE ARMCHAIR at the head of the long table in the dining room of the big house on Atalaia Plantation, Colonel Boaventura Andrade glanced at the distinguished gentlemen around him, all of them specially selected guests, and, raising his voice, spoke to Natário. His words brusquely cut off the eloquence of the public attorney of Itabuna, who was praising the delicacies of the table. A pompous ass, that attorney.

"You're a good man, friend Natário," the colonel declared.

Dr. Flávio Rodrigues de Souza, good at making accusations before a jury, fell silent in mid-sentence when, turning his tongue loose in the name of justice, he was describing the chitterlings as a dish fit for the gods. All the others fell silent as well. The colonel repeated, so there would be no doubts, "A good man, like very few in this world."

So that all the guests—the elite of Ilhéus and Itabuna,

of Sequeiro de Espinho and Água Preta—would know the great esteem he had for the man who had been so loyal and devoted to him for so long.

"How long has it been, old friend?"

"Over twenty years, Colonel."

"You were just a young puppy, but I could see right away that you deserved my trust. You've never let me down in all his time."

A strong statement, but the colonel still hadn't finished.

"They tell me you've built a house outside of Atalaia where you're going to live with your wife and kids. Are you thinking about leaving me?"

"As long as the colonel's alive and happy with my work, I'm your man." Having heard what he wanted to hear, the colonel breathed a sigh of relief. The news of the construction of Natário's house had been troubling him. "But it's true that I'm going to live halfway between Atalaia and Boa Vista. In a place I showed you once. Remember?"

"I remember, friend. I remember quite well, how could I forget? Well, if I brought this up, it was to tell you that I don't know a better man than you. I want it to be known that you've never let me down."

He was presiding over the birthday luncheon for Dona Ernestina, his sainted wife. He filled his glass again with the heavy Portuguese red wine. He'd had two kegs brought from Ilhéus, keeping in mind that lunch, which he didn't want to be only generous and appetizing, he wanted it to be an unforgettable feast. After all, wasn't he also celebrating the presence of his son, just arrived from Rio de Janeiro?

Being who he was, Colonel Boaventura Andrade, more than just rich—a millionaire, a cacao nabob—had been going around rather dispirited of late, hardly talking or laughing. Rumor had it that the colonel's depression was due to the absence of his only son, the lawyer, who'd continued to linger in the federal capital long after he'd gotten his degree, and that was five long and bitter years ago. He was taking courses and more courses, collecting diplomas, graduating and post-graduating. In what fields, the colonel was unable to guess: unless it was in the art of spending money.

The colonel raised his glass in Natário's direction to toast his old friend, foreman, and hired gun. His right arm, as he'd written on a certain occasion to the judge in Itabuna at the end of the struggles for possession of the woodlands along the Rio das Cobras. He repeated, "You never let me down."

He looked around at the guests, his eyes filled with memories.

"Twice you saved my life. To your health, old friend!"

His face ecstatic, sitting at the opposite end of the table, Natário stood up, lifted his glass—"To yours, Colonel!"—and drank his toast. The silence still lingered because the guests didn't know whether or not their host had finished his harangue.

Politicians, magistrates, lawyers, and the parish priest ate out of the colonel's hand and warmly seconded his praise of the ex-gunman. But only the plantation owners, the colonels, were his equals: they knew the way of things, they knew the exact value of loyalty, the price of life and death, they understood the reasons behind such praise.

3

A LUNCH DOUBLY FESTIVE, they all realized. Celebrating the birthday of the adipose and sainted lady and the presence at the table of the couple's only son, Dr. Boaventura da Costa Andrade Junior—Andrade Filho as the colonel's obstinate nationalism would have it—better known in the faculty and the whorehouses as Venturinha the Voracious. He'd arrived from Rio de Janeiro, where he'd gone for a short pleasure trip after graduation and where he'd stayed for more than five years with rare and quick visits to Ilhéus. A plague, that obsession with living in Rio de Janeiro: boys from southern Bahia lost their heads, abandoned their homes and families as if they had no responsibilities or love for their parents.

Young Medauar, at least, wrote articles and poetry for the papers, a profession of doubtful income but generous in reputation and esteem. *Poems of Love Beloved* was the title of the chapbook that Emílio the Arab carried under his arm to show off in his friends' houses and plantations, on the counter of his store, in bars, in whorehouses. Attorney Andrade, Junior or Filho, hadn't published any book or writ-

ten anything for the newspapers; he was accumulating credits, one after the other: the colonel was getting tired of
brandishing diplomas. They were hanging uselessly on the
walls of the office in Itabuna, where the doors remained
shut, and the rooms bereft of a lawyer's vast and expensive
knowledge.

The colonel didn't even have the spirit to mention in
Ilhéus or Itabuna the new titles garnered by the perpetual
student. Perpetual or chronic? Which of the two adjectives
had the mocking Fuad Karan used to describe Venturinha's
profession? Or had he called it eternal? In front of the
colonel he offered unrestricted praise for the young lawyer's passion at studies; behind his back: laughter, mockery.

Colonel Boaventura had given up the struggle to have
his son by his side, finally realizing old plans, filed-away
ambitions, fulfilling the brilliant fate that he'd dreamed
about and had decided for him. But he hadn't lost hope that
on one of those quick, infrequent visits, by some miracle
from heaven, the wastrel would decide to settle down, take
over the office, and get to work the way he should: Dona
Ernestina, having opened her eyes, made promises to the
saints of her devotion for them to send her boy back home.
The colonel didn't want to die without having admired his
son discoursing in court, acquitting the accused, a master of
eloquence and sarcasm, crushing prosecutors.

Venturinha also raised his glass of wine in the direction
of Natário. He'd gotten rather fat and looked like his mother,
but he imitated his father in his gestures and posture, in his
haughtiness. Glass in hand, he looked at the colonel and at
the half-breed; he, too, wanted to have his say in the
conversation.

"What about your marksmanship, Natário, still first
class?"

That habitual quick and fleeting smile passed over the
half-breed's serene face.

"It's still worth something, Venturinha."

In the silence that followed, the public attorney of
Itabuna, Dr. Flávio Rodrigues de Souza, regained the floor
and returned to his praise of the chitterlings, a dish fit for
the gods.

4

"DO YOU WANT TO sell, old friend? If you do, I'm inter-ested." Colonel Boaventura Andrade was joking after having taken a look at Boa Vista Plantation from end to end, admir-ing the groves, the new plantings, cacao trees in healthy growth. Only on Atalaia could one have seen work like that, a plantation so well cared for.

As soon as Venturinha had gone back to Rio de Janeiro— repeating his tired old line: *When the course is finished I'll come back for good, the reason I'm taking so long is for training, I'm not wasting time or throwing money away, don't be upset*—the colonel decided to join Natário for the custom-ary indispensable inspection: anyone who doesn't take per-sonal care of his possessions doesn't deserve to have them, let alone complain. The long ride, begun before dawn, stop-ping from grove to grove, served to gladden his heart, take his son's absence off his mind, ease the poisoned barb tear-ing at his breast. It had also served once more to prove the competence and loyalty of his administrator. Praise wasn't enough: Natário deserved esteem and gratitude. That's why the colonel, instead of going back to the big house, declared, "I want to see your groves, too, *compadre*, and the house you've built for you and your wife in that place: what's it called?"

"Tocaia Grande, Colonel."

Colonel Boaventura Andrade stretched his gaze over the cacao groves, recalling other times, other rides with Natário.

"I've heard of the name. Once in a while I hear it from a drover. An ugly name for such a nice spot."

"That it is, Colonel. But it's too late to change it."

"Everything in life has got its reasons and no one has the right to make changes, Natário. It's like a nickname: once it sticks, there's no way to get rid of it."

Going into the grove, taken by the vigor of the cacao trees blooming in the shadow of the gigantic forest trees, the plantation owner remarked, "There's no prettier sight in the world, Natário, then a cacao tree loaded down like that one." He was pointing to the tree in front of him, trunk and branches covered with fruit that were ripening in all shades of yellow, lighting up the shadows. "The only thing you can compare it to is a beautiful young woman. Two things to lighten up the heart of an old critter like me."

A beautiful young woman like the daughter of the late Tiburcinho and Dona Efigênia, the captain reflected, following the wandering gaze of the colonel. He dropped the name of the coveted girl in the midst of the golden light of the cool of the woods.

"Speaking of pretty girls, Colonel, have you noticed Sacramento, the daughter of the late Tiburcinho?"

The colonel shuddered. The half-breed was reading his thoughts; he'd done it before, more than once. People with Indian blood have a pact with the devil.

"Yes, I've noticed, Natário. What you don't know, *compadre*, you seem to divine."

5

IN ORDER TO CONSOLE himself, to forget about the absence of his son, the colonel had needed something more than inspecting groves and installations: the troughs, the hothouses, the tubs.

In idle moments, with Father Afonso in the sacristy of the church or with the medium Zorávia in the Faith and Charity Spiritualist tent, Dona Ernestina, bathed in tears, spoke about her son's ingratitude: some baser spirit must have entered him. The colonel didn't mention ingratitude, he was always prudent in his use of words: when people said *ambush*, he said *reply*, and the bloody battle for possession of the land, the conflicts and combats, the shootings between gunmen, the deaths—oh, so many!—had been reduced in his words to a series of political inconveniences. When some intimate and trusted friend mentioned Venturinha's long delay in Rio de Janeiro, the colonel would explain, shrugging his shoulders in the gesture of one who gave little importance to the matter: kid stuff. He belittled the delay before they could label it irresponsibility or laziness. He didn't complain, he avoided the subject, locked the bitterness in the depths of his heart. But Natário knew him

like the back of his hand and knew that the silence was as
painful as the excuse: kid stuff.

Dona Ernestina, completely immersed in religion and
indolence—in order to suppress her nostalgia for the mad-
cap, she stuffed herself with sweets and chocolates—was
getting old, fat, and chaste. The debaucheries in bed that
she'd given herself over to with her husband were not to be
remembered—debaucheries in her opinion only; because the
couple never went beyond the modest positions proper for
procreation. She'd fulfilled the duties of a wife, had conceived and given birth to a son. In hopes of having a girl and
in that way rounding out the pair, she'd still accepted the
colonel's visitations for a few years, although more grudgingly every time. She did it for the girl who didn't arrive,
and for no other reason: like the great majority of her married friends and acquaintances, all ladies as sainted as herself, she'd never known, nor had ever heard of the meaning
of the word *orgasm*, or what it was to moan with pleasure in
the arms of her partner. Some few shameless creatures, of
course, carried on in the marriage bed like whores in a
brothel, with no sense of shame, staining the nobility of
matrimony and the sublime status of mother of a family. So
few of them and so unworthy. For the base necessities of
men there were more than enough ladies of the evening, the
public and the private ones. Dona Ernestina had known
about the existence of Adriana, the colonel's mistress, for
more than ten years: it didn't upset her. Nor was she offended by her husband's lack of interest in herself: it had
been ages since he'd been in her; since he'd left her in peace.
Thank God.

Just as well that the sainted lady thought that way,
because with religion and dainties—saints, spirits, chocolates, eggnogs, eggcreams, coconut sweets—Dona Ernestina
had become a fat bystander while the colonel, due to his
age, was becoming more particular. Adriana herself already
seemed less appetizing to him, warmed-over food, stale bread.
The relationship had passed a decade: Adriana had lost her
lust and allure. She complained about her intestines, suffered from flatulence, had headaches, sulked easily, spent
day and night in spiritualist sessions: she was a second wife,
a copy of the first, only less obese, and younger. Young to a
degree: she'd already passed thirty, she no longer had the
bloom or grace of the teenager she'd been when the colonel
met her and fell in love. For an old Jack, a young Jenny.

6

SACRAMENTO STOOD OUT SO much from the circle of women who were swinging knives and cutting cacao shells in the groves that no hired hand, woodman, or trooper had ever dared try anything with her.

Not that she was proud or conceited, but rather reserved and serious; she was already fifteen and, all in all, seemed in no hurry to leave the adobe hut, where she lived with her mother, to join up with a man. Who hadn't looked at her with lust, watching her pass, modest but graceful, fresh as spring, the shape of her body barely hidden by her chintz dress? From Espiridião, an old black man with matted white hair—a trustworthy hand, whose only duties consisted of accompanying the colonel on the road and sleeping in the big house, blunderbuss at his side—to young drovers' helpers, used to satisfying themselves with donkeys and mules, high-haunched mares. Sacramento's high haunches, what a mare, that one!

Venturinha himself had spotted her during the few days he'd been on the plantation and had pointed her out to Natário while, beside the troughs, they gabbed animatedly about the young man's amorous adventures: he liked to boast about his conquests, Natário liked to listen. In the trough, Sacramento was dancing on the soft cacao, the honey dance, to clean off the shells, leave them ready for drying in the tubs and hothouses. The honey was running through the grates in the trough. The hem of Sacramento's dress was held up to her waist, her thighs showing, her hips moving in a light, quick step.

> I'm the color of dry cacao
> I'm the honey soft cacao . . .

"A nice one! Take a look, Natário. She deserves—"

"She doesn't deserve anything, Venturinha. Don't get involved, she's got somebody."

"Are you nibbling at that chicken? Congratulations."

"I wish I were." With a nod of his head he pointed to the big house.

"The Old Man?"

Venturinha laughed: standing on the veranda, the colonel watched the trough where two women, mother and daughter, were working: Dona Efigênia and Sacramento. Natário changed the subject.

"Forget it. So, tell me who it was you finally gave that bauble to, the one you bought from Turk Fadul."

"Gave it to a young German girl, a dancer named Kath. A good deal, Natário, a chili pepper. A married girl, to top it off."

On his last trip Venturinha had told how, when he got back to Rio the time he bought the reliquary, he'd discovered the sublime Adela, the Argentine tango dancer, "nuts about me, Natário," in bed with a croupier from the casino— the gambling was going on in the rear—a certain Aristides Pif-Paf. Both were so involved in their labors that they didn't see him come into the room. Did Natário remember that whip he'd given him, a strong switch? It came in quite handy: he lashed the bastard's face and left the bitch's bottom in shreds. . . .

"You mean you've got a German girl now? You really like your foreigners. . . ."

The German belonged to the past too. She didn't last long: she left for other parts, for other tours, with her husband. At the moment Venturinha was involved with another dancer, but this one was a Spaniard, "the prettiest thing in the world, Natário."

"Have you heard of a dance called the flamenco, done with castanets?"

The foreign term didn't ring a bell for Natário. But once he'd been to a circus in Itabuna, where a woman played castanets while dancing. The dancer wore a tight dress with a long skirt, she looked like a Gypsy, maybe she was Spanish. To make it clear, Venturinha spun his fat, heavy body in a fandango, imitating the rhythm and sound of the castanets with his hands and his mouth.

"It was something like that," Natário recognized.

Venturinha stopped his demonstration, confided, "Crazy jealous, it's scary. I can't even look at another woman, she goes wild, threatens to kill me, she's already made scenes. A Spanish woman is capable of anything when she's in love." Delighted, self-satisfied, proud of himself, the same happy laugh as that of the boy who used to go to the whorehouses of Taquaras and Itabuna, always bragging about his kept woman. "Do you know what her name is? Just imagine: she's called Remédios."

"Remédios? Cures? You learn something new every day! Remédios! That's really her name?"

Off went Venturinha to Rio de Janeiro to chase after his Spanish rose, leaving the colonel sad, indifferent to his cacao groves, unable to lift his head and hold it high. There was nothing that could get the colonel laughing again.

"What you need, Colonel, is to bring somebody into the big house to help Dona Pequena do the sweeping and light the stove. Dona Pequena's getting too old to do things like that all by herself." He didn't say any more; it wasn't necessary.

"You always give me good advice, Natário."

7

BEFORE DISMOUNTING BESIDE THE hitching post next to Fadul Abdala's store, Colonel Boaventura Andrade asked Natário, "How many years has it been, Natário?"

"Seven already, Colonel."

"It used to be a deserted place, as I remember it. I also remember what you said: this here is going to be a town someday. It isn't there yet, but it won't be long."

Standing in front of the door of the store, the colonel took in the view. On the other side of the river the planted fields stretched on as far as the eye could see.

"Nice-looking cornfields. Sergipeans?"

Natário filled him in.

"Most of them. But there are people from the backlands too."

"The other day a family came in from around Buquim," the Turk said. "Five people."

"From Buquim? I come from close by. I come from Estância: a good place to wait to die." How many years had it been since he'd gone back to the town where he was born and had started to work? Since the death of his father, old José Andrade, a solid citizen who brought no trouble home and who played the trombone in the town band, the Lira Estânciana. "Good people in Estância, law-abiding and hardworking. They're not like the people from farther north, from the banks of the São Francisco." He was having fun teasing Natário. "Unruly people, always bragging, isn't that so, Natário?"

The captain didn't react, almost smiling.

"The difference, Colonel, is that in Estância there's only poverty. Along the São Francisco even poverty is a gift, in place of the misery."

"What about your house, Natário? Is that it?" The colonel was pointing at the stone and mortar house of black Tição Abduim.

"No, Colonel. Mine is up on top of that hill. You can see it from here. Unless you want to go up there?"

The colonel raised his eyes to look at the new construction worthy of the owner of Boa Vista Plantation: it dominated the settlement.

"I don't have to go up. I can see it from here. A nice place, yes, sir."

He smiled with affection for his former gunman, his *compadre*: he wanted to give him a present to decorate the newly built residence.

"What about the furniture, Natário, have you bought it yet?"

"Yes, sir. Most of it I had built right here, by Lupiscínio. The rest I got in Itabuna."

The colonel thought, his eyes on Natário's house.

"I noticed that your wife likes music. She's crazy about singing, isn't that so?"

"Too much so."

"Well, then, I'm going to give her a phonograph, just like mine. So she can listen to music whenever she wants to." During the quiet hours on Atalaia, the colonel would relax listening to arias on his phonograph, the latest novelty, a real showpiece, indispensable in affluent homes.

"Thank you, Colonel. Zilda will be thrilled with one."

Fadul repeated his invitation.

"Come in, Colonel, make yourself at home."

The plantation owner went through the door, laid his riding crop on the bar, and took a seat.

"If you want to rest, Colonel, there's a hammock inside. It's a poor man's house, but it's at your disposal."

"I'm fine here, Fadul, I won't be staying long."

The sound of steps outside, someone running. It was a woman with her hair flying, disheveled, an urgent, agitated expression. She came in shouting wildly, without taking a breath or pausing at the entrance of the store:

"Captain Natário! Captain Natário!"

A light mulatto, still young and not worn out, wet with perspiration, her large, pointed breasts pushing through the ragged blouse, the wild eyes of someone who's just witnessed an important event, the woman was panting from her running. Natário stepped forward.

"What is it, Ressu?"

"Dona Coroca sent me to tell you that Bernarda's had a boy. Just now." She took a breath and smiled with her white teeth and pomegranate lips. "She said for you not to worry, everything went fine."

Her smile grew, filled her whole face.

"I watched him be born!"

Not a muscle moved on Natário's face. It was necessary to know him inside out, backward and forward, to catch a sign of excitement, a show of happiness on the face and in the heart of the half-breed. But Colonel Boaventura Andrade also had the privilege at times of being able to read other people's thoughts.

"Go give your blessing to your son, Natário." He put his hand on his friend's shoulder. "But first let's drink to his health."

"I've got a bottle of arrack, a very good anisette; it came from Itabuna, made by the Farhat sisters. Let me go get it," Fadul offered.

"Later, Turk Fadul. Anisette liquor, that's for foreigners, it doesn't fit. To toast the child give us a shot of *cachaça*. And don't forget the girl here too."

Auspicious and festive sounds came from the Caminho dos Burros: a troop was arriving. Decorations hung from the neck and chest of the lead mule, bells jingling.

Agreements and
Disagreements in Love,
with a Flour Mill
and a Bridge Thrown In

1

IT'S EASY TO SPOT a Turk by just his looks, no matter whether he's Syrian, Arab, or Lebanese. It's all the same race, they're all Turks, recognizable by their hooked noses and curly hair, along with their botched-up language. They eat raw meat ground on a stone pestle. That's what Diva had figured out as she walked with her family toward the stone building that afternoon when the Sergipeans arrived in Tocaia Grande, full of fear and uncertainty.

Instead of a Turk, they came upon a very dark black man hammering iron, naked from the waist up, a greasy peccary pelt around his waist, covering his parts. The surprise had made Diva give out with a child's crazy laugh, answered right off by the blacksmith, who gave in to a deep and captivating chuckle.

When she heard him, Diva controlled herself. She became serious, felt peaceful and trusting. Where had it come from, that peace that marked the end of the journey and the end of injustice, that confidence in the future? Sparks scattered over the forge, the fire rose up in flames. Standing before the anvil, a jolly smile, a good omen, the black man looked like a huge, proud animal, a majestic tree, a happy, transparent creature. Diva laughed again, no longer a child's wild laugh, but the bashful, almost furtive smile of a young woman.

Castor tried to guess her age, couldn't make up his

mind. Slim, her legs spindly, her braids hardened with dust, her uncontained laughter, still a little girl. But under her dress her breasts were boldly showing themselves and on her face her eyes were pensive, fugitive, her smile furtive, her expression thoughtful: all of a sudden she looked older, a full-grown young woman. She might be only thirteen or as much as sixteen or seventeen.

The black man went to Fadul Abdala's house with them, his house of business and of residence. Diva went along beside him, her eyes lowered. Tição's eyes looked straight ahead, frank and bold. Wagging his tail, Poor Soul joined the caravan.

2

SHE'D TURNED FOURTEEN ON the road; if it hadn't been for Vanjé, nobody would have remembered. Only Vanjé, because she was a mother and because she was worried about her young daughter's growth. Scrawny, thin, she had no figure, as if she'd stopped developing: she was late in blooming. Vanjé blamed their tribulations for the girl's ungainly body, her shapeless appearance, her sometimes sad, sometimes slightly crazy behavior. She was still a child; the moons would come and go with no sign of staining, the indication that she was ready for husband and child. Would she always be dry?

On that now-distant afternoon when the family arrived in Tocaia Grande, having been offered food by the local inhabitants, with provisions bought on credit from the Turk, they'd lighted their fire in the clearing to cook a meal. Before eating the meager repast, however, the women went to bathe in the river; they were in need of it. Black Tição pointed out the place called the Ladies' Bidet, the name he'd baptized it, a backwater in the middle of the current. Dinorá bathed the child and Diva undid her braids. When the black man saw her coming back, he felt sorry she was so young.

Solicitous and polite, Castor went to his shop to get a piece of salted meat to improve their rations. Then he led

the women to the dwelling that had been built for Epifânia,
where no new whore had yet taken up lodging.

The straw cot, covered by a mat and broad, as was
required by the needs of the trade—the bumping, rolling
and cavorting—had fallen apart in its abandonment. Dinorá
laid the child on the mat, Lia lay down alongside. Agnaldo
gathered some kindling wood, Diva lighted a fire, damp
smoke rose up. Like a thick sheet, the heat enwrapped the
child and the pregnant woman; bedbugs were aroused.

The black man had disappeared, he hadn't even said
good night: Lia was puzzled. But they saw him coming back
right away: he'd gone to the stone and mortar house where
he lived and worked to get a big, ornate hammock, dirty
from use. The hammock where Tição received whores, nestled with his mistresses, Zuleica's and Epifânia's hammock,
to name just two. He himself hung it onto the hooks nailed
in both sides of the shack.

"There's room for you both, it's a hammock for two," he
said, addressing Diva and Dinorá.

Only then did he say good night, after having placed
himself at their disposal. He left in the company of Agnaldo,
preceded by Poor Soul. From the door, an opening poorly
covered by a sheaf of *dendê* palm fronds, Diva watched them
go off: the dog, the brother, and the blacksmith. She stood
for a moment looking at the full moon, motionless over the
river. They'd arrived at last.

3

DINORÁ REJECTED THE HAMMOCK, preferring to stretch out
on the cot alongside Lia, the child between them. With the
heat of their bodies the whimperer fell asleep and his mother
was snoring immediately after, dead tired. Lia's restless,
superficial sleep also calmed down and the pregnant woman
was finally able to forget the weight and volume of her
broad, heavy stomach.

All alone in the hammock, arms and legs curled up,
Diva remained awake, alert to the sounds made in the Baixa

dos Sapos or echoing down from the clearing. Suddenly she heard someone shout the black man's nickname.

"Tição! Hey, Tição."

A drover, no doubt, looking for the services of the shoer of donkeys, who evidently had attended to him, because the call wasn't repeated.

The hammock gave off a strong smell, it must have come from the black man, and it enveloped her. That's where he'd sweated on hot nights in the arms of women, and his masculine smell, his musk, his aroma, had impregnated the cloth. Intoxicating, the heady smell was making her drunk; Diva felt the way she had one past St. John's Night when she drank too much genipap liquor.

She couldn't manage to sink into the depths of sleep, get rid of the memories of the afternoon. At the same time, she wasn't completely awake; she was rocking in the sway of the hammock, caught up in the poison of that smell, which she'd already caught before in the smithy when Tição had burst out into laughter standing over his anvil. In the hammock, powerful and persistent, it seeped in through her nose, penetrating her pores, spreading out under her skin, hardening the nipples of her little breasts, running down her hips and stomach and coming to burn the virgin lips of her treasure. She felt Castor's body swaying in the hammock, the peccary skin covering and revealing his parts. With his powerful arms he was grabbing her and crushing her against his chest.

Finally sleep came over her, but Diva didn't sleep peacefully; she slept with the black man until morning. Except that he wasn't black. Not black or white, or brown, or Indian, or half-breed: he was shining, and a flame glowed between his legs. For a good part of the vision, which was long and uneven, Castor appeared as a huge peccary: he would have been a wild boar if Diva had known what a wild boar was. He was leading her across the valley, flying over hills and river, landing on the full moon. Cornering her in a part of the smithy under a storm of sparks, he mounted her. Diva felt herself flowing, melting into lava.

When she awoke with the crying of her nephew and the noise of mule trains moving along as they left, blood was flowing from the mouth of her body, dark and thick, running down her thighs. An outpouring she owed to the heavy odor that had penetrated her and had made her a woman.

The red stain on the dirty cloth marked the strange deed of black Castor Abduim da Assunção, Tição by nickname, who, after having shoed two hooves on the donkey Lancelot, had slept the sleep of the just for the whole night. All alone, a rare event.

4

WHEN OFERECIDA CAME TO tease him, leaping about, biting his legs, nipping his snout, Poor Soul would join in the play, chase madly after her, roll over on the ground, lay his paw on her belly to hold her motionless: instincts other than those of the merry play of false anger and threats, foolishness and revelry, never crossed his mind.

Oferecida was growing less playful as she got bigger: she would spend hours sleeping by the heat of the forge next to Poor Soul, snuggle up to him. But she hadn't stopped stirring him up for romps across the clearing, inciting him, challenging him to fights that never went beyond innocent merrymaking.

One day, however, everything changed and for no apparent reason Oferecida avoided her companion. It seemed like yesterday and yet more than half a year had passed since Zilda's first visit to Tocaia Grande. Now, suddenly, Oferecida showed her teeth when she saw Poor Soul approaching to start the daily tourney of play. She barked angrily and bit him when he insisted on starting up their usual innocent romping, capering about the clearing.

For a few instants Poor Soul was bewildered, unable to understand what was going on. And lo, he too was transformed; he ceased being the thoughtless jester. The relationship between them changed completely. She began to run away, as if she were afraid of him, to avoid him as if she disliked him, would even chase him off when he got close. But if she ran away, it was only a little way, if she avoided him, it was only a few seconds, and if she rejected him, she sought him out all the more, looking at him out of the corner of her eye, showing him her rear end.

For a few days Poor Soul hovered about Oferecida, subjecting himself with patient stubbornness to the rejections, the dislike, the refusal, the violence of the bites. Ready to conquer her, and he did. But wasn't that perhaps what the bitch wanted? Oferecida was ceasing her growls, her running away, showing her teeth, she let him bring his snout close, smell her puffy rear, let him use his avid tongue to caress her.

One afternoon on the terrace in front of the smithy, before the gleaming eyes of Nando and Edu, who egged him on, in the presence of black Castor, Turk Fadul, and Coroca, involved in a long, drawn-out conversation, Pour Soul succeeded in thrusting his spike into Oferecida's fertile insides. After the ceremony was over, dog and bitch remained stuck together; Nando wanted to throw cold water on them to undo the knot, but Castor wouldn't allow it: let nature take its course.

5

ONE MIGHT STATE, IN a feeble comparison, that the same thing had happened, the identical quid pro quo, between the blacksmith Castor Abduim da Assunção and Diva, at least as far as the way in which he saw her and treated her for over half a year, until his surprise when, one day just like any other, he suddenly noticed the change in her. *Surprise* isn't strong enough a word to describe such an impact: a revelation.

A day just like any other for the people of the village, not for the astounded shoer of mules. Nor for the girl either, more skittish and impetuous than the bitch Oferecida when she went into heat. Those and other singular things that life holds for us—enigmas, prodigies, miracles—nature takes upon herself to explain and resolve. That was what Castor Abduim himself had taught the hasty Nando: it doesn't hurt to repeat such a wise and sensible dictum.

The one who first noticed Diva's transformation, however, was Bastião da Rosa, a prospering stonemason, a solid citizen, a blue-eyed white man, a rare piece in those parts, highly regarded among women, a lover fought over by whores.

Of the five houses made of tile and brick built along the
Caminho dos Burros, the home of Bastião da Rosa—José
Sebastião da Rosa—was far and away the fanciest and most
comfortable, something easily explained: doing the work
himself, he had taken particular care in the firmness of the
foundation and the perfection of every detail. Blue walls,
pink windows with wooden sills, a gutter for rainwater. And
the luxury of an outhouse in the yard, a deep hole and over
it a wooden box for the afflicted to sit on, just like the
houses in Taquaras and Itabuna. The first latrine in Tocaia
Grande, a comfort soon to be imitated by Castor and Fadul.

Too big a house for a single man, it was murmured in
Tocaia Grande that Bastião da Rosa planned to get married,
raise a family. Rumors circulated about a fiancée acquired
in Itabuna, the town he came from. Back there he'd left a
reputation as a lover boy; a tireless gadabout, he'd destroyed the hearts of many marriageable girls.

But time passed and Bastião da Rosa was still a bachelor; he hadn't even thought about having an affair in spite of
there being no end of offers. Including Maria Beatriz Morgado,
a poor cousin of Dona Carmen Morgado de Assis Godinho
and, therefore, of Colonel Enoch de Assis Godinho—poor, but
noble. Bastião had spent time on Godinho Plantation in
charge of the renovation of the big house, and by the by had
won the heart of Maria Beatriz: the noblewoman was no
longer a virgin, her rich cousin had earlier won the same
heart. If it hadn't been so, the poor cousin, in her thirties
already, a distinct fuzz darkening her upper lip, would have
remained intact for the worms. Infatuated the lady was
ready to abandon the bed and board that her cousins offered
her out of charity—in exchange for which she took charge of
the housekeeping, oversaw the work of the servant girls, and
took care of the children—to go live with Bastião without
even insisting on a marriage license or giving satisfaction to
the prejudices, pride, and other crap of the Morgados and
Godinhos. Bastião da Rosa broke it off, slipped away; he
didn't want his bones bleaching on some crossroads, the
victim of an ambush, thanks to some woman.

He'd crossed the river in the company of Guido, invited
by old Ambrósio and José dos Santos to talk about building
a flour mill. Frequently hired, the same as other master
masons and carpenters, to go off and build improvements on
plantations, Bastião da Rosa didn't spend much time in

Tocaia Grande; it had been months since he'd last seen
Ambrósio's daughter. He remembered the quiet, skinny little black girl, her braids hanging down, playing tag with
the boys, selling things at the market alongside her parents
and brothers. She couldn't be the same one he saw now in
front of him, breasts erect, skirt pulled up, hoeing the ground,
the sweat running down her face: this was one hell of a
woman: young, succulent, and as pretty as, what could she
be compared to? The lushness of verdant manioc.

Ambrósio and José dos Santos detailed the plans for a
flour mill, Lupiscínio listened and discussed them. Bastião
da Rosa made comments, his eyes on the girl bent over the
soil, glowing in the sun, the face of a saint, the body of a
queen: with that one, yes, it would be worth hitching up.

6

IT DIDN'T HAPPEN THAT way with Castor Abduim, not so
suddenly, but in spite of that, the surprise and amazement
were no less. The revelation came a few days after Captain
Natário da Fonseca's family had moved into the residence
built on top of the hill: the finest in Tocaia Grande by its
size, comfort, and location. Carrying a basket on her head,
Diva was climbing up the slope, difficult even though it was
well paved with pebbles. It so happened that on his way to
the river, Castor saw her going up and stopped in amazement: that simply couldn't be Diva, he refused to believe his
own eyes. But it was Diva, yes, it was nobody else: having
paused to adjust her basket, she spotted him down below
watching, open-mouthed: her naked thighs were showing
under her skirt. She smiled and waved to him.

Tição remembered that she used to come running with
Cão and Nando across the clearing to get Edu, take him
away from work, so the four of them could hunt lizards in
the woods, set up snares for birds, carve tops—in his free
hours one of Balbino's pastimes was making tops, which he
supplied to a merchant in the market of Taquaras—or fly
kites made by Merência, each one more colorful and high-
flying.

Nando and Ção would go into the smithy, never Diva. She would stay outside by the door, peeking in. Tição would look at her angelic face, lay down his hammer, invite her in.

"Don't you want to come in, little Diva?"

She shook her head no and, without waiting for the others, would run off as if she were fleeing, afraid: afraid of what, for the love of God? At first he was annoyed, then he stopped noticing: rare was the day when she didn't put in an appearance around the workshop, hiding behind tree trunks, furtive and timid, her arms and legs dirty from tilling the soil.

On a certain morning, very early, going into the woods to get some game as he did on an almost daily basis, Castor spotted her following his tracks, slipping along among the trees. In the river too: he was swimming at the end of the afternoon in the deep water, far away from the shallow part with rapids where the women washed clothes and bathed, when Diva emerged in front of him, almost touching his nude body: a wet piece of cloth left her more naked than dressed. If she hadn't been so young, he wouldn't have resisted. He shouted—*Be careful, little Diva!*—in order to warn her of the dangers of the strong current and to break the spell: the river was the dwelling place of enchanters. It lasted less than a minute, she dove again and was already on her way off: she swam as swift as a fish. Or a mermaid.

Castor would often run into her and say something. Diva would smile, lower her head, run off, but not too far. Dumb and blind, Tição didn't understand the strange behavior, the skittish ways of the child, nor did he perceive the change that had transformed her thin toothpicks into well-turned legs, her budding mounds into appetizing breasts: for him she was still little Diva, with hanging braids, running across the clearing. He didn't notice when she stopped playing tag and abandoned the company of the adolescents, the foolishness of urchins, taking to walking by herself or with her mother and sisters-in-law, or spying on him around the smithy. He hadn't seen her take on body and become a woman.

He noticed the changes and became fully aware of her only when he spotted her climbing the trail to Captain Natário's house. He had a shock, he felt his heart leap. He decided to wait there and confirm the miracle. Diva must have seen him frozen out there, but she pretended she hadn't, she didn't look at him or slow her steps. She stopped farther on, however, turned her head around, and laughed as if she were making fun of him. Explain that, if you can!

Ever since he'd seen her turn her head to look and laugh, he had no other thought and no other desire arose in his breast: without Diva, life wasn't worth anything; it wasn't life. He lost heart, however, when he noticed—and it was easy to see—that Bastião was after her too. Blond beard and mustache, thick, wavy hair, the pink face of a foreigner: a foreigner from Europeland—the stonemason had a clear advantage over him. Since she wasn't French, but was a dark girl from Sergipe, she'd prefer the blue-eyed white man to any tobacco-faced fellow. Only French women, as he knew and had proof, gave proper value to the black race. But, even so, he didn't give up: resigning himself, avoiding battle wasn't his nature, much less in those circumstances where the prize at stake was life itself.

7

WATCHING DURVALINO DRAW WATER from the well for use in the kitchen, Fadul nostalgically remembered Zezinha do Butiá and sighed: both the well and the clerk brought the whore back to him. He was satisfied: the well was most useful and Durvalino had been working behind the counter in the store for more than a year, had shown himself to be most serviceable. And honest, as incredible as that might seem. Zezinha didn't flaunt full breasts or broad hips, known preferences of the Turk in matters of women, but he'd never been so drawn to anyone else. She was more attractive than cacao: her face a jewel, her body a statue, her twat an abyss, her heart overflowing. He sighed again, disconsolate.

He realized that he was thinking about her in terms of the past, as if the whore had kicked the bucket, was dead and buried in Lagarto cemetery, which, happily, wasn't the case. In practice, it didn't make much difference: buried in the cemetery or vegetating at home, only in his dreams or in his thoughts would he find her again, listen to her soft singsong talk inviting him to the joys of bed. *Come, Turk, show me your turtledove, I've forgotten what it's like.* She called him names, took his money, completely entranced him, an angel from heaven, a gift of God. She sang lullabies: *Dove, dovey, lovey-dovey.* Oh, how he missed her!

Fadul had received only one bit of news from her after, afflicted, she'd taken off for Sergipe: a letter delivered by her nephew Durvalino, an adolescent beanpole, pants halfway up his legs, face covered with pimples and moles. A letter with scrawls and erasures, without punctuation, large and irregular writing up and down the page in keeping with the unskilled hand, Fadul deciphered and read it so many times that he almost knew it by heart. He could recite it as if it were poetry or a verse from the Bible: "these bad ritten lines are for to tell You Fadul My Love I never forget you or ever be able to forget You because at nite I dream I'm in bed hugging You and wen I come too my eyes are wet and down there You know where too but somday I coming bak God willing." At the bottom of the page, under her signature: "yourse forever Maria José Batista," she'd placed a number of commas, apostrophes, accent marks, exclamation points, and question marks so he could distribute them in the letter where they belonged.

She referred to her brief stay in Tocaia Grande before traveling: "wen I was there I saw how You nock yourself out working like a mule." That's why she was sending him her nephew Durvalino, the son of her older sister, a tubercular widow "with one foot in the grave," to work for him. Anything he paid him, as small as it might be, would be welcome: "a lot better than starving to death hear." She couldn't help teasing him, however, making fun so she wouldn't lose the habit: "Im not worried, I know that youre not a mean guy and I swear by the kid." Angel from heaven, gift of God!

He took Durvalino on with visible benevolence and secret enthusiasm: Zezinha do Butiá—divine providence—was solving a problem once again. But he didn't let the beanpole see his pleasure, because it isn't only with Gypsies that a citizen has to be prudent in his dealings: with people from Sergipe too. Fuad Karan never tired of saying that Sergipeans were the Arabs of Brazil, and Fuad wasn't in the habit of speaking in vain.

"I really don't need anybody, I can take care of the work

all by myself. But since it's a request from Zezinha, I can't refuse to take you."

He got a good picture of the boy's skills: he could read, write, and do arithmetic, said he was ready for any work, it couldn't be any worse than cutting cane from sunup to sundown.

"Let's see, then. Put your things in the storeroom, spread out a mattress to sleep on, and you can start. We'll talk about pay later. That'll depend on you, not me. If I'm satisfied, you won't be sorry."

Finally he let out the question he'd been holding back in his breast.

"What about Zezinha, how's she doing?"

"As good as God allows," the nephew answered. She wasn't living in Butiá or Lagarto, she was living in Aracaju in a house set up by Dr. Pânfilo Freire: a physician though he didn't practice, he produced brown and refined sugar at Funil mill, distilled *cachaça*, made sugar loaves, was stinking rich and over seventy. Shacking up with a moneybags, a good deal. Fadul didn't want to hear any more details: fiery as she was, Zezinha couldn't be satisfied with the limp dick of an old man.

8

FADUL HAD THE WELL dug behind the house on the advice of Zezinha do Butiá. Given for free on that happy and at the same time sad visit of the whore to Tocaia Grande, keeping a promise made and repeated and to put the bite on him, touch him up. "One of these days, when you least expect, I'll put in an appearance," she'd sworn in Xandu's house in Itabuna. The Turk wasn't buying it: on St. Never's Day, perhaps. But Zezinha's father had kicked the bucket in Lagarto, the victim of malaria or *cachaça*, why look too closely?

In Largarto, the old aunts, the madwomen, the children, didn't know what to do; they needed her to give them some direction in their orphaned state: they called for her presence, the little money sent religiously at the end of every month wasn't enough. Before embarking, she'd come to say good-bye, taking advantage of Zé Raimundo's troop to make the trip, lolling on the back of a donkey with a firm step. She arrived unannounced. Fadul was busy in the store when he heard the drover's shouts announcing, "Mr. Fadu! Mr. Fadu! Come and see the present I've brought you!"

Gay and smiling, Zezinha threw her arms around his neck.

"Didn't I tell you I'd come someday, you no-good Turk?"

Then she wept genuine tears when she told him about the death of her father, a good man who never had any luck. While he was strong he worked the land as a sharecropper, turned to *cachaça* when malaria infected his brain. The family worked by the day on other people's farms, the men cut cane for sugar mills. If it hadn't been for Zezinha's help, they would have starved.

It wasn't a good time for welcomes, the mule trains were arriving, drovers and helpers were coming into the emporium to buy food, the whores were hustling customers and a swig of cane liquor. Zezinha, after putting her tin trunk in the bedroom, came out to help the Turk behind the counter and in that way increased the consumption of liquor— everyone wanted to toast her and the thieving Turk: who wasn't wise to his long-standing and obsessive love?

Quite a bit later she accompanied him to the riverbank, where Fadul had gone to fill a bucket with water for the necessities of the house, even greater that day: Zezinha, owing to her fear of venereal disease, had a mania for cleanliness. The fire lighted in the clearing, the lanterns, a star here and there lighted up the pitch-black night. They were holding hands: Zezinha was so happy, she looked like a virgin strolling with her sweetheart out of sight of the family.

"Why don't you have a well dug to supply water for the house?"

"It'll cost money."

"All the work you have to do costs more. Who ever heard of being so stupid?"

He filled the pail, eager to get back, in a hurry to lay her down on the bed; he'd pursued her there so many times in his dreams, trying to catch her. Wanton and cruel, she would offer herself but not surrender, would flee from his arms, laugh in his face. The day for revenge had arrived; he was going to collect with interest.

"Let's go."

"Not yet."

She pulled him by the arm; they sat down beside the river alongside the Ladies' Bidet, their feet in the water, listening to the croaking frogs. Zezinha laid her hand on the Turk's broad shoulder, put her hand inside his shirt to stroke his hairy chest.

"I didn't want to go away without seeing my Turk."

"And without putting the bite on me, isn't that so?" He was speaking in a joking tone, without any hint of complaint or annoyance.

"I came looking for help, I won't lie to you. But it wasn't just for that I came, God is my witness. You're a blockheaded, ignorant Turk; you think I have no feelings."

Fadul wrapped her in his arms and looked into her eyes: the tears were no longer due to her father's death. They were tears of longing and affection, wept on that night of meeting and parting.

9

ZEZINHA DO BUTIÁ GOT UP at the same time as Fadul Abdala, when the whinnying and braying began to awaken the valley and the drovers went to get their trains together. A night of dreaming, not sleeping, a night of sighs and laughter, painful moans, muffled shrieks, words that were good to say and hear. Fadul suggested she sleep a while longer; already on her feet, she refused.

"I'm going to help you."

She looked at the size of the bed, huge, a touch of reproach in her singsong voice.

"This was where you stuck it in Jussa, wasn't it? The whole afternoon . . . Pushy slut!"

A lot of time had passed, but she still remembered the incident with pain and rancor. The Turk touched her naked body with his enormous hand.

"There's no woman like you. And there never will be."

Zezinha took some dresses out of the trunk, selected the one to wear. To serve *cachaça* behind the bar at that hour of the morning she dressed up as she would have for a party.

She decked herself out as if she were going to Ilhéus and not that asshole of the earth.

When the last train hit the road, the Turk gave the key to the house and the revolver to Coroca, put the pack frames on the two donkeys, and accompanied the whore to the railroad station in Taquaras.

They covered the leagues of the journey in silence. Sad, as if saying good-bye forever. When she got on the train, Zezinha reminded him, poking his chest with her finger.

"Have the well dug, don't forget."

"Thanks for the help." He made an effort to smile. "And for everything else." Losing control of herself, she broke into sobs, loud and mournful.

The Turk put his hand into his pocket, took out a large handkerchief with a faded floral pattern, and passed it to Zezinha, who plunged her face into it, standing in the doorway of the coach.

Fadul tried to speak, couldn't. The train whistled, began to move, and Zezinha do Butiá waved good-bye with the faded floral handkerchief.

10

DURVALINO PROVED TO BE a hard worker, tireless in his chores and absolutely honest: he would set aside a coin now and then to feed his vices, such an insignificant amount that Fadul pretended not to notice. Outside of that he was a skinny and gossipy wiseguy. The butt of nicknames because of his spindly size and his lashing tongue: Grease Pole, Fishing Rod, Tale Bearer, Know-It-All, and You'll See. Those were the main ones; there were others, less ordinary, more poetic: Turk Worm, Whore Crutch, Leftover, Dog Flea.

Nobody in his right mind would have tried to dispute Pedro Gypsy's position as town crier for the events that took place in those wild parts, the vast and turbulent territory of the Rio das Cobras. Pedro Gypsy, in his seven-league boots, covered all roads, carrying the latest information from place to place: who'd died and who'd given birth, a bar that had opened or closed, fights, brawls, gunmen's boasts, invasions of property, the killing of Indians, the sale of farms and plantations, the location of whores, wandering the land with his concertina. He was to be trusted because he wasn't one to make things up, it was only necessary to discount the extent and volume of the stories: in telling the tale he would make it grow, he wove a whole wig out of a single strand of hair.

As for what took place within the confines of Tocaia Grande, no one could beat Durvalino, up on the smallest incident, any argument among whores, a passing disagreement among drovers over the distribution of the roundup, the breakup of an affair: nothing happened in Tocaia Grande that Durvalino didn't know and tell about. Tale Bearer they called him, but to that bearing of tales and the habit of exaggerating—in which he resembled Pedro Gypsy—must be added the mania for foretelling the outcome of every occurrence. No wonder that along with Tale Bearer, they'd also dubbed him You'll See.

A familiar figure in the Baixa dos Sapos, he was constantly getting in over his head as a consequence of his rumors, his they-says, whisperings, and murmurs, but especially because of his conjectures and predictions. He fell into a few scuffles, running away from bad-tempered sluts who considered themselves insulted or libeled by Fishing Rod, although he was generally received with pleasure and curiosity when he would appear in the whore colony with his mysterious air and the usual question: *You know the latest?* They greeted him as Know What? when they saw him appear, long-shanked like a geometry compass and eyes wide open.

Thanks to Durvalino, Fadul was doing fine: he no longer had to get up before the sun to take care of the drovers leaving, he'd turned that unpleasant chore over to his assistant. He could come behind the counter ready to hear, besides the cordial "Good morning, boss," the news, the comments, and the predictions from the clerk, who wouldn't go to the privy, the river, or the stove without getting everything off his chest first.

"You know what's been going on between Tição and Bastião da Rosa over Diva? Everybody knows . . ."

Fadul knew too. Durvalino himself had called his attention to the interest of the two aforementioned in the daughter of Ambrósio and Vanjé, following her in front of everybody.

With such a passion for gambling among the population of Tocaia Grande—the settled and the transitory—it should come as no surprise that bets had already been made on which of the two would win in the tourney of pleasures and courtesies for the conquest of the lovely Sergipean's virginity. That Diva was a virgin there was no doubt, not even Know-It-All himself, with his long adder's tongue, had raised any suspicions regarding that.

"Don't you think Bastião is way ahead? Mr. Tição's got a lot of nerve thinking that Diva is going to prefer an ugly black man, a dolt—just between us—to a white man who even looks like he came from German stock? Mr. Tição's going to get burned, you'll see."

"You think Tição's ugly because he's black, but you're almost as black as he is." Durvalino was even darker than his aunt, a mulatto woman the color of dry cacao. "Color doesn't make a person pretty or ugly; a person can be just as pretty white or black." Lowering his voice, Fadul seemed to be talking to himself. "If Zezinha was white, she wouldn't be as pretty. . . ."

For a fleeting moment he saw her again behind the counter serving *cachaça* to the drovers. Then he finished, adding to the confusion of the tongue wagger.

"Well, I'll bet the money you're stealing from me that Tição's the one who's going to win. . . ."

Durvalino swallowed hard.

"That I'm stealing? You mustn't say a thing like that, not even as a joke. I swear!" Having sworn, he went back to the hot topic. "If you say that Mr. Tição is going to be the winner, who am I to doubt it? Ressu thinks so too; she's crazy about him. You never can tell . . . But you'll see: this fight is going to end up bad, it's going to end up in a brawl. . . . You'll see!"

11

DURVALINO DIDN'T CONTENT HIMSELF with foreseeing an inevitable conflict: he set a time and a place for the face-off. It would certainly take place on a Sunday, during the wingding announced to celebrate the arrival of Lupiscínio's wife, Dona Ester. Prudish, bad-tempered, a mass of faults, she wasn't given to festivities; she didn't even dance. Her main diversions consisted of conversations with neighbors, gabbing about illnesses, and comparing the efficacy of strange medicines and infallible prayers.

For years Dona Ester had refused to live in Tocaia Grande, permitting herself to stay in Taquaras while husband and son labored ceaselessly in those backwaters of the earth. Finally, noticing that Lupiscínio's visits to the station stop were becoming less frequent, sending her as a great favor and via drovers what she needed for expenses, she decided to spend a few days with the ingrate and give her blessing to the lad—a small boy when he'd gone off with his father to learn the carpentry trade. Skillful and hardworking, Zinho wanted to become a cabinetmaker and build furniture like Master Guido did.

"Carpenter, huh! Eat your words, I'm a master cabinetmaker."

Dona Ester wasn't for dances, but there was no reason for the people of the place not to give her a party. Besides, the idea for the party came from black Tição, a devoted organizer of good times, no matter what the nature or objective. Especially on that occasion: he'd take advantage of it to shed light on what was getting more and more obscure for him—which of the two suitors had Diva's preference, if one existed. It was hard to tell, since it was a question of such a moody and whimsical creature: sometimes giving everyone a smile, sometimes heavy with gloom, her face apprehensive, clouded by an angry look. He decided, all by himself, to throw the party when he saw the always welcome figure of Pedro Gypsy appear on the Caminho dos Burros. If it was a matter of having some fun, who could be against it?

12

AT THE TURK'S BAR, Pedro Gypsy learned right off from Durvalino about the stubborn contest between black Tição and blond Bastião da Rosa and about the probable tragic ending foreseen by the ever prophetic You'll See.

Pedro Gypsy had been away from Tocaia Grande for quite a spell, livening up dances for a sacred mission in Lagoa Seca, Corta-Mão, and Itapira: there was a German monk, quite something in his pleas against the pains of hell and his gluttony; there was no meal big enough for him, the only one who could have matched him was Father Afonso, remember him?

A pack of urchins passed by the door at the run, raising dust, at the head of them a girl calling names: sons of bitches, jerks, fairies. Pointing to her, the musician wanted to know who she was.

"Altamirando's daughter, Ção. She's out of her head. She spends her time hanging out with the boys. It won't be long before she's got a fat belly," Fadul predicted.

Pedro Gypsy followed Durvalino's look at the vagrants. The clerk wasn't only passionate for gossiping about what other people did, the accordion king smiled to himself, bemused. The girl, on the way back, turned into the store to escape her followers, stopped beside the Turk, panting. Under the rag she was wearing she showed the ripeness of her adolescent body.

"Don't let them get me, Mr. Fadu. They want to take advantage of me."

Huffing on the outside, Nando, Edu, and his brother Peba, eleven years old, were waiting. Certain that she'd come back out to egg them on after drinking the well water that the Turk Worm was giving her in a glass still dirty from cane liquor. But when she saw Pedro Gypsy, Ção forgot about the games of tag and hide-and-seek, disdained the waiting urchins. In the store she found herself among men, one still younger than the other two, tanned by life. She sat down on the floor, sitting straight up, sticking out her tongue at the boys, and forgot about them. Her legs stretched out, her laugh flooding out of her half-open mouth, happy with the way life was.

"Is there going to be a dance? Dancing is the thing I like most of all."

13

DURVALINO CONTINUED WITH HIS interminable gossip, ana-
lyzing the prospects of the two rivals, making predictions,
not accepting bets for the lack of funds. But he fell quiet,
deaf and dumb, when, by chance, he caught some reference
about who might pick the imperiled flower, all too soon, no
doubt, of crazy Ção. A candidate himself, he preferred not
raising the subject. In that risky business of womankind, he
left the fuss and bother to others, those who took pleasure in
boasting aloud. In his quiet way, without bragging about
his expertise, he went along trying out the best whores, one
today, tomorrow another. In the case of Ção, a nutty virgin,
there were more than enough pretenders, fiery and visible.
In the shadows, Durvalino.

Ção didn't pay any attention to Edu and Nando, much
less Peba; they lacked competence. During breaks in their
games, they didn't go beyond hugs, feels, wrestling: when
they tried to lift up her skirt, Ção would run away. The fact
that they all acted together made any greater consequence
impossible and the urchins, deep down, preferred mares
and mules, the experienced ones, easy to find in the pack
trains that spent the night in Tocaia Grande.

The real pretenders were others, boys who were coming
into adulthood, who'd already been with whores and resorted to mules only on dire occasions. Two of them especially worried Durvalino and interested Ção, who incited
them, the same as she did the clerk. One was the Sergipean
Aurélio, tall, crackbrained, given over lately to learning how
to play the *cavaquinho*. The other was Zinho, a long-time
resident of the place, always neat and clean, well-mannered,
discreet, not much given to mischief. Who would be the
lucky one?

Only God, who'd made her like that, hare-brained, could
say whether or not Ção felt a real attraction for any of them.
What's certain is that she never rejected anyone, not even
the boys. Foolish, ignorant, poorly equipped—they could
beat her in a race only if she let them—the boys, in spite of
everything, helped her pass the time and lighted her fire. As

for the three braggarts who sheep-dogged her and sought to pull her down in the shade of the forest or in hiding places along the river, Zinho, Aurélio, and Durvalino, she kept them in agony, their mouths watering and their rods in their hands. She let herself be touched now by one, now by another, letting them place their thing between her thighs or in the hollow of her behind, bring their hands down from her breasts to her pubic hair, but when they tried to open her legs, she always found means to run away.

If someone could have guessed her thoughts, he would have found out what attraction, what vehement greedy desire she felt not for any particular male, but for a singular species of studs. Neither boys nor fledglings: mature men, strong and virile. Hidden behind the trees, she happened to see Fadul and Castor pissing, appreciated their instruments. For once she was able to compare them: the two were chatting. Mr. Fadu's—my God!—a fright, it looked like a donkey's. Castor's—Ave Maria!—a log sparking in a fire, that's where his nickname came from, it had to be. For them, yes, she'd open her legs, anytime they said so. For the accordion player, too, handsome as the devil himself.

14

IEMANJÁ'S REALM IS THE ocean, the wild salt waters, a world without gates: compared to the sea, the land is insignificant. Castor Abduim, fleeing from the death decreed for him, had sailed off in a sloop from the docks of Bahia. During the night he caught sight of Janaína's hand in the moonlight erasing the trail of his escape. The long tresses of the sea foam in the sway of the waves, the burning eyes in the starry sky and, in the sea's silvery womb, the cortege of the drowned. Bridegrooms she had chosen from among the bravest boatmen, fishermen, sailors. They went with her to their nuptial night in her bed at the bottom of the sea, the lands of Aiocá. Like Janus, Iemanjá has two faces, the face of birth and the profile of death. Castor sailed toward freedom on the water flowing out of her breasts: condemned to death, he had been saved by her: Iemanjá was mother and wife to him.

When he got to Ilhéus, Pai Arolu showed him the beach where Iemanjá had her dwelling, a grotto up above the rocks, washed by the waves. He brought her an *ebó*, a collection of offerings: a bottle of perfume, a bar of soap, a blue kerchief for her hair.

Mistress of the sea, ruler of storms, what had she come to do in the narrow bed of that river of peaceful waters? Black Castor Abduim da Assunção, son of Xangô, part Oxalá and part Oxóssi, was tempering the white metal with fire, with primitive tools, giving shape and life to the siren in the center of the *abebê*. Iemanjá's fan is silver, Oxum's is made of gold, since there was no silver or gold, one was worked in white metal, the other in yellow. The priestesses use them in the feast of the enchanted when they dance in the midst of the people. Tição wanted to put the *abebê* among the fetishes in the *peji*: who knows, placed in the workshop, it might attract Iemanjá from her hiding places and secret caves to pick up the peerless fan and light up dawn and joy in the forge.

Coming from the river, a tributary of her kingdom, Oxum had laid claim there and was sovereign, presiding in the hammock where he slept and dreamed. But Oxum, as we initiates know, *ekedes* or *ogans*, is elegance and seduction, whimsical and proud, lighthearted. She's no use as a spouse, only as a lover, and a lover's time is tumultuous and brief. Eipifânia had gone away, bearing the golden *abedê*. Poor Soul had accompanied her for a way along the road. Now the dog was hanging around Diva when she showed up peeking from behind the trees. He greeted her, wagging his tail, eager for the leftovers she brought him wrapped in manioc leaves.

Iemanjá from Sergipe, mistress of the white salt flats and coconut beaches, sweet Inaê. Mother and wife, made for pregnancy and birth, Iemanjá means fertility and perpetuation. It was she who had begotten the enchanted ones when she gave herself to Aganju at the beginning of beginnings, at the start of the world. He, Castor Abduim da Assunção, had been born the son of slaves and fearless, had made himself a freed man, a black without master or boss; the protégé of Oxalá; he wished for a son, one at least: Poor Soul wasn't enough.

He didn't know what fear was, not even when the *capoeira*

fighters were out looking to kill him on orders from Milord the Baron. He didn't know what cowardice was, showed himself like the sun, impulsive and burning bright. That was what the women proclaimed, taking him to the heart of their tittles and tattles: Castor Abduim, one of a kind.

Contrariwise, in front of Diva, he was a different person, not the same Tição, smiling shoer of donkeys, master blacksmith with a skilled hand, seducer of whores, servant girls, and noblewomen, to whose boldness women surrendered, enchanted, submissive. Victim of her spell, the pampered ebony prince, the seductive burning spark, wandered in a trance. Smitten with the blues, gone were his grace and his drive.

Iemanjá had come out of the sea to change him, to make him fearful and timid, cowardly. Where was the courage to go after her, take her by the wrist and drag her home a captive? Where was his hearty laugh, his frank speech, the sun of his strong face, his large nostrils and thick lips, his valiant eyes? What had happened to black Castor Abduim da Assunção, a victim of melancholy, dragging after a white girl? White? She had long hair and a coffee complexion; on the Santo Amaro Plantation she would have been called a light mulatto, never a white.

The siren was swimming across the waves under a sky full of stars. Castor had still to fashion—his chisel was a simple spike—the waning moon, because the moon rules the sea in the absence of Janaína. The *abebê* where she could see and recognize herself was finally ready.

No, he couldn't go on in such apathy, a weakling, a nincompoop, infatuated, wasting his time in a half-breed love with fleeting glances and insinuated intentions. He had to return to being the willful, proud, and haughty black man he'd been before. It wasn't just to drag along like that that he'd put the horns on the baron, a plantation owner, with power over life and death, that he'd prevailed in Madame's bed, on the mistress's mattress, and had finally busted his master in the face. It hadn't been to surrender, to kiss the hand of a white girl, a nobody, the one he wanted for mother of his children, grandmother of his grandchildren, mistress of his house. He had to make an offering to Omolu, the old one, also known as Obaluaiê, father of melancholy and smallpox, malaria and fevers, to get back his health and his strength. He must also provide food for his patron saints, Xangô, his father, Oxóssi, and Oxalá. In order to rid himself of these blues, this curse, this spell. That's all he asked.

Overseeing the construction of the flour mill, Bastião da Rosa spent the whole day around Diva. Anyone who noticed would have said that he'd become an intimate friend of the family; he flattered the old folks, hung out with Jãozé, Agnaldo, and Aurélio. They often could be seen together at Fadul's bar. A difficult contest, full of gossip—Tição had learned all about the bets and the predictions. For his part, with that stern pride of his, he had no desire to compete, to use cheap wiles, to suck around relatives. He wanted to have her, yes, and forever. But only if she wanted to come to him on her own two feet, if that was what her heart commanded. He wouldn't turn to the enchanted ones to cause her to decide to like him and give herself to him under a spell cast by them. It was up to him, Castor Abduim da Assunção, not to the *orixás*.

Iemanjá was glowing in the *abebê*: staring at the mermaid's tail, he couldn't help but see the buttocks of the girl from Sergipe.

15

AFTER THE DROVERS HAD been taken care of in the middle of the night, Tição went to wake up the birdman Dodô Peroba; he couldn't carry out his mission alone. Poor Soul broke trail through the woods, but Oferecida, pregnant, chose to stay behind by the forge.

The sun still hadn't shown any signs of life when Tição and Dodô returned to the black man's house with the results of the hunting expedition: a big, fat *paca*, it must have weighed a good twenty pounds, two *agoutis*, and a *teju*, downed while they were beating the bush in search of a tortoise for Xangô. They also brought in half a dozen snails, Oxalá's oxen. Dodô Peroba went back to get the birds: he'd left the traps set on hooks in the trees, if he didn't hurry, Edu and Nando would have a celebration at his expense.

While Tição was hunting, Ressu, a cook for *orixás,* had already begun the work of preparing other offerings. The night before, Castor had knocked on the door of Ressu's shack and when the whore answered, in hopes of a trick, he'd greeted her by invoking the saint: *Eparrei!* He called for her services: Ressu belonged to Iansan's horses, initiated while still a young girl in Bahia. Ressu had put the dark green beads around her neck and brought the scimitar and the horsetail *erukerê.*

Having finished the hunt, the black man crossed the river, went to Altamirando's plot: pork was indispensable, Omolu's favorite dish. The backlander had just awakened, was taken by surprise: Tição hunted peccaries, different kinds of wild pig, what did he want with a critter out of the sty? "I need him alive," Tição explained. He'd spent the night checking his traps to no avail.

"Is is a suckling pig you're after. I haven't got a big one. I butchered the last one last Saturday."

It would do: even if it was young and small, a suckling was still a swine. Altamirando would accept no payment: what about the pieces of salted game that Ção brought home, sent as a present by Tição? Not to mention that he still owed him a little money for the machetes, made by the blacksmith on credit.

"Take the piglet, we'll settle later."

On the banks of the river the red sky announced the sun. The drovers were still sleeping.

16

IN ORDER TO AVOID brawls and misbehavior, they began by serving Exu a libation of *cachaça.* There he was in the altar, the little iron Exu, lord of the crossroads, the wily *compadre,* his dick longer than his legs. Going on, in order to prepare the meal, they cut the head off the tortoise—there's no critter harder to kill: in the pot the pieces were still quivering and moving, as if there were still life in them. While she poked the fire, without turning around, Ressu asked, "A love offering? I never saw one so big."

"For health, not love."

"Why? Are you sick? Since when?"

"Love is a sickness, too, except it doesn't show. Just the same, it weakens anyone, worse than the blues. A real pain, do you know what it's like?"

"How could I help but not? I've had it and good. It feels like the evil eye, but it's worse: a person loses any will to live."

Even so, her curiosity wasn't satisfied.

"The pig is for Omolu, that's for sure. But why all these other animals?"

"An obligation I've been owing the saints for some time. I think that's why I've been so weak."

"Weak? You?" She laughed scoffingly.

Tição hurried her up.

"Let's go, before dawn breaks."

She fanned the fire under the tin cans and the pots: tortoise meat takes a long time to cook. She joined Tição and they went to the back of the house, he carried a long knife and a gourd made out of a coconut shell. Ressu held the suckling pig's legs; Tição bled him. When the blood spurted out, red and hot, the black man put his mouth to the neck of the animal and sucked in life with eagerness and faith. Then it was Ressu's turn. Finally they filled the gourd for their offering to the saints.

They sang the chants for Omolu. They clapped their hands in the rhythm of the *opanijé*, danced the dance of the *orixá*: those of the sick, hunched over, bent, eaten by smallpox; those of the curer, saving the people from the plague and the evil eye, defeating death. Tição, touching the ground with his head, made his greeting and offered the sacrifice, the offering of blood, begging for the strength to conquer the shock and the spell that had been sealing his lips and binding his hands, suffocating him.

Then came the crack of lightning and the roll of thunder, the growl of the panther and the black leopard. The stars that had gone out flashed again in a red sky, the color of blood. Iansan arrived on a black cloud, mounted on her horse, gripped her saber and her *erukerê*, gave the war cry, danced the dance of combat and victory, clasped Tição to her breast, expelled the demons that surrounded him, cleansed his body of curses. A split second, no more: then Ressu put her slippers back on.

The spell broken, defended on the seven sides dictated by his faith, Castor Abduim could now move on.

17

BLOODY FROM HEAD TO toe, they went to bathe in the river, carrying a chunk of soap. On the way, Ressu said, "They're saying around that Bastião is fixing up his house for a party."

"What party?"

"I mean . . . for the day she decides to go live with him. But the way I see it, he's going to get the brush-off. Specially now, because—" Ressu had faith in the power of the Enchanted Ones, in the strength of the offerings.

They washed themselves with the soap, cleaned the tortoise shell. Tição, thanking her for her help, promised, "I'm going to make it into a cup for you, where you can keep your beads."

They splashed water, dove together, their bodies touched, and, with the sun coming up, they surrendered to the good fun: nobody's made of iron and it takes only a spark to light a fire. Tição, with his thoughts on Diva, he couldn't get her off his mind; Ressu without any hidden thoughts, just for the pleasure of it. It wasn't the first time, it had happened before, except it had been only in the hammock and not there, in the flow of the river.

"Only if she's a fool . . ." Ressu murmured.

They went back to the smithy to salt the meat, set aside pieces for their friends: the Turk, Coroca, Altamirando, old Gerino, and some others: Tição was a born giver of gifts.

"Are you going to take anything to Dona Vanjé?" Ressu chided.

"You can take something if you want. Not me. There are things you can't buy with money or gifts. Love isn't for sale."

From the door of his workshop, when Ressu had left, black Castor Abduim, his old self again, looked over at the opposite bank, where his beloved lived. He'd made up his mind: he'd go meet her with an open heart and, for better or for worse, take her in his arms and carry her to his hammock to show her what a passionate black man is worth. The time had come to put an end to that nebulous infatuation that was getting nowhere, before the blue-eyed white man could take the lead and get the edge on him. *Atotô, Omolu, father of the blues and smallpox, of strength and health, atotô, my father Obaluaiê!*

18

CASTOR ABDUIM WENT OVER to the other side: soon he wouldn't be crossing over on the rocks, wetting his feet in the rapids. Hired by Colonel Robustiano de Araújo, woodsmen were felling trees, sawing up logs that Guido, Lupiscínio, and their helpers would turn into pilings and planks for the projected bridge. The colonel had doubted that the two master carpenters could handle such a big job, had pondered the possibility of sending in competent workers from Itabuna. Lupiscínio, one of the builders of the cacao warehouse and the corral, felt offended by the suggestion: after all, wasn't the colonel more than aware of his skills and competence?

"Put up the money, Colonel, leave the rest to us."

As for the flour mill, its construction was nearly finished. Bastião da Rosa was in charge of two helpers and finishing the walls; Lupiscínio and his son Arturzinho were turning out the grindstones. Women bustled around the site: Vanjé and her daughters-in-law, Dona Clara, Zé dos Santos's wife, and her daughters—the flour mill would stand on the boundary between the lands worked by both families. Altamirando's holdings and crop lands were a ways beyond. But Ção and her mother, Das Dores, came to help too. Ção wanted Zinho to show her how to use a plane; Zinho hoped to teach her the manipulation of a more handy instrument. The women carted stones, prepared meals, traded comments and smiles with the men. Castor couldn't spot Diva in the midst of the turmoil; where could she be? She must have been out in the fields. The black man sat down on the ground, greeted the gathering.

" 'Afternoon everybody."

Old Vanjé came over.

"Good afternoon to you in God's name, Mr. Tição. Ressu brought us a quarter of a paca, said you'd caught it. May God give you back double." She pointed to the building. "See? It won't be long before we'll be making flour and won't have to bring it in from elsewhere anymore. With the first batch I'm going to send you some tapioca cakes."

Bastião da Rosa, hands and chest caked with lime, also came over to chat.

"The first stone and mortar house I built here was yours, remember? I've built houses of tile, wood, adobe, and even straw in this place. I've built troughs, hothouses, corrals— the devil only knows what. People in these parts have got to know a little of everything, just one trade isn't enough. When I finish this job, I'm going to help with the bridge."

He was a good talker and could take in anyone who was listening, man or woman.

"After the bridge is built, I want to build a new house for Dona Vanjé. Get her out of the hole she's living in. Isn't that so, old friend?"

Both of them laughed at the announcement of the project. Bastião da Rosa pulled Vanjé over to him and gave her a hug.

"Good people, these here, Tição."

A sharper, Bastião da Rosa, wily like nobody else. Blue eyes, blond hair, just like a foreigner. So what? That was hardly reason for Tição to give up, put his tail between his legs and run away.

He was going to ask about Diva, when there she was, almost in front of him, carrying a stone on her head, steadying it with her hands. Sweaty, her face flushed, all the prettier! When she saw Castor, she slowed her pace and smiled. Tição got up with the intention of helping her.

"No, that's okay."

She dropped the stone alongside the construction, wiped the sweat off with the back of her hand, came over to where the black man was.

"You here? What a surprise." She kneeled down beside him.

"I came to see you. I made an *abebê* to give you."

"What's that?"

"It's Iemanjá's fan. Didn't you ever hear of it?"

Never. Her saints were different, the saints of the church, coming from Europe on the prows of the caravels. In Sergipe, on sugar plantations and in the canebrakes, they'd got mixed up with Tição's gods arriving from Africa in the hold of slave ships. Diva knew little about that business and those mysteries.

"A fan . . . I never had one."

A real fan, like the one bejeweled ladies carried with grace and elegance at Sunday mass in Maroim? She'd had straw fans, a lot of them: they were good for cooling her face and for stirring up the fire on the stove.

"Where is it?"

"In the shop. You can come and get it whenever you want."

Diva raised her eyes and looked at the black man, thoughtful.

"You want me to pick it up at the shop?"

"You know, the only time you've been in there was the day you arrived. Never since. People would think you're afraid."

"Afraid of what?" She broke out laughing, the same wild laugh as on the day she'd mistaken black Castor Abduim for the Turk Fadul Abdala. "I'll come pick it up today."

19

AT NIGHTFALL DIVA KEPT her promise. She stopped by the door of the blacksmith shop: the forge was lighted, but not a trace or sign of Castor. She took a step forward, went in, looked around, spotted the *peji*. On that distant afternoon of her arrival she hadn't noticed anything except the black man and his naked torso, the greasy peccary skin slung around his waist.

Four dishes with food, pieces of iron, wood, straw, and metal, fetishes. She stared in fascination. All of a sudden she caught the same strong, penetrating smell that had enveloped her in the hammock on that one and only incompara-

ble night, when beneath the full moon her body had bled.
She knew, even before she saw him, that he'd just come in.
She turned slowly: Castor, all smiles, greeted her.

"The house is yours."

What did he mean by that? Diva didn't ask, where was
her courage? Tição went into a corner, where those strange,
dazzling objects were placed. He bent over reverently; with
the fingertips of his right hand he touched the ground before
lying facedown on the floor and kissing the stone in the
ceremony of the *icá*.

He got up and, taking one of the objects, brand new,
made of tin leaf, gleaming, went over to Diva. She felt
anxious and startled at the same time, enveloped in that
atmosphere of mystery and witchcraft. She held out her
hand with fear, Castor gave her the *abebê*: in the blacksmith's eyes a strong red light glowed, light or flame, a
burning ember. His tone was deep, his voice a muffled
breath of air.

"The siren is Iemanjá, but for me it's you."

Diva caught sight of her face reflected in the metal
mirror. Looking at the figure printed on it, she recognized
herself, or, rather, guessed it was she: the hair, the bust, and
the buttocks. She smiled, lowered her eyes, waited for him
to go on and finally say the long-awaited words.

Silent, he took her by surprise, grasping her and squeezing her hard, almost violently. Instead of opening up into
the affectionate words that she was waiting for and expected to hear, Castor's mouth, in a ferocity of lips, tongue,
and teeth, covered her mouth, smothered it, avid and fierce.
She found him strange and felt a dreadful fear. She stood
there cold and feelingless, dead inside. Instead of love and
tenderness, brutality and force. With a great effort she got
free of him and before the devil could try to take her in his
arms again, beside herself, she slapped his face.

"Can't you control yourself?" she said, and ran out.

Tição was so stunned, foolish, that he let her go on
without saying a word, without doing anything to hold her
back. Nor did he notice, astonished and defeated, that after
going out the door, she stopped a short distance away, and,
for an instant, as long as a lifetime, waited for him. Castor's
smell was filling her breath, impregnating her body, circu-
lating in her veins. But he didn't see her: blind with rage,

paralyzed with frustration, he held his dark hand on his bleeding face.

Only when she got home, trembling and out of control, did Diva realize that she was still holding the metal fan that Castor had molded and carved for her as a present. A weapon that had served her at that fateful moment of the breakup, Iemanjá's *abebê*. Iemanjá has two faces, sailors on the docks of Bahia say: the sweet face of the calm sea, the bitter profile of the storm.

20

IN SPITE OF THE fact that Dona Ester hadn't appeared for the dance in celebration of her welcome presence in Tocaia Grande, the happy idea was crowned with total success. A veteran of the settlement, Pedro Gypsy, king of the accordion, couldn't remember a feast as lively and as well-behaved. For a start, the violent confrontation between Castor Abduim and Bastião da Rosa, foreseen and foretold by Durvalino You'll See, never took place. Castor and Bastião not only chatted pleasantly, but drank together, toasting with Lupiscínio, husband of the guest of honor.

In compensation, the clerk saw his other prediction confirmed: it had become clear and patent to anyone who took the time to observe and decide, which of the pretenders had the preference of Diva. Showing off her recently completed fifteen years, she'd undone her braids and tied up her loose hair with a broad pink ribbon, the same width and color as the one around the waist of her printed cotton dress, a flounced skirt, a lace-trimmed top, lovely.

At Dona Ester's party—"I'm scared to death of those wingdings," Dona Ester had explained when Pedro Gypsy brought news of the invitation. "I won't go even if you drag me"—there was no one livelier than the blacksmith Castor Abduim. He danced without stopping the whole night long, didn't miss a single polka, mazurka, *coco*, schottische, and he topped if off by calling the steps of the quadrille. The other one may have looked like a gringo, but the one who sang out *balancê* and *anavantu* in the foreigners' language was he, Tição, rolling it off his tongue like butter. He'd learned to talk European and show their mannerisms on the feather mattress between Madame La Baronne's satin sheets; she was a real milk-colored white, a real honey-colored blonde.

Tição started off the dance with Zilda, but didn't neglect any of the ladies present, virgins or whores. He spun around the dance floor, deft and tireless, with Merência and with Ressu, with Zé dos Santos's three daughters, with Ção and Bernarda, who wouldn't put her baby down even when she polkaed, with Dinorá and Lia, proper married women, and with all the whores, without exception, no matter who they were. The only one he didn't dance with was Diva, the constant partner of Bastião da Rosa, rarely seen in anyone else's arms, spinning around in her print dress, the pink ribbons around her waist and her hair. Only in the contradance of the quadrille, *anavantu, anarriê,* did Castor touch Diva's hand with the tips of his fingers, without looking at her.

Castor was bursting with energy, laughing and joking, buying people drinks, the duty of the party's host.

"Let's have a good time, Jacinta; life is too short."

Coroca went along with the merriment but refused to believe the black man's affected exuberance.

"You're just dying of contentment, God save you! Why is it that when somebody's in love he's blind and deaf, can't see or hear anything?" She said nothing more and he didn't ask for any further explanation.

The party was catching fire the way Tição wanted it to. Dona Ester's party, with the guest of honor preferring to stay away. But Zinho and Lupiscínio, son and husband, made up for her absence and had a roaring good time. Zinho chasing after Ção, Lupiscínio escorting freckle-faced Nininha, a long-standing affair, with the age and mustiness of marriage. Zinho vied for Ção's attention with Aurélio and Durvalino, who, when he had a chance, left the bar a few minutes. "The thing I like best is dancing," Ção had revealed in Fadul's store, and that's how it was. She didn't warm her chair, went from partner to partner, and she herself went after the men, inviting them unceremoniously. "Take me, let's go," she said when she saw one of her

favorites—Fadul, Castor, Bastião da Rosa, Guido—standing
and having a drink, gabbing. She crossed the dance floor in
the arms of Pedro Gypsy: the accordionist was managing his
instrument with one hand, the other he had around her
waist. Mr. Pedro Gypsy, a handsome devil!

Having left Coroca wiggling her hips with Balbino, Castor went over to the improvised bar where Tale Bearer,
seeing him approach, filled a glass and handed it to him
even before he asked, "I've never seen you so lively, Mr.
Tição . . ." Surprise and amazement were in his voice. The
blacksmith wouldn't give in, he must have been eating his
heart out inside, but he wouldn't show it, as if the setback
hadn't bothered him in the least.

If he heard, Castor Abduim didn't answer or comment.
He downed the drink and asked for another. Durvalino served
him, picked up the money hurriedly; he ran over to where
Ção was, free, incredibly, waiting for an invitation.

"I'm going over there, I'll be right back. . . ."

Tição followed him with his eyes and watched him
come out dancing with Ção, clumsy but animated. Bastião
da Rosa was dancing with Vanjé, the wise devil. That was
when Tição felt a shadow and lifted his eyes to the figure
standing in front of him. Looking at him askance, a sly
smile, a dazzling print dress, Diva cooed a complaint.

"Aren't you going to ask me to dance?"

21

EVEN AFTER THE FLOUR mill was completed and put into
operation, the manioc scraped and pressed, the first batch
roasted, Bastião da Rosa still appeared at lunchtime to
sponge a meal or join the men when, at the end of the day,
they came back from the fields and went to bathe in the
river. He whined in Vanjé's and Ambrósio's ears, glued himself to Diva, asking about her likes and preferences, especially as concerned the necessities of a married couple. When
he wasn't working with the other carpenters on the bridge,
he was renovating his own house to make it more comfort-

able: he finished the whitewashing, dug a well, built a wood-burning stove, Merência's was the only one like it, he swore. Vanjé was invited to give her opinion.

One ash-gray afternoon, under a light, steady rain, coming back with Diva from the Ladies' Bidet, where they'd washed clothes and bathed, Vanjé spoke up in a voice like that of someone unconcerned.

"Mr. Bastião's house is all finished. I went over to have a look, it's very nice."

"So I've heard."

They walked on in silence, the subject seemed closed. But overcoming inhibitions and embarrassment, Vanjé went on.

"Mr. Bastião's a straight young fellow. He spoke to me and Ambrósio."

"About what, Ma?"

She delayed answering, as if it were something difficult to say.

"You'll find out."

They stopped in front of the hut built up on stakes, the pigs rooting about underneath, among the remains of jackfruit and guavas. Vanjé looked on in silence, as if she were remembering and reflecting, the question forgotten. Crying from Lia and Agnaldo's baby came down from up above. She made her decision.

"People can't do things here the same as they did in Maroim. There we'd go to church every Sunday, hear mass and listen to the priest's sermon. If some no-good came to me asking about living with my daughter without any wedding, without a ring, I don't know what I'd have said; it wouldn't have been anything nice. Have you ever thought about it? Jãozé and Agnaldo were both married in the church. Imagine you, being a woman."

She opened her arms to emphasize the thought.

"But who can get married here? There's no priest, no chapel where you can pray. On the other hand, we've got more than enough land, we can't complain. Life's been good to us here, the place is backward, let's admit, but it's a lot better than back there."

She was trying to be objective, to see things as they were. Resigned, she looked at her young daughter, a woman at fifteen, at the age for getting married or living with somebody. If she delayed, she'd end up in prostitution, a lady of the evening. If they'd been in Maroim, she'd have gone to tell the priest, set the date. But they were in Tocaia Grande, with no priest, no church, no nothing. Better shacked up than taking on men in the Baixa dos Sapos, poor thing.

"Bastião wants to hook up with you. He gave me his word that as soon as there's a holy mission in Taquaras, you'll get married, that I don't need to worry. He's got everything in his house, he doesn't need a thing. An iron bed, the big kind, a double bed. He bought it in Itabuna. A mirror on the wall." She repeated it in order to convince her and to convince herself. "Bastião's a straight young fellow."

Diva lowered her eyes, smiled with the corners of her mouth.

"Get married? There's no need, Ma."

Vanjé sighed, surprised or relieved? Her eyes on the shack where they lived one on top of the other, just like the animals in the pigsty. She hadn't finished telling her: Bastião had promised that as soon as the bridge was finished, he'd build them a new house: a good boy, Mr. Bastião da Rosa.

Oh, why didn't God send a holy mission straight to Taquaras? Immediately: it wasn't hard for God Almighty, all He had to do was want it. But God had other things on His mind, busy with the kingdom of heaven and the important people on earth, He couldn't waste His time on the nonsense of some old ninny. Unlike Fadul's God, the good lord of the Maronites, fatherly and intimate, serviceable, Vanjé's God was the Eternal Father, the Supreme Being, King of Kings, all high and remote. Who knows when some monks might get off the train at the Taquaras station, cross in hand, fighting sin, handing out penances, baptizing children, marrying people shacked up together. Vanjé sighed again.

While Vanjé was lost in such melancholy thoughts, Diva had disappeared. No need for marriage, she'd agreed, taking a weight off her mind: imagine if she hadn't accepted! Bastião da Rosa, as proof of his good intentions, had asked the consent of Ambrósio and Vanjé to take Diva to his house on the Caminho dos Burros on Sunday after market. If it had been in Maroim . . . but it wasn't. God's will be done. She sighed again.

The shadows of dusk collected, darkening the river and the fields: night was falling quickly over the valley. Diva came down the rough steps, a bundle in her hand, she came over to Vanjé, motionless in the same place where she'd left her.

"Your blessing, Ma."

"Where are you going?" To Bastião's house, it had to be.

"I'm leaving, Ma."

"Bastião said Sunday, after market. There's no rush."

"I'm going to Tição's house. I'm going to live with him."

22

THE FIRST STARS SHONE pale in the ash-gray sky. In the clearing stood the first mule trains, the men covering heads and cargo with burlap bags. In the drizzle, the bundle with her goods in her hand, Diva crossed the river, heading toward the blacksmith's shop, smithy and dwelling. He certainly didn't have a wood-burning stove; he had a forge and a fireplace where he cooked his food. Mirror, she didn't know. In the bundle she carried the metal fan, she could look at herself in it, it was mirror and portrait, the invention of the black sorcerer. She smiled as she thought about it.

She'd wanted and desired him ever since her arrival in Tocaia Grande, filthy with dust and mud, bone-weary, when she'd first laid eyes on him: the broad, smiling face, the naked torso, the pigskin around his waist, hiding his parts. She had expected to find a Turk; instead, she'd found her man. In the hammock that night, the powerful smell—the odor, the aroma, the stench, the perfume—had invaded her, body and soul, made her a woman: she was his before she even knew the strength and pleasure of his member.

Bastião da Rosa was a good boy, blond and blue-eyed, a gringo and all that, with a house richly set up. But her man, the one that made her blood hot and appeared in her dreams, was black Castor Abduim, shoer of donkeys, better known as

Tição. She was going of her own free will; she was carrying the bundle in her right hand, her heart in her left.

Kneeling down, Tição was holding the mule Lamiré's hoof steady, nailing on the new shoe, hammer in the air. Edu, the apprentice, at his side, was holding out the nails. Diva stopped in front of him and smiled. Castor smiled, too, and if he felt surprised, he didn't show it. They exchanged no words: he brought the hammer down on the nail, the mule didn't feel it. Welcomed by Poor Soul and Oferecida, Diva went through the door into the house, her house.

The fire was glowing in the forge, Diva took the kerosene lamp, lighted up the bedroom, where she'd never been: the mattress on the floor, the hammock hanging from the wall, his clothes in a box. Next to the pants and shirts, Tição's few items of clothing, she arranged her two skirts, a couple of petticoats, her blouses, the flowered dress, her slippers. She put out the lamp, got into the hammock, and lay there. From then on, nobody else, no matter who she was, would occupy it. It had a mistress.

She let herself be enveloped by the smell of her man, softly laughed the wild laugh of their first meeting and felt at peace: tomorrow there would be a second bloodstain, hers as well, on the dirty floral marriage hammock.

THE
VILLAGE

A Parade of Pregnancies, amid the Flux of Critters and Croppers

1

BELLIES STICKING OUT, THE pregnant women proudly paraded about Tocaia Grande: they would give birth when summer arrived, at the end of harvest time. At first only Diva and Abigail, youngest daughter of José dos Santos; later on they were joined by Isaura, eleven months older than her sister, and Dinorá, married to Jãozé. With the arrival of the Estâncians, the procession of pregnant women would nearly double, since three of the women in the clan were heavy; they, too, dropped their loads into the capable hands of Jacinta Coroca.

Dinorá had been reborn the day they first spotted Tocaia Grande and Jãozé touched her tired, dusty face with the fingers of hope. She had arrived half dead, miraculously sustaining the life in that scrawny body of the stunted child who whimpered in her arms, certain that every hope had ended for them on that day of the last judgment when they'd been thrown off their share-cropped plot in Maroim. But when she caught sight of the rich and beautiful valley and felt the unexpected caress, her man's callused, loving hand, she thought that maybe in those virgin lands she could go back to tilling the soil, raising animals, feel her body awaken, warmth in her parts, even become pregnant again: ready once more for work and bed.

That was how it happened; although her pregnancy wasn't that soon. Only after the flour mill had been inaugu-

rated, with the help of his father and brothers, did Jãozé
build their own adobe house, where he settled down with his
wife and son. In the family's house, with two small rooms,
they didn't even try to do it. The same with Lia and Agnaldo;
when their appetite grew demanding, they would take refuge behind the trees, in the woods, or by bends in the river
to moan and sigh, hidden and in haste.

In their hut they finally rediscovered the peace of night,
refuge and privacy, and smiled at each other while the
revived child slept soundly. Then Dinorá got pregnant again.

2

HAVING WHITEWASHED THE CHATEAU—that was what Fadul
had labeled the stonemason's residence, in order to distinguish it from the shacks beside it—touched up the paint on
the front and around the pink windows, dug a well, installed a wood-burning stove, bought a double bed and
mattress in Itabuna, the bed of iron, the mattress of horsehair, the airs of a colonel, all that with the idea of shacking
up with Diva, José Sebastião da Rosa didn't harbor any
jealousy. He got rid of it quickly: crude, angry curses and
short-lived bitter meditations on the nature of female senti-
ments but no show of despair or oaths of vengeance.

The one whom he'd had his sights on and in his head,
whom he'd been fluttering around for months, had preferred hanging up her clothes in the blacksmith's shop,
leaving Durvalino and most of the inhabitants of Tocaia
Grande open-mouthed: what do you know! She wasn't the
only or even perhaps the prettiest girl in town. When he saw
her again at the market, strutting on Tição's arm, he congratulated her and stepped aside.

Let's put aside for a moment the surprise of the makeshift prophets, busy stuffing prognoses and predictions up
their asses, and celebrate once again the merits of Coroca.
At the same time that the busybodies were so astonished—
she jilted Bastião, she preferred the black man, how do you
like that—Coroca commented to Bernarda while helping her
with the child, "Remember what I said. . . . Only a blind
man wouldn't see it."

"Friend, don't put down such people, who can only see with their eyes. You see with your experience, not just with your eyes, Coroca."

Coroca equally foresaw the reaction of the one turned down.

"It won't take him long to get involved with somebody else."

Bastião da Rosa really didn't hesitate. He wasn't going to waste any time, work, or money unhappily licking his wounds. He'd fixed up the house to shelter a woman on a permanent basis, to raise a family; he wasn't going to leave it empty for the snakes and bedbugs. There were others in Tocaia Grande besides Diva, young, pretty, capable of tending the wood-burning stove and the children when they arrived. He didn't have to go far: in the flour mill, grinding manioc, stirring the pot, ready to be grabbed were Zé dos Santos's daughters. Leaving aside Ricardina, the eldest, for being cross-eyed and crazy, he could choose between Isaura and Abigail, both young, well-shaped, and virginal.

A half-breed with straight hair, tall and robust, a man of few words and lots of work, Zé dos Santos left the fate of the girls to Dona Clara. He had enough to do tilling the land. He knew that one day or another the girls would go their way: he was worried most of all about the loss it would mean to the work in the fields. Quite the opposite of what her name implied, Dona Clara was rather dark. Kinky-haired, fat, and affable, a round face still attractive in spite of her age: watchful over the girls' behavior, she never really fretted about them.

She'd brought the same prejudices from Sergipe that had embittered Vanjé so much, but she was adapting without any great difficulty to the realities of southern Bahia, a new and rich land, where other values came to the fore and life had a different price. What really worried her, her greatest fear regarding her daughters, was the risk of falling into prostitution, ending up as open-door whores in the Baixa dos Sapos. That really would have afflicted her. In those ends of the earth, living together was like a blessing from heaven, more secure than marriage in a church.

Bastião hesitated between Isaura and Abigail, but his doubts didn't last long, conquered as he was by Abigail's docility. In that particular she had an advantage over Diva, arrogant and sometimes insolent. In order not to mess up

again, before dealing with Dona Clara and Zé dos Santos,
and hinting at a holy mission and the blessing of a priest, he
spoke to his intended and obtained her consent.

"If that's your pleasure, it's mine too." An innocent
dove with no pretentions.

Before she was sixteen, Abigail's belly had already begun to swell. Bastião was never one to waste time. Nor was
Tição Abduim, let it be perfectly clear, for if Diva had
indeed taken a bit longer to conceive, it was a question of
her period and the moon, not her competence. As for Isaura,
before living with her, young Aurélio had initiated her behind the press in the flour mill. With the addition of the
three from Estância, at every moment and on every corner
of Tocaia Grande one would come upon a pregnant woman,
belly sticking out, announcing an increase in the number of
native-born Tocaians.

3

TOCAIANS? IN ORDER FOR the tale of events, the weave of
problems in Tocaia Grande to have a scholarly touch, it
might be worthwhile making reference, albeit superficial and
swift, to the learned debates that took place regarding the
matter of a proper nomenclature to be given to the natives
of that asshole of the earth, and what babies born there
were to be called. What should the citizens of Tocaia Grande
be named? Tocaians, Tocanians, Tocaia-Granders, or simply Tocaios? Fadul brought the matter up for discussion at
the cabaret in Itabuna, at Fuad Karan's table, and in Ilhéus
at a waterfront bar, tippling with Álvaro Faria. From the
two learned men he heard an opinion that, if not analogous
in form, was identical in content.

"There's no doubt about it," Fuad Karan said in a voice
dampened by arrack, perfumed with anisette. "Anyone born
in Tocaia Grande is a bandit, Grand Turk. And the cruelest
kind, certainly."

Álvaro Faria, enjoying the whiskey of the English, was
no less straightforward and to the point.

"A son of Tocaia Grande could only be a gunslinger,
friend Fadul."

A rotten reputation, unjust and undeserved, the Turk countered. If in all the immense cacao country, in all of southern Bahia, there was really a pacific spot harboring little violence, it was Tocaia Grande, where God's peace reigned supreme. What had happened years ago, giving the place its name, the big ambush, and its sad fame, took place before the beginning, when there wasn't a living soul there. Nonetheless, anyone who first saw the light of day in Tocaia was necessarily born carrying the mark of spilled blood on his back, the memory of violent death.

4

IT'S CERTAIN THAT NO one took Ção's stuffed belly seriously, virgin that she was. It was a reason only for mocking laughs and obscene comments. In her desire to be a mother, the poor thing was sticking clumps of sedge under her dress so people would imagine she was pregnant, expecting a child.

One Sunday she appeared at the market showing a huge and strangely restless stomach. She sat down on the grass and, to the laughter and whoops of those present, gave birth to a piglet and immediately, right there in front of everybody, opened her ragged blouse and tried to give it her breast to suckle, happy with life.

5

ON ARRIVING IN TOCAIA Grande, an ardent young man going on eighteen, ingenuous and eager, Aurélio had turned the heads of a handful of whores: mattresses and hammocks were placed gratis at his disposal.

Charmed, he fooled around, courtesy of the whores, until the day when, having put together the necessary sum, he'd paid for a session with Bernarda. He'd planned to have her for a whole night, but Bernarda was even more difficult since her son had been born, and now she limited the obligations of her trade to screwing on a reduced timetable: between the baby's feedings and never after midnight. Even so, a quick job was sufficient to have left Aurélio enraptured with the whore, spellbound. The others ceased to have any interest at all for him. Ção, who would renew his drive, hadn't appeared in Tocaia Grande yet.

He made life hell for Bernarda, dogged her heels, all that was lacking was for him to commit a robbery in order to get enough money to command her army cot, even for a quick screw. He found out, in conversation during a break in his pursuits, that she liked the sound of the *cavaquinho*: that was enough for him to start lessons on the instrument with one of the men at the cacao warehouse, a fine player. He spent all his free time with the whore, insisted on seeing her, even helped her take care of baby Bernardo: he took his mother's name, since he couldn't have his father's.

When Bernarda, without feeling the least self-conscious, suckled the baby in the doorway of the wooden house, the last feeding of the afternoon—the next four hours would be spent earning her living—Aurélio would become so restless that the whore gave up the habit altogether. The Sergipeans hadn't been in Tocaia Grande for two months, when Aurélio proposed living together with her and went even further: if she so desired, they could leave Tocaia Grande, move to a less backward place, where there was a priest. He was ready to marry her in the first church they found, eager to help bring up her son as if he were his own.

Bernarda listened to the passionate outburst, tried to dissuade the adolescent from crazy ideas like that, foolish plans. But she did it without mocking him, and thanked him for the intention.

"Anyone you ask will tell you why I don't even want to hear such things. . . ."

"So why don't you tell me yourself, with your own mouth?"

"Well, I'll tell you, then: I've got a man and I love him. That's why."

Aurélio wanted details, but Bernarda was silent. The rest he found out from third parties: *drop it, boy, leave the girl alone, you're taking a chance on getting into trouble, something bad could happen to you. . . . Captain Natário da*

Fonseca? A tough customer? Less out of fear than from gratitude, Aurélio swallowed his plans, cast off his displeasure—
the hand of the captain had guided the family from Sergipe
to settle down in Tocaia Grande. Youthful temptations,
whims, foolishness: that's how you grow up, through pain
and passion.

He went back to the whores' favors, convalescing. Then
Ção appeared on the scene, completing the cure. Young
Aurélio was seen stalking the nutty girl with the drive that
was peculiar to him, determined to live with her without
worrying about her foolishness. Ção let herself be hauled in,
eager and easy, allowing almost anything, but, at the moment of decision, she'd find an escape. Aurélio was so put off
that he was ready to propose living together with her, to put
an end to that abuse. He attributed the firmness of the
refusal to the girl's fear of being fucked and forgotten, left
alone with no future: he didn't deny her reasons.

One day, when least expected, Ção let herself be possessed. The excitement of victory melted into disappointment when he found out that she wasn't a virgin. Furious,
Aurélio tried to make her say which one of the two, Zinho or
Durvalino, had reached the goal he'd wanted so eagerly. He
got no answer: Ção only laughed and asked for more. By
indirect means he got to know that the boardscraper and
the clerk had suffered identical disappointments, had asked
the same useless question—which of the two?—without getting any answer. In face of which, without any previous
agreement, they all continued laying her in the woods: she
satisfied all three and, laughing, always asked for more.

He'd never laid eyes of interest on Isaura. Zé dos Santos's plots began where Ambrósio's ended, the flour mill
stood on the boundary line. Aurélio saw Isaura daily, but it
was as if he didn't see her at all. At the age of eighteen, in
spite of his haste, Aurélio still hadn't reached the age of
settling down and having a family. At sixteen Isaura was
beginning to exceed the proper time to marry.

At the flour mill, in the midst of the squeezing of the
press, the stirring of the vat, they unexpectedly discovered
each other when their eyes met. Diva and Abigail had both
taken their path, Isaura also wanted to fulfill the destiny
that heaven had assigned her. In the mill, in the vegetable
plots, on the riverbank, they exchanged smiles and words,
and before they realized it, Isaura was pregnant. Aurélio

was going to be a father. As cherries go, hers was hard to get
into and break. Behind the press, with the smell of manioc
shreds, intoxicating.

Ção was puzzled by Aurélio's disappearance, his sudden withdrawal, reducing her evening's delights. The fact
that he was shacking up didn't explain his staying away.
For her married, shacked up, bachelor made no difference,
they were all welcome, independent of their civil status or
age. Nevertheless, she preferred adult men; they were less
foolish, they knew more, they didn't waste time on boring
questions. Adolescent or mature man, hasty or delicate, one
of them, anyone, it didn't matter, would put the seed of a
baby into her belly. A baby to rock in her arms. She longed
to know where Pedro Gypsy might be wandering, handsome
as the devil.

6

A COPIOUS BAND OF animals had moved to Tocaia Grande
along with Zilda. Beside dogs and cats, domestic fowl—
chickens, guinea hens, ducks, and turkeys—the backyard
and front terrace of the house boasted a menagerie of do-
mesticated *currasows* and jacus, a Peba's rhea, a pair of
seriemas, giving off their hoarse cry and killing snakes, and
a hedgehog belonging to Lúcia, the eldest girl. Not to mention parakeets, parrots, and songbirds, their cages hanging
on the veranda and the stoop.

The parrots were three, gaudy and talkative, two of
them relegated to the kitchen and the yard, but the third—a
fidgety and loquacious *maracaña*, possessor of an extensive
pornographic vocabulary—lived loose on the veranda, where
he had his perch, on which he rarely settled: the pet of the
master of the house. The bird answered to the name of
Up-Your-Ass, its favorite expression, which it would repeat
continuously, with or without reason. It would walk back
and forth along the balustrade of the veranda shouting dirty
words, whistling for the dogs, and laughing a shrill and
mocking laugh when it saw them coming in answer to its
call. It would proclaim with pride the title and name of its
master and bosom friend: "Captain Natário da Fonseca!"

The captain would lay it on its back in the palm of his hand and scratch its head and belly. Up-Your-Ass would close its eyes, given over with pleasure. It must have been a female to let itself be handled like that, Zilda declared. Female and faithful, because she allowed only Natário intimacies like that; she would fiercely peck anyone else who tried to please her and would insult him: "Bastard! Son of a bitch! Up your ass!" She almost took black Tição's finger off when he tried to make friends. *Pretty polly, want a cracker?*

The *maracaña*'s foul vocabulary was the result of a long residence in the smoky gaming room of a dive on Mule Alley in Itabuna, the popular House of Clouds. A blend of tavern, where they served *cachaça*, brandy, and rum, and whorehouse—prostitutes working in cubicles on the top floor—and, above all, gambling den, that recreational complex was under the management of Luiz Preto, a champion, sometimes unjustly misunderstood, of dignified idleness. The captain had saved his life on the occasion of a double-or-nothing cut of the cards.

He happened to be in the place at the invitation of a whore he'd known years ago: *It's been a long time, Natário,* the slut had said when they met on the street. Between reminiscences they ended up upstairs at the House of Clouds to celebrate their meeting and relive old times.

Natário was buttoning up his pants, starting to say good-bye, when the noise of chairs and tables being overturned and the enthusiastic shouts of a parrot—*Shitting thief! Faggot!*—reached his ears. The lady, still naked, didn't pay any attention, curses and disorders were quite frequent among the extensive clientele. But since the disturbance went on with threats of death—*I'm going to slit your guts, you bastard!*—and since the captain recognized the voice of Lalau, a gunman who'd been under his orders in the past, a man of courage and true to his word, he got there in time to prevent Luiz Preto's being sent six feet under: Lalau's dagger was gleaming in the smoke-filled room. Once peace was reestablished, chairs and tables back in place, and the gambling going again, Natário lingered to tease the *maracaña* and let out a belly laugh—such a rare thing for him—when he heard the parrot order him: *Up your ass,* while it winked an eye and merrily flapped its green and red wings. Grateful, Luiz Preto had the bird sent to Aunt Senhorinha's boardinghouse, where the captain stayed in Itabuna, a present from someone brought back from the dead.

On Atalaia Plantation, Up-Your-Ass learned to whistle
for the dogs, peep for the hens, imitate the voice of black
Espiridião: *Peace and health, Dona Zilda!* In Tocaia Grande,
Turk Fadul taught her dirty words in Arabic: *Manhúk, ru-h
inták, ibam, charmúta*: the parrot repeated them with the
purest accent of the mountains of Lebanon.

7

COMING FROM ATALAIA, THE colonel had taken the shortcut
and passed through Tocaia Grande to study, with Natário,
where to locate a group of Sergipeans expected in Ilhéus,
coming from Estância, the plantation owner's home territory—
relatives of his, as was discovered later. He took advantage
of the opportunity to ride through the valley: he'd been
there during the last harvest, more than a year before. Even
then the progress of Tocaia Grande had left him impressed,
what would he say now?

The great surprise, however, which brought out the
most enthusiastic remarks, was the work on the bridge,
nearing completion. The size of the undertaking, the quality
and skill of the work, made him marvel. Lupiscínio and
Guido, master carpenters, received the congratulations of
the colonel with modesty and satisfaction. Lupiscínio dis-
closed, without bitterness, "Colonel Robustiano didn't think
we were up to it."

They stopped at Bernarda's house, the colonel wanted
to see the boy who'd been born on the occasion of his last
visit, whom he'd toasted with *cachaça* at Fadul's store. Coroca
brought coffee, Bernarda was all excited showing off the
baby, his father's face.

"Natário's curse," the colonel joked.

They finally went to have a drink at Fadul's store before
lunch.

"What do you think of the place, Colonel?"

"In a few more years it'll be ahead of Taquaras. All
that's needed is for the railroad tracks to reach here."

Stuffed, he left the table, going directly to a hammock
on the veranda to take a nap. Before dozing off, however,

the colonel had a chat with Zilda and gave her the news from Atalaia. Siá Pequena had gotten a helper, the daughter of the late Tiburcinho: do you remember her, *comadre*?

"Sacramento? I remember her well . . . a beautiful girl."

On the colonel's face, weathered by life and time, by bitterness and sorrows, appeared a bashful, almost timid smile.

"Old Siá Pequena can barely walk. The new girl was a gift from heaven, she's a hard worker, no one like her. A good girl, *comadre*. She does a fine job with the house and even takes care of me." Was he talking about her as a servant or a mistress? "Just between you and me, I can tell you that I'm spending more time at Atalaia than in Ilhéus now."

"What about Venturinha? Any news of him?"

The smile left the colonel's face.

"He's still in Rio; I'm beginning to think he's there for good."

"Still studying? He really is funny, I never saw anyone who liked to study so much." Pure words of praise, innocent, with no malice.

"Yes, he is, but it's time he stopped. With too much studying a lawyer can end up a bum."

The nasal shout of the parrot cut off the conversation.

"Son of a bitch! Up your ass!"

The colonel closed his eyes, trying to get the thought of Venturinha drifting about Rio de Janeiro out of his mind. What was the use of worrying? But he did worry, like it or not, that good-for-nothing was still his son, his only one. For his sake he'd worked without rest, day and night. He'd cut down the forest and tamed it, planted leagues of cacao trees. He'd taken up arms, fought, risked his life, ordered people killed and even did it himself. Oh, if it weren't for the girl Sacramento, he would have lost his taste for life completely— money and power aren't everything.

Seeing his eyes closed, Zilda withdrew quietly. The colonel didn't hold her back, he let her leave without picking up the thread of the conversation: he didn't like to talk about his son's absence. Owing, who can say, to his pain with that absence, he was drawn even closer to his old servants, simple people. Siá Pequena, who'd grown old in the big house without a day of rest. Black Espiridião, his trusted guardian angel, with the white kinky hair. When

he'd arrived carrying his blunderbuss, Espiridião was already a middle-aged fellow, and ever since he'd watched
over the big house and the colonel's sleep. Old friends Zilda
and Natário. Natário had ended up being his *compadre* and
a captain because, in addition to his courage and his loyalty, which he shared with Espiridião, he had intelligence,
he knew how to read and write and, above all, he knew how
to command.

Simple, direct folk, the girl Sacramento, too, who never
called him by any familiar term. She always said *colonel,*
sir, but her voice and her ways were a consolation in his
bitterness and despair; she restored his strength and his will
to live. She would scratch him behind the ears, he in the
hammock, she sitting on the floor. She smelled of pitanga
leaves; in bed she would draw him to her breast, laugh and
sigh. Natário's advice, the colonel had followed it. Wise
advice, as always.

8

WHEN THEY SAW THEMSELVES lost and lonesome, reduced
to the money they'd put aside and a little more put up by
Leovigildo Calasans, owner of the sugar mill, Dona Leocádia,
octogenarian, widow, mother, mother-in-law, aunt, and grandmother remembered her relative. In that hour of tribulation
who else could help them but her rich cousin? A cousin
three or four times removed, but not to be dismissed because of that.

Colonel Boaventura Andrade, the last time he'd been in
Estância, a long while before, had recognized and greeted
them at the market, where they displayed and sold the
fruits of their sharecropping. A millionaire, not knowing
what to do with his money, he hadn't spurned them for
their poverty. Sitting on a crate beside Cousin Leocádia, he
stayed to chat, recalling people and events, some funny,
others sad. In addition to being a cousin, Leocádia had been
the lover of the trombonist José de Andrade, the colonel's
father. They'd danced a lot of mazurkas, a lot of schottisches
together at the unforgettable parties given by the Lira
Estânciana band.

"I was almost your mother, Cousin Boaventura."

Touched, the lord from south Bahia opened his wallet and gave her some change for the children. Some change? A fat wad that Leocádia kept for medicine and doctors. When they said good-bye, the colonel offered his services should they need them someday.

"In Ilhéus, I'm at your disposal, anything at all, just write. Just put on the envelope 'Colonel Boaventura Andrade, Ilhéus, State of Bahia,' and the letter will get to me, there's no need for the name of the street, they all know me there."

The story was no different from the others, they always came out the same, with a few variations in details. They'd divided their crops with the landowners, had known prosperous times. Afterward came what we've seen: the land reverted to the owner, sugar cane replaced corn and *manioc*. In Estância there was no way to make a living: no lands to till, no jobs in business, no work to do except as cutters in the canefields of the great sugar plantations.

At a certain point, Estância had come to be a town of importance in the state of Sergipe. Merchandise brought by sea was unloaded at the mouth of the Rio Real, piled up on the Crasto docks. From Estância it went into the backlands, a heavy traffic of mule trains and traveling salesmen. But the railroad tracks that linked Bahia to Sergipe passed far from the town and thus condemned it, if not to death, to decline. The Estâncians were left with no alternative but to leave for the south: the fame of the cacao boom drew the disinherited away. All the more so when they'd lost land, work, and hope.

Then Dona Leocádia remembered the distant millionaire relative. She gathered the clan together, proposed their exodus. They amounted to twenty-three living souls, fathers and mothers, brothers and sisters, aunts and uncles, cousins, all of the same blood: seven women, six men, and ten younger children of different ages.

Dona Leocádia wrote a letter to the colonel recalling their meeting and his promises. "Hasn't he kicked the bucket by now?" asked Vavá, Dona Leocádia's oldest son, in his fifties. If he'd passed away, the news of it would have reached Estância somehow; bad news travels fast, it's never lost or delayed. He won't answer, predicted her son-in-law Amândio, a perennial killjoy.

Not only did he answer, but the fact that he did so by

telegram caused a sensation. They got their things together, boarded a third-class coach for Bahia, where they took the boat to Ilhéus, counting their last pennies. In Ilhéus their cousin would take care of them.

The colonel asked Natário to go meet the Estâncians at the station in Taquaras on their arrival from Ilhéus. After all, they were relatives as well as fellow countrymen, the old woman was going to turn eighty shortly, they deserved more than simple compassion. So Natário took along a docile donkey, gentleness itself, and, to play safe, a hammock and a pole: if the old woman couldn't ride, she could be carried on people's shoulders. He waited for them at the station and led them to Tocaia Grande.

Dona Leocádia didn't look old at all. Thin, wiry, she didn't show her age. Lively and spirited, buzzing with energy, she kept the donkey at the same pace as the fiery mule ridden by her cousin's emissary and she was eager for information.

"Is it an up-to-date place? Does it have a band? What kind of church does it have? Who's the patron saint?"

The thread of a smile crossed Natário's lips.

"There's still no band, but there's plenty of harmonicas and guitars. No church either, but aside from that the place is up-to-date, you'll see, ma'am. As for the patron saint, I have to tell you: if it's got one, it's yours truly, Captain Natário da Fonseca."

9

THE CAGES HANGING FROM the adobe walls of the barbershop were never more than half a dozen. Not counting the *cancã* hawk's, almost always empty because the bird flew around the shack at liberty, catching insects in its long beak. Nor that of the scaled dove. They displayed dazzling birds, especially chosen by Dodô Peroba. What was the explanation for so few, since the birdman brought so many back from the woods each time he set his traps in just the right spots?

Edu and Nando, partners in the business of birds and

small pets, displayed a variety of offerings at the Sunday market to buyers come from the surrounding territory. A songbird makes a house happy, and even the poorest and most desolate home is enriched and beautified with the song and plumage of an oriole, a song thrush, a cardinal, a rice finch, a blackbird, a goldfinch, a seed eater, a siskin: the list is long. As for parakeets and parrots, they make the most intimate, cherished companions.

Not just birds, other creatures too. The widow Natalina owned a honey-colored kinkajou who dozed on the box of her sewing machine, curled up in its long tail. To believe the people, kinkajous, the so-called midnight monkeys, were like the cacao barons: they slept all through the day, spent the night carousing. Whores and children loved to watch the small monkeys cavorting. Merência and Zé Luiz kept a boa constrictor at the brickworks: it was already over seven feet long and still growing. It kept the place free of vermin and drove off poisonous snakes.

Dodô Peroba didn't hunt birds to sell at the market, or just to keep captive in cages, decorating his barbershop—to call the tiny room where he kept the chair made by Lupiscínio a barbershop was bragging that equalled terming the shed a dance hall—but local folks liked to put things that way.

From the abundant harvest of the traps, quite often Dodô wouldn't come back with a single bird. After studying them carefully, subjecting them to curious and strange tests and exercises, Dodô would usually select only a few, based on mysterious conclusions known only to himself. He would free the great majority, if not all of them, and, when he saw them flying happily in their unexpected freedom, he showed such contentment that one could only hit upon an absurd thought: that he kept them prisoner just to have the pleasure of setting them free.

The chosen ones—for their beauty, their singing, their liveliness, who knows?—would go into the cages hanging in the barbershop and would take up the greater part of the birdman's time. Dodô tamed them and with infinite patience and extreme skill taught them to do startling things. With their bills they would move mechanisms made of braided string in their cages, lowering and raising thimbles to fill them in the tin drinking cups, like people drawing water from a well. They would open the lids of wooden boxes to eat their birdseed, open and close the cage door, and so forth and so on, a multitude of skills. Dodô commanded by snapping his fingers.

The birds that Dodô raised and tamed weren't sufficient for the orders and requests coming from plantations, from Taquaras, even from Itabuna. The birdman, however, sent them off against his will, sadly, and only after prolonged negotiations. He wouldn't sell to the first person who came along, to just anybody. First he wanted to know for certain that the buyer really liked birds, wasn't one of those heartless owners of fighting cocks who raised them for the purpose of contests and gambling.

A scaled dove lived in the barbershop that he wouldn't sell for all the gold in the world: it would peck at his toes, alight on his shoulder or on his frizzled head, finding and pulling out the first threads of gray hair with his bill. There was no lack of offers to buy it: he'd already received several and refused them all, losing his temper, awakening from his habitual apathy, if they insisted. How could he live without hearing it continuously repeating the mellow and amusing onomatopeia of its Portuguese name: *fogo-pagou, fogo-pagou,* the fire's out, the fire's out! He could be seen by the door, sitting on a wooden stool, the bird on his head, pecking at his hair.

Well, it so happened one night, when the bustle of drovers was over, when silence came over the clearing, Dodô Peroba awoke from a light sleep surprised to hear the dove making his happy morning announcement: at that hour he should have been sleeping in his cage; the light of dawn still hadn't come up. He got up from his mattress in the dark: the birds were asleep, the call that could still be heard, the insistent summons, wasn't coming from the room. It came from outside: could it be from some lost bird, frightened and half crazy? Who knows, a dove with a damaged wing, unable to fly, pleading for help?

Without making any sound, so as not to disturb the birds, Dodô Peroba slipped out the door. Before he could take two steps he spotted the loony huddled in the drizzle. When she caught sight of him in the darkness, Ção smiled, stood up, and held out her arms.

The Waters of the River Rise and Almost Wipe out Tocaia Grande

1

IN THE TORRENTIAL DOWNPOUR, dripping water, his cape soaking wet, Colonel Robustiano de Araújo dismounted by the door of the shoer of donkeys. He handed the reins to the henchman who was with him, Nazareno, Gerino's younger brother, absolutely trustworthy.

"Wait for me at the warehouse."

In the door, Castor Abduim greeted the plantation owner with excitement.

"Come in, old friend, make yourself to home. Your godson's been born. Come see what a fine mulatto calf he is."

The colonel was also a mulatto. But in those parts the division was between rich and poor: for a plantation owner not to pass as white he had to be coal black, like Colonel José Nique, and make a point of proclaiming his race. *Black Zé Nique! Rich and handsome!*—he would boast from the top of his white horse, cracking his braided silver-handled leather whip. At the beginning of the off-season, Colonel Robustiano would give Father Mariano Bastor, prior of the cathedral of St. George, a donation for the altar of the warrior saint, and an equally liberal gift to Pai Arolu for the *peji* of Oxóssi, lord of nature. Between the two, the saint and the enchanted one, they would keep the rain within reasonable limits so that the blooming of cacao sprouts would proceed normally and the harvest would be even greater. An urgent and necessary promise: the weather was wild at the headwaters of the Rio das Cobras.

The colonel unbuttoned his cape and laid it on the stone next to the forge to dry: *Whorish damned weather, damn it all!*

"I got the message with the good news. I came to pay a call on the little mother. How's she doing?"

"Happy as a lark, smiling all the time."

Living together, Tição and Diva still acted like sweethearts: not even a hint of fights and rows; holding hands, smiling, always together, swapping secrets and kisses; people said they'd been born for each other. He called her black girl, my little black girl, and she called him my whitey. She would rest her head on his broad black chest and he would touch her belly with his open hand, measuring the growth. They were waiting anxiously.

Finally, one dawn, there was a bustle in the blacksmith shop. With the start of the off-season, the coming and going of mule trains carrying dry cacao had lessened. When in the course of the night she began to feel the pains, Tição went out and got the rooster tied with prudent foresight to the guava tree in the yard, sacrificing him to the *orixás*. Only after that did he go to get Coroca.

The female relatives weren't long in following in the midwife's footsteps: Vanjé, Lia, and Dinorá. Dinorá with a huge stomach, bulging so much that it led her to believe the *ibejes* had oiled Jãozé's tool and twins would be born. It did Castor no good to frown, trying to make his presence felt beside the mattress where Diva was suffering. When she stopped moaning, she smiled at him, stoic, as if she were a veteran at bearing children.

"Out!" Coroca ordered, pushing the black man. "Go to your saints." The authority of a midwife, the highest there is.

Sitting by the *peji*, Tição waited, controlling his impatience. Poor Soul and Oferecida stretched out at his feet, restless, too, their snouts sniffing the air, both alert, their eyes on their friend. Something was about to happen, they knew it.

When he heard the cry, Castor leapt up and dashed into the bedroom: Coroca was holding the newborn baby in her hands and exhibiting the small body, dirty with blood, in the light gray glow of daybreak so all could see him: Tição and Diva, Vanjé, Lia and Dinorá, with her big belly. The black man's heart grew in his chest and he felt dampness in his eyes. As far as people knew, he'd never shed tears. Not even when he got the news at the end of winter, after a great delay, of the death of his uncle, Cristóvão Abduim, blacksmith and *alabê*. He'd told Diva, if it's a boy, his name will be Cristóvão, after the uncle who brought me up; if it's a girl, you can give her whatever name you want.

2

ON THE PLANTATIONS THE harvest had come to an end, the drying of the cacao completed. It was a yield beyond all hopes and predictions, twice the one of the year before, thanks to the rich production from the new groves. The colonels' houses were rolling in money, the barons' accounts fattened in the branches of the Bank of Brazil, in Ilhéus, in Itabuna, in the offices of the export firms. In cabarets the plantation owners lavished champagne, presented their mistresses with diamond rings, gold bracelets, pearl necklaces. For a colonel to be really respectable, he had to have, like the president of the Republic, a civil cabinet and a military one: ministering the civil one, an austere and religious wife, queen of the home, devoted to the cares of the family, carrying out the duties of a mother; at the head of the other, a glamorous and chic mistress, dressed to kill, good in bed, jolly company, easy on the eyes, a fine body, an object of envy for all others.

As a measure of the extent of the colonels' outlandish behavior, rumors ran through the streets of the cities, on country roads, how they had lighted cigars with five-hundred-milreis notes. It seems, really, that on a night of some memorable carousing, celebrating the end of the harvest in a cabaret in Ilhéus, Colonel Damásio de Castro, or his son, attorney Zequinha—the versions are contradictory—put a match to a five-hundred-milréis note in order to light Wanda Meow-Meow's cigarette, the supreme homage. He'd lighted not only the tawny Polish girl's cigarette but also his own Suredieck cigar, handmade at the factory in São Félix.

No less bountiful and satisfying was Jacinta Coroca's harvest, a crop of babies. She didn't lose a single one, and instead of seven there'd been nine, one after the other. How could that be, since seven was the number of pregnant women parading around Tocaia Grande in the constant drizzle? Dinorá, in accordance with the predictions of the experts in such things, bore twin girls, with a difference of less than half an hour between the two babies, "two little dolls," the midwife boasted, Marta and Maria, Coroca's first twins. The ninth, besides being the first to be born, was brought into the world by Guaraciaba, wife of Elói Coutinho, from the bay region. It was through them that Castor learned about the death of Uncle Cristóvão Abduim and the devout behavior of Madame la Baronne, now dedicated to affairs of the parish church. More than the years, the tropical sun had aged her, without reducing her appetite one whit, as it continued voracious and unquenchable: in the fervent recital of the *ora pro nobis* she wooed the adolescent altar boys, without distinction as to their color, maintaining, however, a particular weakness for the dark ones, her favorites among the acolytes of God.

3

COLONEL ROBUSTIANO DE ARAÚJO presented Diva with a gift for his godson, a gift worthy of a man who'd harvested over a hundred tons of cacao and had put his brand on so many herds, countless heads of rustic cattle: steers, cows, heifers, bullocks, and two prize Guzerá bulls, bought with gold coins in the backlands of Minas Gerais, sired by the champion imported by the famous breeder Alfredo Machado. A gift in the form of a five-hundred-milreis note, crisp and new.

"Isabel sent this for you to buy some knickknacks for her godson."

A godfather meeting his godson, a happy occasion. Still, Tição noticed a latent apprehension in the tone of the plantation owner, ordinarily chatty and joking. He didn't venture to ask him the cause, but the colonel himself, when he took his leave at the door of the smithy, revealed what it was.

"I'm worried, Tição. Really worried."

"About what, if I can ask, Colonel?"

"It's been raining nonstop at the headwaters of the river, coming down heavier all the time. The river's getting too full. I hope to God nothing comes of it. Just in case, I took the cattle farther inland to that gulley where I keep the calves, you know where."

The rain was washing the valley right there in Tocaia Grande as well, filling the river. The plantation owner and the shoer of donkeys both paused for an instant, examining the sky covered with dark, heavy clouds, listening to the wind whistling through the woods. Colonel Robustiano de Araújo finished his thoughts before going off into the downpour.

"My real fear is for the cacao groves that are blooming: the harvest could be ruined. Let's pray to God the rain stops."

4

MR. CÍCERO MOURA, KNOWN in all of whoredom by the nickname of Dr. Permanganate, short and delicate, the representative of Koifman & Co., one of the main cacao exporting houses, went up and down the Rio das Cobras country riding on Envelope, a slow and steady donkey with a measured, cautious step: on roads through mudholes, gullies, and cliffs, the safety of the rider depended on the quality of the mount.

Not even when going along trails cut through the woods—putting up in the most out of the way places—did he touch his bow tie, his collar, or his stiff cuffs: the tip of a folded handkerchief showed in his jacket pocket, a watch chain hung across his vest, his hair gleamed with all that brilliantine; he was the latest word in fashion and looked as if he were on his way to a formal ball. In a certain way he was, because in the big houses on the plantations, where he stayed whenever he could, his arrival brought a flourish of activity among cooks and maidservants, as he had a taste for a good table and good serving girls. Small and thin, he

would eat his weight at every meal. As for the servants, he
had plenty of reason to prefer them.

Mr. Cícero Moura's best customers were from among the
small plantation owners. Generally in need of cash to take
care of expenses, they couldn't wait to sell when the price
per ton of cacao hit a high, as the large landowners could.
Mr. Cícero Moura bought on speculation at a modest price,
part of the upcoming harvest, paying in advance. On those
lesser plantations he did business and settled accounts sipping coffee or a glass of genipap liqueur; but to bed down,
eat, and spend the night, he preferred the large plantations,
where the fare was first class and the help, the house servants, equally appetizing.

Appetizing, they charmed him with their youth and
their cleanliness. Going to bed with them he felt safe, free of
the danger of any "ugly disease." Venereal ailments—gonorrhea, clap—were rampant in whorehouses in the region,
treated with herbal potions and miracle cures. When he'd
just begun to cover those out of the way places, Mr. Cícero
Moura caught a dose of gonorrhea in a whorehouse in
Taquaras that became a chronic condition and gave him a
rough time. From them on he would carry permanganate
powder on his trips: if he had to settle for a lady of the
evening, he demanded that the slut begin by washing her
parts with a solution of permanganate dissolved in water, a
sine qua non for screwing and payment—he wasn't cheap if
they met his demands. Only as a last resort, however, did he
turn to whores. He felt safer in the arms of maidservants,
since, normally, they'd been deflowered and possessed by
the colonels and consequently must be clean and healthy.
Nor did he eschew their mistresses—he treasured above all
those young and recently deflowered. Mr. Cícero Moura, an
audacious runt, was mad about skirts.

He'd become a popular figure in the districts along the
Rio das Cobras. In his imposing leather briefcase, along
with the notebook containing the number of purchases and
credits, he carried bundles of small colored saints' cards,
which he distributed with equal piety to colonels' ladies,
maidservants on the plantations, and sluts in whorehouses,
a gift always accepted with pleasure.

Every so often Mr. Cícero Moura could be seen dismounting from the donkey Envelope in front of Arab Fadul
Abdala's establishment to swallow a double shot of brandy
and get the latest news about the female population.

"Any new cattle around, friend Fadul? Any calf that's been weaned?"

Beginning his circuit at the start of the off-season and the summer rains, the cacao buyer passed through Tocaia Grande and repeated the usual question. The Turk pointed to the loony standing on the bridge, covered by a burlap bag.

"Somebody popped that girl's cherry and the boys have been laying it to her, including that beanstalk over there." He was referring to Durvalino, washing glasses by the well.

Mr. Cícero Moura still wanted more information about age and circumstances: when had it been, more or less. New like that, her pussy in bloom, not having had time to catch any disease, opening her legs for pleasure, not for money, precisely what he liked. He downed the rest of the brandy, headed toward the bridge, eyes aflame.

5

SERVING THE SCARCE LOCAL *cachaça* to occasional custom-ers, Fadul Abdala was digesting alarming bits of news with his eyes on the leaden sky. Conjectures, predictions, excla-mations of alarm, echoed across the greasy bar. The Turk's heart was tightening too.

Before continuing on to Taquaras in the downpour—it seemed to be the same one that had caught him on his arrival, the cloudbursts poured down so close to one another— Colonel Robustiano de Araújo stopped at the Arab's store to wish him a good day, have a drink as a precaution against a cold, and reaffirm his growing apprehension.

"I'm going to Ilhéus, but I'm coming right back. I haven't seen so much water in over fifteen years. It's no laughing matter."

With the same pressure to get back to the threatened groves, Captain Natário da Fonseca arrived after a pro-longed absence at Boa Vista and Atalaia Plantations, the bearer of bad tidings received from Itabuna. The Rio Cachoeira had overflowed its banks, flooding farms, destroy-ing crops, turning the fields into a vast mud flat and driving

workers off to the settlement at Ferradas. Enormous losses:
the buds of the season had been washed away by the torrent.

Colonel Boaventura Andrade, no less worried, had taken
advantage of the occasion to send Dona Ernestina back to
the comforts of the villa in Ilhéus, but not before the sainted
lady had lighted up the chapel with dozens of candles placed
at St. Joseph's feet, helped by the girl Sacramento, a love of
a girl, dedicated to her employers, serious and diligent. *Docile and warm,* the colonel added to himself, cuddling in
her receptive arms in order to bear up under those new
woes that had been added to his old, heavy afflictions. If St.
Joseph wasn't moved by the candles and promises, if the
flood persisted at the headwaters of the Rio das Cobras,
there, too, as had happened in the valley of the Rio Cachoeira,
the budding would be affected and the harvest in danger.

At the counter, Fadul Abdala listened to the frightening
accounts, the bad omens. All of them, plantation owners,
hired hands, whores—even the accordion player—were fret-
ting over the flowering of the groves, the incipient buds on
the cacao trees, about the blooming and the harvest.

To hear them, one could say that nobody cared about
the fate of living people. They calculated the amount of the
damage caused by the flood on the Rio Cachoeira, but as for
the fate of the refugees—with no place to stay and nothing
to eat, all crowded together in Ferradas—nobody seemed to
feel pity or give a damn. When they finally did ask what was
happening to those poor devils, they learned, more or less
casually, about the outbreak of black pox. Scattered cases of
smallpox were no reason for fear, but when it grew into an
epidemic, death did its own calculating, and the price was
high.

Fadul had almost forgotten the day and the circumstances of his arrival at the port of Ilhéus, an adolescent
recommended to his countryman Emílio Calim, owner of
the Alexandria Bazaar, behind whose counter he suffered
and learned. But one thing he had yet to discover: in his
beloved south Bahian homeland, cacao trees came before
man or woman; they counted above all.

Unexpectedly, Mr. Cícero Moura, who should have been
going from plantation to plantation buying cacao for Koifman
& Co., hitched the donkey Envelope to the post alongside
the store, leaned on the bar, careful not to dirty the sleeves
of his worn jacket, impeccable in spite of the sea of mud.

Fadul began to wonder, because the buyer hadn't asked for any news of women, didn't want to know about any new heifer. His face dark, he didn't hide his worries.

"The situation is getting grim, friend Fadul, nobody wants to do any business. I'm going to wait here until the rain stops."

Fadul was surprised: wait in Tocaia Grande? Dr. Permanganate usually stayed in Taquaras, where he had some distant relations. The Turk didn't ask him for any reasons: behind the counter he would end up knowing the reasons for anything sooner or later without having to show the least curiosity or interest.

6

ACCOMPANIED BY TARCÍSIO, COROCA went to the Estâncians' place on the opposite bank. Crossing the bridge, she noticed the rising of the river; full and turbulent, it gushed along with rage. She spotted clumps of water hyacinths dragged along by the current. A blue flower standing erect between two green leaves kept itself undamaged, fragile, and sovereign in the swirl of waters. The river was a good friend: it gave them fish and prawns, water for all their necessities; they bathed in it, washed clothes, killed time there joking and gabbing, and, on bright nights with a full moon and dark ones with a new moon, infatuated couples used it for wooing and relaxation, diving hand in hand into its tepid waters, moaning in its pools, taking shelter in hiding places among the reeds. It had become an enemy for no good reason, snorting challenges, thundering threats. Coroca reflected but didn't say anything, not wanting to add to the worries of the one who'd come to fetch her.

The young man was walking fast and was tense. It was natural: Zeferina, his wife, had complained about the first contractions, still slight and intermittent. Flustered, he had quickly set out in the downpour for the little wooden house in the Baixa dos Sapos. He wasn't going to wait for the contractions to become stronger or for the patient to begin to break water before running out for the midwife.

"There's no time to lose, Dona Coroca. Let's go!"

Let's go! How many times had Coroca heard that imperative call and obeyed the peremptory summons and left, she, too, in agony? She would control her nerves and her fear, only really getting hold of herself when she reached the place and took command of the battle: she on one side, death on the other. On that particular day the fright, the tightening of her heart, were even greater, because though it wasn't yet three in the afternoon, it seemed that an ominous dusk, long and ugly, had settled over Tocaia Grande.

"Let's go," she agreed with a smile in order to calm Tarcísio down. She protected her head with a sack and off she went to take care of Zeferina's birth. The eighth of the harvest begun with Guaraciaba, the cobbler girl; or the ninth if one bears in mind the fact that Dinorá's were twins.

The gusts of wind threatened to carry off Coroca's wasted body; on the bridge she had to hold on to her companion's arm. With all that rain nobody was setting foot outside his house, but it's not up to the midwife to pick the date of a birth. When Coroca had attended Hilda and relieved her, Dona Leocádia, who understood religious matters, explained that the hour and day are set down in advance on a scroll in heaven. The midwife scoffed at the old woman's superstitions.

"If you mean that when a baby is born before its time it's because the saint made a mistake in counting the moons between the day of the act and the day of the suffering, isn't that it, ma'am?"

Dona Leocádia laughed at Coroca's blasphemy; in addition to being a sinner, she was a heretic: the weather cleared, the work of the birth went well, under the blessing of the Lord.

There was a certain air of expectancy in the village about Zeferina's delivery, even bets had been made on the sex of the baby. In Tocaia Grande, generally anything was a pretext for gambling and raffles—they raffled off cats and dogs, songbirds, carved bird cages, broken clocks, old blunderbusses, God knows what. Four males and four females had been born, it fell to Zeferina to break the tie—the experts laid down their money based on the shape and slope of her belly.

A girl was born a little after nine that night, and Dona Leocádia announced the chosen name: Jacinta.

"Jacinta, oh, don't tell me!"

"Yes, ma'am, the name of the midwife responsible for

the deliveries of three Estância women. Who better deserved it?"

"I don't deserve anything, I don't know what to say, this isn't done." Taken by surprise, Coroca completely lost her composure, and for the first time they saw her blush.

Everything in order, Coroca washed her hands with a piece of coconut soap, another novelty brought by the people from Estância, took a sip of the coffee prepared by Fausta, followed it with a shot of brandy served by Gabriel. She refused any company on the way back—who ever heard of such a thing? Crossing the bridge, she was frightened: the waters, noisy, swift, and rebellious, were engulfing it, running over the boards, uncontainable. She still hadn't reached the door of her house when she heard the deafening roar.

7

THE HEADWATER, FED BY the rain from the deluge, rose at the source of the Rio das Cobras, surged to great heights, and broke. The wave then rolled into the valley, roaring, sweeping everything before it. Held into its banks since time immemorial, the river crashed out of them angrily and its flood inundated Tocaia Grande. A nightmare, Turk Fadul remembered.

In the flooded woods, animals fled in panic, climbing trees, going inland in an exodus where snakes and jaguars, songbirds and monkeys, wild boars, armadillos, and capybaras crowded together, lazy sloths moving from branch to branch. Those who couldn't escape in time fought in vain against the current. Soon the bodies multiplied, floating adrift, wild beasts and domestic animals united by the same fate.

With that roar, whoever was asleep was awakened, those waiting for the worst jumped to their feet, all ran outdoors. The river had gone mad, the mass of water was growing steadily and spreading out, destroying everything in its path. A furious wind joined in, sweeping across Tocaia, as if to wipe out the village once and for all. Shapes could be made out in the darkness, some carrying lamps that blew out immediately, others shouting suggestions, pleas for help, barking orders, who knows what: the gale devoured both words and candlelight. Nothing could be heard except the fearsome roar of the torrent and the funereal groan of the storm.

A man ran by. It was the carpenter Lupiscínio; he was going to station himself by the bridge. Would it be possible to hold it with his hands, defend it with his body? Women poured out of the Baixa dos Sapos, frenzied; people arrived from the Caminho dos Burros; gathering in the clearing in fright and confusion, shouting and weeping. Nobody knew where to go or what to do.

Stronger than the terror and the despair, the thundering voice of the Arab Fadul Abdala rose over the din of the storm and the rage of the waters. Fists raised, he challenged the skies.

8

THE FIRST BUILDING TO collapse and be carried off in the surge of waters, the old straw shed, rotted by time, carried with its ruins the memory of sad and happy times.

In the midst of the broken fronds swept along by the water they recognized the belongings of Mr. Cícero Moura: the celluloid cuffs, the hard collar, the bow tie, the shirt, and the pair of trousers. Where could the cape and the boots, items of greater value, be? And the cacao buyer himself, a distinguished citizen, the representative of Koifman & Co.? If he'd slept in the shed, he must have donned his cape and boots and gone out to witness the disaster.

9

FOLLOWING RIGHT AFTER THE straw shed, rolling along in the murky waters of the river, were the whores' straw shacks, the adobe huts, miserable living quarters. Also, the almost negligible possessions of the rootless women: pallets and mattresses, dirty and torn chintz bedcovers, clay pots, tin cups of various sizes, the trash of penury.

All that was left standing in the whore's hollow was the little wooden house that Captain Natário da Fonseca had had built years back for Coroca and Bernarda. Even so, invaded by the current, articles of clothing and utensils were lost in the sweep of the waters. The kerosene crate, which had served as the baby's cradle, smashed to pieces against a tree in that damnable flood.

No shack was spared, not even the one put up for black Epifânia when she appeared in these parts with her sultry ways, though the men of the place had taken such care with the adobe bricks and the lashing of the poles. It resisted a little longer, but ended up heeling over and breaking up into mud. In two seconds Baixa dos Sapos was finished; only the name remained.

10

WHEN SHE HEARD THAT thunder, Coroca ran to the house, shouting for Bernarda. She didn't wait for her to finish with the customer, but grabbed the child and ran out, splashing in the water, bent over by the wind. As she ran out she shouted to Bernarda, "I'm going to the captain's house, taking Nadinho. Hurry up!"

Bernarda caught up to her at the beginning of the stone steps, panting.

"What kind of rain is this? I've never seen . . ."

Coroca gave her back the baby.

"If it was only just the rain . . . It's the flood, don't you realize?"

"I was busy. Where are you going?"

Coroca turned and Bernarda grabbed her arm: the mud was flowing between their legs, the wind shook them.

"Zeferina gave birth just now, I'm going to see her and the little girl who was born. Help as best I can."

Coroca went down, teetering on the slippery steps, Bernarda continued on up. Edu came to meet her.

"Can I help you? Give me the baby. Ma's expecting you."

"I'm all right. What about you? Where are you going?"

"I'm going to take a donkey and go tell Pa; he's at Atalaia and doesn't know anything."

They heard the noise of the straw shed falling apart. Standing still, they tried to peer into the darkness, but the wind cut them like a knife. Edu slid down the steps.

"Get going!"

Bernarda started climbing again, the baby whimpering at her breast. Zilda's shape stood out on the veranda: she walked quickly over to Bernarda and held out her hands to take the child.

"Give me my baby."

Only then, taking shelter in the house of the godparents, did Bernarda begin to tremble in fear: not because of the dangers of the flood, it wasn't the fear of dying. Much worse: she was afraid of goodness, of life's selflessness. Coroca had given her good advice: when a woman of the streets brings a child into the world, one of the two must be prepared to suffer. Either the child from the shame and neglect of a whorehouse, or the mother, torn apart, her heart cut to pieces.

11

THE EVENTS, LARGE AND small, the latter no less important, had taken place, several at the same time, with the same inexorable rapidity with which the waters spread out and rose, covering the entire valley, reaching out to the hills. A sea, for lack of a better comparison, said old Gerino; he'd never seen the sea, but he knew it was huge.

When they left their dwellings under the impact of the river's drive, slogging through the mud, the inhabitants realized that the water was already halfway up their shins, but they didn't have time to ponder the fact because the water continued climbing up to their thighs, reached their stomachs, engulfed the chests of the tallest, the necks of the shortest. The highest level was measured in the morning in a dim light, as if night were trying to continue on: the flood had touched Fadul's jaw. The people had gone up into the hills, pressing against each other on the stone steps of the slope that led to the captain's house.

After a night of bad dreams came the beginnings of panic: it threatened to spread, was held back only with difficulty. Crazy as bedbugs, the whores ran from the smithy to the store, shouting for Castor and Fadul. Some of the most terrified grew hysterical and announced the end of the world. The rest ran into the clearing, where they saw with their own eyes how the land was being eaten up, the houses on the Caminho dos Burros reduced by half in a matter of minutes. Huts and shacks fell into the torrent, just like rotten fruit falling from a tree. Huts put up in a hurry, provisional shelters for people who'd come without any intention of settling, thinking they'd stay only for the time their business required, but had put down roots and remained. The more solid dwellings stood their ground, those of brick or stone and mortar; inhabited now by waters that flowed in and out of doors and windows, the families driven out.

Astonished, hesitant, perplexed, they surrounded Fadul, not knowing where to turn. There was more than enough to do if they were ready to confront the situation and limit its consequences: they just had to follow the imperative gestures of the Turk, his arms extended. Fadul didn't waver for an instant: he'd just told his God where to go, now he was ready for anything.

The Turk began by picking up his clerk Durvalino and slapping him back to his senses. When he saw Mr. Cícero Moura's clothes floating in the water, Tale Bearer had turned pale and began to shake. His eyes bugging out, pointing to the shirt and pair of pants, he started crying like a newborn babe, close to a seizure, as if the whores weren't enough to handle. Fadul urged him to stop setting a bad example before others imitated him and the panic generalized. The Turk didn't waste any time on speeches and advice, he used the proven remedy: he applied his hand to the base of You Know's ear, a single slap.

"Shape up, you chicken shit!"

In order to bolster the sunken spirits and prevent panic from spreading, Fadul assigned—assigned no, imposed, leaving no alternative—to each one immediate, concrete responsibilities to face and fulfill. As for the people on the other bank, Tição Abduim and Bastião da Rosa, in-laws of the Sergipeans through the bonds of concubinage, would see to them.

12

IT WASN'T LONG BEFORE the captain's house was filling up with people; by morning it was jammed. Even the most discouraged felt secure there, safe from everything and everybody, even the uncontrollable forces of nature, the wrath and punishment of God. Safe by the fact that the house was located high on the hill and that it belonged to Captain Natário da Fonseca.

The newborn babies and new mothers were taken there, along with a whore named Alzira, burning with fever, without the strength to walk, carried on Balbino's back. In the crowded parlor, Nadinho, Bernarda's baby, was attempting his first steps, wobbling on his legs, as the captain's other children ran to hold him up, bursting into laughter. Bernarda had gone down to help, carrying with her that threatening vision of carefree joy.

Diva, too, having turned her baby over to Zilda's care, went down the slope in the rain and the wind, crossed the clearing with the water up to her waist, eager to find out about her kin on the other side of the river. She had to get there, no matter what happened. Confronting the flood, going against her promise to Tição: *You stay with the child, leave the rest to me.*

The little ones on the double bed, the sick woman in Edu's hammock, women weeping, men silent, morose; in that confusion Zilda thought about what she could do to give new courage to the weak and wretched people who were taking refuge in her house. Starting to pray, as Dona Natalina was attempting, was of no use, the melancholy litany served only to increase the distress. Zilda went over to the phonograph, cranked it up, put on a cylinder, and music flowed out, spread and rose up, blanketing the litany, the flood, and the tempest.

13

ONCE THEIR INITIAL FRIGHT had been conquered, the people showed courage, answered calls, lent a hand. In the store some helped Fadul and Durvalino pile the goods on the highest shelves, those close to the ceiling, to save the merchandise. At the warehouse others worked to save the cacao piled up and waiting for the mule trains from Koifman & Co. that were behind schedule.

Pounds and pounds of dried cacao beans were spread on the ground, it required a lot of work. With the help of volunteers, men and women—the women stopped crying, began to banter—Gerino and the two men who guarded the warehouse managed to use the planks left over from the work on the bridge to raise a kind of platform and place on it, out of the water's way, the cacao they were putting into sacks as fast as possible. Even so, part of it was wet and spoiled, losing its classification as superior cacao, dropping down to regular grade. Yet to be decided was who would bear the damages: the colonel or the exporting house? In Ilhéus the plantation owner had alerted Kurt Koifman, the head of the firm: better hurry, because anything might happen in the valley of Tocaia Grande. The rain was threatening the budding of the groves, but the dry cacao stored in warehouses wouldn't be safe if, like the Rio Cachoeira, the Rio das Cobras overflowed.

With startling drive Pedro Gypsy took on the job of recovering the canoe, suddenly necessary in that emergency. Beached on the opposite bank, it would have been natural for the Sergipeans to have taken care of it. But the accordionist wouldn't hear of that and took the job on himself. For a second time Durvalino the clerk began acting strangely, and almost got another cuff. He'd tried to go along with Pedro Gypsy, showing that he, too, had a special interest in the boat. But Fadul grounded him and kept him close at hand, to take and carry out orders.

On instructions from the Turk or by his own initiative, Durvalino, soaking some old rags in pitch and tying them to bamboo poles, managed to make some torches whose flames resisted the wind, allowing people to move about in the darkness. In that way they were able to save some of the animals and possessions endangered by the flood.

Natalina the seamstress who, in order to take shelter in the captain's house, had gone up the slippery steps carrying on her head the Singer machine, her breadwinner, had promised the world and more to St. Mary, Mother of the Afflicted and had begun a litany—with little success, it must be stated. Merência had similarly resorted to her saints, imploring mercy and pity. Not to mention the whores' prayers: due to the weight of their sins, they didn't reach heaven, but fell apart in the floodwaters along with the rotting straw roofs of their shacks.

Godfearing, esteemed on high, Merência won an immediate response to her prayers. In the light of the torch held by Zé Luiz, she saw pass among the debris, curled around a tree trunk floating downriver, the boa constrictor that lived in the brickyard. When she recognized him, Merência ran forward, managed to save him, and put him up onto the branches of the jackfruit tree. Crossing the swirling waters with the snake coiled around her voluminous bust, she had brought on surprise and laughter. In that night of horror, all sorts of things happened in Tocaia Grande. There were good reasons for surprise and laughter, for weeping and despair.

14

DODÔ PEROBA HAD TO stop at the best part of their frolicking, trying to disentangle himself from Ricardina, when he heard the roar of the river, a cannon shot, a deafening, fearsome noise, the sound of death. The wave knocked down the door of the flour mill, covered the embracing bodies, and rolled them along the floor. Dodô managed to stand up, help the terrified Ricardina, and went out to look. The water had invaded the vegetable plots, had eaten up the cornfields.

The cross-eyed girl tried to hold him back, but he pushed her away angrily, brusquely, in contrast to his normally gentle and well-mannered behavior. He ignored the flood, his mind fixed on the songbirds locked in their cages.

"Let go of me."

He got there too late; the barbershop no longer existed, the cages with the birds had sunk. So that the desolation and sadness wouldn't be complete, in order to ease the tears of the trainer of orioles and finches, Guido had saved the bar chair from the waters and, perched on it, the scaled dove. His eyes moist, Dodô picked up the precious bird, and nestled it under his shirt, against his chest, to warm her. He showed interest in the chair, the only piece of his goods that had been saved, only because he couldn't find a trace of the *cancã* hawk, no matter how hard he searched.

15

TIÇÃO ABDUIM AND BASTIÃO da Rosa went down from the captain's house together, having left their wives and the children, Cristóvão and Otília there along with Maria Rosa, the clogmakers' baby, who'd started off the harvest of births at the end of winter. Wooden clogs that now floated adrift like tiny ships before a storm.

Lupiscínio the carpenter was standing guard by the bridge. Zinho had tried in vain to get him to leave, then decided to keep him company. Bastião da Rosa, who'd worked with Guido and Lupiscínio on the difficult undertaking, boasted, "That's what I call a job you should take your hats off to. Hurray for us, Lupiscínio, old friend!"

"It's holding up so far. We'll see what happens next. Where are you people going?"

"To see how the folks on the other side are doing."

"We're going to bring the babies to the captain's house," the black man explained. "Why don't you come with us? You might be needed."

"Let's go, Pa," the boy insisted. "What good is it staying here?"

"None at all, I know. But a thing like this here, that people worked so hard on, that gave them such pride, it's just like a son. While it's in danger, you've got to stay close by. You go along with them."

"I'm not going. I'm staying with you."

The first person they spotted in the flour mill was Coroca. In her dry arms slept the baby she had delivered but a few hours before, the newborn Jacinta. Spread out on the oven lay the other new babies: Dinorá's twins, Hilda's and Fausta's children. Missing was Isaura's, busy suckling at its mother's breast, a dark, full udder: her milk was flowing plentifully. Few men were about: most were off looking for the canoe.

A bevy of restless urchins, kept there with difficulty. A world of silent women. A heavy, sad environment: Bastião da Rosa, trying to lift their spirits, joked, pointing to the babies.

"A fine batch of tapioca cakes."

Except for two or three of the urchins, only Dona Leocádia, sitting on the gear of the press, her legs covered with water, laughed at the master craftsman's sally. Ambrósio failed to see the humor, grumbled.

"It's going to be a long time before we eat tapioca cakes or toast flour again. The manioc's finished, the plots, we've lost everything."

Dona Vanjé took a step over to her husband and, without disputing him, silenced his mournful mouth. What good was complaining?

"That's right, old man, the river's taken them—crops, houses, animals. But it didn't carry off everything, no, sir. The land's still there, we'll plant it again, God willing."

Amâncio, one of the Estâncians, answered back.

"It doesn't look like God is willing. If we are to depend on him . . ."

From the top of her improvised seat, Dona Leocádia scolded the impertinent fellow, backed up Vanjé.

"Shut your mouth, you don't know what you're talking about. I say the same as you, Dona Vanjé. We've still got our lives and nobody's taken our land. All I ask is for God to give us good health."

"Health and a little sunshine," Bastião joked again. "Do you remember the promise I made to you, Aunt Vanjé? The first house I'm going to put up when the flood's over is going to be yours. Don't think I've forgotten."

The conversation didn't go beyond that because the men who'd gone to get the canoe had come back bearing bad news.

As expected, they found not a sign of the canoe. They'd left it upside down between the roots of a tall hog plum tree,

but below the rapids, at a place where the river, free of
rocky narrows, broadened and deepened. How could anyone
imagine that the boat would stay there awaiting its owners?
The river had become lord and master alone and uncontested, giving and taking on its own terms. It isn't even
worth going to take a look, Ambrósio had said. Pedro Gypsy
arrived along with the farmers, they'd found him underneath the hog plum tree: gloomy, his face drawn, muttering
to himself.

Black Castor wouldn't even let them start any discussion about the fate of the canoe.

"Let's go while the bridge still holds, before the devil
carries it off."

Coroca took the lead, showed her newborn namesake to
the stonemason and the shoer of donkeys.

"What a pretty little thing."

She took off her blouse to better wrap the baby, a ray of
hope, the thread of life.

16

MOTIONLESS ON THE SLOPES, the goats were like sculpted
stones. Suddenly, for no reason, one of them set off at a
giddy run; the others followed it.

Between the two of them, Das Dores and Altamirando
carried the fattening pigs up the hill, the pregnant sows and
the one who'd just given birth, the sucklings, more than ten
heavy animals: each step was costly. They'd lost three of the
eight suckling pigs. Speaking of that, where was Çáo, who
hadn't put in an appearance when her help was needed?
She liked to rock the piglets, sing lullabies to them.

Where Çáo might be at any hour of night or day was
never known for certain: a cross to be borne by her father
and mother. In a world of her own, God's simpleton, without the common sense of normal people, it was impossible
to hold her back or to control where she went. Try as they
could, they had no success. Das Dores had said and repeated
to Altamirando whenever she saw him depressed because of
their daughter, "Leave her be. God made her that way, she's

in His care. We can't do anything." She was afraid her husband would get to know everything and, furious, beat the poor thing to death.

That's how it was; they couldn't do anything. Alta-mirando tried to follow his wife's advice, let it go, try not to get heated up. But when Ção would appear herding the goats, cuddling the piglets, or selling things at the market, when she came running and threw her arms around his neck, the man from the backlands, with no outward show, felt like a different person, happy and serene. A good girl, his daughter, it wasn't her fault that she was weak in the head, she'd been born that way. If anyone was to blame, it was God, who hadn't taken pity on them. Though pretty, she was off in the head, defenseless in those wilds; it was better not even to think about how easily trouble could come her way.

Exhausted, with the last of their strength, Das Dores huffing and puffing, they finished lugging the pigs. They hadn't been able to do anything to save the vegetable plot. Das Dores sat down on a rock. Altamirando announced, "I'm going to look around."

"What for?"

"I'm going to look for her. I've got to find her."

"I'm coming with you."

"Why? You stay here and look after things. One alone or two together, what's the difference? I'll come back with her or with the news."

The news: it had to be that. God gives life and God gives death, Das Dores thought. Altamirando went down the hill, waded into the water that was up to his waist, and set off in search of his daughter. Das Dores covered her face with her hands and began to weep.

17

THE SIGHT OF ALTAMIRANDO, confused, wandering all over in the midst of the rising water, asking about his daughter—if they'd seen her, where, with whom, doing what—made such an impression on Durvalino that it brought him to the point of a new confrontation with Fadul Abdala's wrath.

"Mr. Fadu, don't get upset, but I've got to go. . . ."

"Go where, for God's sake. Do you think—"

"I saw, with my own eyes—"

"Damn you! Can't you see this is not time for gossip?"

"I swear by the soul of my mother. I saw the two of them, Ção and Mr. Cícero, underneath the canoe. Mr. Pedro Gypsy saw them too."

"Why didn't you say so before?"

"I tried to; you wouldn't let me."

They learned about the canoe's disappearance from the Sergipeans, while Pedro Gypsy confirmed having seen the harebrain and the agent for Koifman & Co. heading for the shelter of the hog plum tree. What had happened to them afterward, nobody had any idea. When they heard the roar, had they fled or had the flood caught them?

Halfway between the bridge and the flour mill, Fadul and Durvalino met the band of Sergipeans. In spite of the urgency, they were coming along slowly, out of concern for Zeferina, who'd just given birth, and for the handful of babies. Old and young—men, women, and unruly children— all waded with those who'd gone over from the village: Coroca, Castor, Bastião, and Pedro Gypsy. Coming from the faraway depths of his memory, a recollection plagued the Arab: as a boy he'd seen caravans coming out of the desert, loaded down with misery and misfortune. How different and how alike.

18

IT WOULDN'T HAVE BEEN any use to follow the path of Ção and Mr. Cícero Moura: the canoe no longer served as a point of reference. Tição suggested that after leaving the women and children safe at the captain's house, they organize a general search of the area, looking for those who'd disappeared. Who knows, besides those two there might have been others: with so many new inhabitants in Tocaia Grande, how could they be sure that everybody was safe? They gathered the available men. "I'm not a man, but count me in," Coroca demanded. Bastião doubted the feasibility of the idea.

"As long as the water's rising, you won't be able to do anything. We won't even be able to walk in a little while. From here on it's only going to get worse."

Without anyone's having noticed it, Zinho appeared like a ghost, asking for help. The river was carrying off the planking of the bridge. Frantic, Lupiscínio was talking about killing himself if the flood destroyed the marvel.

The flood was growing in volume and in violence. Tição went with Zinho to check the damage. Fadul, with his enormous hands, lifted up the venerable Dona Leocádia, skin and bones and an indomitable will to live, and placed her on his shoulders, her legs wrapped around his neck.

"Are you all right, Aunty?" First he spoke to the old woman, then to the others. "One way or another, we have to cross. Nobody can stay here. It's certain death."

It wasn't easy, but they managed to get everybody to the other side. The black man had dived under the bridge and saw that the river had carried off only some planks from the flooring. The pilings that held it up, stout posts well sunk in, were still resisting; the bases were unharmed, hadn't suffered any damage. Reassured, Lupiscínio was of the opinion that they could cross by holding on to the railings.

They organized a kind of human bridge: one on each of the twelve wooden beams, balancing himself, standing. In that way, going from hand to hand, the children crossed the river. Except for little Jacinta, because Coroca wouldn't trust her to any other hands: measuring her steps. Stretching them if necessary, she made her way from beam to beam, followed immediately by the rest.

The urchins got the idea to use the door of the flour mill as a raft. Using a pole, Nando piloted; they devoted themselves to picking up animals and flotsam. In that confusion of fear and sadness, the urchins laughed merrily. The flood for them wasn't a calamity; it was a stupendous amount of fun, an unexpected adventure. Happy on their pirate ship, they became captain and crew.

Lowered from Fadul's shoulders, Dona Leocádia, before scurrying up the steps to the captain's house with the other women, asked about Das Dores. She'd seen her carrying pigs up the hillside, but when Altamirando passed by the flour mill looking for his daughter, he was alone. They couldn't leave Das Dores there all by herself, defenseless, dependent on her husband's return.

Fadul and Tição looked at each other and, without exchanging a word, set out again for the other bank.

19

SO EAGER WERE THE Turk and the black man that they didn't hear Diva's shouts, lost in the thundering of the flood. Loud cries, half-choked sobs: in her arms she carried the body of the bitch Oferecida, who'd drowned trying to follow her.

Diva had jumped into the water to cross the river and help her family on the other side, unable to bear waiting for news. She didn't notice that the dog had followed her from the captain's house. Only when she got to the other bank and looked all around did she notice, too late. The current had dragged Oferecida down to the bottom and thrown her against the riverbed. Diva spotted her blood bubbling up before she saw the body rise to the surface and give one last quiver.

She managed to reach her and found that the blow had opened Oferecida's head. Diva wouldn't allow the river to carry her off as it had the farm animals. When Tição returned they dug a hole on the same hill where the cemetery was and buried her there, attended by a small cortege of urchins. Poor Soul whimpered for hours, standing guard by the stones that marked the grave.

20

THE BODIES OF ÇÃO and Mr. Cícero Moura were found much farther downstream, caught in clumps of water hyacinths. Captain Natário da Fonseca had spotted them as he hurried in response to Zilda's call, tearing down the road.

On Atalaia Plantation Edu had to search through the groves for Natário, who was accompanying Colonel Boaventura Andrade in an inspection of the cacao trees: the budding was suffering with the rains, the danger was acute. Grim-faced, the colonel and the captain cursed the bad weather, ruminated over the damages.

"Your blessing, Colonel, sir. Your blessing, Pa. Ma sent me to tell you that the flood's finishing off Tocaia Grande. It's terrifying."

"With your permission, Colonel, I'll go take a look there. Tomorrow or the day after at the latest I'll be back."

It was enough to scare you, just as Edu had announced, and to stop your heart. As the rain slowed, the waters had stopped rising, but the river still raged swiftly, spreading out through the woods. The captain, before going to his residence on the hill, covered the valley from end to end, the black mule slipping on the mud. He rode along the base of the hills, where most of the people had taken refuge, stopping to chat, listening to news, hearing wails, calling each one by name, giving his blessing to the urchins. He didn't say the flood was a trifle, nor did he say it was the end of the world. He preferred to ask for suggestions as to what they should do the moment the flood was over: the worst had already passed. Mindful of opinions and judgments, in a little while he was discussing plans for rebuilding and replanting.

"Have you thought yet about where you're going to set up the shoe shop, friend Elói? And what about you, Mr. Ambrósio, are you going to expand your plantings?" They worked out details, made decisions. "It's high time there was a boardinghouse for you girls, don't you think so, Ressu?" Ressu thought so.

He asked for volunteers to carry up the corpses of Ção and Mr. Cícero Moura, and he discovered the whereabouts of Altamirando. He learned that the backlander had returned to the other side, to the knoll where he'd left his animals. He'd taken some *rapadura*, a piece of dried meat, and a bottle of *cachaça*. Das Dores, rescued by Tição and Fadul during the night, thanked them, but went back to her husband, she wouldn't allow herself to be away from her man. At the store the captain had told Fadul, "I'm going to give them the news."

"Do you want company, Captain?" Fadul offered. "It's a dirty job. Altamirando won't bear it."

"Better for you to stay here, friend, and see to the funeral."

At nightfall Natário finally entered his house and greeted the gathering, a crowd of people: from Dona Leocádia, the octagenarian, to Jacinta, newborn, still not a full day old. They surrounded him on all sides. Zilda was carrying Bernarda's son around her neck.

"I'm going to keep him and raise him."

The captain nodded his assent; all about the house were the children Zilda had borne or adopted, all with the same half-breed face, showing that strong Indian blood: *Your blessing, Father.*

21

PLACED IN HAMMOCKS, BY torchlight, the bodies were carried at dusk to the cemetery. There was no place left to hold a compassionate and well-attended wake where, with drinks of *cachaça*, they might recall the good qualities of the deceased. Ção, pretty and simple-minded, had been the joy of the village; who didn't like her?

The urchins would run after her, shouting. The adolescents would pull her down under the canoe, in the underbrush on soft beds of sedge, in clearings in the woods under the eyes of impassive lizards. Not just teenagers, mature men, too, would take advantage, and those were the ones she always preferred. It would have been a compassionate and indiscreet wake, rich in queries: who knows, in the string of memories and suspicions, whether the secret might come out into the open of who had deflowered Ção, a secret that all hoped would go to the grave. Who'd popped her cherry, facing the wrath of God? That it hadn't been any of the three insistent, inept bumblers Aurélio, Zinho, and Durvalino, was known for certain. Who, then? Pedro Gypsy, the accordion player? Dodô Peroba, who tamed wild birds? Guido? Balbino? Mr. Cícero Moura, with his stiff collar and bow tie?

Not Mr. Cícero Moura. He took advantage only by helping himself after her cherry had been popped. There was a lot to talk about Mr. Cícero too: starting with the reason for his nickname of Dr. Permanganate, his mania for cleanliness, his taste for maidservants, the smell of his brilliantine, the part in his hair. An important personage in the byways of the Rio das Cobras, a cacao buyer, the diligent agent of an export firm. Would the one who took his place traveling from plantation to plantation, carrying the briefcase with documents and account book, continue the offering of saints cards, that pious and coveted gift? Whoever it was, he surely wouldn't be as well-groomed and gracious as Mr. Cícero Moura. If a whore satisfied his demands, he didn't argue price or payment.

Altamirando and Das Dores carried the hammock that held their daughter's body. The captain and Fadul took charge of Mr. Cícero Moura's fragile corpse, dressed in his boots, his cape, eyes open, glassy. Almost nobody was missing from the cortege. Zé dos Santos and Dona Clara, and Ambrósio's people, the Estância clan all appeared, with the exception of Dona Leocádia, who didn't like the idea of cemeteries. From the hills where they'd taken refuge, the inhabitants of the Caminho dos Burros and a swarm of whores came down. Merência crossed herself, said a Lord's Prayer. Another riddle to solve: who had managed to pick an intact flower, sky-blue, out of the tangle of water hyacinths, to place in Ção's hands?

Set on a rise, the cemetery remained unscathed by the flood. Among the graves, papaya, banana, cashew, and cherry trees thrived—a wild orchard, happy with colors, rich in aromas. Going from grave to grave, one could tell the whole history of Tocaia Grande, from the remote and hazy beginning of legend and lies to the calamity of the flood that was still under way.

22

THE FLOOD LASTED FOR more than thirty hours of agony until, on the second night, the rain began to let up and the water receded, ebbing back into the riverbed. A baleful sun lit the muddy terrain and revealed a devastation that was widespread, stark, and dirty.

Both banks revealed ruin and desolation: the planted fields inundated, the crops destroyed, the animals decimated. In the village all that was left were the few houses made of tile, stone, and mortar, a half dozen adobe huts, the cacao warehouse, the corral, the oven of the brickworks, the blacksmith shop, the Turk's store, the captain's residence up on the hill. Only Coroca and Bernarda's small wooden house stood in the Baixa dos Sapos.

On plantations the cacao groves, especially those nearest the river, suffered great damage from the flood: less, however, than had been anticipated and feared. It seemed as if the river, following the established tradition of southern Bahia country, had preferred to assault the people than to harm the cacao.

A few days later, traveling to Ilhéus, where Dona Ernestina was going to extremes with promises and masses, consult-ing the spirits of light about the prospects of the weather, Colonel Boaventura Andrade, accompanied by Captain Natário da Fonseca and black Espiridião, passed through Tocaia Grande, now a place of swamps, ruins, and rubbish, where people were still picking through the remains of their belongings. Shaking his head, he said in dismay, "Your wife was right when she said it's finished. Forever! It'll never be the same again."

He was talking to the captain, Fadul, and Castor. The three of them, along with Pedro Gypsy, were busy drinking at the bar in the store. That fleeting trace of a smile crossed Natário's lips: he barely raised his voice, as if there were no need to underscore his words.

"With your permission, Colonel, let me tell you: you're still going to see Tocaia Grande twice what it was."

He looked at the others, he would have liked to have had all of them there: old Gerino and Coroca, Lupiscínio and Bastião, Balbino and Guido, Merência and Zé Luiz, Dodô Peroba and the people from the other side.

"It's not just me who's saying it. Ask Fadul and Tição, anyone you find out there living in these hills."

He looked past the door at the landscape, beautiful again under the bright summer sun.

"I don't know of anyone who's gone away because of the flood. Not even the whores, who aren't people to settle in any one place. The only thing people are talking about is building houses, houses that the water won't knock down. Come back to Tocaia Grande with me one of these days: you'll be surprised."

On the Day Inaugurating the New Shed, the Fever Also Arrives

1

HAD PEDRO GYPSY BEEN a real Gypsy, by blood and birth, certain whores in the habit of lending supernatural character to the drifter's arrivals in Tocaia Grande might have taken him to be God's messenger. But since he was a Gypsy in nickname only, they ascribed the concordance of dates and events to the accordion player's recognized wisdom: none of them believed in simple chance.

"You can smell a party, can't you, sweetie?" exclaimed the plaintive Anália when she saw him cross the threshold of Nora Sweetcake's whorehouse. "How did you find out?"

"A little bird whispered in my ear. Didn't you know that birds take to me? They tell me everything that's going on."

His disappearance had lasted for months on end. Occasional news brought by drovers prevented the women from thinking him dead and buried: he was livening up dances in the four corners of the world and would ask constantly about Tocaia Grande. To explain such a long absence, some stated that Pedro Gypsy was mad at the place, mad or disgusted. It had to be.

The reason could have been the death of Ção in the arms of Mr. Cícero Moura, a midget, a pygmy. The truth of such inventions was never proven, but if Master Pedro had thought that by being the first he'd be the only one to have her under the overturned canoe, he showed a complete ignorance regarding the nature of loonies, another quite singular nation apart. In the fortuitous chronicle of the road, tall tales fed on hearsay; Pedro Gypsy had never boasted of the first crack at Ção's cherry; on the contrary, if someone brought the matter up, he promptly changed the subject.

In any case, by guessing or by wisdom, by having overcome his disgust or unable to resist the nostalgia, no sooner had the date been set for the festive opening of the new shed than, behold, there he was, settled down at the bar in the store, savoring the free swig of *cachaça* proffered by Fadul Abdala in the warmth of his welcome.

"How could I miss it? Who was it inaugurated the first two sheds? Not even death could keep me away: I'd rise up out of my grave and come."

The inauguration was set for Sunday, September seventh, by happy coincidence also the anniversary of Brazil's independence, according to the Turk, an informed citizen and a patriot, the only one in Tocaia Grande. For the rest of them the story of independence was sheer drivel, vague and abstract, beyond any comprehension or importance.

"All that was missing was our friend here," Fadul agreed.

How could he miss it? The bitter tone revealed the accordion player's proper indignation. "Remember the straw one, Mr. Fadul?" Put up on a cold and rainy night by the drovers who'd opened the initial trail by machete and mule hooves in order to cut the length of their journey. He, Pedro Gypsy, had helped put up that first shelter. He saw no reason for their laughter and jokes. Furthermore, he'd proposed that they top off the job and fight off the rain and cold with a fling, and that's what they did. They beat the drums until dawn, eight souls, counting drovers, helpers, whores, and he, Pedro Gypsy, bellows in hand.

"Ask Lázaro if you think I'm lying," he challenged.

"You know, Mr. Pedro? They're saying around here that even Colonel Boaventura's coming to the party," Durvalino the know-it-all announced.

"God be praised! There was a time when the colonel liked a good blast and a fresh young woman. He was younger and not so rich."

"He still likes young women, even today."

Speaking of women, the Turk wanted to know if his friend Pedro Gypsy had been to Nora Sweetcake's bordello.

"She's got a new recruit, a certain Ceci—" Fadul brought

the fingers of his right hand together, plucked a kiss from his lips, and tossed it into the air to complete his praise of the whore.

Pedro Gypsy still hadn't been there; he'd just arrived, but wouldn't fail to pay a visit, meet the woman and to get to know the place.

"A shed, well, this'll be the third one I've opened. But a real bordello here in Tocaia Grande; I never thought I'd see that. Someone told me about it, but I thought he must be kidding."

At Nora's Pedro Gypsy turned down the madam's skills, Anália's languor, and the recommended attractions of Ceci, for Paulinha the Wildcat, whom he'd had his eye on for a long, long time.

2

GRAPIÚNA LAND, SOUTH BAHIA, was extravagant in wealth and exaggerations: you could make an ocean out of a glass of water there. In the coming and going along trails and roads, shortcuts, and highways, drovers, hired hands, whores on the move, gunmen, even colonels, all commented on and inflated the progress of Tocaia Grande. Sacrificed in a fearsome flood—the flood, too, had gained in volume and violence—the village had arisen once more out of the mud flat it had been reduced to: not content with simply returning to what it had been before, a puny settlement, it was taking on the airs of a prosperous town with a brilliant future: it had leapt forward; you had to see it to believe it.

Working night and day, in a spontaneous collective effort paid for by a curious bartering of produce and animals, where possible, and by money when God brought good weather, the inhabitants had remade the topography of the village. Topography, a formal and pompous word, it can't be applied to Tocaia Grande: they changed the appearance of the place.

The Caminho dos Burros, the donkey road, had become the Rua da Frente, front street, with gaily colored façades. Parallel to it was the Rua dos Fundos, back street: there were those who preferred living farther away from the river. In the Beco do Meio, middle alley, which joined the two lanes—two streets, in the proud vernacular of the locals— lived and worked the shoemaker. There, too, Dona Natalina had set up her sewing machine and already couldn't keep up with the orders. One of them, quite recent, brought by Captain Natário da Fonseca: a party dress for Sacramento, the young infatuation of Colonel Boaventura.

In the Baixa dos Sapos, new straw shacks had taken the place of those that the river had carried off, which is to say, all of them. The whores urgently needed a corner where they could stretch their mattresses. Others, however, less pressed, having set down roots in Tocaia Grande—Nininha, mistress of Lupiscínio, to mention one—had built more stable dwellings. In that way, an alley of adobe huts was born and prospered: on the corner, painted yellow, the house of Nora Sweetcake: a nickname that went back to when she was fifteen years old, and made her debut in Aracaju, a soft and tasty sweetcake; at the age of forty a hooker fit for the buzzards. Nora's house and not Ressu's. Ressu, poor thing, incapable of managing her own twat, let alone a bordello, had passed the idea on to Nora for the same price that she'd gotten it from the captain: for nothing.

Worthy of mention is a curious fact demonstrating the fever for construction that dominated the village: the owners of shacks that had withstood the flood ended up knocking them down in order to build more comfortable ones. The brickyard couldn't handle all the orders for bricks and tiles. Zé Luiz and Merência, if they didn't become rich, certainly became the creditors of most of the inhabitants. The surprising thing was that they expected to collect the debts: even though the buds had suffered from the rain, the coming harvest would more than compensate for the damage.

3

FOR SEVERAL DAYS AFTER Çāo's burial, Altamirando walked around aimlessly, not saying a word, distant. Das Dores was killing herself with work, trying to get the plots and the animals back in shape. Altamirando would remain sitting on the ground, peeling off pieces of tobacco and cutting up corn leaves with his knife to roll it in. Smoking was all he did.

He changed beginning with the day when, the sun at its peak, he caught sight of Ção on top of the hill, sitting on the rocks as was her wont: she'd come back to herd the goats and was smiling at him. He called Das Dores so she could see, too, but when the mother arrived, Ção had vanished. Altamirando understood that only he and the goats could see her.

She wouldn't appear every day, only once in a while. Das Dores refused to believe it; he didn't mind, it was a secret between father and daughter. Altamirando went back to work with restored drive and energy. The cattlemen who dealt with him at the corral, selecting steers for slaughter and for the sale of meat at retail, said that Altamirando had a screw loose somewhere: that did not keep him from fulfilling his obligations and commitments. A screw loose, perhaps, but not enough to stop him from working and toiling.

4

IN SPITE OF LUPISCÍNIO'S insistence, and the pleas of Castor and Diva, parents of his godchild, Colonel Robustiano couldn't stay for the shed party. He even resisted the news, confirmed by Captain Natário da Fonseca, of the presence of Colonel Boaventura Andrade: the owner of Atalaia had promised to show up.

On the other hand, Mr. Carlinhos Silva, the new representative of Koifman & Co., on the way back from his usual coverage of the plantations, didn't go straight to Taquaras, but lingered in Tocaia Grande to take part in the dance, putting up at the Central Boardinghouse.

What's this new item of a Central Boardinghouse? In this brief summary of the rebirth of Tocaia Grande, more than one reference has been made already to Nora Sweetcake's house, with details concerning the color of the façade, its exact location, at the corner of the alley of huts in the Baixa dos Sapos. If the street number on the door wasn't given, that was due to the simple fact that there was none, but praise for the qualities of the girls practicing their trade in the establishment has already been lavished elsewhere here by Turk Fadul's sinful mouth. One more proof of the fallibility and frivolity of information and reports that are so often presented as serious and correct. By virtue of its being an inn for whores, given over to licentious activities, Nora's house received excessive notice and praise, while the Central Boardinghouse, owing evidently to its family character, was relegated to oblivion.

STRICTLY FAMILY STYLE proclaimed the sign hanging on the front: it would furnish room and board at modest prices for the eventual visitors to the village. Two rooms, each furnished with three army cots and a small tin washbasin; in the back of the yard a tub filled with water. What more can be said to the benefit of the Central Boardinghouse, the proud property of Dona Valentina and Mr. Juca das Neves? That Dona Valentina, in addition to her merits as proprietress, cook, waitress, and maidservant, would fulfill other needs if the stranger was to her liking or was ready to supplement his daily charges? She wasn't pretty, nor ugly either, but the fact that she was married gave her status, aroused cupidity. Such details, however, along with those referring to the voracity of the bedbugs, were for the guests to discover.

Having cleared up any possible confusion between the two houses, it's time to get back to Mr. Carlinhos Silva, a guest of considerable standing, just the opposite in physique and behavior from his predecessor. Where Mr. Cícero Moura had been frail and scrupulous, Mr. Carlinhos was broad-shouldered and spontaneous.

A half-breed with kinky blond hair and blue eyes, pale as a snail, evil tongues said he was the illegitimate son of Klaus Koifman. If that wasn't so, why had the foreigner sent him to study in Germany as a boy and kept him there for many years? With Klaus's death, the younger brother, Kurt, took over the management of the company, and immediately ordered the return to Brazil of the deceased president's protégé—his illegitimate son? Who knows? But a bastard, most certainly. Young Carlinhos returned to Ilhéus with the status of orphaned son of Benedita Silva, a gem of a black woman who had served Klaus's table and warmed his Teutonic bed. From student in Weimar, he became bookkeeper in the cacao-exporting firm. He was making progress.

At the shed party he revealed an unexpected side to his personality; he took pleasure in performing magic tricks. He was hiding other surprises up his sleeve, as will be seen later, at the moment of truth.

5

WORDS CAN'T DESCRIBE Mr. Carlinhos Silva's success with the acts of prestidigitation he presented. Waves of laughter mixed with exclamations of disbelief issued from the open-mouthed audience, raising the children to extremes of excitement and astonishment. A thunderous success and there's no exaggeration in the metaphor: almost none of the spectators had ever witnessed a theatrical performance of any kind; they knew nothing of sleight of hand, card tricks, or magic. The women crossed themselves—God save us!—the men, startled, didn't know what to think.

Mr. Carlinhos Silva rolled up the sleeves of his jacket and shirt and the magic began: everybody saw that it wasn't child's play. Without using his hands, by the power of thought, the employee of Koifman & Co. transferred penny coins from Guido's pocket to Edu's ear; from Zé Luiz's nose he extracted five dry cacao beans. Repeating cabalistic words, hokus-pokus, sinsalabin, presto, abracadabra, and other fearsome incantations, with the tips of his fingers he drew out from between Mrs. Valentina's breasts the pocket handkerchief that, in plain sight of everybody, he had placed into Aurélio's bag, and it had disappeared from there without anyone's touching it: a feat beyond understanding. He did wild things with a deck of cards, they floated between his fingers, appeared, disappeared, reappeared, the ace of hearts became the king of clubs, the two of spades was transformed into the ten of diamonds, and he plucked the queen of hearts from Bernarda's flowing hair. He manipulated the cards before a stupefied audience that crowded up in front of him, trying to get a closer look, seeing but not believing.

"God save me and keep me from getting into a game with you, sir! I'd rather play against the devil!" stated the drover Zé Raimundo in spite of his habitual deftness with his own cards.

Fadul Abdala applauded, the audience joined in. A lot of them wanted explanations—did he dazzle people's eyes or what?—others swore that Mr. Carlinhos had a pact with the devil. The one who got most excited and applauded the loudest was the young Sacramento. Until then she'd kept her eyes lowered, looking at the floor, sitting in silence beside Zilda on a wooden bench. Even Colonel Boaventura Andrade clapped his hands and heaped praise on Mr. Carlinhos Silva.

"Yes, sir, my congratulations! If you wanted, friend, you could earn your living as a magician in theaters of the capital."

Musicians, amateur magician, an influx of people from outside, and, above all, the presence of the plantation owner had brought the shed feast to those heights. They'd brought Dodô Peroba's barber chair and placed it at one end of the hall so the colonel could sit in it, over by the improvised bar selling *cachaça*, brandy, and genipap liquor.

No one dared ask Sacramento to dance, but when it was time for the quadrille, seeing Castor organizing the couples, Mr. Carlinhos Silva, not being from there and thus unapprised of certain details, and having liked the face and modest comportment of the country girl who had so applauded him, went over to her, inviting her to be his partner in the lancers' quadrille. Alone on the bench, for Zilda had already gone off on the captain's arm to take her place in the dance, Sacramento felt confused, faltering, her eyes lowered, lost in distress. Standing, hand outstretched, Mr. Carlinhos waited. Then Colonel Boaventura, who'd been watching the scene with smiling interest, got up from the barber chair.

"I'm sorry, Carlinhos, but the lady already has a partner, her lancer is yours truly."

Not believing her ears, Sacramento lifted her eyes and smiled bashfully at the colonel, who stood waiting for her. Legs trembling, she accompanied him to the circle of the quadrille under the oblique gossipy glances. Mr. Carlinhos Silva understood, went to look for Bernarda; too late, the whore already had a partner. He contented himself with Mrs. Valentina, she was better than nothing. Black Tição clapped his hands for attention, the lancers' dance was about to begin. He lifted his voice, started the calls in his French patois.

6

DIVA SWIRLED IN THE steps of the quadrille, proud of Tição's roguishness; he had a pact with the devil too. But Tição, who knew her well and could read her mind, sensed that she was restless, worried, no matter how she tried to hide it. Her thoughts were wandering from the dance, drifting to her parents' house on the other side of the river.

Vanjé and Ambrósio weren't in the shed. At the market that morning, selling the produce from the gardens, Ambrósio was burning hot. Zilda, who'd stopped to buy some things and chat, had a bad premonition when she saw him like that. She advised Vanjé to take Ambrósio home and sweat him as soon as possible. Maybe she could still cleanse his blood, get rid of the bad fluids.

At the noisy lunch table, full of guests invited for the feast, Zilda spoke to the captain: it looks like Ambrósio's caught the fever.

"Pray God it doesn't spread."

7

AMBRÓSIO DIED THREE DAYS later and neither old Gerino nor young Tancredo, the son of Vavá from Estância, could attend his funeral: both were fighting the same dreaded fever.

The no-name fever, the plague, the one that people said killed even monkeys. They talked about it in low and reverent voices, a monstrous divinity, an endemic and ancient scourge over cacao country, towns and farms, it went about collecting here and there its quota of sacrifice. They avoided mentioning it in conversation, tried to forget about it to see if, ignored like that, it might move on.

As long as the malignancy killed sparingly, unhurriedly, without greed, they went along supplying it with its ration of corpses, living with it, conformed to it. But when, billeted in a village, it turned into an epidemic and slaughtered wholesale, fear became panic, and instead of the soft weeping of a father and mother, a wife, husband, or child, a clamor of curses rose up to heaven.

It would consume a living soul in a matter of days. It burned and softened the body, the head bursting with pain, off its rocker, evil-smelling farts, the guts breaking out in a pestilential discharge. A certain and ugly death, there was nothing that could be done.

Other fevers had names: tertian, malaria, hoof-and-mouth (which attacks people and cattle), yellow fever, and gland fever, each more dangerous than the other. There was a cure and treatment for all of them, however, even for the black pox: dry cow dung placed on the blisters. But there was no cure for no-name fever, just the fever, with no adjective to describe it, with no diagnosis or prescription, the patient in the hands of God, the merciless God of the plague. They called for sudorifics, cataplasms, enemas, bottled medicine, and tisanes, drinks made with roots and leaves from the forest, formulas passed from father to son. They hit the mark for a lot of infirmities: venereal disease, for example, gonorrhea, but had no effect on the fever, the one that has no name and kills even monkeys. All that were left were prayers, incantations, conjurations, spells, and promises.

It came on suddenly, with no warning. It knocked down, skinned and scalded, emptied guts and brains, reduced the strongest man to a rag before killing him. There was nothing to do but wait for it to fill its maw and, as unexpectedly as it came, go dig graves somewhere else. Completing a cycle or by simple accident, totally at random? Because it was sated or because God had heard their prayers? It could have been anything. If high-class doctors in the cities of Ilhéus and Itabuna couldn't diagnose and fight it, the only thing left for the decimated people in the backwoods to do was run away or wait for the fever to decide to leave, change its quarters, carrying the death sentences without appeal in its sack. A painful, dirty, stinking death, atrocious.

8

IT LASTED TWO WEEKS. It arrived on the Sunday of the party, showing itself at the market with Ambrósio; two Sundays later it took advantage of a strong wind, climbed aboard, and continued its journey to kill farther on. In the prosperous cemetery of Tocaia Grande it left at least nine crosses to mark its passing.

What the flood had not succeeded in doing—making the inhabitants flee, emptying out the settlement—the fever was on the verge of accomplishing without any thunder or fanfare, discreetly, almost unobtrusively. If it had lasted another week, who would have been insane enough to stay there waiting for death?

Dona Ester did her duty by spreading the alarm from neighbor to neighbor, doing it with a certain satisfaction because of the animosity she felt for the settlement, the dislike of living in such a backwater. Among other lesser annoyances was the fact that her husband was shacking up with a hussy. If it had been a case of a mistress decently set up in her own private house, it would have been bad enough. But this one was nothing but a whore with an open door. Dona Ester tried to drag her son along, but Zinho refused to go with her. She shrugged her shoulders, patience! Better to live all by herself in Taquaras than to die a stinking death just to be with her family. She gathered up her goods and left without a backward glance, setting the example.

With increased exaggeration caused by the grimness of circumstances, hair-raising news spread about, fearsome events were recounted on plantations, in towns, at stopover places, on the roads. What was about to happen to Tocaia Grande was the same horror that had befallen an anonymous settlement in the Água Preta region: all the inhabitants had given up the ghost. In the Água Preta region, the Sequeiro de Espinho, or along the Rio do Braço: the geography varied according to each narrator, the size of the place grew, the number of dead increased, but one detail always remained the same: no one had been left to tell the tale. As for Tocaia Grande, even Captain Natário da Fonseca had been reported a victim of the fever, he'd cashed in his chips, he must be in hell paying for his sins. There were those who secretly lifted a glass in celebration.

The whores, wanderers by nature, scuttled away. Having begun its harvest in the plots of the Sergipeans, the fever crossed the bridge and fell on the shacks in the Baixa dos Sapos: in two days three women had died. The flight was almost general: taking advantage of the passage of mule trains or traveling by themselves, bundle in hand or on their heads, the whores took off. One of them, Glória Maria, left when she was already under attack, vomiting and crazy, fever in her brain. She made the trip shitting her way through the woods, died when she got to Taquaras, and there they buried her, thus avoiding the need for a tenth grave to be dug in the cemetery at Tocaia Grande.

Some drovers changed the route of their trains: for a time they avoided the shortcut, and activity at the shed decreased. During the second week the exodus grew—the idea of flight dominated the village. After trying fruitlessly to convince Zé dos Santos and Dona Clara to come—*who can we leave the plots and animals with?*—Bastião da Rosa gathered up wife and daughter and went to seek shelter and safety in Taquaras. When they saw him lock the door to his house, the ones still in doubt swiftly made up their minds.

9

SEVEN DAYS AND FIVE deaths after the Sunday when Zilda had first expressed her fears to the captain, at the same luncheon table, during a silent meal with no guests, she took up the subject at the point where she'd left off.

"It's spread."

The week had been sad and difficult. Natário, somber, looked like an animal of the forest, hard-pressed. They'd come looking for him, anxious, tormented, as if the captain were a doctor or a medicine man, seeking some answer from him, some solution, and he had neither answer nor solution to offer, not even an encouraging word: words were vague and vacuous, they echoed false. The people weren't looking for consolation in their mourning; they sought salvation for the living. Zé Luiz had sat down on the bench on the veranda, bathed in tears: there's nothing more unseemly, more intolerable than a man weeping, his shame and pride lost, stripped of his manhood.

Zilda repeated, raising her voice in order to be heard and get an answer, "It's spread."

The captain was eating with his fingers, rolling a ball of beans and flour.

"They say another relative of Dona Leocádia is down with it. A man or a woman? Do you know? The Estâncians had buried young Tancredo on Friday.

"A boy, Mariozinho, no more than ten, that's all he was. He used to come around here a lot, he was close chums with Peba."

"You talk like he's dead already."

"God forgive me! I don't want to make any predictions, but have you seen anyone who got over it? I don't know of anybody."

She lowered her eyes to the tin plate, played with her food with her spoon.

"I'm scared to death about the kids. What do you think? Wouldn't it be better to take them and go to the farm? Until it's over?"

The captain ran his eyes over the children, who, paying no attention to the conversation, were eating eagerly, some at the table, others sitting on the floor. Then he looked at his wife.

"Haven't you noticed how many houses are shut, how many people have gone away already? If we leave, if we go to the farm with the kids, the next day there won't be anybody left. We can't do that."

Zilda put her spoon down, lifted her eyes to look at him.

"I took on other women's children to raise. I'm responsible for them."

"This is their home here and we're not leaving. Nobody." He wiped his hands, dirty with food, on each other. "Unless it's to the cemetery."

Zilda nodded in agreement: they weren't arguing, just talking. She knew her husband and his way of thinking: the one who holds command and authority has his obligations. It would have been no use arguing, much less going against him. She'd done her part, she'd expressed her fears: it was for him to decide, for her to obey.

10

LATER, IN BED WITH Bernarda, the captain said to her, "Some people are leaving; you should do the same. It's dangerous here."

He was looking at the wooden ceiling, his voice neutral, relaxed: he wasn't giving an order, just offering some advice.

"Go away? Where to?"

"There's a place in Taquaras where you can stay."

"Are you going too, Godfather?"

"I can't leave."

"What about Godmother?"

"She's staying here with me. She and the kids."

"Not you, not Godmother, not the kids. Why should I have to leave? Why do you want me to be far away? Why are you sending me off? I haven't done anything to win either reward or punishment. If I have to die, at least here I'll be near you and Nadinho."

She rested her head on her godfather's chest, as she'd done ever since she was a little girl, but with her arms and legs she clutched him against her naked body.

"Are you tired of me?"

"I didn't say for you to go away, I was only thinking out loud."

He'd done his part, the same as Zilda at lunch. Captain Natário da Fonseca ran his fingers over his goddaughter's face, his lover for so many years. When he spoke he already knew what the answer would be.

11

MERÊNCIA'S WAS A DEATH deeply felt. Had she been the victim of any other illness or bitten by a snake, she, too, would have merited a lively wake, for more reasons than the loony or the cacao buyer. There were so many things to remember, amusing incidents, moments of exaltation.

A married woman, she kept her distance from the whores, but that didn't stop her from standing up for them when the cattlemen tried to impose the law of force. With the callused hands of a tilemaker, she was tireless in putting up walls and installing roofs in the desolation that was Tocaia Grande after the flood. In idle moments she made kites from paper and stalks with her slender and skillful hands and gave them as presents to the children so they could launch them into the sky high above the village. She came to appreciate the skills of her favorites and clapped her hands in applause for the altitude of the flight and the spins of the kite. She'd wanted a child, oh, how she wanted one! But she had an inverted uterus, barren ovaries. Lacking a child, she spoiled the urchins, raised animals. Who could forget her with the water up to her waist the morning of the flood, the boa constrictor coiled about her bust?

When Zé Luiz went beyond the limits, in *cachaça* or whoring, drunk or horny, Merência would get angry and lay him out without his daring to protest. She would go looking for him in the Baixa dos Sapos and bring him back home with blows and curses. At burials it was up to her to recite the final prayer. Oh, she would have been the cynosure of so much laughter and so much remorse!

She'd been buried in haste like all the others taken by the fever. So the miasma wouldn't spread out into the air and get into the blood of the living. Religious, knowing her catechism and prayers, Merência would have liked an accompaniment of litany and lauds. So deserving, yet in her last moments she had none of it: no wake, mourners, or prayers. Not even a chorus of whores to say amen. The fever killed quickly, but even more quickly were the deceased dispatched to the cemetery in a fearful anxiety. In the precipitous haste there was scarcely time for Fadul to sputter an Our Father in Arabic.

12

THREE DAYS HAD PASSED since Merência's burial, and no new fatalities had occurred in the village, now bereft of animation and joy, when Pedro Gypsy appeared in Castor

Abduim's smithy on a mission of life and happiness. He
came to discuss the idea of a dance: they had to forget the
dark days, put an end to weeping, erase the memory of the
fever, cease remembering the dead: the dead would only
rise again on the Day of the Last Judgment.

Right after the inaugural party for the shed, Pedro Gypsy
had vanished from Tocaia Grande and some evil tongues
took advantage of his disappearance to backbite him. He'd
turned tail so fast and so frightened of the fever that he'd
left his accordion in the Turk's store: when there was a
revel, you could always count on him, his five fingers bringing out the fine points of the music, his mouth wide open to
drink at the expense of others. Envious accusations of his
gifts as a minstrel, his free wanderlust, and his constant
love affairs, awful things, were promptly dispelled: quick as
a flash, Pedro Gypsy was back, bringing quinine and other
pharmaceutical drugs obtained in Taquaras, good to combat malaria, but useless in cases of the fever that had no
name, no cure. He not only returned, he stayed there passing out preventative doses of quinine to the inhabitants,
lending the piss of Tocaia Grande a blue tint.

Certain that the curse had come to an end, he went out
in search of support for his proposal of a good wingding,
capable of chasing off the blues and bringing back laughter.
In the shop he held back his enthusiasm as he remembered
that old Ambrósio, Diva's father, had been the first victim of
that malignant feast. But Diva wasn't offended, she agreed
with the accordion player: nothing better than shaking a leg
to scatter the ashes and restore a love of life. Tição agreed,
and Pedro Gypsy went off in search of more support.

13

DIVA DIED AT DAWN, cleanly and quietly, stretched out in
the hammock, feeling the coolness of Tição's flesh against
her burning body, hugging him, listening to him murmur: "ô
iiá, my black girl, my little black girl, ô iiá." The surge of
calm waters, waves on the beach, the distant sound from a
conch shell. She said, "My whitey," and left him.

She'd caught the fever when people were already thinking about celebrating the end of the outbreak and setting a date for some hipswinging. The morning after Pedro Gypsy's visit, Diva complained of a weakness in her legs, warmth on her face, and a pain in her stomach. It lasted a day and a night.

Lia and Vanjé had come to keep her company and help. The baby was taken to stay with Dinorá, far from the danger of contagion. Tição stayed, squatting by the mattress where Diva was expiring minute by minute, a caressing hand, here and there a word; she tried to smile, couldn't. He'd sacrificed a pig to Omolu, knowing, however, that it would be as useless as the two offerings the week before had been. The fever shut off the path to the enchanted ones, it opened the door to the *eguns* and any creature on whose head it laid its hand belonged to them. Tição knew that for certain, but he'd decided that the curse wouldn't take Diva away alone. If it didn't knock him down onto that same mattress, dirty with vomit and discharge, Tição knew what to do. Squatting there, he'd thought about it and made up his mind.

Diva moaned softly and more than once her mother and sister-in-law cleaned the filth while Tição held her against his chest. But the rags didn't do much good; she still felt filthy and smelly. She asked them to heat up some water for a bath. Lia and Vanjé were against it: taking a bath with the body burning up, a foolish wish, a delirium of the fever. "For the love of God," Diva begged, fainting. Tição ordered them to do it: be it absurd, be it delirium, be it the fantasy of a dying woman, she had a right to what she wanted. He went to get the tub.

They took off her dirty slip, sat her in the lukewarm water. Vanjé and Lia withdrew into the shop, leaving her in Tição's company. Naked, clean, smelling of soap, she wanted to get into the hammock with him, to have them lie down together.

Under the hammock, motionless, his snout between his paws, Poor Soul waited.

14

A HOWL OF DEATH, Tição's cry cut the grayish dawn, laden with dread and mourning, woke up the people: the same thing had happened that summer when the headwaters had burst out and the river brought devastation. What new affliction was being announced? Weren't the misery and suffering enough?

Dawn lighted up and those who gathered saw the fever run and leap onto the gale: God willing, it was tired of slaughter. Nine deaths, ten counting Glória Maria, not too bad: a fair part of the population of that asshole of the earth. When everything had been toted up, subtracting the dead and the runaways, only a very few inhabitants were left. Even they couldn't feel totally safe. No-name fever, the one that killed even monkeys, was scouring the cacao lands; it came and went from place to place. It might declare a truce, but would never go away for good.

Lia was the first to come out, running madly, calling for help, asking for Fadul's aid. Then a group of drovers, whores, inhabitants formed, wanting to know what was happening. With slow steps, a ghostly zombie, Tição was crossing the clearing toward the river, followed by Poor Soul. In his arms he carried Diva's body, dressed in the mist of dawn. He wasn't going to let her go alone: in the depths of the water, in the bed of the river were the lands of Aiocá. Sacrilege! A dead person should be buried in the cemetery, and it's for the living to weep and remember.

Vanjé was caught by a blast of wind and fell in the mud before she reached Castor and begged him to show respect for death and its pomps. Bernarda appeared and helped her up. Rushing like the devil, Coroca ran into the whirlwind. In the sky the cover was breaking up into shreds of clouds. After the tragedy, blasphemy.

Fadul barely had time to pull on his pants. He hurried out to confront the blacksmith and to try to stop him. He shouted as he went, "What the hell are you doing? Are you crazy, Tição?"

Castor Abduim didn't slow down, nor did he speed up; he simply kept on walking. He wasn't the blacksmith Tição, a good fellow, liked by everyone, he was a soul from the other world. He growled in a toneless voice, terrible to hear, "Back off."

A circle was closing in around him, the people ready to put a halt to the sacrilege. The Turk approached, the circle closed.

"We'll dress her, put her in a hammock, see to the funeral."

"Back off!"

In his eyes the emptiness of death, Tição tried to break through, shoved at Fadul. The people all around, ready to intervene: helpless against the fever, they weren't going to allow that outrage.

Fadul lifted his huge hand, closed his fist, and let go the blow before the people could come forward and do anything more. Vanjé, Bernarda, and Lia picked up the body. Tição stood up, ready to kill and to die. But the one he found posted in front of him was Coroca, the mother of life.

"Have you forgotten, damn you, that you've got a son to raise?"

Dona Leocádia's Epiphany Parade Marches In: Quilariô! Quilariá!

1

CASTOR ABDUIM WAS HARD at work shoeing the mare Empress, Colonel Robustiano de Araújo's favorite mount, a delicate job, because the animal, besides being mettlesome, had fragile hooves, when Poor Soul's barks, unexpected and welcoming, drew his attention. The dog had pricked up his ears, stood up, wagging his tail, and ran off to meet someone outside. Poor Soul was not normally of an expansive nature. Faithful to his master, he reserved all effusiveness for him; he wasn't one to chase after and leap about strangers. At the end of a summer's afternoon a bonfire was burning in the Tocaia Grande sky, a glow of reds and yellows.

Giving Edu the mare's hoof so the lad could finish the job with the butteris, Tição, focusing his eyes, caught sight of somebody silhouetted against the light and shadow of the sunset. In the blacksmith's thoughts a fleeting and absurd thought passed: the mystery of Poor Soul's appearance in Tocaia Grande would finally be cleared up. After all those years someone had come for him, who knows, ready to take him back.

The hazy outline of a woman wrapped in light and dust, the figure bent over, dropped her bundle to the ground, the better to receive and reciprocate the dog's greeting. At that precise moment, without making out the features or the shape of her body, the black man knew who it was: it could only have been she, nobody else.

Graceful step, relaxed body, swinging hips, Epifânia
approached, her face serious. Quiet in her manner, without
any outbursts, she didn't flash her teeth, didn't insinuate
flirtation. She didn't even look like that bold and brassy
woman, ostentatious, who turned men's heads and disturbed
the peace. She stopped in front of Tição, the bundle under
her arm, the dog leaping about her.

"I've come to take care of the kid. I'd dropped out, I was
living with someone. Three days ago I ran into Cosme. He
told me about things. I felt sorry for you."

Her voice was calm and firm.

"Where is he? Where's my boy? I won't leave even if
you tell me to."

Without waiting for an answer, she crossed the shop,
followed by Poor Soul, and went into the house. Bathed in
blood, the sun was drowning in the river.

2

IN THE COMPANY OF her granddaughter Aracati, who still
hadn't had a party for her fifteenth birthday due to the fever
that had raged that winter, Dona Leocádia covered the half
league that separated the fields of the Estâncians from Vanjé's
people. A good walker in spite of the burden of the years
that bent her shoulders, she made the girl maintain a brisk
pace in order to keep up with her.

The two of them went along talking about matters unusual for those backwoods. They were discussing shepherdess costumes, shepherdesses of the stars as could best be
made out, and they referred to characters whose names had
a strange and seductive ring: Dona Deusa, the lady goddess,
Besta-Fera, the wild beast, Caboclo Gostosinho, the tasty
half-breed. These and other marvelous beings, in addition to
the beautiful shepherdesses of the manger, would soon be
parading through the brambles of Tocaia Grande under
the direction of Dona Leocádia. Summer had begun, an
occasional rain washed the sky, rinsed the sun, beautiful,
hot days, lightened hearts. Dona Leocádia had set out on a
mission of courtesy: she would listen to the opinion of her

neighbors, but she had made her decision and no one would make her give up. That was what she said to her people.

"I'm not going to let another year go by without having an Epiphany parade going down the street."

With her sunken eyes, two holes dug in her hollow face, she scrutinized relatives and friends to observe the reaction of each. Doninha, Vavá's wife, lowered her head and Sinhá looked away.

Her son-in-law Amâncio couldn't help putting his two cents in. In a mocking tone he asked, "Where have you seen any street around here, ma'am?"

"If you're against it, you don't have to play the role of Jaraguá, I'll get someone else."

"I didn't say a word. You're the one in charge."

She was the one in charge, the matriarch. They didn't question her decisions, and, as for Amâncio, nobody enjoyed the Epiphany celebration as much as he. No one could match him as Jaraguá, a wild and frightening Besta-Fera. He was just talking for the sake of talking, drivel, babbling on: there are people like that. Dona Leocádia cut off the conversation before some woman, Doninha, Sinhá, or some other ninny remembered the dead.

"The people will go wild, don't you think?"

The year before, newly settled in Tocaia Grande, they hadn't even been able to think about the Epiphany. In Estância, for more than forty years, Dona Leocádia's Epiphany procession, coming from the farm, had vied with those from town for the people's applause. It wasn't the richest or the biggest, but it was the happiest and most inspired. In pomp and glitter none could dare be compared to the Epiphany of the Alencar family, people who, in addition to their wealth, had education and background. Dona Adlaé and Mr. Alencarzinho rehearsed the whole year and even studied every step and every line in books in order to follow the plot and dance to the letter. Even so, measured against all their wealth and learning, Dona Leocádia's Epiphany didn't do badly: when it appeared at the entrance to town, lanterns aglow and Dona Deusa clutching the standard, people ran to greet it, and, with applause and cheers, followed it to the Praça da Matriz, the square of the parish church. In the parade, Dona Leocádia always wore shoes, and on the top of her white hair, a fancy comb.

Grandmother and granddaughter hardly noticed the long walk while discussing the Epiphany parade. In Tocaia Grande

it wouldn't be the same as in Estância; there were some
things missing, starting with the indispensable bass drum:
they would have to be satisfied with accordion and *cavaquinho*. Where were the plazas, the broad streets lighted
with kerosene lamps, the mansions and houses with two
front parlors: the crèche in one, the other cleared for dancing, tables loaded to receive the shepherdesses and the rest
of the procession? In Estância the festivities began with
midnight mass on Christmas Eve and continued until the
Feast of the Magi: on the bandstand the Lira played marches
and schottisches, there was dancing on every corner. But
Estância had been on the edge of civilization until the cultivated fields were replaced by greenish canebrakes. In Tocaia
Grande were neither kerosene streetlights nor colonial mansions and houses with two front parlors and a crèche set up:
three and a half dozen inhabitants, not counting itinerant
whores, drovers sleeping over in the shed, hired hands coming from the plantations for a holiday and to take care of
their urges. That was no less reason for Dona Leocádia's
Epiphany to be any less brilliant or inspired.

3

THE EPIPHANY GROUP IN Estância had never failed to parade and dance in the streets—even on the occcasion of the
death of Fortunato, Dona Leocádia's husband, head of the
family, who gave up the ghost while working in the field,
without uttering a sound, without complaining of being
sick. For ever so many years he'd played the part of the
Caboclo Gostosinho and, according to the people of Estância,
not even Mr. Leonardo himself of the Alencars' Epiphany
group could compare with him when it came to the lines
about the ox:

> My lowing ox
> Has died of the pox

With Fortunato missing, the part of Caboclo Gostosinho
ceased to belong exclusively to this one or that. Each year
Dona Leocádia would choose one of the men of the group
to take the part and recite the lines. When they were almost

at old Vanjé's house, Aracati dared to ask, "Who are you thinking about for the part of the Caboclo, Grandma?"

Funny, Dona Leocádia had been thinking about that very problem.

"I'm going to do everything I can to get Mr. Tição. Up till now you'd think he buried himself along with his wife."

"I think it's nice, Grandma, so much feeling. Don't you?"

"A young fellow all wrapped up in mourning like some old widow? No, I don't think it's nice."

Mourning, a figure of speech. Covering oneself in black from head to toe was the custom of rich people in cities and in the big houses on the plantations. Mourning for the common people consisted of sadness and gloom, agony inside; it wasn't expressed in clothes. It was called sorrow, and didn't last long. In their life of weariness, there wasn't much time for nostalgia and tears.

4

MR. CARLINHOS SILVA CHANGED the look of the cacao warehouse inside and out, even enlarging it with two new additions. One served him as residence and office; the other was to lodge the guards: before that they had slept on mats beside the stored cacao, bathed in the river, and they relieved themselves in the woods. With the improvements they got canvas beds and a privy. It well might have been said that Mr. Carlinhos had a bit of the gringo in him, fussy as he was. He'd built two small houses: one for the guards and one his own, kept for his exclusive use and under lock and key.

There were those who were puzzled to see him in the warehouse one day, busy with Lupiscínio and Zinho, drawing plans, setting up contracts, giving orders. But the news soon got around: Colonel Robustiano de Araújo had turned the warehouse over to the firm of Koifman & Co. The reason for the colonel's decision could be found in the death of Gerino, victim of the fever that hadn't respected his status of a southern Bahian.

Due to so many burials in such a short time, no reference was made at that moment of the size of Gerino's wake, capable of outdoing in normal times those of Ção and Mr.

Cícero Moura and of equaling Merência's: but the four wakes were nonexistent. The fever killed perversely, then to top it off, forbade remembrance and praise.

The plantation owner, still depressed by the death of the irreplaceable Gerino—a fellow whose trust could be equalled only by that of his brother Nazareno, and the latter never left the colonel's side, God be praised!—suggested turning his warehouse over to the company, an advantageous deal for both parties. That was how it ultimately happened, allowing Mr. Carlinhos Silva to set himself up in Tocaia Grande, bag and baggage, a comfortable and practical solution: he would go to Ilhéus once a month to hand in his report.

Along with the double bed, he brought a small desk from the city and a bookcase filled with books, most of them in a foreign language. To those who were puzzled by a double bed in a single man's house, he answered in a friendly but blunt way: *Bachelor, yes, jerkoff, no.* He was an affable person, cordial by nature; when he wasn't traveling buying cacao, he liked gabbing with the people, fascinated by all sorts of matters: recipes for home remedies and syrups, outlandish cures for asthma and tuberculosis, tales of superstitions, sayings and proverbs, small and silly things. He took notes in a small notebook with a pencil stub: you see all kinds of things in this life! For that and other reasons, Bráulio, one of the depot guards, said that Mr. Carlinhos was an interesting fellow. Bráulio had heard the word in a whorehouse in Itabuna and had incorporated it into his meager vocabulary, using it sparingly, when he had to explain the unexplainable: *interesting!*

Listening to Dona Leocádia unfold her plan for the Epiphany parade, Mr. Carlinhos Silva applauded the idea with enthusiasm and placed himself at her disposal: how could he be of help? Dona Leocádia took advantage of his offer to mention the serious matter of the bass drum: without a bass drum, Epiphany wasn't the same. Mr. Carlinhos promised to get the donation of the instrument from Koifman & Co.: rest assured, it won't be for a lack of a bass drum that the Epiphany parade will fail to get off the ground. In exchange, he made a request: he wanted to attend the rehearsals, would that be possible? Of course it would, all he had to do was come to the shed, where they practiced three times a week. In Estância each rehearsal had been a party, with flirting, singing, and dancing. Sometimes they ended up in marriages.

5

CAPTAIN NATÁRIO DA FONSECA gave the corn leaves and tobacco back to Espiridião, put the knife back into his belt, and passed Dona Leocádia's message on to Colonel Boaventura Andrade.

"Dona Leocádia sends word that she's counting on you for the Epiphany parade."

An urgent message, don't forget to tell my cousin, Captain. The colonel smiled, remembering.

"Penniless old woman! I can still remember her Epiphanies. I never saw anybody more devoted to parties than the people from Estância."

"She said your father played the part of Matthew and was a great dancer."

"Old Zé Andrade was the life of the party. He danced in the Epiphany parade, played the trombone, raised hell. Until the day he died."

Until the day he died. In Estância, old José Andrade, trombone player in the Lira Estânciana, had had a good time until he died. On the veranda of the big house, Colonel Boaventura Andrade, a powerful millionaire, reflected on the many courses of destiny.

In Ilhéus and Itabuna there was a hubbub of lawyers, a knavish and suspect race; Masonic lodges and chambers of commerce thrived; the Ursuline College turned out schoolteachers; newspapers circulated, some every week, dipping into politics, a nasty and necessary business; dancing girls showed off in cabarets; hospitals were founded; every week lecturers got off the ships of the Bahiana Line, amusing ones told stories, dull ones recited poetry; even a literary society had been founded in Água Preta on the occasion of the recent visit by Colonel Emílio Medauar's son, who wrote poetry and had been Venturinha's classmate at law school.

Notables discoursed and wrote about civilization, progress, liberal ideas, elections, books, and other nonsense, all blather and gabble. If they, colonels and gunmen, hadn't tamed the woods and planted the land, the Cacao Eldorado— theme of the perorations and dithyrambs—wouldn't have existed, even in dreams.

Listening to Natário talk about the Estâncians, the colonel laid affectionate eyes on the two strongmen and felt esteem and gratitude in his heart. He'd grown old: he was no longer the same stud or authoritarian boss, lord who held the reins and the knife, determining politics and the law, master in court and in notaries' offices in Itabuna. If he still hadn't relinquished the reins of power and held them tight to avoid tricks, it was because, in spite of all, he still had hopes of seeing his son back home, assuming command, and letting him rest in peace.

Old Zé Andrade, a poor man, an amateur musician, had had fun until his dying day, had never let go of anything that life offered, so many things.

"Tell Leocádia I'm too old to dance in an Epiphany parade."

"She said you should at least come and watch. So you can have a little fun."

6

LIFE OFFERED VERY FEW THINGS to provide the colonel's old age with any joy. Two of them, however, were balm and consolation: cacao and the girl Sacramento.

The sight and care of the cacao groves was a sublime spectacle, a sweet, jubilant task. He'd just completed the off-season inspection in Natário's company, grove by grove, the old ones and the new, each one more flourishing and loaded than the next in that glorious summer, perfect in its balance of sunshine and rain, compensating for the damage of the flood in the previous year. An exceptional bloom, the strong, bountiful shoots warmed one's heart.

He'd also gone through the groves at Boa Vista. The cacao trees were no different from those at Atalaia: the same treatment, the same richness that was a pleasure to see. Natário had been rewarded, if not in the degree that he deserved, at least he had a piece of land planted with cacao: hardworking and wise, he'd end up wealthy. Espiridião, on the other hand, had nothing to his name: he kept his meager possessions in a windowless room, a lean-to behind the big house. A light sleeper with a sharp ear, he slept in the parlor, guarding the bedroom and the boss's rest.

He'd never opened his mouth in complaint, wanted nothing and asked for nothing. He'd arrived at Atalaia Plantation at the dawn of the fighting in the company of a small daughter: the mother had died of tuberculosis, coughing up blood during the drought in the backlands of Conquista. At the colonel's instigation and not at the father's request, the girl, Antônia, brought up in the big house, had gone to the Ursuline College in Ilhéus: the only dark black girl on a roster of pupils who were more or less white. A schoolteacher with a diploma, she was doing her best to teach reading and writing to children at the little school in Taquaras. She wore glasses, had never married, and raised birds. Black Espiridião had a true veneration for his daughter and treated her formally; all that was missing was his calling her ma'am, and when he mentioned her name, he added the titles "my daughter, Professor Dona Antônia."

Espiridião sat on the veranda steps, Natário on the edge of the bench, and between the two of them sat the colonel, reflecting on life, old age, and the few pleasures he had left. Sacramento's voice came from the kitchen, singing a *modinha* from Breja.

> The blackbird's got a touch of blue
> The nightingale is cinnamon hue
> When you've got your love along
> Serenade her, sing your song

Venturinha was loafing in Rio de Janeiro, squandering the colonel's money. Dona Ernestina, his sainted wife, was praying and making promises in Ilhéus; Adriana, his whore, on her way to sainthood, too, was always at spiritualist sessions; wife and mistress, each with their defects and devotions: his people, the rich side. On the plantation, where he was spending more and more time, were Natário, Espiridião, and Sacramento, his people, too, the other side. Sacramento had given him life so that he wouldn't die a solitary creature. It was too bad he'd waited so long.

Sacramento stopped singing, appeared on the veranda with the coffee, freshly brewed, warm and fragrant. While he sipped it, blowing on his cup, the colonel cleared his throat to say, "Espiridião could use a little *cachaça* ..."

"Just him?" The girl joked, familiar with the plantation owner's ways.

"I think Natário might just accept some too. What do you say, old friend?"

"If you'll have one with us, sir, I'll accept with pleasure."

The colonel laughed, comforted. The simple presence of the girl, just like the sight of the cacao groves, warmed his heart. Sacramento cleared the coffee cups, returned with the bottle and the glasses. Stemware, thin and fragile, holding no more than a drop of *cachaça*. When Sacramento leaned over to serve, the colonel caught sight of the full curve of her breasts in the neckline of her dress and he felt them against the back of his hand, lifted on purpose. Desire dimmed his eyes, burned in his chest, mingling with the warmth of the liquor.

On the veranda of the big house, the colonel pondered life and old age, the few joys and the many miseries that man is subject to: With the passage of years the distance between desire and erection grows greater, between hot fantasies that long to be fulfilled and a limp prick, a shriveled stem, refusing to rise. Natário and Espiridião respected his silences; with them it had never been necessary to waste words in order to be understood: the captain could even divine intentions.

An Epiphany festival, fun for the young people, what the devil did he and Leocádia have to do with farmboys and shepherdesses? She with one foot in the grave, he on the verge of impotence? Crazy old woman, wanting to keep reveling until she died. Strong people, they wouldn't let themselves be beaten: they'd lost two in the epidemic, a young boy and a child. Old Zé Andrade, too, had enjoyed himself till the end.

The cacao groves were his own Epiphany celebration. The girl Sacramento was his shepherdess, his Senhorita Dona Deusa. All he had left. He turned up the glass of *cachaça* and halfway between a command and joke he ordered, "Leave the bottle here, tightwad. That's no kind of drink to give Espiridião."

He turned to Natário, his voice tired.

"Tell Leocádia that I won't guarantee I'll go; it's most likely I won't. Even though I'd like to. But most likely Ernestina will come here or I'll go to Ilhéus for the holidays. To make an idle promise is not my way."

The afternoon was agonizing above the cacao groves.

On the riverbank the croak of a frog dying in the mouth of a snake. In the colonel's parlor Sacramento had lighted the kerosene lamp.

7

BATHED IN BLOOD, THE sun was drowning in the river. Son of Xangô, part Oxóssi and part Oxalá, black Castor Abduim stood stock-still by the door of the shop where black Epifânia had slipped in in search of the child. "My boy," she'd said. Red clouds ran across the sky, light and shadow mingled in an atmosphere of treason, the threat of an ambush, the announcement of danger. *What can I do?* Castor asked himself. *How can I stand up to her and say no?*

Behold a wind, abrupt and abrasive, blowing out of the east, stirring up the waters of the river, crossing through the forest and the center of the clearing between the shed and the Turk's store, spreading out a thick mantle of dust, cutting the world into two parts, the upper and the lower: one in the light of day, the heat of life; the other in the shadows of night, the coldness of death. And soon that mantle of divided light and shadow was no longer a whirlwind of dust but a gigantic and frightening apparition. The lower part was immersed in night, dressed in dirty rags with vomit and offal, legs and arms held by filthy rusty chains; the upper part glowed with light, burned with flames.

The full figure, hair of pure gold, cloak of stars, and crown of blue seashells, could only be seen later, when the skyline was dressed in purple, and the *egum*, free at last, dove into it and departed forever. It wasn't something of this world.

Black Tição Abduim saw it rise up out of the void, frightening, growing in the air, spinning in the wind, rising up in a spiral that touched the sky. He hunched over in fear, bowed with respect, closed his eyes to avoid blindness, and uttered the greeting for the dead: *epa babá*. Muttering phrases in Yoruba, the *egum* commanded him to open his eyes and come closer to listen to what it had to tell. Turning his weakness into strength, the black man walked toward it.

Epifânia of Ogum, an *ekede* able to bring on the enchanted ones, for she'd been an initiate for fourteen years, might have seen it with her eyes that could glean and perceive, but she wasn't there, she'd disappeared inside the house looking for Tovo, with Tição unable to stop her, taken by surprise as he was. Edu, busy cleaning the hooves of the mare Empress with the butteris, putting the new shoes on her, and the cowboy who'd brought the mount on Colonel Robustiano de Araújo's orders only saw, as their eyes could not glean or perceive, the swirl of dust raised by the unexpected windstorm, startled at the height and force of the whirlwind.

Tição went forward to meet the *babá*, dragging his feet: he'd lost control of his own movements and, as he advanced, he felt a weight growing on the back of his head, a feebleness, a weariness, as if he were going to die right then and there. It was Diva's *egum* manifesting itself, a pressing reason had made it embark on the desert's wind of fire: it was coming from the Beyond to fetch him. He had been waiting.

His head swirled in that mist of dizziness, his legs giving way. With difficulty he managed to get to a rock and sit on it, obeying the *babá*'s command. He found himself at the gates of night, still closed, before the *egum* of Iemanjá, but he saw her only from the waist down. Filthy rags covered her, they gave off the stench of the fever, displayed their repugnant filth, feet wrapped in chains, the same chains he'd seen as a child in the slave quarters of the sugar plantation: chains used to bind the feet of slaves to prevent their flight to freedom.

Tição couldn't succeed in making out the face that was showing up high, but he did recognize the surge of Diva's voice whispering the familiar words of enticement and tenderness into his ear: *My whitey, I'm your black girl and I'm here.* A suffering voice, cut by sobs, overflowed with plaintive grief, with bitterness. What's the reason for such great suffering? *Do you want to know? I'll tell you, listen!* She began her accusation. She asked why Tição hadn't freed her, hadn't given her the *axexê* coin to pay for the death boat. Why was he keeping her in a world that was no longer hers, bound with chains of sadness and revolt? *I died in the tide of the plague and I'm obliged to live, while you, who are alive, seem dead, everything backward and vice versa, everything contrary and out of place. Oh, my whitey, your little black girl*

*is suffering, you condemned me, I've got no peace. Why do you
want to keep me weighing you down?*

*Free my death and keep my living memory in your heart.
Why do you keep my clothes along with yours in the kerosene
crate with the* abebê *that you chiseled for me one day? Free me
from these chains: get my clothes and take them to Lia and
Dinorá, they can still get some use out of them. Put the* abebê *in
the* peji *of the* orixás, *because I'm an enchanted one now, an*
egum *of Iemanjá. Call Epifânia of Oxum and Ressu of Iansan
and dance my* axexê *with them: you haven't danced it yet.
Free my death, which you took to your breast, and go back to
living the way you lived before you knew me. I want to hear
your clear and merry laughter. I don't want to see you weeping
in despair. Go back to being Tição again, a man.*

The sobs ceased, the complaints, the accusation, and
what had been lamentation became warm tenderness again:
My whitey, oh, my whitey, listen to what I have to tell you. She
said it and repeated it three times so what had been said
and repeated would sink into his hard, stubborn noodle: it
had been she, Diva, his departed, his little black girl, Tovo's
mother, who'd guided Epifânia's steps, bringing her back to
the shop to take care of the child. A man alone never knows
how to bring up children; Tovo hasn't even learned how to
laugh, he looks more like an animal of the woods than a
child. It had been she, Diva, who sent him Epifânia to take
care of Tovo and him, Castor Abduim da Assunção, too, once
a *tição*, a burning ember, now a useless wooden log. *When I
died, I didn't geld you, my whitey. You've become a beast, an
apparition, a werewolf. Why are you crying when I want to
hear you laugh?*

Only then did he see the luminous face, glean the full
figure of the *egum*: free of the bonds, the tatters, bathing in
light. Diva, the braids of a girl, Iemanjá, the long hair, they
were two and they were one and the same, they're not
things to be explained but to be understood. Diva flew over
the river and the clearing. With her lips she touched the
black man's face, blew life into his mouth, revived his member, and, at peace with death, disappeared into the void.

Those who had seen black Tição Abduim sitting on a
stone, his eyes on the glimmering light that was breaking up
into dust, say that he got up, still in a trance, and executed
the ritual dance steps, the macumba rites. Informed by some
onlookers, Fadul Abdala hurried over from his store.

"Is something wrong, Tição?"

Surprised, he saw the black man smile.

"No, it wasn't anything. I'd been asleep and I just woke up."

He'd awakened smiling, good news.

8

FOR EPIFÂNIA OF OXUM, Tição had crafted a golden *abebê* during the days of loneliness and blues: the loneliness, a heavy weight; the blues had stifled him. Oxum had come to keep him company and help him in the task of bringing together those who had lived indifferently and aloof from one another, as if their neighbors didn't exist. Together the two blood brothers had broken the loneliness and organized the festival, at a time of meetings and farewells.

For Diva of Iemanjá, Castor Abduim had forged a silver *abebê* during the days of doubt and bewitchment: the doubt, an open wound; the bewitchment was consuming him. Iemanjá had come from faraway Sergipe in the hold of the moon boat and had dropped anchor in his sleeping hammock. *My whitey, my little black girl, oh!* The world had begun and ended in the hammock.

With Diva's death, solitude returned, another, different kind. This time it didn't come from the loneliness of the place: it was inside Tição's chest, not around him. He didn't want to give the child to its grandmother or aunts, and refused Zilda's offer: *I'll take care of him, bring him up along with my own.* But his son's presence didn't compensate for Diva's absence, didn't console him: on the contrary, it made her memory all the sharper.

Tovo was a child without a mother, reared in a vacuum. Sometimes Tição felt guilty keeping him, but how could he be separated from his Tovo? Coroca's shout, on the night of damnation, still rang in his ears: *Have you forgotten, damn you, that you've got a son?* In order to fulfill the responsibility that Diva had left him as an inheritance, black Castor Abduim hadn't killed himself. In solitude, in desolation, the three creatures inhabited a house of stone and mortar: Tovo,

Tição, and Poor Soul. In the waters of the river, in his father's arms, Tovo was learning to swim; in the workshop he learned to walk, stumbling, clinging to the dog. He had a big rattle a drover had given him, and Turk Fadul had brought him a little celluloid swan from Ilhéus, which Tovo would bite as his teeth began to come in. A child without a mother.

Tição stopped in the doorway of the shop when he heard a child laugh once, and then again, coming from inside. He stood there listening. Tovo didn't know how to laugh, Diva had complained, he looks like a wild animal and he, Tição, a lonely ghost. It was true. He responded to the child's crying only to feed him or to clean his bottom. He'd take him into the woods in the morning, to the river at the close of the afternoon. The rest of the time, the dog took care of him. He, Tição, had become a werewolf.

The three of them were playing on the mattress: Tovo, Poor Soul, and Epifânia. Tição squatted beside them. Epifânia had heard that the shoer of donkeys was no longer the same person she'd known, that he'd forgotten how to laugh, just lived to keep alive. Who'd made up such a tale? There he was, laughing, the same old Tição. No one knew how to laugh with as much pleasure as he.

"Did you come to stay? Really?"

"Didn't you hear what I said? I'm not leaving even if you send me away."

She didn't say it with a challenging voice; she said it so he would know and agree. She lifted her eyes up to Castor Abduim, once her lover. She'd sworn to herself, proud and unsubmissive, that she'd never come back to him. But as soon as she learned about the purgatory he was going through—unhappy, a condemned dog, his feet no longer obeying him—there she was. But she still had her old spirit.

"I didn't come here to sleep in your hammock. You can have any woman you want, I don't care. If I have to sleep here to take care of the boy, I'll sleep on the mattress with him. I didn't come with the intention of shacking up with you, but to be a mother to him, I swear to God. I want you only to let me play with him, take care of him. All children need to have a mother, and all women must have a child, even if it's only a rag doll or a full-grown man. Did you know that I had a child once? I never told you, why should I have? He was Tovo's age when he died. I also wanted to die once, Tição."

"You did the right thing in coming. She brought you here."

"She? Could be. I found out from Cosme, on the road. I was going to Itabuna, I kept on going. I hadn't gone half a league when I noticed I was heading in the direction of Tocaia Grande."

The child was crawling, looking for Epifânia's lap.

"Tovo likes you." The black man spoke as if he were giving her his welcome.

"Is that a name or a nickname?"

"His name's Cristóvão, for my uncle. Tovo's the nickname she gave him."

The child stretched out his arms to his father.

9

ALMIGHTY GOD, THE SUPREME Wisdom, only he and no one else could know if Dona Leocádia's Epiphany would in time come to be a tradition in Tocaia Grande, repeating what had been the case in Estância. Mr. Carlinhos Silva foresaw that it would receive the same favor there: but that was the opinion of a mere mortal, no more than a doubtful conjecture. On the streets of Estância the parade had been taking place for more than forty years: the fabulous figures of the Bull and the Caboclo, the groups of shepherdesses, the blue and the scarlet, the orchestra of accordion and *cavaquinhos*, the bass drum beating time. The bass drum pulled in the urchins, took wing, raised up the people. What would happen with Dona Leocádia's Epiphany in Tocaia Grande after that year of triumph and glory only God knew, if He was up to knowing.

What was certain and nice was that there was drumming, a shaking of legs, flirting, affairs, merriment turned loose while the rehearsals went on, from mid-December until the day before Epiphany eve.

Day by day the excitement grew with the rehearsals of the music and dance steps, the marching and the recitals, lines memorized by everyone. Just as Dona Leocádia had told the meritorious Mr. Carlinhos Silva—he'd managed the donation of the bass drum—the festivities began with the first rehearsal and went on for almost a month.

Those present when the roles were decided used and abused the right to applaud the selections made by Dona Leocádia: mistress of the parade, she brooked no arguments, cantankerous and iron-handed. Captain Natário da Fonseca commented to Turk Fadul how much it all resembled the appointment of candidates for intendente and councilmen in Itabuna: the assembled politicians automatically acclaiming the names proposed by Colonel Boaventura Andrade. It wasn't by chance that the old woman and the landowner were relatives.

The participants and the curious gathered together in the shed—the whole population, actually—and Dona Leocádia handed out the roles. Senhorita Dona Deusa, the lady goddess, would be her granddaughter Aracati. Dressed as a clown, Vavá would triumph once more in the part of Mateus, dragged off as a prisoner by the soldiery. Amâncio would have died of chagrin if anyone else had been chosen to play the part of the Besta-Fera, the wild beast, also known as Jaraguá and Temeroso, the fearsome one. Aurélio would wear the hide of the bull so that Vanjé's people would figure in the Epiphany cast. Zinho, Edu, Durvalino, Balbino, Zelito, and Jair would make up the contingent of soldiers meant to arrest Mateus, accused of killing the bull. As for the Caboclo Gostosinho, the principal male role, who plays opposite and has a dialogue with Senhorita Dona Deusa, Leocádia had gone to the blacksmith's shop that morning to invite Castor Abduim to play it. In her eyes the Caboclo Gostosinho in the Tocaia Grande Epiphany parade could be no one else but the black man: he had the hearing, the arrogance, the roguishness. He was heartbroken, she knew, but maybe the invitation would boost his spirits.

Had she gone a week earlier, she would certainly have received a resounding no. Dona Leocádia took advantage of the visit to offer black Epifânia a part as a shepherdess, but the whore thanked her and declined the honor; she'd be too busy with the boy.

10

STARTING WITH THE FIRST rehearsal, the initial
meeting to decide some important points, Dona Leocádia's
Epiphany as it prepared itself to parade in Tocaia Grande
was hardly the same as the one that had cheered the population of Estância for four decades.

To begin with, how could the groups of shepherdesses
be organized in Tocaia Grande without the participation of
whores? To begin with, there weren't enough young girls in
the place to make up the two groups of eight shepherdesses,
and, generally, the married women or those living with
someone offered excuses, a child, a husband, or a boyfriend,
and turned it down. The solution was to resort to the prostitutes, and because in Tocaia Grande it was impossible to
draw the line between them and family women.

What beautiful shepherdesses, ah! So well-dressed, so
graceful and exciting! It was necessary to increase their
number, however, because, in toto, adding up whores and
girls, there were twenty-three candidates vying for the two
groups of eight shepherdesses each. Dona Leocádia, ever
magnanimous, decided that since there was only one Epiphany parade in Tocaia Grande, such conventions made no
sense: why only eight? She raised the blue and scarlet groups
to twelve members each, and, to make them equal, invited
old Vanjé; and she didn't have to plead with her: a shepherdess at her age? Only there in that asshole of the earth!

11

RIDING ALONGSIDE COLONEL BOAVENTURA Andrade, Natário
found him quite worn out. Old age had lighted on the plantation owner overnight, accentuating his wrinkles, adding
to his white hairs and to his silences.

Accompanied by Espiridião and the drover Joel, they
were going to the Taquaras station to meet Dona Ernestina,
coming to spend the holidays on the plantation with her

husband. The donkey Himalaya, so called because of its girth, plodded along beside the drover's mount, on its broad back a made-to-measure seat to hold the colonel's sainted lady and her fat bottom.

Seeing him at Atalaia day after day, Natário hadn't noticed how much the colonel had aged. But that morning, their two animals keeping the same pace, side by side, the half-breed was able to see the devastation of age on his old friend's flaccid face, and noticed his shortness of breath: it made him afraid.

Signaling Natário to follow him, the colonel nudged his mare and went on ahead. The bodyguard and the drover kept a discreet distance.

"Tell Leocádia that with Ernestina on the plantation I won't be able to attend the Epiphany. I'm sorry, because Sacramento would have liked it. I told her to go, to stay with Zilda. Do you know what she answered me? Just imagine: she said she wasn't going because if she went, Ernestina wouldn't have anyone to help her. She's a good girl."

He fell silent for a moment, as if thinking about Sacramento's refusal, then he lowered his voice.

"Listen, Natário, there's something I want to ask of you."

"Anything you say, Colonel."

"You've never let me down in life. I don't want you to let me down when I die."

Concerned, Natário became alert: what was the colonel going to ask him to do? He would probably make him promise to serve his son as he'd served him, keeping the title and responsibility of administrator on Atalaia Plantation. Natário had no intention of keeping any such promise. Only he knew how much his beloved Boa Vista suffered from having the colonel's land under his care: seeing to plantings, harvests, improvements, workers, a burdensome and difficult job, a huge responsibility. Another boss, never. Colonel Boaventura Andrade had been the first and only one, he would be the last. Tense, he waited.

"Listen, Natário. Promise me that when I die you'll look after Sacramento." He added, "She's a good girl."

Relieved of his concern and fears, Natário promised, "If it so happens that you go before me, sir, you can rest easy about her. For me, she'll be the same as if she were my child. I'll watch over her."

They covered a good stretch in silence. The worry had
disappeared from the colonel's face, tired but serene, his
voice calm. That was the way it always was when he'd
made a decision.

"Taking an old man's abuse without anything in return!
You know something, Natário? I'm going to buy a house in
Itabuna and put it in her name."

"With your permission, Colonel, I must say I think you're
doing the right thing."

12

THE SHEPHERDESSES' LANTERNS WERE twirling, a flight of
fireflies, on the climb that led up to Captain Natário da
Fonseca's residence where Dona Leocádia's Epiphany would
begin its performance on the night of January 5th, the eve
of the Feast of the Magi. Behind them waited the whole
population. Only one person hadn't run to enjoy the maneu-
vers of the pastoral groups: the backlander Altamirando.
His festival was made up of Ção's appearances on the hill
with the goats. He didn't need anything else to celebrate.

The two groups of shepherdesses, surrounding the characters, stood on the terrace that stretched out to the foot of
the mulungu tree. At a signal from Dona Leocádia they began
the "Song of Entry to the Parlor," addressed to the owners
of the house in their Sunday best, Dona Zilda and the captain, waiting at the front door.

> It's here, it's here
> The dark girls have arrived
> The girls and their Epiphany
> The nicest little dance alive

There wasn't enough room in the parlor for the antics of
the group: the high jinks of the bull, the twirling of Senhorita Dona Deusa and the Caboclo Gostosinho, the somer-
saults of Mateus the clown, the running about of the
Besta-Fera, the entry of the soldiers—bandits, that is. Not in
the captain's house, much less in the others to be visited. In

all of them the Epiphany had the same routine—in addition to permission to enter, blessings were sung in honor of the Christ Child:

> Blessings and praise upon him
> Blessings and praise upon him
> The Christ Child has been born

The accordion and the *cavaquinho* drew out the humble melody; the bass drum, brand new, kept the beat. Dressed in colorful flowered chintz, with lace, bows, and frills, their straw hats decorated with cloth foliage and flowers tied with blue and pink ribbons—the blue of the Immaculate Virgin, the scarlet of the Passion of Christ—the shepherdesses danced and sang for the Christ Child born in a manger in Bethlehem and, no one knows why, found in Rome.

> The Christ Child has been born
> And found up there in Rome
> And found up there in Rome
> All dressed up on the altar bar

With the blessings over, there was a pause for drinks and a full and tasty repast. Bottles of *cachaça* went from hand to hand; they drank straight from the neck: glasses and cups were reserved for the genipap liqueur served the shepherdesses. Wiping their mouths with the backs of their hands, the principals in the Epiphany began the "Farewell Song" as they left.

> So I say good night
> Ladies of the house
> I'm leaving now
> With tears in my eyes

Awakened by the singing and the beating of the drum, the parrot Up-Your-Ass stirred on his perch: he flapped his wings and shouted foul words as the whole group joined in singing the final verses.

> I'm leaving now
> For the lands I call my own
> Oh, good people, I'll return another time

One last turn around the parlor and the Epiphany waved good-bye.

> Quilariô, quilariá
> Alone on the sea
> Shines the Morning Star

The flickering light of fireflies, the lanterns of the shepherdesses descended the hill; behind came the retinue of Tocaia Grande, enlarged by Captain Natário da Fonseca, Dona Zilda, and the couple's children, those by blood and those by adoption.

As the Epiphany lit the way, they suddenly crossed paths with a rider who had burst out of the shadows of the night: riding bareback, wildly, coming at a gallop, shouting for the captain. When he came up to him, he leapt off his mount and started talking. It was black Espiridião.

"Natário! The colonel's kicked off. He died before my eyes without saying nothing. His eyes bugged out, his face twisted, his mouth bent sideways, and he slammed to the floor." He spoke fast, trying, perhaps, to get rid of the picture he carried in his eyes and his heart.

Colonel Boaventura Andrade had dropped dead before the eyes of Espiridião, who guarded the door of the boss's room to protect him from any bandit paid by some enemy to do him harm. Espiridião had been unable to use his shotgun against the stroke that had been lying in ambush, biding its time. In the distance the pastorale was saying its farewell.

> Quilariô, quilariá
> When I die, that day
> The world can fly away
> Quilariô, quilariá

Zilda burst into tears. Captain Natário da Fonseca, his face frozen, a gargoyle of stone or wood: *With your permission, Colonel*, what a tragedy! *Quilariá, quilariô*, the world is finished, I know.

CITADEL OF SIN, LAIR OF BANDITS

A Visitation to Tocaia Grande by the Holy Office, Along with Requisitory, Condemnation, and a Good Fling

1

CARRYING THE SACRED CHALICES, vestments, incense, holy water, sacramental wine, and the word of God in two metal trunks, the Holy Mission reached Tocaia Grande just as the thick and heavy winter dreariness descended: a steady, depressing rain, mud ruining the roads, the light of the days growing shorter, the darkness of the nights longer. Two mendicant friars descended from their catechising toil at the headwaters of the Rio das Cobras. In the breadth of the valley, keeping pace with the development of cacao groves, settlements were springing up, villages growing, some more miserable than others, all, without exception, living in iniquity and sin.

Frei Zygmunt von Gotteshammer and Frei Theun da Santa Eucaristia arrived after covering that vast province of paganism and heresy in two months of arduous and punishing preaching; as they drew near Tocaia Grande, riding slow and cautious donkeys, they carried hearts bursting with pity and wrath. Pity in the heart of the young Frei Theun, Dutch by birth, a novice ordained in Rome and sent by the order as a missionary to Brazil. Wrath in that of Frei Zygmunt, thin and wizened, with an ascetic look, his finger held up, upbraiding, his mouth full of anathema and condemnation.

The round face of Frei Theun, a new priest on his first holy mission, showed fatigue from the endless crossing of desolate regions that lacked material comfort even for a mendicant friar, not to mention any spiritual support. The inhabitants lacked everything in spite of the lush, rich production of cacao, a product almost as valuable as gold. Twenty years older than his preaching companion, and with more than ten of them spent in the irreligiosity of southern Bahia, Frei Zygmunt, if he was weary, didn't let it show and continued the task of unmasking and defeating Beelzebub.

On the banks of the Rio das Cobras the absence of order and the disregard for morality were total and absolute. The mission to install order and morality, to implant the fear of God, had been given to Frei Zygmunt not only by the superior of his congregation, when he sent him to preach and convert in those ends of the earth. He had received it directly and without appeal from Christ Our Lord. In the solitude of his cell, on sleepless nights of prayer and penance, he would flagellate himself with his scourge in order to tame his body, free it from the seductions of the world, from idolatry and lechery. The only decoration on the naked wall was a print of the Sacred Heart of Jesus, blood pouring from the hallowed heart because of the sins committed against the glory of God. The image took on life, the blood spreading out, spattering the thighs and stomach, the buttocks and torso of the tormented monk. Jesus was commanding him to depart and fight sin with steel and fire until its complete extirpation.

In Frei Zygmunt's opinion, the Holy Mother Church possessed no saint of greater virtue, none more deserving of honor and devotion than Torquemada, the Grand Inquisitor of Spain and Portugal: he hadn't been canonized, an injustice that made him no less venerable. He was captain of the hordes of virtue and doctrine in the armies of God, and Frei Zygmunt had enlisted under his banner to do battle without quarter against heretics, degenerates, and blasphemers. The fury of the Illuminated sustained him. Illuminated by the fires of hell.

During the fatiguing journey from settlement to settlement, the two priests had become aware of Tocaia Grande's dark and sinister reputation. From what they had heard, heathens lived there without religion or law, without dogma or codes—pagans, concubines, bandits, sluts—there were even blacks practicing macumba and Mahometan Arabs.

The name of the place said it all. In biblical terms, Tocaia
Grande meant Sodom and Gomorrah rolled into one, united
in the abominable worship of the seven deadly sins.

2

DOGGING THE TRAIL OF the monks, splashing through the
mud, went their gadabout rival, the popular accordion player
Pedro Gypsy. Whenever the arrival of monks and priests on
a holy apostolic mission was announced—preaching, performing baptisms, weddings, confessions, exorcisms, and
expiations—echoing down the same trail, an integral part of
the great event and at the same time its negation was Pedro
Gypsy's accordion, brightening up the festivities with which
the village would celebrate its baptisms and weddings.

From having taken part in so many missions, Pedro
Gypsy could have served as their sexton, aiding in the celebration of mass. In spite of that, Frei Zygmunt, when he
spotted him listening attentively to the fiery words of the
sermon in the first row of the devout, felt his guts twist in
his fanatical insides: he saw Satan seated before him in
flesh and blood, the smile of debauchery on that simple
face. A missionary suffered a great deal in primitive places
with backward customs, with the Holy Office of Inquisition
disbanded and sacred institution of slavery abolished.

3

EVER SINCE HE'D SOLD his cacao warehouse to Koifman &
Co., Colonel Robustiano de Araújo's stops in Tocaia Grande
had been less frequent. Still, every so often he would use the
shortcut and take a look at the corral, have a chat with the
Arab Fadul and Captain Natário, pay a visit to his old friend
Castor Abduim, give his blessing to his godchild.

He had a high regard for the black man, he'd helped

Castor set himself up on his own. The colonel had been concerned when he saw him so gloomy and spiritless, with no interest in anything after Diva's death. There hadn't been a trace of that expansive fellow, quick to sense things, to start bragging and meddling, the one who'd enlivened Santa Mariana Plantation with his joviality and whose inventiveness had transformed the customs of the settlement.

The sudden resurrection of the blacksmith had made the colonel happy. His old friend had told him in confidence about the episode of the *egum* that had shown itself in the clearing, putting an end to his mourning and restoring the joy of living to his empty, suicidal body. It had touched him in the head, the heart, and the member. To make Epifânia come take care of him and the child, the *egum* had altered the whore's route, guided her steps. Diva's *egum*, a star glowing above the ocean waves in the faraway lands of Aiocá.

Contrary to the efforts of many, Colonel Robustiano de Araújo didn't try to hide the black blood that flowed in his veins, abundant and powerful. A pure white by grace of being rich, a cacao planter of more than a hundred tons harvest, a cattleman with a considerable herd, a pillar of the church, the father-in-law of a Frenchman—his youngest daughter had married a Laffitte of the Gas and Light Company—not even because of that had he forsaken the *orixás*. His mother, the mulatta Rosália, dark and beautiful, had been initiated as an *iaô*, becoming sanctified without being aware that she was pregnant by her employer, the elementary-school teacher Sílvio de Araújo, handsome and penniless, weak in the chest. Oxaguian, on entering Rosália's head, at the same time became lord and master of the child she carried. To win back his right to live, Rosália had to buy the child from the Enchanted One, paying a high price for his document of manumission, and she was successful in her endeavor: she freed the slave and gained him the status of son of Oxaguian. The boy grew up healthy and strong, and while still young he left for the cacao war and came out of it victorious.

Before dying, his father had recognized him, but all he had to leave him was the family name. Young Robustiano joined up with Basílio de Oliveira in the legendary struggle against the Badarós: he cleared the forest, marked out land, faced gunmen. With an armored body, protected by Oxaguian, he didn't suffer a scratch. He planted cacao, bred herds, married a rich girl, a relative of the Badarós, as should be noted: young Isabel. They didn't have any male children, the daughters were sent off to study at the Colégio da Piedade with the good Ursuline sisters. They would be elementary-school teachers like their grandfather, but would have no need to teach—dark beauties, rich heiresses, there would be no lack of suitors. And that was how it was: the medical doctor Itazil Veiga married the eldest; the second in line, Kátia by name, hit the lottery on the day of a fair in honor of St. George by winning the foreigner Jean Laffitte, an engineer educated across the ocean. The colonel was a generous contributor to ceremonies of the Church and to those of Pai Arolu's *axé*. He helped carry the litter of the patron saint in Catholic processions. He didn't dance in the circle of *orixás* at the *candomblé;* but in his home he always put out food for Oxaguian.

4

ON A CERTAIN OCCASION the summer before, the colonel had lingered a bit in Tocaia Grande, a little longer than the usual stop of a few hours to check the corral and bat the breeze with friends. He'd done so in answer to the request of Captain Natário da Fonseca, for whom he'd always shown a special regard. He'd promised to visit the Boa Vista Plantation, whose production was causing surprise and comments: a minimal piece of land in comparison to the spread of Atalaia or Santa Mariana, its harvest, from the last crop, had topped four tons, and the captain predicted that he would double that figure in a few years.

By keeping his promise—he covered the plantation from one end to the other, grove by grove, examining the improvements one by one, troughs, hothouses, bins, workers' housing—the colonel got the answer that always intrigued him: he finally learned what had really happened between Natário and Venturinha, when the only son and heir of the late Colonel Boaventura Andrade had finally taken possession of his property. Rumors had been heard about the delicate matter; there was talk about a misunderstanding and an exchange of harsh words.

On the occasion of his father's sudden demise, Venturinha was in Europe, at the start of a planned excursion that was to stretch out through cabarets and whorehouses in the great capitals of London, Paris, Berlin, and Rome. He didn't get to visit Berlin and Rome because the news, sent on from London, caught up with him in the midst of his passion and prodigality. A bit delayed: the colonel had been resting in the cemetery on Conquista Hill in Ilhéus for almost a month— after an endless funeral cortège and interminable perorations beside the mausoleum. The seventh-day masses had long been sung, and those of a month were drawing near— the ones arranged for by Dona Ernestina and by Adriana. The colonel's spirit had even taken on flesh for more than an hour in the skinny and nervous body of the medium Zorávia at the Faith and Charity Spiritualist Center, beseeching Adriana for masses for the repose of his soul and alms for the poor, in that way helping him depart the lower circles of the Beyond, where he was wandering. In the streets of the cities, especially in Itabuna, the backbiters, informed of such psychic phenomena, promptly translated *lower circles* as the depths of hell. Viper tongues have no respect for the dead.

It was also said, right and left, that the immediate cause of the stroke that downed the colonel was the letter from Rio de Janeiro in which his son announced his departure for London aboard a packet of the Royal English Mail Line. A trip to further his studies that would last three months. It asked for a letter of credit to be assigned to a bank, likewise English, as a loan to underwrite the trip. It was a voyage decided upon at the last moment; Venturinha was sorry he hadn't had time to inform his parents earlier: when the letter reached them he would already be in England. Still without an address where he could be reached, he gave them that of the bank through which, with natural urgency, a goodly sum of money should be sent; being who he was, he couldn't play the role of penniless pauper in Europe. He asked for a large amount and quickly: studies at Oxford and the Sorbonne cost your eye teeth.

According to black Espiridião, the colonel had barely

finished reading the letter. He'd taken a step toward Dona
Ernestina, holding out the sheet of paper, but hadn't been
able to give it to her, he'd dropped dead between his bodyguard and his sainted wife, at the feet of Sacramento. How
had Dona Ernestina been able to bear the tragedy and not
fall dead right there at the same instant, beside her husband?

With a scream she threw herself onto the inert body,
and when Sacramento succeeded in raising her, she hugged
the girl and they wept together. Her husband dead, her son
far away, all alone and lost, Dona Ernestina found shelter
and consolation in her prayers and in the devoted and tireless Sacramento. She took the girl with her on the special
train the following morning as it bore the body of the deceased to Ilhéus. Having arrived in haste in the middle of
the night, Natário took charge of the arrangements. His
tight face remained locked in a hard and opaque silence.

5

IF, AS WAS COMMONLY said, and he himself, Colonel Robustiano de Araújo, could confirm, the care given to the groves
of Atalaia was identical to that dispensed by Natário to the
cacao groves of Boa Vista, Venturinha was more than right
in being angered by the refusal of the administrator to
remain in his position. An absolute refusal, no amount of
money, no additional incentives, would alter Natário's decision. "What was the reason?" asked Colonel Robustiano de
Araújo, curiosity showing itself amid the praise for the richness of the groves and the edenic bloom: nothing was closer
to the beauty of Paradise than the moving sight of a cacao
plantation loaded with flowers and buds.

Captain Natário da Fonseca heard the question without
moving a single muscle of his half-breed face: the bronzed
skin, the tiny eyes, the thread of a smile on the lips that the
lawyer and poet Medauar had once compared to the thin
cut of a razor blade. An enigmatic smile, some thought it
was mocking, others found it frightening.

"I'll tell you, Colonel, if you've got the patience to hear
me out. I came from Sergipe; I was just a boy, I'd got into
some trouble up there. Nothing important, the guy wasn't

worth the bullet I spent on him. I had a recommendation to
the colonel and he took me in."

Colonel Robustiano's mare Empress and Captain Natário's
black mule were going along side by side with a slow
and careful pace on the path through cacao groves. The
colonel made no comment and the captain went on with
his account.

"Colonel Boaventura was already mixed up in the troubles, as you know, sir, you were involved in them together.
He trusted me, gave me a repeater, and took me with him. I
might say that he raised me, he always treated me the way
a man should be treated, I owe him what I am and what I've
got. I don't remember my father: he knocked up my mother
and took off. The father I knew was Colonel Boaventura."

"But I heard him say himself that you saved his life
more than once. Boaventura wasn't just doing you a favor
when he had the ground we're riding on put in your name."

"The colonel protected me and he paid me a gunman's
salary to look after him. I'm quick on the trigger and in my
thoughts. I only did my duty. If he didn't want to, he didn't
have to give me land or title. I won't say I didn't deserve it, I
damned well did, just that he wasn't under any obligation
because I'd been taken in and had been properly paid for
what I did."

The captain had dropped the reins onto the saddlehorn,
letting the mule go at its own pace along the familiar path;
he was following other trails, those of the past, where sometimes there weren't any paths.

"Colonel Boaventura was the bravest and straightest
man I've ever known and it wouldn't have bothered me if I'd
had to die for him. That's why even after I owned the land
and had planted cacao, I never left his service, I continued
taking care of Atalaia. I told him on more than one occasion: 'As long as you're alive sir, and you want me, I'm at
your service.' I promised him only one thing for after his
death and I'm keeping that promise. But it hasn't got anything to do with cacao groves or the job of administrator."

"They told me that Venturinha offered to pay you whatever you asked."

"Colonel, I think every man wants to be master of his
own fate. When I started earning my living, going along
with pilgrimages up there on the São Francisco, I heard the

people say that a person's fate is written up in heaven and
nobody can change it, but to my way of thinking it's different. I think that everyone has got to look out for himself and
I always wanted to be on my own. I served the colonel for
more than twenty years: I was seventeen when I got here, I
just celebrated my forty-second birthday. I never promised
to serve his widow or his son. And he never asked me to."

He picked up the reins. The mounts were leaving the
cacao groves, heading along the trail that led to the living
quarters that Colonel Robustiano hadn't yet seen. Natário
softened his voice.

"I like Venturinha a lot. When I arrived on the plantation he was still a little boy. But it's a different liking from
what I felt for the colonel. The colonel gave me a hand, I
was nothing but a fugitive from the police. Now the only
one who gives me orders is me. I'm the one who decides."

"Did Venturinha understand your point of view? Did he
agree? I hear he didn't."

"I didn't ask. I didn't want to know. He's going to get
involved in politics, take his father's place. I told him that if
he needs me to defend him against his enemies, all he has to
do is let me know, I'm still a good shot. But as an employee,
he'd have to excuse me, not for him or for anybody else."

Before they dismounted, his curiosity satisfied, Colonel
Robustiano de Araújo closed the conversation.

"If you're interested in my opinion, Natário, you should
know that you did the right thing in serving Boaventura, the
same as refusing to serve Venturinha. There should always
be a certain distance in standing between the one giving
orders and the one carrying them out." He changed the
subject. "A beauty of a big house. Congratulations."

"Big house? This is just a little house where Zilda can
stay with the kids. A month doesn't go by without her
coming to the farm."

6

ON ATALAIA PLANTATION, THE workers' quarters—adobe or
wooden huts—were grouped around the big house and the
stream, along the side of the road; a few of them were

isolated, scattered among the more distant groves. Natário
had made it his business to stop by all of them and spread
the news that he was leaving, offering his thanks; he maintained a good working relationship with all the field hands
and drovers, one of friendship too: he was godfather to the
children of some. Night had fallen over the cacao groves and
the woods, and, in spite of its being winter, the evening was
tepid, caressing.

As he went along he noticed the light of a lantern in the
shack of the late Tiburcinho. He had just seen Dona Efigênia
taking care of Idalício, a young cacao picker bitten by a
snake that afternoon. A competent healer, the old woman
had been nursing him. She'd filled her toothless mouth with
plug tobacco and applied it to the bite on the patient's
ankle: she was sucking up the venom and spitting it out,
muttering prayers:

> Good Saint Benedict
> Club the snake
> Kill the snake
> Snakes belong to Satan's nation
> Free me from poison
> Free me from temptation

Idalício was burning with fever but holding his own;
the old woman had succeeded in reducing the amount of
poison and softening its effects, which were nearly always
fatal. The captain found her by the patient's bed and chatted with her there before leaving Atalaia. He hoped for
Idalício to escape with his life, maybe he would, thanks to
the powers of St. Benedict and the folk wisdom of the prayer
woman. They talked about Sacramento, and Dona Efigênia
complained: she missed her daughter, whose lingering in
Ilhéus to care for the colonel's widow was hindering the
implementation of plans nurtured ever since she'd found
out Sacramento was owner of a house in Itabuna, a gift
from Colonel Boaventura Andrade, grateful and magnanimous.

Dona Efigênia and Sacramento had learned about the
house acquired by the plantation owner and put in the
name of his concubine, a document worked out in a lawyer's
office with all the necessary whereases and wherebys, from
Natário; the captain was the only one privy to the hush-

hush matter: the colonel didn't want the news spread about. The rent brought in a few good coppers every month, enough for mother and daughter to live free from worry. Dona Efigênia had dreamed ever since of quitting the plantation to open up a greengrocery in Itabuna or Taquaras, where she could sell bananas, breadfruit, peppers, *gilós*, and other garnishes and spices.

Since the colonel had been in good health, however, and mad about the girl, the prayer woman had put off the project for when the landowner would get tired of Sacramento: you know how it is with a rich man's mistress; it can all end overnight. The colonel never had a chance to get tired, he went before that; death blew the stroke into his head and he fell hard, his mouth all twisted. Selling squashes and pumpkins in the store, with all those people pouring into Itabuna was a golden opportunity: Sacramento wouldn't be long in finding another fat cat who would set her up in a house and give her charge accounts in clothing stores and shoe shops. That was what Dona Efigênia was pondering, ambitious and practical.

But Dona Ernestina had inherited Sacramento along with the colonel's rural and urban properties: the plantation, the streets of rented houses in Ilhéus and Itabuna, the money out on loan, the immense fortune. Dona Efigênia's greengrocery dreams were postponed until God knows when.

Colonel Boaventura Andrade's estate, the main theme of conversation and gossip on streetcorners and in bars, wasn't the object of inventory and division. "Someday or other it shall all belong to him"—the widow had decided, ordering masses from Father Afonso, and referring to her son— "as soon as God calls me to His bosom." Since that's the case, why divide up lands and houses, major and minor possessions, capital and promissory notes? As soon as Venturinha got back from Europe, after stops in Rio and Bahia, his mother turned management and mismanagement of the fortune over to him. Dona Ernestina kept one single belonging for herself: the maid Sacramento.

7

SO WHOSE SHADOW WAS it the captain saw outlined against the lamplight in the house of the late Tiburcinho? Just what was going on in that shack in the absence of the widow who lived there? It couldn't be anything good. Natário shoved the door open with his left hand, his right resting on the butt of his revolver. He came face-to-face with Sacramento, covered with dust: the girl gave a small cry when she saw him, not a cry of fright, but one of surprise and satisfaction.

"Oh, Captain! How good to see you! They told me you'd gone away."

"But you, what are you doing here? Did Dona Ernestina send you away?"

"I never would have left there on account of Dona Ernestina. The poor thing must be thinking badly of me, imagining I'm a good-for-nothing. I ran off without saying anything to her, but what was I going to say?"

"You ran away from the colonel's house? What bee got into your bonnet?"

"It was the doctor. He wanted to have me."

The captain didn't seem surprised: a chilling, almost imperceptible smile was sketched on his lips.

"Venturinha?"

"Like you say, sir, he came into the room where I was, all worked up, drooling, smelling of drink. I was lucky. I pushed him, he fell down, puking. He didn't have the strength to get up. All he did was say he was going to get me. I was so scared I didn't even get my things together. I grabbed whatever I could find, along with the handkerchief where I had a little money tied up, and I ran to the train station. From Taquaras I came here on foot to see Ma and talk to you."

The captain didn't make any comment, but his eyes tightened, the same as his smile. Sacramento raised her eyes and looked him in the face.

"He grabbed me, knocked me down, hit me, bit me. If you don't believe me, have a look." She showed him the purple welts on her arms, the marks of sucking and teeth on her neck.

Natário's silence continued. *Who knows*, Sacramento

thought, *maybe he doesn't think those marks are enough reason to explain my running away.* She lifted up her skirt to her thighs and showed them: black and blue marks at the place where the knees of Venturinha, a full, fat figure of a man, had dug into the dark and appetizing flesh. The captain's stare lingered, and Sacramento lowered her skirt but didn't lower her eyes.

"How could I go to bed with his own son? God save me and protect me! When he came in he offered me money, called me pretty and I don't know what else. I asked him to leave me alone and he talked about the colonel, shouted that he knew all about us and wanted some of the same. I pleaded again, for the sake of his mother, for the soul of the colonel. But he'd already taken his jacket and his pants off. That was when he grabbed me. He was falling-down drunk, that's what saved me."

Captain Natário da Fonseca didn't say a word; he only touched the girl's tense face with his fingertips and wiped away a tear. Sacramento took the hand that was stroking her face and kissed it.

"On the train I was thinking of you. Except for Ma, who can't do anything, you're the only one I've got in the whole world."

Then she lowered her eyes to the floor again.

"Just the other day I remembered you, I remembered so well that I could almost see you beside me telling me what I should answer Dona Misete."

The name sounded familiar to the captain's ears.

"I know a Misete. She's got a whorehouse on the Ilha das Cobras."

"She sent a message asking me to come be one of the girls in her house. That was when I remembered you and your telling me that the colonel wouldn't like seeing me leading that kind of life. Better to stay on as a servant in Dona Ernestina's house. But with the doctor living there, it just can't be. I took the train, I got off in Taquaras, hit out for here. I just got in, I don't even know where Ma is. But I found you and that's enough for me."

She turned and looked straight at him, declaring in a calm and firm voice, "I'm not going to bed with anybody trying to pay me or force me." A smile flickered amid the tears. She examined her arms, dusty from the road, touched her hair, caked with dirt, and spoke softly. "I've got to take a bath, I'm a mess. As soon as Ma comes, I'm going to wash in the river."

Natário told her where Efigênia was and what she was doing. With a look somewhere between bashful and bold, Sacramento announced, "In that case I'm going to take a bath right now, before she gets here. I'm filthy, so ugly you don't even want to look at me."

"Dirty or clean, you're the prettiest thing there ever was. If the colonel hadn't laid his eyes on you, the one to make a woman of you might have been me."

"It could have happened. How could I have resisted when all I ever did was think about you?"

She went to the door, brushed past him; her full breasts touched the captain's chest. He followed her in the direction of the riverbank: *With your permission, Colonel.*

8

FUAD KARAN, AT HIS table in the bar, savoring the aromatic arrack that was his favorite drink, smiled at the Grand Turk, his friend Fadul Abdala, and declared emphatically, "A sexual cataclysm has fallen upon Itabuna, friend Fadul, and we're living under its sign. Listen to this poetic and mysterious invocation: Ludmila Gregoriovna Cytkynbaum. A line of poetry, eh?" He repeated it, raising his open hand and the pitch of his voice in a declamatory gesture. "She came from the taigas of Siberia: Ludmila Gregoriovna Cytkynbaum!"

For a second he stopped to listen to the echo of the limpid pronunciation of the high-sounding name, in evident applause for his own voice.

"You've heard tell of a femme fatale, haven't you, Fadul? Ludmila Gregoriovna is the perfect specimen, she's the prototype, the paradigm of the femme fatale, and we're all chained by her enchantments, we're her slaves, happy in our servitude."

Fuad Karan sipped the arrack to soothe his throat. His face irradiating profound intellectual pleasure, Fadul followed him. Enrapt, he was listening to the sybarite, one of his gurus: the other was Álvaro Faria, who lived in Ilhéus.

"A devourer of men, my Grand Turk. Dark ones by preference, the more Afro, the more they touch her psyche and dampen her vulva. She belongs by right but not de facto to our new lord and master, Dr. Boaventura Andrade, Junior, heir to the United Kingdom of Itabuna and Ilhéus. We're in the reign of Boaventura II, the Merry, grand successor to Boaventura I, the Stud."

For Fadul, exiled by the good Lord of the Maronites to the backwaters of Tocaia Grande, trips to the busy city streets to replenish his stock, pay off outstanding loans and take out new ones, visit bars, cabarets and whorehouses, and watch the sea turn to foam on Ilhéus beaches were a rare privilege; there was, in addition to everything else, the delight of conversation with the two eminences, the two men of letters: Álvaro Faria, in the port of Ilhéus, and Fuad Karan, in the backlands of Itabuna. The two were alike in their low regard for any work that wasn't pure intellectual lucubration: conversation, poker games, and comments on local events. Fuad Karan had a small advantage over his peer in Fadul's mind, by being an Arab and speaking the tongue of the Prophet with honey and dates, with sugar and anisette. Up on all events and all tricks, Fuad would analyze them with knowledge and skill. Fadul would listen in ecstasy.

"Pretty?" Fadul wanted to know, in a voice of lust and hunger.

"Pretty is an improper adjective for the description of Ludmila Gregoriovna: let us say beautiful, preferably. I like to think that she's Eurasian, a mixture of Slav and Semite; she might even be a distant relative of ours and we should be proud of that. In addition to her beauty, being Russian she's mystical and dramatic; since she's Jewish, dark and mysterious, and due to her Arab blood, romantic and sensual. If your luck as Grand Turk still holds, during the day you'll be able to catch a glimpse of her crossing the street, going into shops to sneer at what's for sale, or, accompanied by our young monarch, reigning at night in a cabaret with a long jade cigarette holder and her green eyes." He summed up his feelings in Arabic: *ia hôhi*!

"How'd she land here?"

"Venturinha brought her, how else?"

"Why did she come with the little lawyer?" Fadul still didn't feel that he had all the facts.

"Because she's a whore, that's her trade. She disguises it by singing Russian ballads. She murders 'The Volga Boatman' with extraordinary deftness. Her brother, by the way, plays the balalaika rather well: I've got to admit it because it's the truth."

"Is he really her brother?"

"I did some investigating and I concluded that the ties binding Ludmila Gregoriovna and Pyotr Sergueinovitch are really of blood and not bed. Brother and sister by the same mother. As for her being a whore, we mustn't condemn her just like that. She sells herself for money only to our noble Venturinha; the rest she does for free, for the pleasure of fornication, and we know, my dear Fadul, that there's no other pleasure in the world like fornication."

"I can't fault you there, my friend."

Fuad Karan's exaggerated rhetoric matched the commotion in the city, still under the impact of the intoxicating presence of Ludmila Gregoriovna Cytkynbaum: in cabarets as well as in church, bustling places, both, her appearance of fire and ice, hanging on Venturinha's arm, caused a sensation, provoked disorders: everybody wanted to look at her, bask in her smile, swoon before her green eyes. In the cabaret she would silence the wine-wet tumult, in church she would break the devout silence, *ohs!* and *ahs!* of lust and enthusiasm were heard all about and a flame of desire burned around her like a divine halo, the fiery tail of a comet.

9

THE NEWS OF COLONEL Boaventura Andrade's passing had interrupted Venturinha's fascinating studies at the Sorbonne de la Place Pigalle, hastening his return to Brazil. On that night the attorney drowned his remorse and displeasure in vodka and went on the binge of his life.

Ludmila Gregoriovna, too, upon learning of the tragedy that had befallen her "sugar daddy," suffered a nervous

attack and fell into an agonizing wail, but not any ordinary
weeping, with two modest tears: she began sobbing in the
Slavic manner, pulling her hair with wild cries and reciting
Russian prayers. Impassioned from his gullet down to his
gonads, the self-appointed continental decided to take
Ludmila to Brazil in his company, the best way to import
the culture of Europe, of which she was most representative.
She was accompanied by her brother, Pyotr Sergueinovitch,
but her lover, Konstantin Ivanovitch Surkov, had stayed
behind in Paris, gnawing on the rim of his "pisspot," to use
the folkloric expression of the triumphant Venturinha.

Count and colonel in the imperial guard, Konstantin
Ivanovitch Surkov was a relative of the imperial family,
but, fallen out with the tsar, had confided a state secret to
Venturinha, Baron Boaventura Boaventurovitch, as he had
become known in Slavic emigré circles. Ludmila Gregoriovna
also had noble blood although she didn't flaunt it, due to
the misfortune of being obliged to sing melancholy ballads
in Gallic cabarets. She'd fled the court because of the ignoble harassment of the Grand Duke Nikolai Nikolaievitch
Romanov, who wanted her for his mistress. Uncle of Tsar
Nicholas II, generalissimo of the Russian armies, he made
her life a hell. Since Venturinha seemed to find it odd that
she had not given in to such a powerful and eminent figure,
Konstantin Ivanovitch explained to his dear Boaventura
Boaventurovitch that the little Ludi, delicate and sensitive,
could not bear the smell of garlic on the generalissimo's
breath: the grand duke's kisses made her nauseated, uphold-
ing her virtue. That was why she had gone with Konstantin
when the dissident colonel had exiled himself to Paris. Theirs
was a tragic relationship: they couldn't get married because
he had a wife in Moscow, also a cousin of the tsar, but
they'd sworn eternal love and they were abiding by their
oath. Venturinha paid the bills and did so with justified
pride: it isn't every day that you can put horns on a member
of the imperial family of all the Russias.

At the Datcha, a Muscovite cabaret on the Place Blanche,
Ludmila sang, accompanied by her brother, Pyotr, a virtu-
oso on the balalaika. "Pedrinho, brother!" Venturinha would
beg at the height of passion and drink. "Play that guitar of
yours and make me cry!" Ludmila sang Russian melodies
and did dances from the Caucasus, displaying the perfection

of her legs. At a nearby table Count Konstantin, of ancient lineage, and Boaventura Junior, a recent baron, applauded, downing vodka and cognac. At the end of the night and the show, Pyotr would gather up the cuckolded Konstantin, leaving to the care of the Brazilian, an international champion in liquor consumption, the timid and long-suffering Ludmila: in bed an impetuous mare of the imperial cavalry, glory of the court of the tsar. At the moment of orgasm she would recite Pushkin and intone Orthodox prayers.

Ludmila's version of events in Moscow diverged somewhat from what had been proclaimed by the count and colonel. Not with reference to the Grand Duke Nikolai, the garlic chewer, however: he had, in fact, chased her like a hound from hell, forcing her into exile with her brother. But it was not true that she'd fallen madly in love with Konstantin. Taking advantage of her sad status as a fugitive and emigrée in Paris, he'd imposed himself on her in her entertainer's bed, getting her contracts and protecting her from the lustful aggression of customers at the Datcha. Thankful, she accepted and tolerated him, but between that and an oath of eternal love there was a distance as great as that from Kremlin Square to the Place Pigalle.

In both versions there were hiatuses, contradictions, blanks, incongruities, all no doubt due to the precarious mastery of the French language by the parties in question, although Ludmila did show a talent for languages: from Venturinha she'd learned dirty words in Portuguese and would repeat them with her adorable accent between kisses. In any case, there must have been some truth in the astonishing narratives, for when Ludmila Gregoriovna agreed to accompany him to Brazil, the Brazilian's hotel room was invaded by the count-colonel, who threatened him with scandal and death, challenging him to a duel, dagger in hand.

You could say whatever you wanted about Venturinha, and always come near to the truth, except to call him a coward. On previous occasions he'd found himself mixed up with infuriated husbands and lovers and had never backed off. He plowed into the tsar's relative, took his dagger, and kept it as a trophy. He ended the matter with a show of good breeding and generosity, with French francs and English pounds in the absence of rubles. He set sail for Rio de

Janeiro on a ship of the Chargeurs Réunis Line, carrying along as extra baggage Ludi and Pyotr, the balalaika and the dagger, the spoils of imperial Russia.

10

IN THE CABARET FADUL ABDALA saw how accurate Fuad Karan's exalted words had been, and he repeated the exclamation that came from the depths of his soul: *ia hôhi*! He even had the pretext and the opportunity to touch the Russian woman's exceedingly white hand with the tips of his huge fingers, for Venturinha, on seeing him, had given him a cordial wave. The Turk had then ventured over to the lawyer's table to greet him and take a closer look at the flaming redhead who had set the city of Itabuna and the sea of Ilhéus on fire. According to Fuad's venomous tongue, she was partial to blacks: an ideal tidbit for Tição Abduim, a black man adept at pleasing foreign women.

11

THE ANNOUNCEMENT OF THE imminent arrival of the Holy Mission sped like a trail of gunpowder, causing a sensation, stirring up the inhabitants of Tocaia Grande, a wild piece of news. There was great commotion on both sides of the river.

Natalina had no rest from pumping her sewing machine. Orders flooded in from the womenfolk in general and the May brides in particular: it was the middle of May, the month of the first rains and, according to what they had learned from the monks, that of the Virgin Mary. There was only one bride worthy of wearing a white garland and a veil: the girl, Chica, firmly promised to Balbino. She lived in her parents' house while the rest of the candidates for the nuptial blessing were all shacked up, some already with children.

Even in the case of Chica, in spite of her being so young and still living in the parental house, nobody was about to thrust a hand into the fire as proof of her virginity. In Tocaia Grande, as elsewhere in the length and breadth of southern Bahia, maidenhood didn't normally endure very long; on plantations it was one woman to every ten men, and the virgin flower was often plucked while still a bud.

Chica let herself be seen in Balbino's company in secluded spots along the river and in clearings in the forest; if she still had her cherry, it was one of two possibilities, either Balbino couldn't get it up or a miracle had occurred. Be that as it may, Dona Leocádia came in person to put in an order for her granddaughter's bridal gown and explained to Dona Natalina that she wanted it Sergipe style, with all the fixings and decorations fit for a virgin.

The others didn't ask for so much; they were satisfied with simple dresses—they didn't want to get married draped in old rags. Cleide, also Dona Leocádia's granddaughter and Chica's cousin, had a full belly; she ordered a blue dress, the color of her group in the Epiphany celebration, the blue of the Immaculate Virgin. Now that we're talking about Dona Leocádia's granddaughters and the Epiphany has been mentioned, let it be noted that also on the roll of girls to be married, waiting for the Holy Mission, was young Aracati, the girl who took the part of Senhorita Dona Deusa in the parade. To the surprise of her relatives, even her watchful grandmother, immediately after Epiphany eve, she showed up at home on Guido's arm, saying they were going to live together. The Estância people had contributed three pregnant women to the season of births; they were coming up with three brides for the marriage harvest.

Long-standing concubines ordered dresses from Dona Natalina or sewed them at home. Abigail brought hers from Taquaras, where she and Bastião da Rosa had been living ever since the flood: the monks would be going there, but she wanted to get married in Tocaia Grande, at the same time as her sister Isaura: a big party was planned at Zé dos Santos and Dona Clara's house. Couples came from the plantations in great numbers, it wasn't every day that a Holy Mission appeared in the Rio das Cobras.

12

NO LESS EXCITED WERE the parents of children waiting to
be baptized. Some dozen heathens were waiting in Tocaia
Grande for the opportunity of becoming Roman Catholics,
escaping limbo if they died in childhood, hell if they got to
be adults. There was a harried search for godparents, their
choice brought on arguments and laughter. Zilda sent a
message to Bernarda: she had to choose godparents for
Nado; the boy was going to be baptized when the Holy
Mission came through.

In bed with Natário, Bernarda brought the matter up
for discussion.

"Godfather, have you thought about anyone yet?" She
was resting her head on the captain's chest, he was stroking
her loose hair.

"If you want, we'll do it this way: I'll pick the godfather
and you the godmother."

"As far as I'm concerned, the only godmother can be
our old friend Coroca. I owe her more than I do my own
mother, poor thing."

"For godfather I was thinking about Fadu, for me he is
already a *compadre*." He ran his hand from his goddaughter's
hair down to her breasts, from her breasts to her stomach,
and played with the hair on her pussy.

That was how godparents were chosen for little Nado,
Bernarda and Captain Natário da Fonseca's son by blood,
Zilda's son by adoption, by Zilda, godmother to Bernarda
and wife of the captain.

13

"GET THEE BEHIND ME, Satan!" exploded Frei Zygmunt
Gotteshammer at the climactic moment of the confession of
young Chica, not so young, as she would turn fourteen on
the eve of St. Peter's Day: the only one of the May brides in

condition to wear the garland and a veil at the marriage
ceremony.

Revealing a decided penchant for details and an inordi-
nate innocence regarding what was and was not venial or
mortal sin, Chica, without blushing, told the indignant Frei
Zygmunt about the curious advances her boyfriend had subjected her to. Balbino had lived in Ilhéus, and he knew
foreign women's tricks: Chica had enjoyed them all.

Not for being bloodless was the struggle that ensued in
the improvised sanctuary between the holy inquisitor and the
girl with the scarlet sash less demented. She merrily told
him all about scabrous episodes with finger and tongue,
sodomy—ah! Sodom reborn!—in light of which the monk
forbade her the veil and garland, symbols of virginity. But
the bride, with obstinate respect, demanded her rights to
the orange blossoms fashioned by the skillful hands of Dona
Natalina, because inside there, in her pussy—"Father, I swear
by God!"—Balbino never penetrated. The other things they
did were precisely meant to stop him from popping her
cherry: where had the reverend father ever heard that taking it from behind was the same as giving her treasure? In
Estância girls got married as virgins, most of them, but in
order to bear the waiting, they'd take it in the thighs, in the
rump, nobody's made of iron, Father.

Frei Zygmunt chased her out with his Latin. *"Vade
retro, Beelzebub!"* In other times he would have used the
scourge to exorcise her, drive the demons from her body:
those were the good old days of the Holy Inquisition. Chica
went away satisfied, believing that the priest had been blessing her and sanctioning the bridal gown. She said three Hail
Marys and one Our Father, since the good friar had neglected
to assign her a penance.

14

THE MONKS, WITH THE consent of Mr. Carlinhos Silva, had
improvised two confessionals in the dry-cacao warehouse, one
at each end of the place. There wasn't the usual separation
between confessor and confessee, but the few women who

went to fulfill the sacrament—the most important of all in the learned opinion of Frei Zgymunt von Gotteshammer— had no shyness about looking at the priest at the moment of unburdening themselves of their bag of sins: they didn't know, poor things, the meaning of shame.

Few women, no men. Church and priests are women's things, said the men, renegades all. Homicidal criminals many of them, starting with that certain captain, whose reputation for cruelty and whose criminal past they'd heard about in fearsome references as they covered the leagues of ground along the Rio das Cobras.

Frei Theun and Frei Zygmunt had reserved the first day of the Holy Mission for an examination of life in Tocaia Grande, receiving sinners in confession, acquiring knowledge of the state of the paganism and immorality of the place. Since the confessional and its penances and absolutions were minimally sought after—in the voice of Frei Zygmunt von Gotteshammer, the Hammer of God, absolution sounded more like censure and punishment—the monks decided to go out and learn about things from house to house, person to person.

They returned to Mr. Carlinhos Silva's residence, where they were staying, Theun with his heart heavy at seeing God's law so forsaken—*oh! poor unfortunates!*—Zygmunt, taken with indignation and horror, trembling with righteous wrath as he observed the state of abomination those renegades were living in: *cursed, cursed culprits!*

Unbaptized children, illegitimate offspring conceived in sin, couples breeding like animals without the consent or blessing of God, licentiousness, crime, ignorance, and neglect of the affairs of Holy Mother the Church. Larger than the houses built about the center of the village—two lanes and an alley—was the foul cluster of adobe huts and straw shacks in the Baixa dos Sapos, *whoredom,* in the inhabitants' coarse expressing. They spoke of it with a note of pride, the biggest infestation in all those parts.

On the other side of the river, where they planted what was needed for the weekly market, morality was no better, nor piety. In their new surroundings the Sergipeans, God-fearing people, on coming in contact with south Bahian impiety, had lost their fear of God and wallowed in the slime of the place's depraved habits.

The Arab who did business there, robbing poor devils, whether residents or visitors, loan shark to the poor, an exile, wasn't exactly a Mahometan, but was close enough. Far from being an exemplary son of the Church of Rome, he belonged to the eastern sect of Maronites, hardly worthy of trust: he stood no more than two steps from being a Muslim. If he'd been living in Spain during the good old days, he wouldn't have escaped the blessed Christian sword of St. James the Moorslayer.

As for the fetishist blacks, there was the cynical black-smith at their head, always laughing, persisting in an ever-lasting and perverse attempt to defile the purity and dignity of saints canonized by the Vatican by confusing them with the devilish *calunga* spirits of the slave quarters, offering animals in bloody sacrifices. The alter of this fetishism could be found in the shop of the shoer of donkeys, reprobate that he was.

Frei Zygmunt Hammer of God planned to uplift the spirit of the faithful during his sermons—who knows, maybe he could get them to destroy that impious altar erected behind the forge for the monstrous African devils that the blacks, freed from slavery through the conspiracies and tricks of freemasonry, called Enchanted Ones and dressed in the glowing mantles of our blessed saints. *Sacrilege!*

15

RESTING AFTERWARD FROM THE barbaric—and delicious—repast of fruit and game at the end of that first day of the Holy Mission, Frei Theun bewailed, saddened and compassionate, the fate of those sinners, victims of ignorance and backwardness, whose souls were condemned to hell without their deserving it, perhaps. Above all, the lack of any moral code, or the control of any laws, or any limitations imposed by rules, had brought them to the practice of such errors, in a life of delinquency and sin.

Mr. Carlinhos Silva, speaking German with the fluency and accent of a learned man—a redheaded mulatto, just imagine, the surprises that mendicant friars encounter on a

holy mission—with a soft and affable voice, like someone
with no ulterior motives, who is simply chatting, defended
the place and its inhabitants. He was like a professor giving
a lecture from his chair in Weimar, and Frei Zygmunt eyed
him suspiciously. With good reason, because the half-breed
was absolving the rabble of any blame. The inhabitants of
Tocaia Grande—he said—lived there apart from preconceived
ideas, unhindered by the limitations and constraints of current laws, free of moral and social prejudices imposed by
codes, whether the penal code or the catechism. A more
law-abiding people could not be found in the whole cacao
region, all of southern Bahia, despite their reputation and
supposed bad habits. "And do you know, Reverend Fathers,
why? Because nobody here orders anybody else around,
everything is done by common consent and not out of fear of
punishment." If it had been up to Mr. Carlinhos Silva, such
peace should never be disturbed, the happy life of the people of Tocaia Grande, who in his eyes were most certainly
deserving of the blessings of God, the true one.

"If you reverend fathers will permit my opinion, I can
tell you that the natural paradise of the Bible is here. . . ."

Frei Zygmunt Gotteshammer, Hammer of God, stood
up suddenly, knocking over his tin plate, his rosary in hand,
as if it were a whip raised against sin and sinners and, most
especially, the heretic before him. In Ilhéus he had been told
that the illegitimate mulatto now sitting before him had
been educated in Germany and had the pretentions of a
university graduate: an enemy of the Church of Rome, he
was an infamous Lutheran, even more pernicious perhaps
than the *macumba* people, certainly more dangerous than
the Maronite. He was a symbol of the worst things that
existed in the world: a proclaimer of the infamous ideas of
the French Revolution, the Encyclopedists, the enemies of
God and monarchy, fanatical bombers, clutching an incen-
diary bottle to hurl at emperors and noblemen, a dagger
raised for a new strike at the heart of Jesus Christ. Besides
being a Lutheran, an anarchist!

16

THE CARPENTERS LUPISCÍNIO, GUIDO, and Zinho, in the center of the clearing, halfway between the river and the shed, across from the local marketplace, had erected a huge brazilwood cross, quite tall, a monument comparable only to the bridge. Whoever came down from the headwaters of the Rio das Cobras or from the station at Taquaras, would from far off on the trail, already glimpse the Holy Cross signaling the passage through Tocaia Grande of the first Holy Mission to reach those ends of the earth, preaching virtue and the condemnation of sin.

A broad platform of worn boards had been set up in front of the cross, and on it the friars placed the utensils and accoutrements for mass, benediction, and the sacraments of baptism and matrimony. The friars changed into their formal habits for the divine offices and sermons.

Frei Theun preached in the morning, at the eucharist, Frei Zygmunt preached in the evening, at benediction. The inhabitants were unanimous in considering Frei Zygmunt's sermon superior in all ways to that of the Dutch monk. There was no comparison. Frei Theun, chubby and squat, speaking Portuguese almost without an accent, lingered over God's goodness and mercy, described Paradise, spoke of its beauties and rewards.

Tall and thin, sunken-faced, bony-handed, mingling German terms and Latin expressions with his Portuguese, which had a doberman accent, the German enthralled his listeners, a goodly crowd, even bigger than the one brought together by Dona Leocádia's Epiphany during the summer. His themes were apocalyptical. Beelzebub, the fallen angel, sin and fire consuming the damned. Hammer of God, as his name indicated, Frei Zygmunt Gotteshammer had a success that was almost the equal of Mr. Carlinhos Silva and his magical sleights of hand. Frei Zygmunt was one hell of a preacher!

17

BY COINCIDENCE—NOVELS ARE full of coincidences, life even more—the second and last day of the Holy Mission marked the arrival in Tocaia Grande, on his way from Itabuna to Atalaia Plantation, of Dr. Boaventura Andrade, Junior, less and less called by the familiar diminutive of Venturinha. He was accompanied by Ludmila Gregoriovna, his lover—*lover* was the term the lawyer used because it indicated a loving and noble female, a person of quality, expensive to maintain, placed in a high position never attained by whores, mistresses, hookers, or other kept women of that ilk. Copper hair the color of fire, strong musk perfume, in an elegant English riding habit with culottes, Ludmila could have been a mare from the corrals of the tsar of Russia or from the stables of King Solomon, as Turk Fadul, a reader of the Bible, would probably have said.

During the days of the troubles, when run-ins with bands of gunmen were common occurrence and every guava tree was an ambush, the colonels traveled well protected by groups of armed men; there was always the possibility of an attack. With the end of the fighting, the guard had been reduced to a single trusted man quick on the trigger. Colonel Boaventura Andrade, whose life had been threatened so many times, in recent years had been accompanied only by black Espiridião. Sometimes Natário went along: chatting with the colonel, getting instructions, no longer in the capacity of strongman as before.

Venturinha, however, in his comings and goings between Itabuna and Atalaia Plantation, or wherever he went, was never without a following worthy of a Basílio de Oliveira, a Sinhô Badaró, a Henrique Alves in the golden years.

At the head of the patrol of four men armed to the teeth rode a fighter celebrated in those past struggles, Benaia Cova Rasa, Shallow Grave, a fitting nickname, no need to elaborate. "I counted twenty. After that I lost track," the vain Benaia would say about his victims, the ones he'd dug graves for, whether deep or shallow. He was a short, thin man of black-Indian mixture, with a sucked-in mouth and few words, good with a carbine and better with a knife.

18

AT LUDMILA'S INSISTENCE, VENTURINHA decided to tarry in Tocaia Grande until the time for the blessing, the baptism, and the weddings, with Frei Zygmunt von Gotteshammer's final sermon: she wouldn't miss that for anything.

"In that case we'll have to travel by night. I want to sleep at the plantation."

"Voyager dans la fôret dans la nuit c'est romantique, mon amour."

Mon amour agreed, earned a kiss, and, in the company of Pyotr and Cova Rasa, he and Ludmila had lunch at Natário and Zilda's. A merry and sumptuous feast, celebrating the visit of the Holy Mission, it included the presence of godfather Fadul Abdala, who wore his traveling clothes for Nado's baptism.

After coffee Venturinha stretched out in the hammock on the veranda, took out a Suerdieck cigar, and stayed chatting with the captain and Fadul. He'd hired an agronomist to take Natário's place in the administration of Atalaia Plantation and went on about the fellow's competence, a doctor's degree: he was revolutionizing the working methods, the planting, and the harvesting. He promised to triple production: what did Natário think? Natário didn't think anything, he didn't make any comments nor did he attempt to compare knowledge learned in books with the rudimentary and precarious wisdom of colonels and foremen. Except that on his lips was that thread of a smile, a sign of doubt or indifference, who knows?

Espiridião's name came up, and Venturinha couldn't understand why the black man, following Natário's example, hadn't accepted the position of head of his personal bodyguard now filled by Benaia Cova Rasa: he'd left the plantation to live with his schoolteacher daughter in Taquaras. He called the old gunman ungrateful, but Natário disagreed. If anyone should be grateful, it wasn't the black man, but Venturinha, the colonel's son, whose father's life Espiridião had saved and whose sleep he watched over for so many years. The lawyer changed the subject; while still a boy he'd learned to respect Natário's opinion; if the respect rankled him, he didn't show it. Nor did Natário speak to him in tones of reproach or remonstration; he was just chatting, his voice neutral, his face impassive.

The one who did remonstrate with Venturinha was Fadul, reminding him that passing through Tocaia Grande one day the lawyer had declared himself extremely pessimistic as to the future of the place, predicting a short and miserable life for it. This place here has no future; it'll never go beyond a pigsty. Fadul hadn't forgotten the words, which had bothered him: if it hadn't been for his pact with the good Lord of the Maronites, his confidence might have been crushed. Laughing, Venturinha confessed that he'd been wrong in his predictions.

"Yes, sir, I'll eat crow. The pigsty is progressing. It's got the look of a city."

He took time to explain that *city* was an exaggerated term, and he was using it only to stress the growth of the settlement in contrast to other places in the region, because the category of city really couldn't be applied, properly speaking, to either Ilhéus or Itabuna, municipal seats, nor did they merit it, not even Bahia, capital of the state, nor Rio de Janeiro itself, if the comparison were made to Paris or London. Those, indeed, were cities. What women! Furthermore, his two old friends could judge from the Russian woman he'd conquered; had they ever seen anything like her?

They'd never seen anything like her, neither the half-breed nor the Turk. But Natário remembered that pretty girls had always been the lawyer's daily bread, his bedcovers. It was going on seven years from the time he'd put Tocaia Grande down. Venturinha, a recent graduate, with a penchant for foreign women and entertainers since those days, had at the time been involved with an Argentine woman, did he remember?

Venturinha remembered with pleasure. Adela La Porteña, a great woman, she sang tangos, great in bed. But alongside Ludmila Gregoriovna Cytkynbaum she was nothing but a streetwalker, trash!

19

THEIR STEPS GUARDED BY Benaia Cova Rasa while Venturinha chatted on the veranda, Ludmila and Pyotr went down the hill to have a look at Tocaia Grande.

The Russian woman was mad about that trip on horseback through plantations and villages. On Carrapicho Plantation, the delegation's first stop, Venturinha and his lover had been received in grand style by Colonel Demósthenes Berbert. The colonel being a bachelor, three handsome young women took care of the big house and the whims of the moneybags, elegant and fortyish, with a French grandfather in the mixture of his Brazilian blood. Speaking French fluently and correctly—learned from his ancestor—he introduced the three graces to Ludmila: the *Cunhã*, the *Minhotan*, and the *Malê*, his three Marias, the Indian, the white and the black girls, all chosen by Colonel Demostinho personally, a fine connoisseur with cultivated taste.

The owner of Carrapicho Plantation was an avis rara in that cacao jungle: he had a library in the big house, a wine cellar, and, in addition to a phonograph, a piano that he himself fingered for the delight of the three servants who hovered about. Fuad Karan, a frequent guest, referred to them as Colonel Demostinho's harem, and Álvaro Faria, sequestered from waterfront bars, spent a week on the plantation knocking off bottles of wine and cognac, both Portuguese and French. In the opinion of the man of letters from Ilhéus, Colonel Berbert was the only truly civilized creature in all of that south Bahian universe.

They visited the groves in full harvest—the farmhands' work began at five in the morning—and the corrals with the milk cows where, taking advantage of Venturinha's distraction as he looked over the heifer Sulamita, Colonel Demostinho ran his hand over Ludmila Gregoriovna's noble backside and whispered to her, his breath tickling the back of her neck, "Anytime you want, make yourself at home here, or in my other home in Ilhéus, on the beach." He said it in his best French, in a murmur that was like the morning breeze.

Ludmila replied with an enigmatic smile, as the smiles of Russian heroines are wont to be. The good colonel, before withdrawing the hand that rested on that elegant rear end, gave it a delicate pinch to underscore his offer, to close the deal.

An unforgettable trip for Ludmila Gregoriovna Cytkyn-baum's eyes. The road wound along the edge of the cacao groves: the yellow pods gleamed in the morning light, a more beautiful growth didn't exist anywhere, not even the ripe wheatfields of the steppes compared. They stopped from plantation to plantation to quench their thirst, accepting a drink of water here, a cup of coffee there, tasting rolled banana sweets or marmalades, delighting themselves with a glass of juice made from the nectar that encases the cacao seeds, an invention of the gods.

In order to meet the Russian singer they knew as Dr. Venturinha's whore, the colonels' ladies left their kitchens and prejudices behind and presented themselves with elegance, their Sunday dresses hurriedly put on. Ludmila extended the tips of her fingers for the plantation owners' kisses, smiled beautifully and modestly at the ladies, and said *merci* and *vous êtes très gentille*, Madame. A jewel of a Russian singer she was.

All of that fiery and delicious tropic land, with millionaire colonels and wretched farmhands, sumptuous big houses and miserable adobe huts, was quite the opposite but also the equal of the plains of Russia, with its nobles, kulaks, and serfs. Ludmila Gregoriovna exchanged a few words with Pyotr, her brother, expressing the hope of receiving, one day or another, from the generous hands of her sugar daddy Boaventura or from somebody else just as rich, the gift of fields and a village with black serfs. She was living in an exaltation of discovery; everything seemed romantic to her, with just a touch of danger from the snakes and the bandits.

On returning from her walk, her eyes gleaming, her face pearled with sweat, her voice hesitant with emotion, Ludi asked Venturinha, still stretched out in the hammock, prolonging his siesta, "Does this village belong to you, Daddy? Are these savages your serfs?" She leaned over the hammock, her breasts heaving, enticing. "If you really love me, you'll give me a village with many serfs as a pledge of your affection."

20

DELIVERED IN THE MORNING, during mass, Frei Theun of the Holy Eucharist's sermon, emotional and forgiving, lamented the state of degradation and disorder that the people of Tocaia Grande took pleasure in, but he called upon God's charity, His supreme goodness, His heart bleeding with sorrow for the strayed sheep of his flock; he summoned their repentance and tears.

If the Tocaia Grandeans hadn't been so hardened, their sobs would have poured out freely and clearly, their hands would have beaten their sinful breasts: sinful, alas, were all of the inhabitants of the place, without exception. It would be pious and edifying to give a place in the chronicle of events in Tocaia Grande to that august moment of compunction and penance of the tiny multitude huddled together in front of the Holy Cross, listening to the words of the preacher in relative silence. But how can it be done if there were no signs of compunction or any attempts at penance?

Though his speech was a failure, Theun himself was a success with the whore delegation: while wearing the white surplice on top of his worn cassock and moving about the improvised altar and mourning the fate of the living, whose salvation seemed so threatened to him, the sluts exchanged commentaries of doubtful taste and base intention about what they would do if they had the privilege of holding the chubby friar with the crybaby face in their arms. On the other hand, Frei Zygmunt, with his sermon of fire, threats, and insults, worked up the men especially: *a real brimstone!*

Only a few small children cried when they were carried to the baptismal font, an enameled tin basin loaned by Turk Fadul, an expensive item in the stock of utensils on sale at his store. Fadul, in addition, played an important role in the collective baptism ceremony, having on his right Coroca, who bore little Nado in her arms, and on his left Bernarda, the flustered mother, beautiful in her full skirt and cotton blouse, a lighted candle in her hand.

With pagans of all ages gathered together, among whom
there were lanky urchins from the plantations, Frei Theun
received them into the bosom of Holy Mother Church, making them Christians one by one, wetting their heads in the
basin filled with holy water, anointing them with salt and
soil. He declaimed the words of the Credo: "I believe in God
the Almighty Father." Parents and godparents repeated them
in a confused babble, the gabble of an open marketplace.

Fulfilling a promise they had made, Colonel Robustiano
de Araújo and his wife, Dona Isabel, arrived early in the
morning to witness the baptism of Tovo, son of the late Diva
and of Castor Abduim: there they were, present at the dis-
pensing of the holy oils. Black Epifânia had embroidered a
cloth for the ceremony and had wrapped the restless Tovo
in it, declaring herself the presenting godmother, according
to custom. Poor Soul growled at the monk and tried to bite
him when the child burst out crying as he tasted the sancti-
fying salt in his mouth.

On their way to the railroad station in Taquaras after
the baptism, accompanied by the bodyguard Nazareno, the
colonel and Dona Isabel crossed paths with Venturinha's
entourage and exchanged niceties in the middle of the mud.
From up on her saddle Dona Isabel took in that woman
from faraway lands: she couldn't deny her uncommon beauty;
she was the picture of the Virgin Mary on the flight into
Egypt, modest and pure. "Ones like that, looking like saints,
are the worst kind," Dona Isabel commented to her husband
as they went on their way. As for the corpulent lawyer, to
her mind he was nothing but a spoiled brat.

21

THE BRIDES OF MAY, some pregnant, others accompanied
by their children, born in the abomination of concubinage,
took their places alongside the platform before the cross
facing the altar. Tição Abduim had turned out metal rings
for the rustic brides. Smiling and animated in the morning
during the baptisms, he'd become somber and silent in the
afternoon during the weddings, giving away Bastião da Rosa

and Abigail. Epifânia, in the middle of the crowd, was looking at him, worried; she knew the black man was thinking
about Diva.

To say which bride was the prettiest and the happiest,
would have been difficult and imprudent; about who was
the youngest, however, there was no doubt, it was young
Chica, not yet fourteen and with her honor intact. The only
one in that condition, as she had already said, even to Frei
Zygmunt: where did the reverend father ever hear that taking it in the ass was the same as in the twat? And Balbino
the groom had never put his tool in her twat; Chica wouldn't
let him. All right, but at the moment of the holy sacrament
of matrimony, the enraged monk made the poor girl take off
that beautiful veil and garland where Dona Natalina had
outdone herself embroidering orange blossoms. A farce! Dona
Leocádia, who wasn't one to keep quiet in the face of an
insult, wanted to fight or at least withdraw from the ceremony, but she contented herself with the threats she leveled
at Frei Zygmunt: if it weren't for that cassock, he would
have found out a thing or two. She heeded Frei Theun's
appeal and they reached a compromise—the veil remained,
the garland was removed. Chica was married bathed in
tears, loudly proclaiming her maligned virginity.

With the weddings and the blessing, the Holy Mission
came to an end: the next day, quite early in the morning,
the two missionaries departed for Taquaras, a larger and
less abject place. Frei Zygmunt's sermon closed the religious part of the event that had shaken and stirred Tocaia
Grande for forty-eight hours of wild animation. The last
part didn't have the monks' participation; it was solely
under the direction and management of Pedro Gypsy, the
accordion player, a citizen of note. In order to celebrate so
many baptisms and marriages in one single fling, the party
had to go on all night, as indeed it did. Urged by Venturinha,
Ludmila Gregoriovna Cytkynbaum left for Atalaia Plantation before the wingding was over, but not before having
danced the French lancers' quadrille under the direction of
Castor Abduim, black Tição, caught up by so many emotions that day. He was an Ethiopian from the court of the
Negus, Ludi said to Pyotr, her brother and confidant. She
felt at home in the celebration; it was as lively as the dances
of her poor peasant childhood.

The sermon by Frei Zygmunt von Gotteshammer was

what might have been called the golden key, the diamond clasp that closed off the Holy Mission. The strong and burning words, if they didn't thrive in the arid soil of Tocaia Grande's stony souls, did echo in other ears, bringing on reflection, determining procedures, all in accord with edicts and good behavior.

The name, bestowed as homage to the crime, says it all: that was how the grand inquisitor began his sermon. At the end he accused Tocaia Grande of being a citadel of sin, a lair of bandits—a land without law, neither God's nor man's—a place of degradation, lechery, impiety, sacrilege, and the foul practices of the devil: the realm of Satan's damnation. Sodom and Gomorrah all wrapped up in one, defying the wrath of the Lord. Someday the anger of God will burst into flame, punishing the infidels, destroying the walls of evil and profanation, and turning that den of scandal and iniquity to ashes. That was what he prophesied.

At the moment of the benediction, in the dying light of the setting sun, Frei Zygmunt Hammer of God raised his stern talon of righteousness, carved the cross of excommunication in the air, and put a curse upon the place and all of its inhabitants.

With the Arrival of Law and Order to Tocaia Grande, We Interrupt the History of the City of Irisópolis Here While Still at Its Beginning

1

TOCAIA GRANDE: REFUGE OF bandits, murderers, the unlawful and the unruly, gunmen and sluts—excommunicated by the envoy of God. It was imperative to put a brake on the violence and debauchery, an end to disorder and villainy: thus decreed the bigwigs and their flatterers. The rumors grew into demands in the courts, in City Hall, at the cathedral, in the cabarets.

The tradition was fighting, ambush, gunplay, that was what property and law were based upon. At the head of his army, the king mounted his steed and rode out to impose rules and order, authority and obedience, where only freedom and dreams had ruled before.

From the anathema of the inquisitor to the march of soldiers was a short step, covering precisely the distance between the winter of sermons and the summer of gunshots, between life and death, between lord and subject. Even shorter was the time of the showdown: from threat to domination, what happened, happened in a few days.

2

COLONEL ROBUSTIANO DE ARAÚJO'S message reached Captain Natário da Fonseca on his return from Boa Vista Plantation, where the harvest was just over and the crop, with the vigor of the new groves, had surpassed the most optimistic predictions. The captain had calculated a harvest of a little more than nine tons; it had come to over twelve. His cacao groves were only as well cared for as those of the Atalaia Plantation of the past. In spite of the presence of Dr. Luiz César Gusmão and his advanced theories regarding the cultivation of *theobroma cacao*—a sterculiaceous tree, in the pretentious expression of the engineer-agronomist—even that plantation's production lagged.

Dr. Luiz César Gusmão, with all of his agronomical science, was on the verge of being fired once Venturinha, his boss, on his return from Rio de Janeiro, where he'd gone to take a quick bath in civilization in the company of Ludmila Gregoriovna and her brother, Pyotr, discovered the drop in the harvest as compared to the previous year. He made a great fuss, threatened all kinds of things, and demanded an explanation. The engineer-agronomist, thumbing through books specializing in the subject, explained that that was precisely as it should be: positive results of the application of modern and scientific methods require time and patience. *Time and patience, fuck them both!*—Venturinha upbraided him, indignant. But he ended up giving in to the arguments of Dr. Gusmão, a first-class slicker, because once again Natário had refused even to consider the insistently renewed proposals to come back to work at Atalaia.

Venturinha was wounded and offended by the refusal because he'd even promised Natário a share of the profits, something unheard of and condemned among the principled opinions of plantation owners. Anger leads to excess: Venturinha spoke, for anyone who wanted to hear, about disloyalty, and he used the word *traitor*. Natário hadn't even respected the memory of his boss and protector, to whom he owed everything, and, immediately after his death, had set up a house and financed a greengrocery for Sacramento, the colonel's whore, putting post-mortem horns on him, an ignoble affront. He said *post mortem* and *affront* with the same pedantic tone as that with which the agronomist had spoken of *theobroma cacao,* a sterculiaceous tree.

3

"I HEARD TALK, I didn't like what I heard, watch out"—that was the message from Colonel Robustiano de Araújo, brought by the half-breed Nazareno, a man to be trusted, who didn't have any details to add other than what he knew. At first the captain thought it was a matter of Venturinha's spiteful mutterings; they'd already reached his ears and Natário had laughed at them: *the griping of a bossy kid, next time I see him in Itabuna I'll pull his ears, we'll have a drink and talk about women and that'll be the end of it.*

Going over the matter with Fadul Abdala, however, he was surprised to learn that the Turk, with a small difference in time, had received a note from Fuad Karan, couched in allegorical, one might even say poetic, language. *The* fellah *plants a grove of date palms in the oasis, but the one who picks the fruit is the* zanguil: *have a care, my good Fadul, because the fruit is starting to ripen*—it was a warning in delicate Arabic calligraphy. The note had been entrusted to the drover Zé Raimundo, a veteran of the shortcut, to be delivered directly into the hands of the storekeeper.

They put their heads together without success, Natário and Fadul, and they asked the advice of Castor Abduim, and even then they couldn't find the key to the riddle, something that would unlock the sibylline meaning of the colonel's message or the learned man's allegory.

"I'm going to Itabuna next week, I'll clear this thing up," Natário said, already smelling a rat.

What talk could it have been that Colonel Robustiano didn't like? Watch out for whom? What was the conceit in the charade of ripening dates that Fuad Karan had so cautiously put forth? Adding the message to the note, discounting the wild cards, the answer couldn't be anything to be ignored.

4

THE PROJECTED TRIP NEVER came about: there wasn't time, events had begun to unfold, and they were immediately thrown into a frantic pace of storm and turmoil.

Captain Natário da Fonseca had just sat down to lunch, when his son Peba ran into the house: he hadn't come for lunch. Hastily he told his father, "There are two men down there shooting the pigs, they say they're from the government and they've already killed—"

The captain didn't wait for Peba to finish his sentence: he grabbed his belt with the six-shooter hanging on the wall and ran out the side door. He got to the clearing in time to see Altamirando struggling with one of the strangers. With their weapons in hand, shouting threats, the two newcomers had made a slaughter of the pigs, most of them part of the backlander's herd.

Altamirando, a knife in his hand, and the stranger, whose revolver had been dropped in the fall, were rolling on the ground. Still at a distance, all Natário could do was scream when the second stranger aimed at Altamirando and fired his carbine three times: the hog breeder slumped, a stain on his back where his blood was spurting out. Almost at the same time the killer fell dead from a single shot from the captain's pistol. People came from all sides and Tição Abduim grabbed the arms of the fellow who, free of Altamirando's body, was trying to get up.

When the man saw himself surrounded, he fell to his knees and begged them to spare his life, for the love of God: he had a wife to feed and kids to bring up. He and the other had come there with specific orders. Both constables were from the municipality of Itabuna, with jurisdiction in the city, villages, and hamlets. The settlement, or whatever it was, of Tocaia Grande, was located within the territory of the municipality. They'd come to enforce the ordinance that prohibited animals from running loose in the streets: orders from the sheriff of police instructed them to kill all four-footed animals found wandering in the streets.

They finally released him, rather the worse for wear, and allowed him to get on the donkey he'd come on. First,

however, they disarmed him—in addition to the revolver he
was carrying a knife, a switchblade, and a whole arsenal of
bullets—and undressed him, leaving him the way he'd come
into the world. On the saddle of the other animal they tied
the corpse of the dead killer, and, as he sent him off, the
captain told the terrified constable, "Tell whoever sent you
that here in Tocaia Grande no stranger walks in and med-
dles in our affairs. The one who's telling you this is Captain
Natário da Fonseca, and you've got the proof with you.
Don't forget to relay that message."

5

AFTER GATHERING TOGETHER THE household items needed
for the stay on the plantation, Zilda sat down beside Natário
on the veranda. The children, with the exception of Edu, in
the shop helping Tição, were going up and down the hill,
carrying the bundles and metal trunks to the ox cart waiting below. Zilda remained silent for a good while, but finally she spoke.

"I'm leaving against my will. I'd change my mind if I
could."

"I don't see why. I thought you were happy about it.
Ever since the house was ready, all you talked about was
going to the farm."

"That was then. Ever since the constables came by here,
I've lost my urge. What do you think their coming here
means?"

From up on the hill, sitting on the bench on the veranda
of his residence, the captain studied Tocaia Grande. One
faraway day, when there hadn't even been the start of a
cemetery, he'd shown Colonel Boaventura Andrade the unknown valley. He turned to his wife, stared at her usually
serene face, cloaked at that moment in a shadow of uncertainty. Zilda had never been a beauty, but she had delicate
features and still kept a few traces of youth on her thin face:
the years and the children, the ones she'd borne and the
ones she'd adopted, hadn't succeeded in breaking her, di-
minishing her good temper and disposition. Carried by Peba,

the parrot Up-Your-Ass went by shouting foul words of protest. Even during the worst moments of danger during the troubles, Natário never failed to tell the truth when Zilda, dropping her usual reserve, inquired about difficulties that had to do with troubles or with women.

"It might not be anything, nothing but the meddling of Sheriff Orígenes, trying to show off, or the administrator, Dr. Castro."

The administrator of Itabuna was still the same lawyer, Ricardo Castro, who, ten years before, after having served Colonel Elias Daltro, had gone over to Colonel Boaventura Andrade, bag and baggage. His bag and baggage were subservience and ambition: with such traits, there couldn't have been anyone better for the job. Elected and reelected, almost for life, Attorney Castro, although no more than a figurehead, liked to make a show of strength and power, strut his authority. Natário would seek out the truth.

"When I get to Itabuna, I'm going to talk to Venturinha and give him a little hell about this shit. In the colonel's time, nobody would have dared, he kept them on a tight rein, but Venturinha lets things go any which way."

"You think they did it without his knowing?" She was quick to add, "I think he might even have wanted to stir things up."

The captain agreed with a nod. Who knows, it could just as well have been Orígenes's idea: Dr. Castro was too dumb to have thought of it. The conversation seemed to have come to an end, but Natário kept on talking. He didn't want to leave his wife, the mother of his children, aware of only half of what he was thinking: he owed her the same loyalty she gave him. Sometimes he didn't talk to her about this, that, or the other subject, but he'd never hidden anything from her, no matter what, when she asked him about it.

"It could be something more serious. It could be something worked out beyond the sheriff or the lawyers. Tocaia Grande's growing, it wasn't worth a penny before, but now it's got a lot of people looking at it because of politics and business. There are people who'd like to get their hands on what's here. Only I'm not going to let them."

Having cleared up his thoughts, he considered the conversation at an end.

"You be on your way with the kids."

"I don't feel like going."

The captain took his eyes off the glorious landscape lying in the summer morning, and once more fixed his gaze on Zilda's taut face.

"Remember when we were up against the fever and you wanted to go off to the farm with the kids and I said no? It wasn't the time for you to leave here—not me, not you, not the kids. We'd stay here even if it meant dying. Now I'm the one to say: take them away. The way things are right now, it's enough for me to stay."

"Wouldn't it be all the better if I stayed with you?"

"How did we first get together? Tell me. What did I do that time? Have you forgotten so soon?"

He reminded her in his normal voice, not angry, not excited, as if he were talking about unimportant things, feeling in his heart the tenderness for that woman whom he'd won with bullets in the middle of the road.

"You always stayed with the kids, you did the right thing. I know how to take care of myself, this whole business used to be the way I lived, a gunman's life, you know that very well. Go on, take the kids, fix up the house, and wait for me there."

"You won't be coming right off?"

"Maybe I will, maybe I won't. I've got a lot of things to do at the farm, but first I've got to go to Itabuna and find out what's going on."

From the bottom of the hill came the noise of the children loading the ox cart. Peba ran up to tell them that everything was ready for their departure. The captain went down with Zilda to give his children his blessing. Zilda held out the tips of her fingers to him, their hands touched, and Natário, with a gesture that was very much like him, stroked his wife's face.

The calm of a sun-kissed morning covered Tocaia Grande with a cloak of peace. The sounds were the usual ones, the breeze was rippling the waters of the river, women were washing clothes and singing modas, pigs were rooting among the rotting fruit beneath the jackfruit tree. Fadul stood in the doorway of his store, Durvalino was drawing water from the well, and the sound of hammer against anvil could be heard coming from Castor Abduim's smithy. Bernarda and Coroca arrived to wish Zilda a good trip and to kiss Nado good-bye.

At the cemetery, another grave, a shallow one, just like the others: that of Altamirando, herder of goats and pigs. They'd buried him near Ção, guessing that was what he wanted.

6

THE SAME DAY AT dusk, naked because of the heat, Captain Natário da Fonseca and Bernarda, his goddaughter, his mistress, were resting in their bed, when they heard someone lift the latch and push open the door of the wooden house. It was probably Coroca coming back from her visit to Dona Vanjé. Thinking along those lines, the captain was ready to resume the fun, but Bernarda had her doubts and, with a shudder, slid out from under him. She'd been on tenterhooks ever since the constables had killed the pigs, a foreboding in her mind, a weight on her heart.

In the shadows of the bedroom a figure took shape, came in from the parlor, shouting, "Your day for dying has come, Natário da Fonseca, you piece of shit captain!"

He aimed at the captain, but the one who caught the shot was Bernarda, who'd stood up suddenly, covering her godfather. The bullet hit her in the chest, piercing her left breast, and she fell on top of Natário.

At the same instant a shot fired from the door felled the gunman. Black Espiridião could be seen in the dim light, but he didn't come into the bedroom, stayed waiting in the parlor. Bernarda was dying in the arms of her godfather, just as she'd been told by the Gypsy woman on that distant day when she'd had her palm read.

"My love," she murmured, bleeding from her breast and her mouth. For the first time she'd called him *my love*, the only love of her life. She repeated it again before her voice gave out. "My love . . ."

Bernarda's blood covered Natário's chest, running down his stomach and his thighs. He lifted her in his arms, laid her on the bed, and covered her with the sheet. His face motionless, his jaw firm, his teeth clenched, his eyes dull, his mouth a razor-thin slit, the captain paused for a moment, standing there over his goddaughter's corpse. The sight inspired pity and fear.

7

"DALVINO, DO YOU REMEMBER him?" black Espiridião asked, moving the body with his foot.

Natário remembered the albino well, one of many who'd sworn to kill him during the past troubles. They'd come face-to-face back then, the gunman signed up in the troops of Colonel Dalton Melo of Ferradas, he watching over Colonel Boaventura. In a whorehouse in Itabuna they'd also had a falling out over a woman, but the squabble hadn't gone very far: Dalvino, drunk, could barely stand up. His tongue, thick with *cachaça*, had been limited to vain threats and promises of revenge. One of the girls took him to bed with her.

There he was, suddenly resurrected in Tocaia Grande, bent on liquidating Natário. Carrying out old threats, a long-delayed vengeance, it was hard to believe. He'd been hired to do the job by someone familiar with the layout of the village and the captain's habits, moves, and love life.

"Taquaras is filled to the brim with gunmen, a new bunch arrives every day from Itabuna," Espiridião went on. "If you want to know why, I'll tell you: they're getting together to attack Tocaia Grande."

It had been a long time since so many outlaws had come together for no apparent reason, because peace had reigned among the flock of colonels, the land was divided up among the bigwigs, and politics went along smoothly, elections still a long way off. With nothing to do but admire the knowledge of his daughter, the teacher Antônia—watching her at the blackboard writing figures for the children filled his heart and opened his mouth in a broad smile, showing off his toothless gums—he'd gone out in search of information: why such a concentration of gunmen in Taquaras, some of them with fearful and well-deserved reputations? All of them armed to the teeth, money bulging in their pockets: in whorehouses *cachaça* was flowing like water.

Most of the bravos didn't know much, just the invitation sent by Sheriff Orígenes for a detail that could bring in some good dough, with a guarantee of raids and booty and the future of the place in the military police, depending on the individual's performance. Hitching up with the military police, with the right to wear a uniform and behave with impunity, was the highest ambition of an unemployed gunman. In Taquaras, the gathering place, they'd get their orders at the proper time.

One or another knew a little bit more, and the name of Tocaia Grande was mentioned several times. Dalvino, tying on a monumental binge at Mara's house on the Beco da Valsa, waltz alley, a braggart as well as a drunkard, was boasting about having been assigned a special job, one of great importance, to precede the gunmen's action. A pleasant task, because it would allow him to settle an old score.

He ended up mentioning the captain's name, and from then on Espiridião didn't let him out of his sight. He stayed on his heels, watching his meeting with Corporal Chico Roncolho, assistant chief of police in Itabuna, who'd come in on the train and, keeping his distance so as not to be seen, he dogged Dalvino's tracks when the half-breed set out for Tocaia Grande. His friend Natário knew the rest of the plot.

The black man was only sorry that he hadn't got his shot in before the son of a bitch did, avoiding the death of Bernarda. But he couldn't make out the inside of the bedroom too well from the door; it was swallowed up in the shadows of the night. He was afraid of hitting the girl or Natário; he was only able to aim at the flash of Dalvino's shot. It was sad, Bernarda's death: she was the prettiest whore in all the length and breadth of the Rio das Cobras; no one could be compared to her: pretty as a picture.

8

JACINTA, CALLED COROCA FOR such a long time, finally began to look as decrepit as the name implied, as if age and weariness had suddenly hit her all at once. She crouched like an old woman at the foot of Bernarda's deathbed, star-

ing into her face. Now a bed of death, an old army cot where
once Bernarda's beauty exercised its calling of whore for so
many years and where for all of those years she had been
the woman of only one man, her godfather.

A godmother twice over, old Coroca had delivered
Bernarda's baby, then baptized him at the altar of the Holy
Mission. And Bernarda herself, more than a grandchild, like
her own daughter, because when they met in Tocaia Grande,
Coroca had adopted her. What was Bernarda but a child
beset by suffering: her virginity stolen by her father; her
mother paralyzed in bed; she and her younger sister growing up amid hunger and beatings? Had she been her own
daughter, Coroca couldn't have loved her any more.

With the passage of those years, the two of them living
in the same tiny house built for them on orders from Captain Natário da Fonseca, never an ugly word, an evil action,
a disagreement of any kind, never did the least mistrust
come between the two of them. *My God, what was it going to
be like from now on?* Coroca shook her head, she didn't want
to think about it.

9

MY SILENCE TELLS YOU, my old friends, comadres *and*
compadres: *in bygone days in this south Bahian land where
cacao grows, the richest, most beautiful soil on earth, you had
the honor of a man's word, a nobility in people's dealing. There
was no need for stamped papers or signed documents. Citizens,
rich or poor, colonels or gunmen, had equal stature when it
came to loyalty and respect, courage and honor. And the price
of betrayal was death.*

*A lot of things have changed, outside and in, ever since that
yesterday when you crossed the road, gun in hand, when trust
between cacao barons and brave men was a precious and
respected commodity. Other people are in charge now.* Natário's
face, a stern rock, didn't let his bitter thoughts show through,
didn't reflect his pain at the loss of one who'd been both
lover and godchild, almost a daughter. But the men and
women who were his old friends, a confraternity born of

free people living together, *compadre* and *comadre* understood the meaning of his silence as well as his words and
warning.

Come what may, he would honor his pledge, tacit and
understood, keeping the promise he had made in the flow of
events and circumstances, big and small, fortunate or ac-
cursed, an alliance forged by life.

10

ESPIRIDIÃO HAD HEARD IN conversations here and there—
on the drowsy station benches, at the noisy cane-liquor
bars, in the merry whorehouses—rumors, gossip, talk about
sudden and surprisingly intense goings-on at the intendente's
office, among notaries, at the Briosa barracks, at the jail,
everywhere you looked in Itabuna. The schemes, if one was
to believe all the talk, were dubious and diverse.

A lot of hints all right, but too vague for anyone to draw
any precise conclusions. The captain thought about dropping by Itabuna, to smell out, detail by detail, what was in
the wind, force things into the open. But the others, and
later on Coroca, someone with a nose for those things, advised him against such a trip as imprudent and perhaps
even dangerous: it would be like walking right into the
enemy's camp, delivering himself bound hand and foot.

In the sound and measured opinion of Espiridião, hadn't
they sent a gunman to Tocaia Grande to kill Natário? Why,
there'd be a bandit waiting to ambush him on every street
corner in Itabuna. Fadul Abdala and Castor Abduim agreed
in every detail. Espiridião had instructed his daughter—
Professor Antônia was in contact with everybody, was trusted
and respected because of her knowledge and the eyeglasses
that attested to it—to get as much information as possible
and send a messenger to deliver it in person. All on paper, in
nice writing, he explained, because no one could write as
nice as Professor Antônia.

Not even then, however, would the captain have listened had it not been for the arrival of Mr. Carlinhos Silva.
He'd been to Ilhéus for his monthly report, and brought

back concrete news with an express order from Kurt Koifman in person to clean out and close up the cacao warehouse, then hightail it back to the firm's headquarters. When the hot times that were looming cooled off eventually, they'd make a decision concerning the location of the warehouse: depending on how things went, they might even stay in Tocaia Grande.

11

ACCOMPANIED BY HER THREE sons, Jãozé, Agnaldo, and Aurélio, old Vanjé stopped by the veranda of Captain Natário da Fonseca's house.

"Beg your pardon, Captain, but I'd like to have a word with you."

Sitting on one of the wooden benches cleaning his six-shooter, the captain was chatting with Fadul and Tição. Weapons piled up in the parlor at the foot of the phonograph caught the Sergipe woman's attention.

"Sit down, Aunt Vanjé." Natário pointed to the empty benches. "The rest of you too. There's plenty of room for everybody."

Jãozé had come back from Taquaras with his eyes a-boggle, his ears ringing with what he'd heard and seen. He'd gone off to the market with his brother Aurélio, on their donkey's back the basket of hens and two hampers full of produce from their farm: squashes, chayotes, *onguria* fruit, okra, *jilós*, sweet potatoes. Well, he'd headed back confused, alarmed, in a hurry. He'd seen a bit too many gunmen, the market all a stir, he'd heard murmurs that made your hair stand on end.

"Captain, sir, do you know what Jãozé heard in Taquaras? He told me things I still can't believe they're true!"

The captain got up to get some mugs; the visitors should have some *cachaça*.

"Keep on talking, Auntie, I'm listening."

Before sitting down, he refilled the mugs of the black man, the Turk, and his own. He left the bottle within reach.

"Well, they're saying that we're all a bunch of criminals

here, that we're living on other people's land without the permission of the owner."

"That's right," her son confirmed. "They're calling us land thieves."

Vanjé picked up again.

"And saying that they're going to kick us all out of here, that the owners are on their way to teach us a lesson."

"Backed up by gunmen," Jãozé explained.

Captain Natário da Fonseca laid his six-shooter on the bench, let his stare linger on the face of the old Sergipean woman, then swallowed a sip of *cachaça*, wiping his mouth with the back of his hand.

"There are folks who want it that way, Auntie. And if we let them, that's the way it's gonna be."

"Spell it out, Captain. I don't get your point."

The three brothers, the same as Castor and Fadul, were following the dialogue between the old woman and the captain in silence, slowly sipping their *cachaça*. Tension was in the air, so strong and concrete that you could almost reach out and touch it. Jãozé spat; a thick wad went over the rail.

"How many years has it been since you arrived here with your departed Ambrósio and his people? Tell me if the land had any owner then or if it was vacant. When you people occupied it, cleaned out the underbrush, began to plant manioc, did anyone show up to complain, claiming to be the owner?"

"Nobody."

"And there couldn't have been anyone, because it didn't have an owner. How many years ago was that? Now that it's been cleaned up and planted, with a flour mill, and you people selling things here and in Taquaras, they've got their fat eyes on it. You saw that business with the constables. Whose pigs were the ones they killed? Didn't they belong to Altamirando? They killed him too. They say it's law, that we've got to obey it."

Agnaldo opened his mouth in a rage, got up to say the law, horseshit the law, but his mother wouldn't let him go on.

"Wait a bit, son. Captain, you were saying just now that they'll take over if we let them, weren't you?" She repeated for confirmation. "If we let them?"

"That's right, Dona Vanjé. The men in Itabuna have

done some flimflamming, and now they're saying that this boondocks where we've set up Tocaia Grande has an owner, that it's had one even since the start, that the land on both sides of the river, whether it's where you've planted your fields or where you've built your houses, belongs to someone else. The crops and the houses that were carried off by the flood and that you and us together planted and built all over again. Land that belonged to you people and to us they say has got an owner now and always did. It's written down and registered at the notary's office. All that's left is for us to go along and agree."

"Agree to let them take our land?"

"Listen hard, Auntie Vanjé, listen to what I'm going to say. You people, too, Jãozé, Agnaldo, Aurélio. We can say all right and give in: you keep on working by shares, I start paying rent on the hill, or we can fight to defend what's ours."

"Would it be worth it?" Jãozé spat again. "I never saw so many gunmen."

"It'll be a mean fight. . . ." The captain looked the Sergipeans over with his tiny eyes, lowered his voice. "Most likely we'll lose. But even so, I'm of the opinion that it's worth the try, and my friends Fadul and Tição are of the same mind. We've decided we're going to buy us a fight."

Agnaldo tried to interrupt; the captain made a sign for him to be patient.

"I'll be through in a minute, Agnaldo, then you can talk. Everybody's free to do whatever he wants, Auntie. You and your sons too. Make a deal, leave right now and come back later or pick up a shooting iron."

"As far as I'm concerned, I know what I'm going to do. It's not going to be like the last time, when they didn't let us . . ." Agnaldo exploded, almost shouting.

Vanjé spoke again; there was no change in her tone.

"Do you remember, Captain, when you ran into us on the road running away from Sergipe? It was the second time for me, it had already happened to my father's land. I know what Agnaldo's thinking, he never forgot. I don't know about the rest, each can decide for himself. But I can tell you this, Captain Natário, you've been like a father to us: what we've made of this land, which was nothing but wild scrub when we got here, I'm not giving to nobody, not halves, not thirds. To nobody. And I'll leave it only when I die. I don't know about the others. . . ."

"We'll do whatever you say, Ma." Jãozé got up; the crops needed tending. "Let's get back to work."

"God bless you, Captain, Vanjé said, and left, followed by her sons. But Aurélio, the youngest, who hadn't said a single word during the meeting, dropped behind.

"Can you arrange me a six-shooter, Captain? Back home the only one who's got one is Agnaldo. And I'm not a bad shot."

12

THE LAW, MY GOOD friends. In the barrel of a repeater, in the trigger of a revolver, in the muzzle of a shotgun, the law was on its way. On the heels of flood and fever.

Anyone who wants to leave can take off, hit the road, stay far away, wait for the fuss to be over in order to return nice and tame, head down, to receive the yoke and obey the lord and master's orders. Anyone who wants to can turn tail and run, take to his heels, catch a train and beat it. There's no room anymore in Tocaia Grande for yellowbellies or scoundrels.

Having decided what to do, before making final arrangements Captain Natário da Fonseca, a veteran leader of gunmen, a clever half-breed—sometimes in the company of Castor, sometimes that of Fadul, if not both—went from house to house and explained to each soul what was already going on and what would happen soon enough.

To many, though, because he knew them well, he counseled prudence and urged them to flee; if they weren't absolutely fearless, they didn't have the same reasons to pick up arms and resist. It would be more difficult—oh, much more, there was no comparison!—than facing up to the flood; the law was far more deadly than the plague.

13

ON THE LAST NIGHT of waiting, the good Lord of the
Maronites appeared to his son Fadul Abdala in a dream, as
had happened on many previous occasions. The two lived in
close contact, exchanged impressions about events, the Arab
thanked or complained accordingly, praising the provisions
taken by the Lord or accusing Him of being careless and
capricious.

With his majestic appearance—an immense cloud,
which, in order to talk to Fadul, took on human form, a
gigantic old man with beard and long flowing hair—the
good Lord had interrupted a dissolute night of bacchanalia.
The Turk had started things off by copulating with the
widow Jussara Ramos Rabat—a married woman, no less,
because she'd reverted to that condition some time ago by
having taken on a new husband: a still young country bump-
kin, newly arrived to the region, who had proudly taken
over the Orient Shop and the horns of the late and lamented
Kalil.

In order to complete the orgy of that solitary night,
even the maiden Aruza—vanished from the wide bed with
its sedge mattress and bedbugs, ever since some lawyer had
led her to the altar deflowered and with child—showed up
to offer her still intact pussy, and Aruza's pussy became
Zezinha do Butiá's twat, that unfathomable abyss. On more
recent nights, when the waiting grew long and tedious,
Zezinha had been his constant companion.

The good Lord of the Maronites touched him on the
shoulder, tugged on his arm, pulling him away from the
breasts and buttocks of such women to alert him to the
menace now approaching Tocaia Grande. He opened his
eyes and the Lord had been transformed into skinny Durvalino,
his clerk, who told him, all excited, "Mr. Fadu! Gunmen are
arriving, Mr. Fadu!"

An extraordinary excitement had come over him: for a
fellow whose main characteristic was a state of continuous
agitation, you can imagine his condition now. Fadul jumped
up.

"How do you know?"

"Pedro Gypsy told me! He's in the store, he wants to talk with you and the captain. Only the captain isn't at home."

While he was washing his face in the tin basin, the Turk asked for details, and Durvalino told him what little he knew.

"Mr. Pedro ran into them coming this way. He hid and followed them to a place close by."

Tattletale was twisting his hands, scratching his balls, he couldn't hide his nervousness. Fadul finished drying his face.

"You're leaving town, right now."

"Me? Where to? Are you firing me? What did I do?"

"That's not it. You haven't done anything. I just don't want you around here. I don't want your aunt to blame me tomorrow if anything should happen to you."

Durvalino laughed in his boss's face.

"Aunt Zezinha, when she sent me here to you, told me: 'Lininho'—that's what she calls me—'you go stay with Mr. Fadu, you take care of him, don't you leave his side for a minute, because my Turk is just a big kid, he's always getting himself in a tight spot.' Well, there can't be a tighter spot than this one. How can you send me away? What would my aunt say?"

He looked at his boss seriously and ventured an opinion, attempting to size up the whole mess they were involved in.

"You'll see, Mr. Fadu. We're all going to die at the hands of those gunmen. Nobody'll be left to tell the tale. You'll see!"

14

LEANING AGAINST THE COUNTER, without waiting for an invitation, Pedro Gypsy was serving himself a morning drink to rinse his mouth. He'd spent a good part of the night crawling through the underbrush, following the movements of the gunmen who'd come from Taquaras on a forced march.

In an automatic reflex, Fadul noticed the dent made in

the bottle of *cachaça* by the vagabond. He shrugged his shoulders; it wasn't a proper time to complain. He only commented, with a touch of harshness, "You picked a mighty fine time to show up here. You couldn't have done worse."

"Why is my friend Fadu saying something like that? Is he mad at me?"

"Who knows better than you; you saw that lot, didn't you? They're on their way to attack Tocaia Grande, didn't you know that?"

"Have I ever missed anything? If I missed anything, you tell me. I'm not bragging, friend Fadu, but I'm even less inclined to run away when the shooting starts. Ask the captain; he's known me a lot longer than just today."

He put the glass down on the greasy bar, scratched his kinky hair.

"What do you say, friend, to our having a slice of dried meat to break our fast? An empty sack can't stand up by itself and we've got to line our bellies before things get hot." He handed the accordion to the Turk. "Take care of my concertina, will you, so we can celebrate afterward."

15

THE ACCURACY OF THE news furnished by Pedro Gypsy had been proved; it coincided with the written message from Professor Antônia sent in her own hand by a student of hers, the rascal Lazinho, son of Lourenço, the stationmaster. Used to carrying letters and telegrams to Colonel Boaventura Andrade at Atalaia Plantation, the urchin, riding a donkey bareback, had arrived ahead of the gunmen, making it possible to take measures. Urgent measures and not entirely easy ones.

It hadn't been easy to convince black Espiridião to go to Boa Vista Plantation, but he decided to do it out of friendship for Natário: he went at the request of his companion of so many years and so many scraps to look after his wife and children so his friend could take charge of the defense of Tocaia Grande with less on his mind. When the captain brought up the subject, the black man was almost offended.

"The farm? Don't you know me, Natário? Leave here, now? Like a weak-kneed old man? Not on your life."

"Is there anybody in the world who would ever think you were a weak-kneed old man?" The captain was so surprised that he even started to laugh, something that happened only rarely. "Get that out of your head and listen to me, please." He put his hand on the black man's shoulder in an affectionate gesture to convince him. "Why did you come here? You didn't come because of Tocaia Grande; you came to help me because we've been like brothers. Am I telling the truth?"

"You're telling the truth."

"Well, then, you can help me most by staying with Zilda and the kids. She hasn't got anybody she can rely on. What we don't want is for any cutthroat to find his way there."

Natário didn't give Espiridião further time to reflect.

"If any guy comes snooping around, gun him down, then send Peba to tell me."

With his hand still on the black man's shoulder, he confided his distress.

"I really wanted Edu to go along with you, but he wouldn't hear of it. 'I've never disobeyed you, Pop, until now' is all he said." He quoted the words with concern and pride, content with his son's rebellion.

"It had to be that way, being he's your son."

Natário took his hand off Espiridião's shoulder and, abandoning his customary reserve once more, took him in his arms. Ever since Bernarda's death, the captain had been a different person.

"Tell Zilda to stay put there, not to leave the farm for anything in the world, to take care of the kids and to wait for me."

16

IT WAS EVEN MORE difficult to convince black Epifânia to leave for Santa Mariana Plantation at the headwaters of the Rio das Cobras, taking Tovo, the godson of Dona Isabel and Colonel Robustiano de Araújo.

Son of Xangô, god of war, Tição Abduim had on one side Oxóssi, the hunter, and on the other Oxalá, the great father. Epifânia belonged to Oxum, mistress of rivers and arrogance; being queen, she took orders from no mortal, whoever he might be. At dawn, before the sun shone down on inhabitants and gunmen, the shoer of donkeys called on Ressu to help offer the *ebó* of blood: they sacrificed four roosters and offered one of them to Iemanjá, goddess of the dead Diva.

First Iansan mounted her horse, then Ressu danced the war dance, set out for battle, and returned with the dead and opened the path in the *axexe* for the *egum*.

The black man shuddered, covered his eyes with his hands; pursued, he ran from one side to the other, his mouth red with the blood of the cock offered to Iemanjá. An unexpected wind arose, a cloud descended from the sky and became a being: it was not the good Lord of the Maronites, it was the queen of the waters, mistress of the ocean, Dona Janaína. Tição received Iemanjá, his wife. She took the child in her arms and lifted him up with her hands. She showed him to everyone and, before giving him to Oxum, she sang of joy and life.

Epifânia had no choice but to obey orders from the *ogum*. A woman of strength and conviction, hard to down, her eyes had never shown the trace of a tear, nor had her lips uttered a whine of complaint. Only when she was living with a man or having a good time did she moan and sigh: moans of delight, sighs of pleasure. Epifânia tried to resist, she couldn't, the *ogum* pointed the path of life with a bony finger. As it had done before, giving her the child, imposing its will.

Black Epifânia went off weeping; anyone who saw her wouldn't have believed it. Poor Soul accompanied her for a good stretch of road. Then he came back to his friend, who was gathering his weapons.

Tição, bidding farewell, had hugged his son against his chest.

"Tell the colonel to make a man of him."

17

AROUND ELEVEN O'CLOCK IN the morning the law appeared in the calm and shy, runty person of Irênio Gomes, a bailiff from the criminal courthouse in Itabuna. He arrived in Tocaia Grande accompanied by two soldiers from the military police, hoping to assert his authority, and enforce it if possible. The soldiers were armed to their rotting teeth and Irênio displayed a rusty, obsolete pistol on his belt.

Without dismounting, with a recruit on either side, this officer of the law proclaimed in the public square—or, rather, in the clearing, in front of the cross erected for the Holy Mission—the edict issued by the honorable court judge and ordered by him to be published in *A Semana Grapiúna*, the south Bahian weekly, and proclaimed to the four points of the compass.

It instructed the citizens of Tocaia Grande to lay down their arms and surrender themselves to the above-mentioned authority; at the same time they were to hand over and place at the disposal of the authorities—to stand trial for the crime of murder, the accused Natário da Fonseca, against whom a warrant for arrest had already been issued and who was ordered to appear in court.

Having concluded his solemn notification, to the jeers and laughter of those present, Irênio Gomes began his retreat. And he did so peacefully, or nearly so, since the people who had gathered to listen chose merely to disarm them, the three saps. The most aroused of the citizens told the law to go fuck itself and the judge could do it to the whore who bore him.

18

THE FIRST SHOTS WERE exchanged at two o'clock in the afternoon at the flour mill, on the boundary line between the farms of Zé dos Santos and old Vanjé, and the last ones came after midnight on Captain's Hill: bodies were piling up along the rocky path mounting the slope as if the garrison around the house were made up of a whole gang of ballsy fellows. They may have been the equivalent of a platoon, yet there were only two of them, stationed behind the trunk of the mulunga tree, which had broken out in bloom.

Encirclement, assault, and occupation took ten hours and twenty minutes, counted second by second on the big old nickel-plated pocket watch of the nervous Sergeant

Orígenes. Between three and four o'clock, that is, between
the massacre of the Sergipeans and the second charge, led
by Corporal Chico Roncolho, there was a cease-fire. Taken
advantage of by the attackers to complete their encirclement and by the inhabitants to bury their dead in hurriedly
opened graves, the last individual sepulchers. Afterward there
was no time to bury anybody and on the following day the
bodies of the fallen on both sides were quickly and indis-
criminately dumped into a common ditch dug by the
outsiders.

In the recruitment of gunmen in Itabuna, police agents
had promised a wild party, an incomparable orgy, limitless
booty in the festivities celebrating victory. With the lack of
whores, the affair was reduced to stuffing their guts and
swilling *cachaça*, but what fun is it to eat and drink without
the lively company of *putas*? They're the only ones capable
of calming anxieties and building spirits subjected to the
vicissitudes of combat and dispelling the cold fear that knifes
through a man's balls, making dicks limp. Aside from that,
the only reward was the sacking of the emporium; they
found very few items of value in the private homes. Those
who'd abandoned Tocaia Grande before and during the attack had taken most of their belongings with them, regular
drovers' donkeys, they seemed, they were so overloaded. A
good thing Dona Natalina's sewing machine was driven by
hand and not by foot, so she was able to bear it off on her
head. Dona Valentina and Juca Neves sweated and cursed,
carrying huge bundles in which they had rescued clothing
and bedlinens and tablecloths from the Central Boardinghouse.

It's no use wasting any time talking about those who,
out of cowardice or greed, abandoned the settlement, refusing to take up arms. Suffice it to say, however, that neither
the captain nor Fadul and Castor, his lieutenants, had forced
any decision on anyone, no matter who it was. Nothing was
riskier than leading people who are afraid; Natário knew
that better than anybody.

Those who fled, saving their lives and a few belongings,
lost everything else, including their self-respect and the good
opinion of others, as if, by deserting their relatives and
neighbors, they'd contracted leprosy or acquired the marks
of black pox on their faces and in their souls. It happens
that way.

Not included in that gang of weaklings were those who went off on missions or went along with the wounded and children. Zinho, besides taking care of Lupiscínio, his father, who was badly wounded at the end of the day, had the mission of spreading the news of Natário's death with the aim of weakening the enemy's vigilance, as the captain himself had enjoined him. Jãozé, his arm in a sling and his shoulder all bandaged, led a caravan of women and children toward the headwaters of the Rio das Cobras. In the cemetery of Tocaia Grande he left behind his mother, his three brothers, his sister-in-law and one of her daughters, not to mention his *compadre* José dos Santos.

Zinho, Lupiscínio, Jãozé and the other wounded— Elói, Balbino, Zé Luiz, and Ressu—appear in that way on the list of the valiant to be proclaimed loud and clear so that they may be remembered if there is occasion, opportunity, or interest in it, a dubious hypothesis. Because for once at least Durvalino had been more or less accurate in his predictions; those who hadn't died were sorely wounded: Zé Luiz was lame in one leg, a gunman had dug out one of Ressu's eyes with a dagger.

To do honor to the proper judgment of all, the tale of the valiant must begin with the name of the popular clerk Durvalino Tattletale, inscribed on the rolls immediately after in the rush of battle along with those of Lupiscínio, Zinho, Balbino, Guido, the foreman Zé Luiz, the wooden-shoemaker Elói, Pedro Gypsy, Zé dos Santos, Jãozé, Agnaldo, Aurélio, and Dodô Peroba, who had given his trained birds their freedom. Thirteen souls not too familiar with firearms and disorder, except for the accordionist, who had seen quite a bit in his day and had been in his fair share of shootouts already.

After a while they were joined by the Estâncians Vavá and Amâncio who, unlike other members of the family, hadn't run off on their mules. The clan had gathered after the captain's visit and had decided to keep out of the fighting, at least unless they were attacked: the problem of ownership of the land and terms for working it could be discussed later. Dona Leocádia, against her better judgment, agreed, turning over inside. Faced with what had happened to Vanjé's people, the Estâncians split up, the majority ran off, seeking refuge on neighboring plantations.

Those under the orders of Castor Abduim, Fadul Abdala,

and Captain Natário da Fonseca added up to about eighteen all told, but it would be an awful, unthinkable injustice not to include women among the ballsy just because they didn't have any. Balls, and not bravery: when it came to courage, no one could be compared to Jacinta Coroca. Along with her, leaving their lives there were Dona Vanjé, her daughter-in-law Lia, Paulinha Marisca, a revelation, and Dona Leocádia. Blinded in one eye, a slash across her face, Ressu had lost her cherubic features, was left looking like a demon.

It would be even more unjust to pass over Edu and Nando because of their young age. Nando had come to Tocaia Grande as a boy of eleven; he'd grown into a womanizing adolescent, darling of the whores; he died among his own. The same as Mirinho, the son of Tarcísio, Dona Leocádia's grandson, who, without the knowledge of his parents and his aunts and uncles, had put the expertise of his restless twelve years at the service of Natário, having been of real use in spying on the enemy's movements. Captured on one of these missions, he was killed in cold blood, left with his guts cut out. Edu fell fighting alongside Fadul: he'd inherited his father's fearlessness and good aim.

The final balance sheet of those ten hours of firefights, ambushes, and hand-to-hand combat showed a total of forty-eight dead, made up of twenty-two inhabitants of Tocaia Grande, including the old, the young, and even children, and twenty-six attackers, among them Corporal Chico Roncolho and the perverted Benaia Cova Rasa. Not even in the days of the battles between Basílio de Oliveira and the Badarós had a slaughter that size occurred in such a short time.

19

IT WOULD BE USELESS to accuse anyone, assign blame, incriminate this or that person; events would have gone that way in any case; the disproportion of forces led fatally to the final occupation of Tocaia Grande.

The military police contingent—eight regulars and more than twenty recruits to guarantee the legitimacy of the operation, under the command of Corporal Chico Roncolho and Sergeant Orígenes—only unleashed the final, major assault after news of Natário's death, when the captain's forces had been reduced to six sound men and one woman: Coroca, whore, midwife, and lieutenant in the place of Fadul and Castor, both fallen in combat. The previous incursions had been effected by gunmen without uniforms—the detachment didn't own enough tunics—another twenty at least, to judge by the number eventually found wandering the roads, causing disturbances in villages, threatening one and all.

The truth, however, impossible to hide, demands that we admit that the mad gesture by Agnaldo at the appearance of the first triggermen unleashed the initial slaughter, setting the tone henceforth for the cruel character of the expedition, transforming battle into butchery. Cutting through the underbrush, a group of gunmen led by Felipão Zureta, the Madman, advanced more rapidly than the others and occupied the flour mill. Natário ordered Castor to cross the bridge at the head of four volunteers, Dodô Peroba, Balbino, Zé Luiz, and black Ressu of Iansan, goddess of war, with the objective of dislodging the invaders or at least preventing them from advancing on the settlement. Without waiting for the patrol to get closer, Agnaldo picked up his carbine and ran toward the flour mill.

Ever since those distant, humiliating days of Sergipe— the expulsion from their land in Maroim, the stake where he'd been tied like an ox to be slaughtered, the blows of a whip that likened him to a slave—Agnaldo felt the thirst for vengeance burning in his chest and throat. It would have been really good to have taken a shot at the senator, but since he wasn't there, those sent by other lords to uphold and renew the iniquitous law would pay the price.

He went forward firing the carbine he'd carried uselessly on his shoulder during their crossing as refugees. He hit one thug who had a shotgun and immediately fell himself, riddled with bullets; those were the first two deaths. At Agnaldo's heels, who knows, trying to hold him back, Lia, his wife, pursued him: she took a shot point-blank and fell on top of her husband's body. Behind her came Aurélio, the weapon the captain had given him in his hand; he never got to fire it.

Furious at the unexpected attack, Felipão ordered a violent reprisal, and the gunmen began it, even though they didn't get to finish it as they would have wanted. Not content with killing or putting out of commission Zé dos Santos and Jãozé, who were armed, they slaughtered old Vanjé, who was running up to the sound of the shouting, and the urchin Nando, whose weapon was a slingshot, and one of Dinorá's twins: stumbling on her little legs, the innocent child held out her arms toward the bandits.

The only reason they didn't totally finish off the two Sergipean families—Ambrosio's and that of José dos Santos—was because Castor's patrol got there from the other side of the river and caught them off guard, since they'd left the cover of the flour mill in order to kill more easily. They beat a hasty retreat.

20

WHEN TURK FADUL SAW himself all alone, Edu and Durvalino fallen on the ground, one dead, the other dying, without any bullets in his revolver or on his belt, he flung himself onto the closest gunman, who was none other than Benaia Cova Rasa. With his two hands, those huge hands that he'd used to break up fights and convince the more obstinate, two tongs, he squeezed the bandit's throat, but didn't get to strangle him: he took two pistol shots, one in the shoulder, the other in the neck; he loosened his grip and dropped. They didn't kill him right off: on orders from Benaia, who, huffing and puffing, was having trouble breathing, they tied the giant up and dumped him in the corral, where they were holed up. Benaia planned to take care of him when the fighting cooled down.

For a few minutes Fadul lay motionless, gathering his strength. He was bleeding from the neck and shoulder, but he managed to fill his chest with air and, inflating his thorax, he burst the ropes used for tying oxen with which they'd bound him. With a leap he got hold of one of the gunmen's revolver and began shooting. He sent two down to hell and he couldn't do more because Benaia emptied six bullets into his body. Unable to finish him off with a knife,

nice and slow, as he'd planned, Cova Rasa roared, furious at
being cheated.

Thus was the death of Fadul Abdala, the Grand Turk,
Turk Fadul, Mr. Fadu to farm workers and drovers, a peddler with long experience, a shopkeeper, an outstanding
citizen of the village, celebrated for the size of his deal,
respected for his brute strength, well liked for the affability
of his manners, loved for his frank and loyal nature: hadn't
he been the one to decree in times gone by that in Tocaia
Grande they were all for one and one for all?

In the beginning he'd made a pact with the good Lord
of the Maronites, who'd led him there by the hand. He had
fulfilled his part right down to the end in spite of all the
hardships, and now at the hour of death he'd been abandoned by his Lord. In a mist before his hazy eyes he saw the
fleeting figure of Zezinha do Butiá, waving an embroidered
handkerchief from the door of a railroad coach. She opened
her mouth, but instead of stammering some tender phrase,
she exploded with Siroca's cry when he'd popped her cherry.
With so many beautiful creatures to think about, it was the
black girl he thought of when he surrendered his body to the
Lord God, to the good Lord of the Maronites. Good Lord?
Think what you will, he was indignant before he vomited up
his soul: "A trickster, no better word for it—a scoundrel, a
fine son of a bitch who'd gone back on his word and reneged
on a deal: *iá-rára-dinák!*"

21

WHEN EVERYTHING WAS OVER and done with, when the
law had already been installed and was making itself obeyed
with the prerequisite rigor, a lot of stories were told on the
roads, highways, and byways of south Bahia country regarding the showdown at Tocaia Grande and its subsequent
occupation. According to reports in the press, it was the
largest and most violent battle in the region since the end of
the fighting over ownership of the land, fighting which coin-
cidentally had come to an end with that memorable big

ambush, triggered in the same place, hence its name, Tocaia Grande.

In the scrub forests of the backlands and in the fields of Sergipe, singers picked up their guitars and sang of the fearsome events, rhyming vengeance with remembrance, knavery with bravery, on one side cowardice and evil, on the other valor and honesty, freedom crushed by iniquity.

If in the press of the state capital, with arguments pro and con, each paper carried its own version of the truth, the opposite was true of the rhymes and verses of street poets: the massacre was condemned universally, with an obvious stand on the side of the people of Tocaia Grande. They brought clearly to light the causes of the raid—envy, greed, profit, the imposition of force. They denounced the heroes proclaimed by the newspapers and government, they branded the victors with the stigma of evil and violence and defended the cause of the vanquished—a subversive attitude of ignorant people put forth in verses of the poorest kind. For all of its lack of meter and proper grammar, the poetry traveled about, reaching the distant regions of Paraíba and Pernambuco. It was a small glow, the flicker of a lamp lighting up the dark side.

Some names were cursed, others exalted. The poetry spoke of injustice and intolerance, hypocrisy and treachery, blood and death, but it also mentioned beauty and joy. Men of true hearts who'd built their houses and planted their patch of beans.

> The captain's house on the hill
> Built with love and good will,
> The same you could also say
> Of the bean patch of Dona Vanjé

The True History of Captain Natário da Fonseca under the authorship of Filomeno das Rosas Alencar, a poor relation of the erudite Alencars and their folkloric studies, described Natário's deeds. None of them were as true as the author of the narrative had proclaimed, but even the invented verses fit the measure of fearlessness and decency that the half-breed had.

> He was a gallant captain,
> An iron man in command,

A curse to enemies and badmen,
With women a lover grand.

They spoke of how during the siege the captain had
been seen in every corner of Tocaia Grande leading and
fighting. How, singlehanded, he'd faced a whole troop of
cutthroats, and, given up for dead, had gone on shooting
down gunmen right and left.

Dudu Matias, a guitar player from Amargosa, had dedicated his inspiration and rondels to Pedro Gypsy and Dodô
Peroba, "two minstrels of life." He did a good job singing
about the arrival of the "king of concertina players and the
emperor of birds" in Paradise, where, to attend the celestial
court, Pedro Gypsy immediately

Organized a ball and everybody went
Where Jesus danced a dance with Mary Magdalene

while Dodô Peroba drew out of his riddled chest an oriole
that he offered as a gift to the Eternal Father.

As consolation for the Christ Child
And to sweeten all eternity

All of the guitar players without exception spoke of Fadul,
his giant's strength, the potency and size of a "tool bigger than
the enormous palm of his hand, but smaller than his great
heart"; and they remembered Coroca, "blessed birther of babies, soft, succulent snatch, the older she got, the better she
hatched, in a fight she was the same as two men, maybe
three."

Jesus da Mata, a native of Feira de Sant'Ana, incomparable at improvisation, playing his guitar where the backlands
began, from the canebreaks about the bay to the cacao
groves of the south, spread the "ABC Song of Castor Abduim,
alias Tição," in verses where hemistitches of six or seven
rhymed syllables traced the saga of the black man, a person
of a thousand loves and countless adventures.

... In French things he was ever a challenge,
Of maids and mistresses a love,
He gobbled the good, the best piece of all,
Danced schottische, *miudinho*, quadrille.

With an exaggeration worthy of poets, he swore that the black man had "brought down his hand on counts and barons, put horns on his lordship, and prelates too." With emotion he referred to the death of the blacksmith at the shootout by the bridge.

> Shot in the back was he,
> Black Tição fell down stone dead,
> The best at casting spells,
> The strongest blacksmith's hand
> In all that far spread land.
> Dying with him, faithful yet,
> The dog Poor Soul, his favorite pet.

Dudu Matias sang of the universal repercussions of Castor's death.

> Great was all the weeping
> In the court of France, in Bahia,
> For the rascal made no distinction,
> Taking women, white or black,
> With enduring satisfaction,
> All of them serving him well,
> Ending his lonely spell.

The poetry spoke of thunder and lightning during black Castor Abduim da Assunção's last moments, an adolescent ebony prince regaling himself in the bed of a baroness and a servant girl's, shoer of donkeys, designer of tin jewelry, son of Xangô, Oxóssi on one side, Oxalá on the other, lover of Oxum, flame of Iemanjá. In a flash of lightning, a roar of thunder, the thunder and lightning of shotguns, up to heaven went Tição and his Poor Soul; no one knew where the dog had come from: an offering from Exu, there was no other explanation.

They went up to heaven in a flame and there they can be seen, even today, by black, mulatta, and Indian women, whites and noblewomen, in the wake of the moon, in the field of stars, flying over the canefields of Santo Amaro and the Rio das Cobras, in the captaincy of São Jorge dos Ilhéus.

22

AS FOR THE AFOREMENTIONED newspapers of the state capital, they started a noisy polemic, a bloodless, albeit furious
campaign: it took place in the annals of Bahian journalism
because of the dazzling talents taking part in the show, a
pleiad of eagles!

The sole opposition newspaper had vibrant scribblers
yelling in their articles, both unsolicited and assigned, sparkling, all of them, with indignation, shame, and blood, speaking about a return to those ignominious times when the
south of the state was a land of rampant criminality, heartless monsters, and lawless brigands. The three newspapers
that supported the government, no less vehement, riposted
by stating that quite the contrary, what had taken place was
an imposition of law and order on the remnants of a den of
bandits, confessed and condemned criminals, and fugitives
on the run from the police. A simple, routine cleanup operation that had finally put an end to the last remains of a
period of infamy and barbarism.

In spite of the insistence of higher authorities, in their
reckless haste, Sergeant Orígenes, before giving his final
order, waited a good half hour after the scattered shots had
ceased—a sign that, dead or wounded, that stubborn bunch
was in no shape to go on fighting.

The sergeant's prudence had been dictated by the losses
incurred. He hadn't foreseen so many casualties among the
ranks of gunmen and soldiers. Out of eight regulars, only
three were left, five having fallen, in addition to Corporal
Chico Roncolho. Some fifteen triggermen—he hadn't counted,
but the figure ought to be fairly exact—had rendered up
their souls to God or the devil. The Tocaia Grande people,
some of them taking up arms for the first time, had acquit-
ted themselves like professionals, selling their lives dearly.
Why the devil they'd done it, the sergeant didn't know, but
coming from an old line of gunmen, he could admire their
conduct. His good luck had been the death of Captain Natário
da Fonseca. With him out of the way, the rest had been easy.

As the calm became prolonged, marking a half hour on
his old watch, Orígenes ordered his contingent, still numer-

ous in spite of serious losses, to advance on the shed, carefully, slowly, with arms at the ready. You can never be too careful dealing with madmen; they exist everywhere and they come up out of nowhere.

Had he bet on it, he would have won. They were near the cross when out of the depths of the night a strange figure loomed up, holding and waving a kind of flag while with its free hand firing an old worm-eaten blunderbuss: aimless shots, dangerous for that very reason.

The sergeant immediately ordered them to fire and they obeyed. The volley brought down the solitary shooter; the flag twirled by itself and came to rest at the foot of the cross. It had served as a standard, but it was only an Epiphany banner, scarlet and blue. The one carrying it and using the blunderbuss was Dona Leocádia, who, instead of following her relatives' withdrawal, waiting to see what it would be like afterward, had preferred to stay in Tocaia Grande, risking her life. A crazy old woman of eighty, she'd put on the Senhorita Dona Deusa costume worn on the Feast of the Magi by her granddaughter Aracati, took up the standard and the blunderbuss, and came on to parade down the clearing. There she lay, riddled with bullets, the venerable and lively old woman from Estância—"crazy old coot," the sergeant had muttered—with her invincible Epiphany banner.

The gunmen went on to occupy the shed. Whereby Sergeant Orígenes Brito of the military police of the state of Bahia, the commissioned chief of police in Itabuna, considered his military mission accomplished and proceeded to organize his restless gunmen into an honor guard to welcome, with proper solemnity, the municipal authorities, that worthy and gallant delegation still waiting in the Baixa dos Sapos. Only after the victory ceremony would the sergeant turn loose those under his command for looting and lust.

23

IN THE GLOW OF the full moon hanging over the violated land, over the assassinated river, over the death unleashed, at the hour of midnight, by the trunk of the mulungu tree up on Captain's Hill, Jacinta Coroca and Natário da Fonseca, she with her repeater, he with his six-shooter, were waiting in ambush, enjoying the beauty of the landscape. Down below lay Tocaia Grande, occupied by gunslingers and Briosa's cutthroats.

"The best of all," Coroca said, "nothing can compare to it, Captain, is birthing a baby. Seeing that weight of flesh come out of a woman's belly, grabbing onto your hand, full of life. The first time I brought one out, I fell to crying."

The captain let the thread of a smile show on his lips.

"You brought quite a few babies into the world. You got to be a fine midwife."

"We changed and grew with the place. You, too, Natário; you're not the same roughneck you were before."

"Could be."

There was a brief silence and, coming up from the river on this summer night, the breeze wrapped them in a warm caress and spread the smell of jasmine in the air. The heat and the breeze were mingled in the calm voice of Coroca.

"I never saw anyone love another person, any woman love a man so much as Bernarda loved you." She was pensive for an instant, then went on. "I think that's the love they talk about. I know what it's like, I knew it when I was a young girl. His name was Olavo, he took me, he was weak in the chest, and died with the blood running out of his mouth. I remember him like it was today."

The delegation of notables drew closer to them. They were coming up from the desolation of the Baixa dos Sapos: the gunmen had set themselves up in the huts abandoned by the whores, after cutting down Paulinha Marisca, the only one who'd stood guard in whoretown. She'd learned to shoot in Alagoas from the many pistol men in her family. In the wooden house, in the adobe huts, the intendente, the judge, the prosecutor, the boss, and the whole jolly entourage, the distinguished court, was taking shelter, waiting for the moment of triumphal entry.

They stood out in the moonlight, a cavalcade to be seen and applauded: fat, strong, handsome, well dressed, well disposed, they were bringing the law to Tocaia Grande. Jacinta Coroca rested her repeater against a branch of the tree. Captain Natário da Fonseca said again, "No prettier place to live!"

"There's none like it," Coroca agreed.

Riding a splendid mare in the center of the cortège,

with the prosecutor on one side and on the other Ludmila Gregoriovna, was the chubby figure of Attorney Boaventura Andrade, Junior, political boss, top dog. His face filled with laughter.

Natário took careful aim at Venturinha's head. In over twenty years he'd never missed. *With your permission, Colonel.*

24

And here we have a pause in the beginnings of the history of the city of Irisópolis when it was still Tocaia Grande, the dark side. What happened afterward—progress, emancipation, a change in name, elevation to county seat; the town hall, the church, the bungalows, the villas, the English cobblestones; the mayor, the vicar, the prosecutor, and the judge; the courtroom and the jail; the Masonic lodge, the social club, and the literary society; the luminous side—isn't worth mentioning, holds no interest. Till next time.

This novel was written from house to house: in São Luiz do Maranhão, in the home of Jean and Eduardo Lago; in Estoril in Portugal, at the Hotel Estoril-Sol; in Itapuã, in Bahia, at the home of Rizia and João Jorge; in Petrópolis, at the home of Glória and Alfredo Machado.